A SCIE

CITY

OF THE

SAINTS

A SCIENTIFIC ROMANCE

CITY
OF THE
SAINTS

D. J. BUTLER

WordFire Press
Colorado Springs, Colorado

CITY OF THE SAINTS
Copyright © 2015 D.J. Butler
Originally published by D.J. Butler 2012

ISBN: 978-1-61475-347-6

Cover design by Janet McDonald

Art Director Kevin J. Anderson

Cover artwork images by Nathan Shumate

Book Design by RuneWright, LLC
www.RuneWright.com

Published by
WordFire Press, an imprint of
WordFire, Inc.
PO Box 1840
Monument CO 80132

Kevin J. Anderson & Rebecca Moesta, Publishers

WordFire Press Trade Paperback Edition November 2015
Printed in the USA
wordfirepress.com

DEDICATION

For my grandmother Alexandra, who was always a saint among the Saints.

An Adventure in Four Parts

Acknowledgements

My wife Emily carefully read the entire book and made many helpful observations. Thanks to all the Story Monkeys, as always, and especially to E.J. Patten, who was the first person after me to finish the story.

Thanks to Chad Ogden and Dea Draper, fantastic readers and friends. Thanks to Tom Carr of Residual Hauntings Revived and also Wasatch Paranormal Investigators, for being an early believer and promoter.

Thanks to Mia Kleve, Bryan Thomas Schmidt, Quincy J. Allen, and Michelle Corsillo for their work on the text and other formatting aspects of the WordFire Press edition of *City of the Saints*. Thanks also to Kevin J. Anderson and Peter J. Wacks for bringing me onto the team—I believe Kevin hearing my verbal pitch of *City of the Saints* was the first contact anyone at WordFire ever had with me.

The Deseret Alphabet as reproduced in this edition is in the Bee Skep Serif font, by Joshua Erickson. See that and his other Deseret fonts at:

http://copper.chem.ucla.edu/~jericks/index.html.

Part the First

ᛚᛖᚹᛣᛟᚼᛑ

Liahona

CHAPTER ONE

"Ihis is insubordination, Dick!" the man in the tall top hat and cravat hissed.

"Well then, Abby," Burton growled back at him, "you have something to write in your little notebook for today."

"You may address me as *Ambassador*," the younger, paler man whined, and removed his hat for a moment to mop sweat from his brow with a white silk handkerchief. The ceiling of the *Jim Smiley*'s engine room was high enough for the two men to stand in comfortably but the heat that its boiler gave off, even on a low idle, made the chamber feel smaller and infernal, like a smithy with the windows all shut.

The heat might make Absalom Fearnley-Standish wilt, but it wasn't any kind of serious bother to Burton.

"If we are to stand on rules of address," he snarled, "you may call me *Captain Burton*." He picked up a heavy tool, spanner at one end and spike at the other, from a steel crate of similar implements and hefted it. He leered at the diplomat, knowing that the red light coming through the furnace's grate would give the scars on both sides of his face a devilish cast. "This will do well enough."

"Again, I protest," Fearnley-Standish said, eyes darting around in the Vulcan gloom. "My commission letter says nothing of sabotage."

"Well then," Burton answered in as reasonable a voice as he could muster, examining the three brass pipes that rose from the iron furnace to the enormous boiler, "you should have exercised a little more imagination when you wrote the damned thing."

With a grunt and a swing of his powerful shoulders, he slammed the spike end of the tool into one of the pipes.

Clang!

Fearnley-Standish jumped. Hot air rushed from the hole Burton had made; the room becoming perceptibly more stifling.

"Egad, stop that!" he spat out, and Burton grinned.

"I find that your inexperience in the dark art of sabotage comforts me," he told the younger man. "It restores my faith in the moral rectitude of Her Majesty's Foreign Service. Moral rectitude, if not effectiveness." He swung again. *Clang!* "Still, must do the job right."

The second pipe was well-holed, and Burton looked at the boiler's pressure gauge. Its needle, already low as the boiler idled, steadily dropped now toward zero. Burton was no mechanick but he thought that meant he had done the job. For good measure, he smashed the gauge as well.

"That's enough! The Americans will hear us!" Fearnley-Standish wiped sweat from his face again. He was trembling.

"I forget," Burton mused, "how young you are. You've never cut through impenetrable jungle, never traveled in a foreign country in disguise, never taken a spear to the face." He raised his weapon a final time. "Great Kali's hips, you've probably never even sailed the Nile."

"Blowhard!" Fearnley-Standish squealed.

"Coward!" Burton retorted. "Stuffed shirt!" *Clang!* He smashed a hole in the third pipe. "That should hold them for a day or two, especially," he gestured at the crate of spanners and other implements, "if we take their tools with us."

Fearnley-Standish stepped away and crossed his arms. "I'm not carrying those."

Burton grunted. "Say something that surprises me, *Ambassador.*" He stuffed the spanner back among its fellows and then picked up the box. "You might, for starters, explain why you bothered to accompany me on this little sortie. If you're so convinced the Americans are not our enemies, or at least our rivals, you might have saved yourself a little hysterical panting and remained on the *Liahona.*"

"Did you hear that?" the diplomat hunched his shoulders and twisted his neck, cupping a hand to one ear while he craned to look up the stairs that led to the *Jim Smiley's* deck.

"Pshaw!" Burton dismissed his fears and pushed past, slipping effortlessly up the iron-grilled steps. He was nearly forty, he thought proudly, but he was as muscled as he'd ever been; as strong as he'd been when soldiering in India in his twenties.

Fearnley-Standish hesitated, and then tapped up the stairs in Burton's wake.

"I am Her Majesty's representative," he buzzed in Burton's ear, "responsible for whatever happens on this expedition. I couldn't risk that you might run off alone and do something foolish."

Burton laughed harshly. "Instead, you witnessed the foolishness!" The deck of the *Jim Smiley* was reminiscent of a sailing ship, a flat space with a railing around it and cabins fore and aft. Everything was iron and India rubber. "I hope you're taking detailed notes in your little memorandum-book."

"Yes, well," Fearnley-Standish harrumphed.

Something flickered in the corner of Burton's vision and he snapped his head around to look at it. Nothing. Just a shadow, a well of darkness thrown into the lee of the *Jim Smiley*'s wheelhouse by the Franklin Poles, the great crackling blue electric globes standing guard in front of Bridger's Saloon. But was there a darker shadow within the shadow, a slight stirring?

He stared.

Nothing.

He listened, and heard the raucous, muffled sounds drifting through the plascrete walls of the saloon but nothing more, nothing that indicated any danger. The shadow was too small to hide a man in any case, Burton reassured himself, and he turned and headed for the rail. The grated iron floor, the *deck*, since these truck-men all insisted on talking about their vehicles as if they were sailing ships, jutted out a few extra feet to the ladder, to get over the strangely rounded and rubber-cloaked hull of the vessel.

"What is it?" the diplomat asked him.

"Nothing," Burton dismissed both the other man and his own fears with one word. He dropped the crate of tools to the ground with a rattling *crash!* and slid effortlessly down the ladder after it.

Fearnley-Standish descended more awkwardly. Halfway down, the starchy young man missed a rung. He dangled by his hands for long and flailing seconds before he managed to reattach himself.

"What are you going to do with those?" he demanded shrilly.

Burton laughed again at the pusillanimity of the other man. "I'll put them in the one place where Clemens and his goon won't be able to find them in the morning!" he cried over his shoulder.

Bending at the knees to pick up the crate again, he headed across the yard towards the great shadowy hulk that was the *Liahona*.

ᒪᗴᘺᡐᓍᔨᘺ

"Your road ahead is shadowed and perilous," muttered the gypsy. He held Sam Clemens's right hand clutched in his own, which were armored in fingerless black kidskin gloves, and peered closely at the creases in Sam's flesh.

Close enough, Sam thought, *that the man could just as easily be* smelling *his future as* seeing *it.* The man's hair was long and greasy, as befitted a gypsy, and his coat and vest were threadbare.

"Your future is one of failure, disaster, and great sorrow. You should reconsider your course, sir. You should turn back."

The gypsy fell silent and arched an eyebrow at Sam, as if underscoring the fearfulness of his message. The silence between the two men was filled with the babble of the saloon around them.

"That's refreshing," Sam quipped, chomping fiercely on his Cuban cigar.

The air inside Bridger's was heavy with smoke but it was the smoke of cheap American tobacco rolled into cheap cigarettes, mixed with gas lamp emanations and the occasional ozone crackle of electricity. Sam filtered the stink, as well as the rancid smell of sour, sweaty human bodies and the drifting odors of horse and coal-fire, through a sweet, expensive Partagás. *Nothing,* he thought, *beats a government expense account.*

The gypsy stared at him. His gray-streaked black mustache hung asymmetrically under his bulbous nose, and was no match for Sam's fine, manly soup-strainer. His jaw looked misshapen, too, sort of hunched sideways into the thick, mostly gray, beard that veiled it. Above all the facial hair and the badly-cast features, though, the man had dark, intense eyes, with baggy pouches under them, and those eyes stared at Sam in surprise.

"Did you hear me right, sir? I told you that your future is bleak."

"Yes," Sam acknowledged. "Your honesty is marvelous. Most fortune-tellers would take my two bits and tell me what they thought I wanted to hear. *Beautiful willing women, rivers of smooth whiskey, and horses that run faster than the sun itself are in your future, sir! Come again soon.*" He grinned, took another suck at the cigar and winked. "I respect your integrity." *And besides,* he thought, *you're most likely right, anyway. If the Indians don't kill me, the Mormons will, and that wily codger Robert Lee must have agents out there somewhere as well.* Failure, disaster, and sorrow, indeed.

Sam heard a clatter from the corner of the common room. A squad of Shoshone braves, proud and alien, with their beaded vests and fringed leggings, their strange hair, clumpy on top and then falling long about their shoulders, and their long magnet-powered Brunel rifles, had shoved aside several tables and were beginning some sort of coordinated movement that looked like it might be competitive interactive hopscotch. They tossed flat disks across the floor and then raced in hopping motions, each to another man's disk and then back to his starting position. They looked like big, hairy, dangerous, possibly slightly inebriated, versions of little girls. Sam forced himself to take a second look at their guns and suppressed an urge to laugh.

Those Brunel rifles hurled bullets faster and farther than any gunpowder-driven weapon yet made, and punched awful holes right through a man's body. They were English in design and manufacture, portable railguns, and Sam wondered how the Shoshone found themselves so well armed. He sobered up quickly at the thought. For that matter, as he looked closer, he spotted electro-knives and vibro-blades here and there. Somehow, though it was in a picaresque and highly individualized, even chaotic, fashion, the Shoshone had gotten themselves serious hand-to-hand weapons. Might they have larger armaments, too?

At this rate, he began to think all the wild talk about phlogiston guns being tested out in the Rocky Mountains might not be so wild after all. Maybe he ought to consider his mission objectives broader than dealing with Deseret alone, or at least get that recommendation back to Washington. It was bad enough that Deseret had airships, and might have ray guns that rained fiery death on their targets. Once such things got into the hands of the natives, there might be no end of mischief.

Two of the saloon's bouncers, heavy men in buckskins with knives and guns, didn't look like they wanted to laugh at all; they moved a little closer with expressions on their faces that were downright grim.

The gypsy shook his head, perplexed. What had he said his name was …? Archer? He wore a tall boxy beaver hat, a long duster, brown corduroy pants, and a shirt that was striped vertically in purple and gold. Round smoked glasses that might have hidden his burning eyes rode low on the onion-like bulge of his nose. He didn't really look out of place here, Sam reflected, surrounded by New Russia Trail pioneers, steam-truck mechanicks, black Stridermen from President Tubman's Mexico, cowboys, and the usual clutter of low-life entertainers that filled any bar west of the Mississippi.

Sam knew that he looked much more at odds with the environment in his self-consciously modern attire. He wore a jacket, without tails, because tails were inconvenient, and white because Sam liked to think of himself as the hero of the story, even though, if pressed, he wouldn't admit to believing in heroes. He wore Levi-Strauss denim pants, brand new and shipped straight from the factory to the U.S. Army at Sam's request. They were comfortable and rugged, and they snapped up the front with a row of metal buttons for convenience as well as for a certain masculine flair that shouted *mechanick*. At least, that's what they would have shouted to Sam if he ever took occasion to look at another man's crotch and saw it protected by a row of steel snaps.

"You don't understand," the gypsy said. "You take me for a huckster."

"I take every man for a huckster," Sam agreed. "I find it saves time."

"You're on an errand," the palm reader pressed, looking down again into Sam's close-held hand. "You are a knight, and your quest is of supreme importance to your people … your family, perhaps … but your errand will end in irretrievable disaster. You should turn back now, sir."

Your family, perhaps. Sam felt sick to his stomach, and another swallow of cigar smoke did nothing to relieve him. He pulled his hand away.

"Gentlemen," interrupted a crisp New England accent at his shoulder, saving Sam from the terrifying void of his own thoughts. "If you have a moment …"

Sam turned to look at the intruder, who was brushing his long overcoat aside to reveal his hip. Sam found himself staring at a long metallic pistol, holstered but menacing and obviously meant to be so. The holster itself was unnaturally bulky, with a flap that covered much of the actual weapon and hid it from view. Sam wondered what kind of gun it must be concealing. Something new by Hunley? Maxim? Colt? Its wearer was a tall, muscular man in a bowler hat. He glared at Sam and the gypsy, and in his right hand he thrust forward a black calotype printed on a sheet of cheap paper.

Where the hell is that Irishman? Sam wondered irascibly. This sort of thing was supposed to be his job. Then again, maybe Sam should start wearing a pistol himself.

He spotted O'Shaughnessy against the far wall of the saloon's common room and tried to catch his eye, but the Irishman, Sam's bodyguard and designated man of violence, pulled his porkpie hat as low as the little thing would go over his brow, threw his scarf over his shoulder, and slipped through a doorway into the back hall.

"Pardon the intrusion," Bowler Hat continued, his smooth, polite tones in sharp contrast to the implied threat of his revealed gun. "Have you seen this man?"

Sam dragged on the cigar to steady his nerves and shot a look at the gypsy; the other man was as composed as a wooden Indian. Finally, Sam looked at the calotype and almost choked. It was his Irishman, Tamerlane O'Shaughnessy, in black and white and large as life, large as his own hawk-like nose, though the picture was not half so vicious as the genuine article, no doubt because the calotype hadn't been drinking.

"I suppose," he said slowly, "you've already concluded that I'm not your man."

"Suppose what you like, seeing as you're neither cuffed nor dead." Bowler Hat rested his hand on the pistol grip. "But answer the damn question."

A second man stepped up, similarly wrapped in a long overcoat but wearing a stovepipe hat the color of charcoal. Sam almost liked the man for his neatly trimmed goatee.

"Easy, Bob," Stovepipe cautioned his comrade. "We're not looking for either of these two gents."

Bob snarled and backed off, champing his teeth like he meant to bite off the smoldering tip of Sam's Partagás. Sam eyed him coolly, taking another drag of sweet smoke. If Bob could have shot bullets from his eyes and sliced Sam in half with that glare, he would have. *Well,* Sam thought, *give Horace Hunley and his crew another twenty years, and they'll be grinding out soldiers that look just like real men and* do *shoot bullets out their eyes. This war cannot be allowed to happen.*

"You know the fellow's name?" Sam asked. "Image that fuzzy, could be anyone. Mercy, boys, I'm *surprised* you didn't think it was me."

"He may be using the name Seamus McNamara," Stovepipe informed him.

"Hmmn." Sam chewed his cigar and raised both his thick eyebrows at the gypsy, who continued to be impassive. "You boys haven't shown me a badge, so I reckon that means you're bounty hunters. What's the dividend on this fellow?"

"We're with the Pinkerton National Detective Agency," Bob grunted.

"Like I said, bounty hunters." Sam smiled a practiced sarcastic grin at them that he knew was sweet and self-righteous and infuriating at the same time. He wondered why the Pinkertons would be after O'Shaughnessy. Oh well, it hardly mattered—he couldn't let them have him in any case. "Only you're the kind of bounty hunters that are too proud to subcontract."

"I oughtta—" Bob choked out, stepping forward again, but Stovepipe restrained him by the elbow.

"Have you seen him, mister?" Stovepipe asked Sam directly.

Sam felt the thrill of danger in his blood and grinned. The gypsy's face hadn't twitched a muscle but his posture looked taut, like a spring ready to bounce. Sam wondered if he was packing and concluded that he probably was. Every man in the room but Sam was probably packing.

He looked back to the two Pinkertons.

"I haven't seen the fellow," he told them. It was a lie, but a half-truth like *I don't know any Seamus McNamara* or *I don't know where this man is* would have been just as much a lie, and Sam didn't really object to lying anyway. Lies could be useful and downright entertaining.

Bob snorted but didn't argue. The Pinkertons faded, backing away one step at a time until the jostle of the saloon swallowed them. Now, what had that gypsy been saying about Sam's family?

Sam turned to ask the gypsy to explain himself, but the ugly man was gone. In his seat instead was a beautiful young lady, her brown hair curled on her head and high on the back of her neck, long pearl-drop earrings hanging from the cherry lobes of her ears. Her face was serious but cheerful, with a thin mouth that was all business. She smiled at Sam, and he had to take another puff of the cigar to keep the sudden explosion of songbirds contained within his chest. He glared at the smoldering stump—at this rate, he was no more than a minute away from having to light another, just as a defensive measure.

"I'm Annie Webb," the lady said, "and you're the most handsome man in this saloon."

Sam almost choked. "I'm Sam Clemens," he identified himself, "and I'm certainly the luckiest."

"Yes," she agreed. "Yes, tonight you are."

ᒪᎬ∽ᐱᲚᎤᏂ∽ᐱ

Poe pressed himself deep into the cracked leather seat of the corner booth and let himself feel inconspicuous, unworthy of attention, invisible. He scratched himself with the bare fingertips protruding from his kid gloves and allowed his head to slump with his body, falling into a posture that said he was just another frontier drunk with idiosyncratic taste in clothing. The scratching was not part of the disguise but the result of it—Poe's hair was longer and more oily than he liked under his tall beaver hat, and he couldn't be sure, but he thought he'd picked up fleas somewhere between St. Louis and Fort Bridger.

I'm just a gypsy fortune-teller, he thought; it was a role he enjoyed playing, especially when his mark was a man as shrewd as Samuel Clemens. The role was outrageous, and playing it with a smart man made it a game; in this case, it was a game with high stakes.

Clemens would have a mission counterpart to his own, of course. Ascertain the truth of the phlogiston gun rumors. Influence Brigham Young and the foreign policy of the Kingdom of Deseret or render Deseret harmless.

But what about the strange request from the Madman Pratt, the one that had come directly from Pratt to Robert, the one Robert had told Poe was secret from Brigham Young and Jefferson Davis as well? Was Robert playing some game with Pratt alone or did Pratt act very discreetly on behalf of his country? And what were the strange objects that Poe had agreed to give to the Madman in exchange for the airship designs? Robert had mentioned ether-waves … ether-waves were also Poe's best guess as to how the scarabs worked, and the same technology could certainly be put to other uses … were the canopic jars communicators of some sort? Of course ether-wave communication was experimental at best, even in Hunley's laboratories in Atlanta, but he couldn't imagine what else ether—the mysterious particles that filled the universe, including the apparent void between the planets—could be used for. An ether-wave weapon? A transportation device for small objects?

A secret hope that maybe the objects were healing devices of some sort rose up in Poe's breast, and he strangled it.

Through his smoked-glass spectacles, Poe continued to survey the room closely.

The Pinkertons had made him nervous. His heart was still beating a little fast, and the whistle around his neck felt very heavy. He wondered if he was even close enough to be able to use it, or if the cotton batting packed into the crate would muffle the sound too much. If only one of the men came after him, of course, he could probably disable the attacker with some simple baritsu. Two men, though, would be more of a challenge.

Ah, Robert, he thought. *What have you gotten me into?*

Bridger's Saloon was the heart of Fort Bridger. There were also a commissary, dormitories, and a mechanick's workshop for the steam-trucks that arrived limping at this junction of the New Russia, California, and Mormon Trails, and in any kind of decent combination of good weather and daylight, the stockade yard thronged with merchants of one kind or another. Trappers sold furs; cattlemen sold meat, generally on the hoof; worn out, desperate pioneers sold furniture, books, and family heirlooms to lighten their loads. They all came to spend their earnings at the saloon.

Out front were two Franklin Poles, huge blue electric globes on iron lampposts but the interior of Bridger's place was lit with gas, little lamps glowing in sconces all along each wall, smudging the red wallpaper behind them black with soot and heat. The saloon used electricks, too, though Poe wasn't exactly sure what for, other than the lights in the yard—to cook, maybe? or to operate locks or security systems?—but he could smell the ozone now and then.

The bar crawling down one wall of the common room was like any other, heavy and dark and scarred and stained, clinking dully in the eternal dance of glass- and bottle-bottoms. The faro and poker tables could have been snatched from saloons in the Dakotas, Kansas City, or New Orleans.

The people, though, were a mix such as you'd see nowhere else. Even the pioneers were wildly heterogeneous: there were sober-faced, still-wet-behind-the-ears Mormon immigrants from northern Europe in their thick clouds, and more mixed, smaller bands heading for New Russia, and the California-bound prospectors so excited about the future they couldn't stop talking about how they'd spend their fortunes, if they hadn't already done so.

There were Russians from the northwest and Frenchmen from Canada and black men from Mexico. There were hunters, trappers, and Indians. Were those Shoshone in the corner? Poe wondered. It was out of his area of expertise—they might have been Blackfoot or Ute.

There were soldiers, lawmen, outlaws, gamblers, musicians, dancers, dry goods salesmen, and even a whore or two. They all rubbed elbows and bumped against each other like so many different species of bees, shoehorned unexpectedly into a single hive and surprised to find themselves not entirely displeased.

Poe watched them. He took it all in and he forgot nothing.

Jedediah Coltrane, the dwarf, drifted across the barroom floor, eyes carefully probing all the corners. He'd had a shot of something at the bar and he moved slowly among the faro tables and the dancers, but it was a slowness of deliberation, not of indecision. Despite his height, he fit in well with the saloon's crowd, unshaven as he was, his face craggy under his shapeless hat, and his striped shirt, wool trousers, and jacket fine but frayed, his suspenders holding on by a few impatient threads. He looked like he had purchased the Sunday outfit of some child second-hand and thrown away the necktie. He was coming to Poe to report.

"The Irishman slipped out early," Poe told Coltrane as the little man eased into the seat opposite. "Did he see you?"

Coltrane shook his grizzled head. "The mark didn't see me. Ain't nobody seen me. Then again, wouldn't matter if they did, 'cause I ain't had to do nothing."

"You're charmingly cryptic." Poe laughed softly. "Would you care to explain your statement?"

"The limeys did it for me. Beat hell outta the boiler pipes and then went and stole all the tools. No way the *Jim Smiley* sloughs it and rolls outta here in the morning, not under her own steam. She's gaffed."

"Mmm." Poe considered.

"Whadda we know about the Brits, boss?" Coltrane asked. He fidgeted with the pommel of the knife in his belt, one of several knives Poe knew he kept on his person at all times. "I was damn surprised to get to the *Smiley* and find 'em there ahead of me."

"Captain Richard Francis Burton," Poe reported, seeing before his eyes Robert's handwritten files he had memorized in Richmond. "Soldier, swordsman, linguist, explorer. A dangerous man, and very nearly a famous one. Author of several books, decorated inventor of a dueling maneuver, arguably discoverer of the sources of the Nile, and erstwhile ersatz hajji."

The dwarf shook his head irritably. "Jebus, boss, you buffalo me with the big words. I coulda swore you jest called that feller an *arsehole horse hat sod gee*, but that don't make no damn kinda sense."

"He made the pilgrimage to Mecca in disguise," Poe explained, thinking about the scars on Burton's face, lingering evidence, he understood, of a spear that had once been thrust entirely through the man's head. A man who could survive that sort of attack, Poe worried, was an antagonist to be feared.

"That so hard?" Coltrane wondered.

"It's very difficult," Poe affirmed. "The second man is Absalom Fearnley-Standish, a junior member of Her Majesty's Foreign Service.

Harrow and Cambridge. His only posting prior to this expedition was to a consular position in the Principality of Liechtenstein."

Coltrane spat on the floor. *Ah*, thought Poe, *this was what it was to live in the West. Hard liquor and spitting indoors.* The sight of the dwarf spitting made his own lungs ache, and he clutched reflexively at a handkerchief in his pocket while he fought down the urge to cough.

"Sounds like small fry, don't he, boss? But don't he also sound like a feller you'd expect to play the game straight?"

"Yes," Poe agreed, "and that worries me. What is such a man doing on this mission? Are we mistaken about what the mission might be? Do we overestimate the importance of this to the Crown? Are Burton and Fearnley-Standish a ruse, distracting us from the real operatives? Or might Fearnley-Standish be more than he appears upon first inspection?"

Coltrane grunted. "You think a lot, boss."

Poe coughed once, then stifled the cough's siblings. He wondered if he thought *enough*, and felt dissatisfied. Was he a fool to believe war could still be averted?

"There are Pinkertons here," he told his aide. He nodded almost imperceptibly to where Bowler Bob and Stovepipe stood on the other side of the room, waving their calotype in the pasty faces of a clutch of denim overall- and straw hat-wearing Scandinavians, who answered them with shrugs and uncomprehending stares.

"After us?" Coltrane dropped a hand to touch the knife in his belt again.

"I don't know." Poe wondered. "They claimed to be after Clemens's man, the Irishman, O'Shaughnessy. Though they knew him as *McNamara*. Clemens didn't bat an eye, lied bold as daylight, said he'd never seen the man."

"Brass balls on that guy." The dwarf's voice sounded admiring. "So we're safe. Maybe we oughtta find the Irishman and hand him over to those boys. That'd burn the lot, wouldn't it? Slow Clemens up another few days."

Poe squinted at the Pinkertons and considered. "Unless the Pinkertons are in league with Clemens, and their confrontation was a ruse to try to flush us out. We rush to the Pinkertons to turn in the dangerous wanted Irishman, and they clap us in irons and send us back to Washington."

"Damn, you think?" Coltrane asked. "You're making my head spin."

Finally losing his struggle with his lungs, Edgar Allan Poe coughed, hard, several times, into his handkerchief. He balled the white square of cotton up quickly, hiding the blood spots from Coltrane. "Best to be careful, Jed," Poe said to the dwarf as he rolled with a show of laziness and bad posture to his feet. "We're in the jungle here, and surrounded by man-eaters." But then, he reflected, he was a man-eater himself.

That was why Robert had sent him.

ᒪᐁ ᗯᒍᑕᐆᒡ ᗯ

Tamerlane O'Shaughnessy huddled his birdlike head deep into the nest of his scarf as he kicked the back door of the saloon open and slipped into the sizzling blue half-light of the stockade yard, leaving behind all the idjits lowing into their shot glasses like cattle bound for slaughter. It was a crisp, cold night and his neck was thin, but the real reason to burrow into the scarf was the bloody-damn-hell Pinkertons. Stupid rotten cheating bastards. He'd known when he'd crossed them that they'd send men after him, but who would have guessed they'd follow him out to the Wyoming Territory? *You should have got a pardon, Tamerlane, me boy.* Or if not a pardon, at least the Pinkertons could have the decency to look the other way, since he was a paid agent of the Union Government, and they were more or less supposed to be on the same side.

The Union. Tam sneered at the word in his own inner monologue. *You don't have a* side, *you stupid Irish lunkhead. Besides, it's the* United States, *you idjit, and it's best it stays that way. Pray Brigit and Anthony that this bloody war don't ever come, war ain't good for no one except them that sells guns.*

Crime, now, crime paid. Crime had paid Tam when he was on the Pinkertons' payroll, digging coal mine shafts in Pennsylvania and listening to the grumbling small talk of would-be dynamite tossers. It had paid even better when he'd thrown his lot in with the Molly Maguires and been on two payrolls at the same time, and robbing from the rich mine owners to boot.

It had paid great, right up until that snoopy little Welsh bastard Pinkerton Bevan had told Tam that he knew the score, and he would keep quiet so long as Tam sent a little money the Welshman's way every month. Tam had no objection to greasing palms, of course, but he couldn't trust the little Taffy to keep his mouth shut, so he'd had to slit his throat, burn the body, and go west.

Another man in Tam's boots would have crunched the gravel of the stockade yard loudly, but Tam had a long-practiced step that was silent without being stealthy, effortlessly inconspicuous and unnoticeable without looking sneaky. He floated like a ghost around the side of the saloon, figuring he'd hide in the *Jim Smiley* for the night.

He knew Clemens would never give him up, not that stubborn son of Missouri, good old Sam Clemens. He'd spit in the devil's eye, tell him a joke, and swear he'd never seen no Irishman in all his born days before he'd knuckle under to another man. Sam Clemens had taken Tam under his wing, recruited him into Intelligence (*ha!* Tam thought, *as if*) when the Pinkertons were on his trail and scuttled him out of the country right under their noses.

Clemens was the first person since Mother O'Shaughnessy herself who had ever taken an interest in whether Tam lived or died. Also, Sam had cash.

"Egad, what if we're caught?"

Tam stopped. The words almost sounded like part of his own stream of thoughts but the voice was the frightened whine of some bloody effete aristo Englishman, some useless Etonian fop. It came from the corner of the stockade yard, ahead of him and to the left, where the blue light of the electricks splashed ineffectually against the bulk of steam-trucks resting from their east-or west-bound labors. The voice was followed by a loud, rattling *clank!* of metal on metal.

"Great thundering Ganesha!" barked another English voice, this one stronger and harsher. "*You* insisted on coming along, now the least you can do—and I *do* mean the *very least*—is not get in my way!" A grunt, then more rattling.

Tam thought he could tell where the sound was coming from, and a great hulking beast it was, a track-borne iron behemoth, many times larger than the *Jim Smiley*, hunched in the shadows. Two dark figures lurched across its deck, one straining its shoulders against a heavy load.

"Besides, they've only a few hours to catch us, and they can't possibly even know what we've done yet."

The figures sank into the deck of the big steam-truck, presumably climbing down some hatch or stair into its belly.

Suddenly, Tam had a bad feeling about the whole thing. First, the Pinkertons showed up on his trail, and now, suddenly, here were two English bastards up to no good. If there was only the one of them, Tam would kill him without a second thought, just to be on the safe side, but two men always made an attack a little more of a throw of the dice.

"Hell and begorra."

Tam gave the strolling Englishmen a few seconds to get well inside their truck, then crossed the yard to the *Jim Smiley*. He had to skirt out of reach of the electricks' blue light, which made his scuttling circuitous and piled additional time into his state of anxiety, but a couple of minutes later, heart beating a little faster than he would have liked, Tam stood next to the *Jim Smiley* and surveyed her for visible damage.

She looked fine from the outside. All six of her enormous, heavy India-rubber tyres bulked full and unscathed. The immense inflated India-rubber skirt that wrapped all around her hull was also fine. The big elephantastic wheel in back sat on its axle, unimpeached and unassailed, as far as Tam could see. Black smoke puffed, wispy and hard to spot in the blue-black gloom, from her raised exhaust pipe. Tam almost relaxed.

Almost.

He sent himself up the ladder quickly, conscious that he was visible here from the doorway to any vulture that knew where to look, and then slipped into the wheelhouse for a moment to scan the shadowed deck through its large windows.

Nothing. Bloody-damn-hell nothing.

You're jumping at shadows, me boy.

Tam crossed the deck again and started down the stairs into the boiler room. He flicked the light switch in the iron stairwell and nothing happened. He flicked it again, still nothing. That wasn't good. He wasn't a mechanick like Clemens, but he knew that unless the emergency battery was engaged, the lights were powered by the electricks, which were powered by the boiler. No lights meant the boiler wasn't on.

Tam drew his pistol, a shiny Webley Lonsgpur (not his, originally, but Bevan's. The weaselly little Taffy didn't need it now, did he, with him all singing away, "Bread of Heaven" in the celestial men's choir?). Saints Brigit, Patrick, and Anthony on fire. Could be he let the coal run too low in the furnace and the fire had gone out. Sure, that was it.

No, you idjit. There's smoke out the exhaust, means the fire is going.

Could be a burned out bulb. Didn't they burn out? They burned out, he was sure of it.

Sure, it could, and it could be bloody leprechauns opened a valve and let out all the steam. *Put your balls back on, O'Shaughnessy, and stop fooling yourself.* He shook his head to clear his thoughts, then cocked the hammer of the Webley.

Gun first, he sprang noiselessly into the boiler room.

Nothing.

Empty, no one there, just the shovel and the pile of coal and the boiler throwing out its mad red grin into the room through slitted teeth.

He quickly checked the other rooms below decks—locker, galley, bunk room—and determined that he was alone on the *Jim Smiley*. Alone on a steam-truck with no functioning electricks.

He stood, Webley uncocked and reholstered, in the boiler room, scratching his head and beginning to feel relieved, when he saw the holes. All the pipes connecting the furnace to the boiler were smashed open. No wonder the electricks didn't work—there was no steam to power them.

With no steam, the truck wouldn't go anywhere either, couldn't budge an inch if it was pulled by ten Clydesdales. Well, Sam was a dab hand with steam machinery and electricks, he'd fix it proper in short order. He had patches precisely to cover this sort of an occasion, right in his toolbox.

Still, how in hell did something like this happen? Some kind of explosion? But that couldn't be right; the holes in the pipes looked like they'd been smashed inwards, not blown out.

Then Tam noticed that Sam's well-used crate of tools was missing. He heard the rough Englishman's voice in his mind. *They only have a few hours to catch us.*

"Bloody hell!" he yelled, his voice gigantic and booming in the engine room. He remembered the Pinkertons, and squeezed his voice back down to a whisper. "It's sabotage! We're holed by the English!"

He rushed back up the stairs to the deck, whipping out his revolver again, and flung himself prone to survey the stockade yard. No sign of the Pinkertons. *And isn't that a blessed relief, after me going stupid and shouting my head off inside a great metal drum?*

But there was a fellow on his hands and knees just below the electricks, vomiting on himself, and two men in frock coats strolled casually across the yard, from the far shadowed corner where Tam had heard the English voices, near the saloon doors.

A little too casually. Forced casual, like people pretending they hadn't just been having a quarrel. Squinting, Tam saw that the older fellow, with the big wild mustache, looked like he might bite the head off a mountain lion any second, and the younger, who was clean-shaven and wore a top hat, appeared on the edge of tears, like a little girl.

That'd be the bloody Etonian.

Tam lay flat and out of sight, waiting for the Englishmen to go inside the saloon.

LE⅄⅄O⅄⅄

"All ticketed passengers on the *Liahona*, Fort Bridger to Salt Lake City! Attention, all ticketed passengers on the *Liahona*!"

The man yelling looked to be about fifty, with a square face, serious eyes, and curly hair under a shapeless blue cap. He was dressed in white shirtsleeves under a brass-buttoned blue vest, and his accent was some kind of English-Irish-something-er-other. Jed had seen enough of the world to know there were different kinds of Brits, but he couldn't really tell them apart. Jed had been twenty years old when he finally saw Little Rock for the first time, and there hadn't been any English, Irish, or Scots there.

"This is Captain Dan Jones of the *Liahona*, attention, all ticketed passengers!"

Captain Jones had the lungs of a professional barker but he didn't rely on them alone. He bellowed through a speaking trumpet, an S-bent copper tube with an India-rubber mouthpiece on its lower end and a broadly flowering cone on top, like a periscope for the mouth. His voice came out tinny but clear, and loud enough to be heard over the rumbling din.

A boy, a little dark-haired kid in overalls, sailor's jacket and a gray slouch hat who couldn't be older than five or six but might be as young as four, knocked against Jones's knees and threatened constantly to be squashed underfoot, he stuck so close to the older man. He kept one hand out and tugging at the Captain's pant leg, as if reassuring himself that the man wouldn't evaporate.

The sight of the kid made Jed shake his head in irritation; he'd been that kid once, only even smaller, and a hell of a lot less awkward. You can't afford to get underfoot when the feet belong to a mule pulling the family plow.

"Departure time will be eight o'clock sharp, by my watch!" Captain Jones warned his passengers, stumping a circular route among the gaming tables and turning his head as he delivered his message. The din rumbled a little louder and hands waved here and there in acknowledgement. "There is a return trip and a time table to make, and we will not be late. To those of you who are not accustomed to operating on a schedule, I say, *Welcome to Deseret!* I will fire a ten-minute warning gun. No refunds or exchanges will be offered to passengers who sleep in and miss the departure, but you may hold your ticket, and I will honor it on a future run.

"Any passengers desiring to sleep in the *Liahona* tonight may do so for the very affordable price of ten cents, payable in American, Mexican, Californian, New Russian, or Deseret. Breakfast will be provided for an additional five cents. Any passengers who have not yet purchased their tickets may see me now or in the morning at the *Liahona*.

"Thank you."

Jed dropped off the barstool where he perched, plunking down two bits for his drink, rectangular like all of California's coinage. He ambled in an intercepting course into Jones's path.

"Captain Jones!" he called out. He'd done a bit of barking in his own time and knew how to make himself heard.

"Aye," Jones answered, and his voice was crisp and pleasant. "How may I help you?"

The little boy hid behind his legs and peered out between them like they were prison bars. Jed made an effort to smile at the kid, knowing that on his homely mug, it could only come out as a grimace. Not that he cared about the kid's feelings, but no sense pissing off the captain if it wasn't necessary. The boy shuddered and closed his eyes tight, the ungrateful little shit.

"I'm paid up for the journey tomorrow morning, party of two," Jed explained, and he waved their two dog-eared tickets as a sign of good faith. "I reckon I'd like to book two berths for tonight." He shot his winningest grin at the boy, who only cringed further away from him. *Good money after bad, Gramma would have said.* "And two breakfasts, if you'll vouch for your cook."

"I'm the cook, boyo," Jones said, "and St. David himself will vouch for my work." He beamed a warm, trust-inspiring smile. "That'll be thirty cents."

"I reckon I can believe St. David," Jed smiled back as friendly as he knew how, "whoever he might be." He paid with six tarnished nickels, three of them American and three rectangles stamped with the California bear. The Captain dug a pencil stub out of his vest pocket and marked both of Jed's tickets with the initials DJ and some obscure symbol.

"Bring your gear aboard whenever you want," the Captain invited his passenger, and then extended down a friendly hand. "I'm Dan Jones."

They shook. "I'm Jed Coltrane, Captain Jones."

"Just Dan will do, when we're not aboard. This is John Moses, my midshipman." He gestured to the boy hiding behind his knee, who heard himself talked about and took a deep breath to swell out his chest. "Your first journey to the Great Salt Lake City, is it?"

Jed snorted. "Can't be many folks as've been twice, can there? Thirty-odd years ago there weren't nothing there but dust, buffalo, and Paiutes, and old Jim Bridger paddled around the Salt Lake in a boat sewn outta his own shirt. Hell, even twelve years ago, the Mormons was all living in tents and possum bellies."

"Ah, but that was twelve years ago," Dan chided the dwarf gently, "and travel gets easier every year."

"You find easier travel brings better passengers?" Jed joked.

"A passenger who pays full fare is a fine passenger," Dan Jones said, his eyes opening up and twinkling, "and it's a very good passenger indeed who pays full fare but takes up only half the space."

Jed was caught off guard by the jest and found himself laughing hard. "You'll think better of it, Dan, don't you worry," he roared, "when you find out I *eat* three *times* my share!"

Dan Jones joined in the laughter. "Is that what brings you to the Kingdom, then, boyo? You've come to enter all our pie-eating contests?"

"No, I've come to bring you high culture," Jed tried to say with a straight face, but instead had to wipe tears from his eyes.

"Oh, aye?"

Jed took a deep breath and managed to still his riotous laughter. "Yeah, as a matter of fact, I have. I'm with a traveling showman, feller name of Doctor Jamison Archibald. He's a scholar of anquiquities … anquit …"

"Antiquities," Jones suggested, his own laughter subsiding.

"Really old shit," Jed finished. "Egyptian, mostly. We heard as there might could be some interest in it in the Great Salt Lake City."

"Mummies?" whispered John Moses. He had inched around Jones's leg and stood trembling, eyes wide open and round, both hands gripping Dan Jones by the knee. His voice was so soft that a man of normal height wouldn't have heard it.

Jed nodded, then let his arms fall suddenly slack, held half-up at a forty-five degree angle in front of him, fingers drooping. Reaching deep into his bag of medicine show skills, he rolled his eyes back in their sockets until he could see nothing, and he knew the lad could only see the yellowish whites of the dwarf's eyeballs.

"Muuuuummmmmieees …" he groaned, and lurched forward half a step.

John Moses yelped and jerked back behind Captain Jones, trembling. Both men laughed, though Jed thought that Jones's laughter was more forced this time, for his benefit rather than out of real amusement.

"Maybe you'll show us these mummies aboard the *Liahona*," he suggested politely. "It's not a long ride from Fort Bridger to Salt Lake, but there's time enough to spread the word among the passengers in the morning and put on an exhibition in the afternoon." He smiled, and Jed found it a shrewd and calculating expression. "If you were to charge, say, a nickel a head, I could take two cents of that and let you use the *Liahona*'s stateroom."

Jed nodded as if he thought that were a good idea, and maybe, he reasoned with himself, maybe it *was* a good idea, from the point of view of maintaining their cover story. Of course, Poe would overthink the thing six ways to Sunday before agreeing to anything, so odds were it could never happen anyway.

"I'll pass on the suggestion to Doctor Archibald," he told Dan Jones, and the Captain nodded. "We'll load in tonight, then, and I reckon I'll most likely see you again at breakfast."

They shook hands again.

"Boo!" Jed hissed at John Moses before he turned to go, and the boy looked like he might cry.

LEⱯⱲꟼO⅃Ⱳ

Absalom Fearnley-Standish hunched over the bar and wrote furiously in his Patent Metallic Note-Paper-Book, racing to record all of Dick Burton's offenses of the evening before he forgot them. The morning, of course, had already filled a page. Now he had to add to it.

A lesser man might have surrendered, deciding that Burton had already seen through him and it was no longer worth continuing to write down the misdemeanors and felonies of the famous explorer. Absalom carried on, because he hoped Burton might yet come to believe in Absalom's authority, because it was proper to make a record of material infractions, that was just good Foreign Office procedure, and also out of sheer bloody-minded pride.

That at least, he thought, *we have in common.*

Evening of 22 July 1859. Persists in calling me by woman's name. Will not use correct form of address. Accuses me of cowardice, stupidity. Repeatedly disobeys direct orders. Questions my authority, accuses me of forgery. Commits likely crime (check Wyoming Territory statutes—burglary? trespass to chattels?).

He fortified himself with a sip of whisky from the shot glass in front of him.

Upon consideration, he scratched out the last item and sighed. Any crime Burton had committed, he'd committed, too, as an accomplice.

What are you doing here, Absalom? he asked himself. *You're thousands of miles from home, on a fool's errand, and shackled to a baboon.*

There is a war to avert, he reminded himself. *Or if it cannot be averted, then the Empire's interests must be protected. England, as everyone knows, expects that every man will do his duty.*

And, of course, there is Abigail.

He looked up from his Note-Paper-Book and his eye fell on an Angel. She sat one-quarter-turn pivoted away from him, as did the man graced with her presence, so Absalom could see them both clearly.

He—he was nothing; another brute American, a surly-looking thug whose brushy mustache and gorilla eyebrows would have suited some redcoat in India but here looked overstated, an exaggeration, a false and overly masculine swagger. Something in the back of his mind told him he should recognize the man, but he had no patience, either for the man's face or for the nagging thought. He was focused entirely on … her—she was grace and refinement and elegance and beauty, all bound in the delightful package of perfect, freckle-kissed feminine charms under a crest of curly brown hair. Absalom thought he could smell her perfume, over all the human stinks of the saloon, from where he sat, twenty feet away.

"Why no," the Angel was saying to the Brute, "I know shockingly little of the Mississippi River, really. I was carried across it as a small child and have not been back since. Please, tell me all about it."

"Your first problem with the Mississippi, Miss Annie," the Brute began to spout back in answer, "is distinguishing fact from fiction."

"Does that make it different from any other place, really?" she asked.

"Some would say not," the Brute admitted with a chuckle. "But when a man's riding a river that's so wide he can't see either bank, I find that he becomes particularly susceptible to the pernicious influence of fable."

"Tell me more," the Angel urged him on.

"Consider the case of the famous Mike Fink," the Brute mused. "You'll have heard of Mike Fink, I take it?" He stubbed out his cigar. The cigar, anyhow, smelled sweetly civilized to Absalom, and he regretted its disappearance but the Brute immediately fumbled in the inner pocket of his coat for another.

"He was a boatman of some sort, was he not?" Clearly, distinctly, unmistakably ... the Angel looked Absalom in the face and winked at him.

Absalom's heart froze, and he was dimly aware of his Patent Metallic Note-Paper-Book falling to the saloon floor from nerveless hands. Some time passed, and some conversation between the Angel and her Brute, and all Absalom could hear was the rushing of his own blood and the outrageous hammering of his own heart.

"... but he did in fact, that scalawag, ride a moose," the Brute was saying when Absalom's hearing returned. "Saddled an ornery bull and rode it around the muddy streets of St. Louis when that good old town wasn't much more than a trading post for Frenchmen and Injuns."

Absalom swallowed with a very dry mouth and, feeling suddenly terrified, raised his eyes to look upon the face of his Angel. She was nodding at the Brute's droning oratory, and smiling, but when Absalom looked at her, she shifted her eyes slightly to look back at him, and her smile widened a little more.

"Mr. Fink sounds terribly brave," she observed to the Brute.

Instantly, Absalom dropped his gaze and stared at the floor. *Good heavens, man, get hold of yourself!* He tried to seize command of his suddenly shaky spirits. *Are you a Cambridge man or aren't you? Don't shame the Foreign Office by acting the overgrown child!*

He swallowed again, still dry, and couldn't raise his eyes. The drone filled his ears—he found he couldn't make out the Brute's words at all, but every *mmm*, *hmmn*, and *I see* of the Angel rang like a church bell.

On the floor he saw his Note-Paper-Book. He must pick it up, mustn't leave work papers on a saloon floor. Those were property of the Crown really. He stood from his stool, shaking slightly in the knees, stooped to the floor, wrapped his fingers around the paper—

—and suddenly found himself propelled face-first across the room.

Absalom gasped for air and almost dropped the Note-Paper-Book. Midsections of dancing people and the startled faces of gamblers swerved in and out of his vision as he was launched horizontally forward. His trousers seemed to be dragging him ahead as if possessed, and when Absalom twisted to look back, he saw that he was gripped with both hands by the belt by a wild-eyed man with a gnarled and bushy beard.

"Unhand me!" Absalom meant it as a manly command, but even in his own ears it rang as a shrill squeak.

The wild-eyed man swung Absalom through the doorway and into the back hall of the saloon. There were heated lavatories, he knew, in this hallway, and an exit, but little traffic. The stranger slammed Absalom up against the wall, held him there with one fist twisted in his shirt, and stared into his face.

Absalom gulped. The stranger wore an eye patch, and his one unveiled eye drilled into Absalom with the piercing blue stare of a madman. His face was scarred and weatherworn, his beard tangled and streaked with gray, and whatever hair he had was hidden under a large bear-fur hat like that worn by the Coldstream Guards, though shabbier and more thoroughly used. He stank of meat, smoke, and sweat. He was half a foot shorter than Absalom, but somehow he seemed enormous.

"You use me ill, sir," Absalom managed to protest, though he felt it was a weak expression of his true sentiments.

"I need to be sure I got your full attention," the stranger growled. His free hand disappeared from Absalom's view, and when it returned, it held a long, triangular, straight-edged knife.

CHAPTER TWO

Burton threw the whisky back and let it burn. He looked to the bar again and saw that Fearnley-Standish's stool was empty. *Where had that pompous little pigeon-fart gone?* He was probably off getting into trouble, trying to exercise the authority of his patently fraudulent commission letter over the Shoshone and Burton would have to go drag him from the fire again before he sizzled. At least the Shoshone weren't cannibals, like the Kwakiutl, or like the Iroquois had once been. Not that Burton had anything against cannibals—he'd had more than one good friend who'd been an eater of man-flesh.

Why the Foreign Office had really sent Absalom Fearnley-Standish, Burton might never know. *Why* or *whether*. He seemed like a paper-shuffler, a time-server, at the best of times, a passably competent civil servant, and not like the diplomat he made himself out to be. Burton's own letter gave him wide discretion and referred only to a *companion who may assist you in diplomatic appeals, directed as you see fit.* He poured himself another shot. He'd been told he'd be getting a skilled bureaucrat and instead he got a two-penny Napoleon.

"Is there enough whisky in that bottle that you'd be willing to share?" a woman asked in a husky voice. She sat down opposite him, and Burton completely forgot about Absalom Fearnley-Standish and all the obnoxious things he had ever done.

The woman was small, with a face of straight lines and a natural grace to her movements that made Burton's heart stammer. Her appearance was ageless, though faint lines around the eyes suggested to Burton that she might be his age or even older. Not that that put him at ease—the she-wolf can bite to her last breath.

Her dress was a shiny scarlet crinoline with what looked like whalebone snaps down the front of it. It was the most eye-catching thing in the saloon, without the steel bell around the hips that so marred the fashions of London, hiding women's legs and buttocks, their most naturally fascinating lures. The nearly unveiled glimpse of her form made him regret the frock coat and waistcoat that hid Burton's own excellent, manly physique. At least he had good, virile facial hair.

"Permit me to get another glass, ma'am," he told her after a hesitation that seemed to him to last forever.

In answer, she lifted his shot glass to her own lips and took a sip. "If you feel you need one, sir," she said, mocking him with her arched eyebrows and poker face.

Burton heard her statement as a challenge and his blood boiled within him. Still, something held him back and it took him a moment to identify the restraining impulse. "I must tell you, ma'am, that I am not entirely at liberty. I am affianced, betrothed, engaged to be married."

"You make it sound so lawyerly," she commented, eyes and brows smiling at him though the lines of her lips were rather pursed and skeptical. "Shouldn't love be an adventure?"

Ishtar's pearly teeth, but wasn't that the truth? "I will not tell my solicitor that you have so thoroughly dismissed his profession," Burton managed to riposte, weakly.

Who was this woman?

She took a second sip, smaller this time, and shrugged. "And yet I don't mean to. I have a lawyer myself, a good one. For that matter, I have a husband. And I also have ... adventures ..." Her dark eyes glittered. "Sometimes every cog must slip its casing."

Burton wanted to resist but he felt himself becoming intrigued. "Are you a traveler as well, ma'am, or do you reside in Fort Bridger?"

The woman laughed lightly. "You mean, am I a woman of virtue passing through, or am I some disreputable Wyoming whore? Have no fear, sir, your wallet and your venereal health are both safe from me. I am here *di passagio*, on my way to the Great Salt Lake City and merely looking for company with which to pass a slow and chilly evening."

"I meant no disrespect to you, ma'am." Burton joined her in laughing, a little ruefully. "Nor, for that matter, to whores. The history of the race is replete with powerful and—" he leaned forward to whisper the word "—*sexual* women. Think of Bathsheba, for instance." He wanted to claim the initiative of the conversation and wrest back some of the control he had lost to this aggressive houri.

"Nefertiti," she countered.

"Cleopatra." Part of Burton mutely rebelled against the conversation. What if Isabel could see him now? But he felt compelled, by pride, and also by lust, to press on.

"The Queen of Sheba." She smiled.

"Her name was Balqis, according to the Arabs," Burton offered. "They should know, they're experts in all things pertaining to the *harim*." Was he sweating? He thought he could feel drops of moisture beading onto his forehead.

"And are you an Arab, then, sir? You might be, with that dark, wild, romantic look of yours, those mustachios and those scars, and your foreign accent."

Burton laughed out loud again. "No, ma'am, I'm a true subject of Her Britannic Majesty Queen Victoria and an Englishman of Anglo-Irish heritage, though it's been suggested I might have Traveler blood in me." He effected a slightly awkward bow, still sitting in his chair. "Richard Francis Burton, at your service. I'm known formally as *Captain Burton*, but I'm often called less flattering things."

"Such as?"

"*Ruffian Dick* is my favorite," he offered. "Most of the others are unprintable."

"My name is Roxie," she told him, "Roxie Snow." She made a small curtsy from the waist up. "I've been called more than one unprintable thing myself." She took a third sip from the shot glass.

Burton hesitated. He felt quite strongly attracted to Roxie, who was obviously being very forward with him. He was by no means averse to *adventures*, as Roxie named them, but now he was engaged to be married, and being engaged meant he was no longer a free man.

Not only did he have Isabel to consider, but there was also Fearnley-Standish. Burton tried to look about the room and spot the Foreign Office man but found he couldn't take his eyes off Roxie. Fearnley-Standish, too, was an anchor chained around Dick Burton's neck. Burton was chained to orders, chained to a mission, chained to authority, chained to a useless companion and a cold, boring fiancée. He was totally unfree.

The weight of his servitude hung on him hard and heavy.

He took the glass and raised it. "To the unprintable," he toasted, and drained the glass.

ᒐᛱᛠᛝᏬᒐᛱ

Tam poked his head up out of the stairwell first. Like a bloody woodpecker, he thought, sticking its feathered face out the tree trunk for a look around. The *Liahona* was much bigger than the *Jim Smiley*, with multiple cabins, two levels below decks, and great crushing metal treads where the *Jim Smiley* had its India rubber tyres, but its lights were dimmed and most of its crew and passengers seemed to be away, probably washing down the dust of the road in the saloon. The few men whom Tam had run into aboard had exchanged hat-tips with him (and wasn't Tam as good as any other man, and as worthy to share a doffing of hats with?) and passed by without a second glance.

That was the America he loved, Tam thought. You leave your baggage lying about unwatched like you own the whole bloody-damn-hell country, and if anyone touches it without permission, you shoot the presumptuous bastard full of hot lead.

He knew it was the *Liahona* (*What is that, anyway,* he thought, *some kind of bloody Indian name?*) because he'd listened to the talk in the saloon, and nothing else in the yard could approach this beast in size or sheer rhinocerontic majesty. He wouldn't have known it from the side of the vehicle—where its name should have been painted, in plain bloody-damn-hell English, which Mother O'Shaughnessy had taught Tam to read, instead there was a stream of some odd-looking characters Tam didn't recognize. Squirrelly, curling letters, like the work of some idiot genius who couldn't read English and was trying to imitate the Book of Kells. Maybe, he reflected, it *was* an Indian vehicle after all.

The deck was empty, so Tam wrapped his scarf around the lower half of his face, hoisted the box off its resting place on his knee, and finished his climb, emerging out of the dimly-lit hall into the chill darkness of night. The metal crate was heavy in his arms and *clanked* but it looked like it had all of Sam's precious tools and Tam didn't have that far to carry it. And of course it had the patches; Mother O'Shaughnessy hadn't raised many idjits and the ones she *had* raised weren't named *Tamerlane*.

The man vomiting at the door of the saloon had collapsed now, facedown onto the gravel. *Out of sheer sympathy for fellow human beings,* Tam thought, patting himself mentally on the back, *I hope the fellow passed out before he fell into his own vomit.* Tam didn't see anyone else and, for lack of a better means, he got the tools down to the ground by simply dropping the crate over the rail.

Crash!

He slipped down the ladder and looked around. Was that a shadowy figure, standing over in the darkness of the stockade yard, hidden by the building's corner from the fuzzy glare of the Franklin Poles? Tam couldn't be sure.

Making a show of adjusting his pants, he undid the leather cord that held the Webley Longspur strapped into its holster and checked the thin, spring-loaded stiletto tied to his right wrist.

The shadowy figure, if figure it was, didn't move.

Tam stretched to pop his neck and all the joints in his arms, then picked up the crate again. He walked softly across the yard, making extra sure that his pace looked natural but displaced no gravel, like a ferret, like a blue tit hopping across the yard after a fallen seed, so he could listen over the soft *pad-pad-pad* of his own footfalls and hear anyone approaching from behind. It wasn't quite as good as eyes in the back of his head, but Tam's hearing could be shockingly sharp.

His precautions were rewarded with a *crunch* sound behind him. *Heavy boot in gravel,* he thought.

Bloody Pinkertons, that's who's hiding in the darkness.

No, Tam, you damnfool idjit, that could be anybody. Could be someone else getting off the Liahona, *or maybe the drunk fellow came to his senses and is standing up.*

Or maybe it was someone lurking in the shadow of the building, waiting for Tam to come out of the *Liahona. Could be one of the English.*

Or a Pinkerton, of course it could be, by damn.

Another *crunch.*

Tam forced his brain to analyze the situation as his steps brought him closer to the *Jim Smiley.* Could the Pinkerton know it was him? Didn't seem likely. Better bet was that the Pinkerton was hiding in the yard to see what he could see and it was just Tam's rotten Irish luck that the Pinkerton had seen *him.*

If it was a Pinkerton, Tam had to kill him. He was spotted now, and there was no way to simply disappear from view. And if it wasn't a Pinkerton, Tam might have to kill him anyway—it could be some other enemy of his, or maybe someone badly in need of a lesson that you don't follow other people around in the dark, that's just creepy, and if you aren't careful you're going to get yourself knifed.

Thank Brigit for the scarf, for the cold and for the disguise. Tam made a show of dropping the crate to the gravel and arching his shoulders back to display how heavy it was and how much pain he was in. Then, without delay, though at the same time making a pantomime of how slowly he moved, he turned to see the approaching party, source of the ominous *crunches.*

Tam recognized the man from his conversation with Clemens; he was the Pinkerton with the stovepipe hat. He approached at a calm but determined pace, one hand holding a sheet of paper in front of him and the other hand invisible inside his long duster. *Probably holding a gun,* Tam thought. *Bloody-damn-hell Pinkertons.* Tam shaded his eyes as if to protect them from the glare of the electricks and quickly scanned the yard while his features were in shadow. There was no one in sight—the time to act was now, and quickly.

"Good evenin', suh," Tam said pleasantly, trying to fake a Virginia drawl through his scarf and wishing he were better at accents. "I wonder if you might give me a hand with this load? I find myself not quite up to the task and you are a tall and strong-looking young man." *Don't overdo it, Tamerlane O'Shaughnessy me boy,* he chided himself. *The fewer bloody words, the better. Plus, you don't want to make the fellow think your interest in him is* romantic.

"Pardon me," Stovepipe said, holding out his sheet of paper and stepping closer, "but could you tell me if you've seen this man?" He squinted.

Alarm bells went off in Tam's head and he didn't wait. Releasing the spring of his stiletto, he grabbed the hilt of the knife as it leaped into his hand and punched straight out, swiping Stovepipe across his Adam's apple. Stovepipe lurched back, but not fast enough to get out of reach and blood sprayed forward and down onto Tam's arm and shoulder, hot and wet and sweet stinking.

Tam slashed again and took a second slice out of the Pinkerton's throat. Bloody bastard could take all the time in the world he wanted to die, so long as he didn't call out to anyone.

Chunk! Chunk! Small craters of gravel exploded around Tam's feet. *Is someone shooting at me?* He wondered. *But I don't hear shots.* Then he saw the holes in the front of the Pinkerton's duster, heard a sharp *zing!* and saw another hole rip open just as an explosion of gravel kicked up beside him.

A Maxim Husher, he thought. *Bloody self-righteous Pinkertons with all their high talk and rules and principled objections to a little bit of traditional graft, and the bastard's shooting at me with a silenced gun.* He stabbed at Stovepipe's eye— another *zing!*—at the same moment, Tam sank his stiletto deep into the private detective's skull and felt a sharp bite in his thigh.

The Pinkerton collapsed backward with Tam off-balance and flailing on top of him. For a moment, Tam could do nothing but catch his breath and fight to calm his wildly beating heart. *Got to move, you dumb Irish bastard,* he cursed himself, *the Pinkerton didn't come here alone,* and he forced his body into action.

He took the Pinkerton's Husher (*and aren't you a strange-looking little fellow?* he thought, looking at the pistol whose barrel looked like two onion bulbs stitched together front-to-back), along with powder, shot, and bullets, and shoved them into his own coat. Stovepipe was larger than he was, but Tam's wiry frame was all sinew, and the adrenalin in his body now made it easy to drag the corpse a few dozen paces across the gravel, hiding it in the shadow of the *Liahona.*

He searched the man's coat and took the calotype. No sense leaving that to float around; he'd ball it up and throw it into the boiler of the *Jim Smiley,* and good riddance to it.

When he stood up from that effort, the pain shooting through his leg reminded him that he'd been shot and must be bleeding. He couldn't see, so he felt with his fingers for the slickness to determine how bad the bleeding was (*not so bad, all things considered*), tied his scarf around the wound and then hop-walked quickly back to the crate. He examined the ground. The gravel was scuffed where the body had been dragged, but he doubted it would show footprints with any clarity at all and Tam didn't think he was leaving a trail of blood.

He grunted, picked up the crate, and headed for the *Jim Smiley. Be careful, O'Shaughnessy,* he reminded himself. *There's still another one of those two-faced dirty bastards around here somewhere.*

ᒣᕃᘈᐚᘚᐚᕂᒣ

Burton led the way, but in his heart he knew that Roxie was directing his steps. It felt good, though, to wrestle with a woman who was his match. To feel at risk in the contest of the heart, that was what he wanted, what he needed.

He shut thoughts of Isabel, his fiancée, out of his mind.

A niggling worry about Fearnley-Standish tried to creep into their place, and he slammed that out as well.

The transition through the saloon doors was a plunge from a warm, smoky, amber bowl full of placid human goldfish into the cold, crackling, blue ocean floor, among sleeping leviathans who could, with a single bite, swallow you. As he crossed the crinkled gravel carpet, the spitting blue balls of the saloon's Franklin Poles propelled him out of their own sphere and into the bone-white realm of a dusty, enchanted moon. A carpet of pale moonlight, like a silver dusting of snow, lay across the nearest mountains, visible over the stockade walls, and all thoughts of Burton's fiancée and his nebbish associate vanished. This was a wilderness, he was a man, and he was about to have the experience of this mysterious, exciting woman.

He tightened his grip on her hand, which squeezed him back with a surprising strength, and headed for the near-side ladder, but Roxie pulled him to the right, underneath the ship-like prow of the vehicle and just beneath the exotic characters that Burton assumed must spell out its name; they looked vaguely like the Devanagari script, he thought distractedly, though not cursive. She pulled his body into hers. Her mouth was sharp, salty, and exhilarating, a foamy wave concealing deadly shoals beneath, and he was hard put to breathe between kisses.

"Dick," she moaned.

"Roxie," he breathed.

"Nefertiti," she corrected. Her body blazed against his like a fire.

"Nefertiti," he agreed, intoxicated.

"Cleopatra," she continued. She smelled like an entire orchard of sweet pollen. He tightened from head to toe, poised for intimate combat.

"Cleopatra," he said, "Bathsheba." *This, by the fires of Vizaresh and the House of Lies,* this *was what a woman was supposed to do to a man!*

"The Queen of Sheba," she added. He thought her mouth was on the verge of drawing his very soul up from his chest and consuming it.

"Balqis," he agreed, then suddenly jerked to his full height, pulling away from her. "Vishnu's beard!" he barked.

"Yes, Vishnu," she murmured. "Don't pull back!"

But Burton did withdraw his mouth from hers and his hand went to the gun at his belt, the well-worn and deadly accurate Colt 1851 Navy Revolver. Behind Roxie, on the other side of the *Liahona*, invisible to the saloon, someone lay on the ground. All he could see of the person were two heavy boots, toes up, poking around the corner of the vehicle.

"There's someone there," Burton muttered. The boots weren't moving, despite all the noise the pair had been making, and he didn't hear any snoring. "Or a body."

"Yes," Roxie breathed, but then she caught his tone, stopped, and looked where he was looking. "Oh," she said simply.

"It could be Isabel," Burton said, and edged forward for a look.

"Isabel?" Roxie asked. "Is that your fiancée, then?" There was no accusation in her voice, only amusement. Still, Burton gritted his teeth for his humiliating slip. "She has large feet."

"I ... I mean Absalom," he corrected himself. "I mean my colleague, Absalom Fearnley-Standish."

"Is Mr. Fearnley-Standish a drunk?"

"No." Burton frowned, and turned the corner of the *Liahona* to finally look at the body lying on the ground. "And neither is this man. He's dead. Been cut several times to the head, neck, and eyes."

"Be careful, Dick," Roxie whispered, hanging slightly back. "Too much of that kind of talk may cool my ardor."

"I wouldn't want that," Burton murmured, and he meant it.

He considered what his obligations might be. The dead man was one of the Pinkertons who had accosted him in the saloon, demanding to know if he had seen some Irishman, McNamara. He owed the Pinkertons nothing. Ought he to inform some kind of law enforcement officer of the Fort? He didn't know who that would be, but didn't he owe at least that much to the general principles of law and order?

Roxie looked past Burton's elbow at the dead man. "Yes, Dick, I believe he's dead. Now I'm going up the ladder, and if you want an opportunity to show me how lively *you* are, you'd better move quickly." Then she was gone, and Burton heard her shoes *crunch* on the gravel and then *click* on the ladder of the *Liahona*.

It surprised him, but this was as dangerous a country as he'd ever been in. It made him wonder if perhaps he ought to be carrying his sword around, as well as his pistol, rather than leaving it in its case with the rest of his luggage. He had brought the sword thinking he might at some point have an opportunity for a little exercise, but perhaps he actually needed it as a weapon in this lawless place.

Burton turned and admired Roxie's form, lithely flitting up the iron rungs of the ladder.

Perhaps it took such a country to make such a woman.

He would inform someone on the *Liahona* of the body, he resolved as he gripped the bottom rungs of the ladder to throw himself up after her. It was hard to see that he had any more obligation than that.

ᒪᗱ𐤔ᗱ𐤔

Moments after Annie excused herself and disappeared, the Irishman slammed down into her chair. He had his porkpie pulled low over his face and the collar of his coat (not his coat at all, actually—Sam's long moleskin overcoat, and Sam didn't recall offering to lend it to him) turned up, giving him the ridiculous appearance of skulking in a room full of people. He was pale and sweating, and Sam found that he resented his associate for not being a beautiful, interesting girl.

"You don't look well, O'Shaughnessy," he observed mildly.

"Damn fookin' straight," the Irishman agreed. "I'm not well. I'm bleeding is what I am."

"The Pinkertons catch up with you?"

"One of 'em, and not to his own gain." The Irishman huddled deeper into his collar. "Was it you that turned me in, Sam Clemens?"

Sam snorted, unwilling to answer such a stupid question. "You're welcome to borrow my coat, by the way. But shouldn't you be hiding?"

"Yeah," O'Shaughnessy agreed, "I should. The other one's in the loo, so I've only got a minute. And I had to tell you something, something right bloody damn urgent!" His pointed nose, green eyes, and reddish blonde hair made his apparent anxiety comical. He looked like an irate fairy, Sam thought.

"I'm listening," Sam said.

"Sabotage!" the Irishman hissed. "Filthy underhanded tricks, and it was the English that done it!"

Sam took a punch in the stomach from cold fear, but he wasn't about to share his feelings with Tamerlane O'Shaughnessy. "What is it you think the English did to sabotage us?" he asked mildly. "Did they steal your coat?"

"You ought to be thanking me, Sam Clemens, and not taking the bloody mick," O'Shaughnessy pouted. "Those bastards punched holes in the precious bloody boiler pipes of your precious fancy truck, and then they went and stole the tools and patches. And who was it, if it wasn't me, that went and snuck onto that big hump of the *Liahona* and stole the tools and patches back?"

That was an interesting development. "Good job, O'Shaughnessy," Clemens complimented the man grudgingly. "When Washington asks, I'll tell them you're earning your paycheck. Now unless you happen to know that that Pinkerton is a world champion at Endurance Micturition, you'd better take a powder."

He watched O'Shaughnessy slink back out the front door of the saloon. The man had some nerve, demanding that Sam thank him after Sam had saved his bacon by hiding him from the Pinkertons. Well, that might not be such a bad thing; nerve, after all, was one of the principal things Sam needed the Irishman for.

He considered his situation. The Englishmen were riding on the *Liahona*, which meant they were going to the Great Salt Lake City. They had poked holes in the *Jim Smiley*, which meant that they wanted to be sure they got there before Sam. That made them rivals, competitors of some sort. Likely an English mission to old Brigham Young, and Sam thought he could predict what they wanted. *There's a war coming, Mr. Young,* they'd say, *and England wants you in it on her side, with your airships and with your phlogiston guns, too, if those are real and not the product of Rocky Mountain moonshine, thank you, very much.*

England would be on the side of the South, with all her cotton exports that fed England's many mills. Not that Sam hated the South, not at all. He was from Hannibal, Missouri, and if you drew the Mason-Dixon line straight out west all the way to his native state, you'd find Hannibal on the same side of it as Georgia, if only by a hair. Sam loved the South, but he loved the Union more. *The United States of America, that was old Ben Franklin's dream, that's what makes us great,* he thought.

And Sam hated war. War killed young men, young men like Henry. If the English got the Kingdom of Deseret into the game on the side of the secessionists, then the so-called Confederate States would be emboldened. They might think they could actually win. That would make war more likely. The Confederate States would stop being a dream that fools like Robert E. Lee and Jefferson Davis talked about in salon society and would start being something that killed young men.

Maybe a lot of young men.

Sam had to get to Salt Lake City first.

He lit a cigar and pondered.

Repairing the *Jim Smiley* was one thing; Sam could do that in a few hours, if it was only a matter of patching some holes. Sam had seen the *Liahona* arrive at Fort Bridger earlier in the day, and she had come in fast, growling up the road west like some giant wild animal, chewing up the hard earth and throwing out a cloud behind her that settled for miles.

That thing probably went fifteen miles an hour on a straightaway and if he didn't do something to slow it up she would drop the Englishmen off on Brigham's doorstep while Sam was still cranking away with a wrench in Fort Bridger.

One of the Shoshone apparently won the hopscotch game they'd all been playing and erupted into a yelp of victory. The yelper collected winnings from his friends, barking and hooting all the while, and then broke into some kind of spinning, ecstatic dance. All in all, the Shoshone reminded Sam of the drunk white boys he had seen every weekend growing up in Hannibal, Missouri.

The bouncers must have viewed the matter differently. They moved in steadily, beady eyes squinting in faces like smoked hams. "You're gonna have to keep it down," one of them directed the Shoshone.

Other patrons of the saloon were staring. The dancer didn't slow down or quiet his voice, if anything he became more frenetic.

Sam took a puff on his cigar.

Both bouncers raised their fists to show that they were wrapped in brass knuckledusters, studded with low, ugly little spikes. "I said quit yer caterwauling," the bouncer repeated himself. "You wanna get noisy, get noisy in the yard."

The dancer's friends gave the big white men hard stares of rejection and did nothing else. The dancer kept right on whirling.

Sam sensed impending violence and wondered idly if he ought to start wearing a gun. He scooted his chair back a step so as to be able to stand up quickly without getting tangled in the table.

"I *said*," the bouncer grimaced as he waded into the Shoshone youth, "shut *up*!"

He swung his brass-encased fist at one of the Shoshone's heads—

—and another brave stepped in, turning aside the blow with his long rifle, as if it were a quarterstaff—

—the dancer himself leaped forward, drawing a long, ugly knife, quick as lightning, and pointing it at the bouncer's face—

—other rifles snapped to the ready, held by Shoshone or by other customers of the saloon—

and the bouncers' pistols—

—two scatterguns came up over the bar—

—silence fell over the Saloon.

Everyone took a slow breath.

Electricks crackled in the background.

"I *told* you, you got to keep it down," persisted the talking bouncer. *Give the man credit for taking his job seriously,* Sam thought. *And for guts.*

One of the Shoshone, who held his rifle pointed squarely at the bouncer's chest, shrugged, his face impassive. "We're done taking orders from white men," he said.

More silence. Sweat.

These boys would do very nicely.

Sam blew a dragon puff of blue-gray smoke out into the already-thick air and clomped noisily to his feet, stamping the thick rubber soles hard to get everyone's attention.

"This impasse is uncomfortable for everyone," he began. He turned at the waist as he spoke, smiled at the whole saloon. "But I think I may have a solution."

There was a brief pause.

"I'm listening, mister," the bouncer said.

Sam counted the Shoshone braves and pulled a twenty-dollar gold double eagle from his pocket for each of them, seven in total. No employer more generous with expense money than the taxpayers. He held his hand forward as he approached, showing the gold to the Indians, and damn who else might see. He'd be gone in the morning, anyway, and if anyone was fool enough to attack him aboard the *Jim Smiley*, he'd fry them in their boots.

"I have business to conduct with these fine Shoshone gentlemen," he explained, stretching the truth just a little. "I've been waiting for an opportunity to get their attention, and now seems like a fine time."

The bouncer blinked and looked back at the Indians. The Shoshone stared at Clemens with hard eyes, and for a moment Sam thought they were just going to shoot him and take his money. *Oh well,* he thought, *if I'm dead I won't care so much when war breaks out.*

Plus, I'll finally know the truth about Henry.

"Yes," one of the Shoshone finally agreed. He was a young man, tall and straight and strong-faced. "Let's talk business." He lowered his own rifle first, and then his comrades, the bouncers, the bartenders, and the various armed saloon patrons followed, in rough synchronization.

"Thank you, very much," Sam said to the Shoshone, taking another comforting draw on his cigar. "Though I will confess to a little disappointment. For a moment there, I thought I was about to get my glimpse of the much-storied afterlife, and I'd finally know what all the fuss was about."

LƐ⅄ꟼ0ꚝᴎ

"You have my undivided attention, I assure you," Absalom gulped. He'd known as an abstract fact that dangerous frontier types were one of the risks when he'd come after Abigail, but the Foreign Office hadn't trained him for this.

"Listen close," the one-eyed, bear-hatted, grizzled man barked. "I will say this one time—"

He cut himself off abruptly, cocked an ear in the direction of the common room, and then whirled on his heel, jerking Absalom in his wake. Absalom stumbled after the little bear of a man, pulled by his shirt front, past the dented brass doors marked *Bucks* and *Does*, past an automatic boot-polishing machine that squatted sullenly against the wall, hissing softly as it waited for toes to work on, and then out through the rear door of the saloon, ducking as it rebounded from his captor's kick and nearly caught Absalom in its trap-like jaws.

"I should warn you," Absalom squeaked, "that I've done my fair share of bare-knuckle boxing."

Bear Hat dragged him around the back of the saloon, into the darkest quarter of the yard, out of sight of the idling steam-trucks, out of sight of the dormitories, lit only by an indifferent moon and distant, dimly twinkling stars. He tossed Absalom against the saloon wall—the plascrete hurt as Absalom crashed into it and his vision spun. The wild man spat in the gravel.

"Like I give a shit," he said.

Absalom felt like begging, but wouldn't let himself. He had to keep his dignity. "I'm a representative of Her Britannic Majesty Queen Victoria," he pointed out.

The wild man laughed and brought the knife up, its glinting blade flashing dangerously close to Absalom's eyes. "I ain't afraid to borrow trouble," he grunted. "I'm a representative of His Rocky Mountain Majesty Orrin Porter Rockwell, the notorious Danite! How does that sit with your liver?"

Rockwell! "Your, er, master is a dangerous man …"

Absalom's mind cranked away, gears spinning. How could he get this fellow to take him to Rockwell?

The bear-hatted man turned up his eyepatch, revealing that he had two perfectly good eyes.

"By representative, what I really mean to say is that I *am* Porter Rockwell."

"Rockwell!" Absalom gasped. Abigail … "But you're … you're just the man …"

"I didn't kill Boggs," Rockwell grunted sourly.

Boggs? "No, what I mean to say is—"

"Nor none of them others, neither."

"No? Well, I—"

"Leastways, not all of 'em. Now, look here, Absalom—"

Absalom gasped. "You know my name!"

"You must think I'm stupider'n a fence post. I married your sister, dumbass. Just 'cause I ain't never seen you before don't mean I don't know your name!"

Absalom tried to take this information in stride. "So ... you know why I'm here, then?" The little four-shot derringer tucked into his waistband, the pistol that Ruffian Dick had mocked as a lady's gun, had never seemed so inadequate as it did in this moment.

"Everybody knows why you're here, you numbskull!" Rockwell barked, and then, as if startled by the loudness of his own voice, he peered both directions into the darkness. When he spoke again, it was in a hoarse whisper. "That's the problem! You're here with that other Englishman, the Nile explorer, 'cause you want to talk Brother Brigham into lending you airships to bomb the hell outta the Yankees, yeah?"

Absalom breathed a sigh of relief. "Yeah," he agreed, the word foreign in his mouth. "Well, more or less."

As if this admission gave him renewed purpose, Rockwell hoisted Absalom up by his shirtfront again and waved his knife in his face. "I ain't gonna say this twice!"

"You said that before," Absalom noted reflexively, then cringed at the sound of his own words. "I mean ... I meant ..."

"Shut up!" Rockwell snarled. "Go back! Go back to London, tell your Queen that the passes were all snowed in, you couldn't make it through, you were tortured by Injuns, you were robbed by bandits, you lost your money at the faro tables, your boat sank in the Mississippi, you were eaten by the damn bears, tell her whatever the hell you gotta tell her, but *GO BACK!* Don't go to Salt Lake, as if your life depended on it!" He scowled ferociously, but the eyepatch chose that precise moment to *snap* back into place, ruining the effect. "Ow!"

"I ... I can't ..." Should he tell Rockwell? Should he have it out with the man now?

"Mind you," Rockwell cut him off again, "your life *does* depend on it." With a simple twist of his wrist, Rockwell turned his big, sharp knife and it carved a large crescent out of the stiff brim of Absalom's hat. The discarded snippet fell to the ground, forlorn.

No, Absalom decided, *best to say nothing to the man now. Best not to say anything ever. Best to simply get Abigail and leave, and never see Porter Rockwell again.*

"I understand," he said carefully, as if trying to talk reason into a mountain lion. "I shall discuss your position with my colleague, Captain Burton."

"Fine," Rockwell spat. "Tell him I'll knife him just as happily as I'll knife you, even if he ain't family."

"He will appreciate your fair-mindedness," Absalom said, and then wanted to kick himself.

"I'd sooner see you floating dead in the Bear River than alive and walking the streets of Salt Lake," Rockwell said. "I hate—" he paused and strained at the air to listen. Absalom thought he heard the low conversation of men's voices somewhere, but he couldn't be sure.

"Dammit!" Rockwell cursed in a whisper. Dropping Absalom to the ground, he turned and sprinted, cat-like and quiet, into the darkness and was gone.

"Great thundering Jove!" Absalom quipped, sinking into a puddle of his own coat, but the Burtonesque oath lacked Burton's panache and gave him neither courage nor comfort. He sat shaking and trying to calm his breath, took off his circumcised top hat, and let the cool night breezes blow through his sweaty hair.

"Looks like you've had a scare, brother," said a warm, kindly baritone above him. Absalom lifted his head and found himself in the gaze of a clean-shaven, square-headed man with protruding jug ears and a broad smile. "That isn't the happy grin we prefer to see on first-time visitors to the Kingdom," the man said.

He wore a heavy brown wool coat over a yellow waistcoat of rough wool and a red bowtie. One of his waistcoat buttons was tortoiseshell, but two of them had been replaced with whittled wooden disks.

"A grin that happy'd make me feel bad to see it on the face of my worst enemy," added another voice, more nasal and higher-pitched than the first, and Absalom saw that a second man stood at Square Head's shoulder. He was lean and bent, with a stubbled chin and eyes that didn't look quite the same direction. Each man wore two pistols on his belt and held a rifle in one hand. "Name's Bill Hickman," he introduced himself and extended his free hand in greeting.

"Absalom Fearnley-Standish," Absalom presented himself. He rose shakily to his feet and then took the proffered hands of both men and shook them. "Representative of Her Britannic Majesty Queen Victoria."

"Oh, you're one of the Englishmen," said Square Head. "My name is John Lee. Bill and I are both simple ranchers and horse traders, but we sometimes run errands for Brother Brigham or the Twelve."

"You mean Brigham Young?" Absalom clarified.

"President of the Kingdom of Deseret," Lee nodded proudly.

"And the Quorum of the Twelve Apostles," Hickman added.

"Yes, the Foreign Office is well aware of the identity of Brigham Young," Absalom said, dusting off his hands. "I am to see President Young on my arrival. My colleague and I are to see him, that is."

"We can't none of us wait." Hickman grinned, and his missing teeth and stray eyes together gave him the appearance of a madhouse resident. Absalom shuddered.

"In the meantime, Brother Absalom, maybe you can help us," Lee suggested. "We're aiming to meet a friend of ours, a man named Porter Rockwell, but we haven't been able to find him."

"It wasn't him as scared you, was it?" Hickman demanded, staring at Absalom with one eye while the other wandered about the back wall of the saloon.

Absalom looked from one man to the other. They stood respectfully back and smiled in a friendly fashion, but their friendliness and their interest in Rockwell made him nervous.

"I'm afraid it wasn't, gentlemen," he lied. "Unfortunately, you've caught me after an argument with my colleague that's left me rather shaken. I don't know your friend; have you checked inside, and in the dormitories?"

Hickman squinted suspiciously, but John Lee nodded and smiled. "Thanks very much," Lee said. "Welcome to the Kingdom of Deseret. I hope we get to see more of you around the Great Salt Lake City."

Then he walked away, tugging Hickman with him by the elbow.

Absalom stood watching them go, nodding affably, and when they were around the corner, he collapsed like a marionette with cut strings.

LEWTOHW

Sam sat on the edge of a bunk in the cheap section of the dormitories. Two gas lamps lit the whole room, which looked about a hundred feet long and held maybe fifty beds, upper and lower bunks, all flat and hard and appealing only to the truly exhausted. In the corner opposite the entrance was the all-ages-and-sexes latrine, a squatpot-and-bidet unit whose modesty could be preserved by a tattered and unfortunately stained curtain. As usual in these caravanserais, the Indians, Mexicans, and other non-Anglos ended up bunking around the latrine end of the room, so Sam sat staring into twenty-odd copper faces and feeling grateful for the jet of steam and hot water that flushed out the squatpot after each use and kept it smelling, if not nice, then at least not abominable.

Still, the sight was distracting. "Would you gentlemen mind closing the curtain?" he suggested mildly. "I find my sensibilities are more delicate than I had imagined."

They were mostly young, all male, wild-looking, and armed to the teeth. Just what he needed.

"I'm not looking to start a war," he informed them. "I just need to delay the *Liahona* a bit."

One of the older men—maybe as old as fifty, a man who had been identified to Sam as Chief Pocatello—nodded. "The white men of Deseret are not our enemies," he said, "but we sometimes have small disagreements with Brigham and his people. Sometimes those disagreements even go so far as skirmishes."

"Tell me what sort of thing might cause such a disagreement, Chief Pocatello," Sam urged the older man.

"Money talks," said the older Shoshone. "I hear you speak its language."

Sam tossed a small bag of gold coins to the floor; the bag (the strings of which Sam had deliberately loosened) opened and spilled its dully gleaming contents onto the plascrete floor. The crowd gave an appropriately appreciative collective grin and one of the younger men collected up the coins and gave them to Pocatello. "How's that for a parley-vouz?" Sam asked.

The old Indian shrugged, but his eyes twinkled. "Is that all?"

Sam grinned broadly. The hook was in the fish's mouth. "No, Chief, it isn't. I've got an idea how you can turn an even bigger profit out of this deal, provided you're willing to do a little trading in commodities."

LƐⴑⴎⵀ0ⴕⴑ

Jed crouched behind the pipes above one of the squatpots. The two 'pots sat side by side in the saloon's donicker, in booths separated from each other by a thin slab of plascrete, and the pipes that ran up behind the 'pots and into the ceiling shared a crawlspace behind them for occasional maintenance. A full-grown man might have wormed his way back into the crawlspace with a ladder and some patience; Jed found it a comfortable waiting place, as well as a tactically shrewd one.

Sooner or later, he thought, *everybody shits*. When it really came down to it, that's all people were anyway, skin bags full of blood and snot that sloshed around all day processing their next shit.

He had a length of piano wire wrapped loosely around one hand and a little ebony canister, inscribed with hieroglyphic writing, beside him in the shadows. He couldn't read what the hieroglyphs said, and he didn't care to. Hell, he wasn't even sure Poe could read them, though that man could fake his way out of an iron box if an army of angels was guarding it with flaming swords. If pressed, Poe would no doubt be able to spout acres of bullshit and claim it was the interpretation of the funny old pictures. Jed knew what was in the canister and he knew how to use it and that was all he cared about.

The latrine door opened and the Pinkerton sauntered in. It was the one with the Bowler Hat, and he seemed to be looking for someone. Jed crouching extra low in the shadow of the crawlspace just in case Bowler Hat decided his quarry might be a spider or a monkey. The Pinkerton peered under both the stall doors and called out, "Diamond!"

Was that all he wanted, to find his friend Diamond? Would he have to spend more time up here waiting, ignoring the vile noises and breathing in the rotten stink of his fellow human beings? As he thought of it, the image struck him as a pretty good description of life generally.

But no, Bowler Hat had the urge. He selected the stall with the cleanest 'pot, shut himself in, hung his duster over the stall door, and dropped his trousers.

Why is it, Jed wondered, *that naked men looked so damn silly?* At least the Pinkerton kept his shirt on.

Jed wasn't certain that the Pinkerton had to die. But he had chewed the matter over after his conversation with Poe, watching the two men work the room and flash their calotype, and had come to the conclusion that it was best if the two detectives disappeared. He couldn't be sure whether they were his enemies or enemies of his enemies, and the uncertainty would complicate all his decisions. He hadn't discussed his resolution with Poe, had decided to take it into his own hands to cut the Gorgon knot, as Poe himself was fond of saying, and just wipe the problem out. The world was uncertain, unclear, dirty, and dangerous and a man still had to act.

Bowler Hat grunted, tensed the muscles of his shoulders, emitted an unpleasant odor, and relaxed. Now he was vulnerable. Jed stretched the piano wire from one hand to the other, waited until he heard his target exhale, and then jumped.

Long years of playing the acrobat or the geek or the animal wrestler in one-horse southern towns made his attack possible. Jed dropped easily onto Bowler Hat's shoulders and simultaneously threw a loop of the wire around his neck.

The hat hit the filthy floor as the big Pinkerton jumped back, smashing Jed against the plascrete wall of the stall—

—*thud!*—

—Jed grunted, but held tight—

—the Pinkerton pulled, kicked, strained—

—Jed squeezed tighter, just like holding shut the jaws of an alligator—

—the Pinkerton clawed, scratching Jed's arms, and smashed Jed against the walls several more times—

—*oomph!* —

—but by the time the big man realized that his only chance was his pistol and grabbed for it, he was passing out.

Jed landed hard, wedged into the corner of the stall as Bowler Hat fell back onto the squatpot. He continued the garroting until he was sure the Pinkerton was dead, then climbed down, feeling more irritated than sickened by his surroundings. He quickly stripped the man of interesting personal effects—a Maxim Husher (he raised his eyebrows and whistled), a wallet, a badge—before climbing the cold water pipe back up into the crawlspace where he'd left the canister.

The attack and the theft had together taken two minutes or less. Now Jed popped open the lid of the canister and shook its contents down onto

Bowler Hat's prone body. Several dozen brass beetles, *scarabs* Poe would call them, fell onto the bare lower half and into the clothing folds of the dead Pinkerton.

Inside the hinged lid of the canister there were two buttons. Jed pressed one of them, and the scarabs set to work. With fine brass mandibles, relentless brass claws and tiny jets of powerful acids, they made short work of the corpse, squirting acid onto the man's body and then plucking away the dissolving and scorching bits and consuming them, like a woman plucking the flesh off a boiled chicken. Like a snowball tossed into a campfire, the man's body just melted.

Jed watched, fascinated and a little bit disgusted, though he kept one nervous eye on the door. Not that he was surprised at what the inside of another man looked like, but it wasn't the sort of thing he looked at every day, not by choice, not if he could help it.

In thirty seconds, bones showed through the flesh all over; in a minute, only bones were left; in two minutes, the bones were gone too, and the brass swarm *clicked* and *clattered* uncertainly around the 'pot and rustled the empty clothing.

Jed pressed the second button. Instantly, the swarm stopped its random runabout motion and headed his direction. Slightly unnerved, despite his knowledge, he set the canister on the edge of the crawlspace and edged back into the darkness, as if that would save him. He watched uncomfortably as the scarabs marched in orderly ranks, like they were under the spell of some bug-herding Noah, back into the canister, made one last scuttling sound, and then were still.

Jed closed the lid of the canister on tight and tucked it inside his jacket. *Creepy little sons of bitches, but they did the job.* He dropped to the ground, washed his hands in the low trough sink, and headed back into the Saloon. Time to pack their gear into the *Liahona*—he'd deal with the second Pinkerton later.

CHAPTER THREE

Sam sat on the deck of the *Jim Smiley* and scowled into the pale mountain sun of the early morning. He made good and sure that every face that turned from the much bigger and much higher deck of the *Liahona* to look at him got a scowl in return, fierce and wild, eyebrows on full furrow and jaw jutted out. He could have sat in the wheelhouse and scowled, but he'd dragged the wooden captain's chair—one of the few things he'd bribed the salvage teams working on the wreck of the *Pennsylvania* to give to him—out into the sunshine and plunked his narrow hips into its welcoming arms to make sure he was good and visible to all and sundry. He positioned himself carefully to catch the light of the rising sun on the crotch buttons of his Levi-Strauss denim pants.

He sipped at a mug of hot coffee for show, but he'd already poured two down his gullet since the sun rose. Sam Clemens hadn't slept and sleep wasn't on his mind now. He'd worked through the night, which was hard to do in the dark of the boiler room when the electricks weren't cooperating, and two of the pipes were already patched, with the third on its way. Once the *Liahona* pulled out, Sam would finish the repair job and be on her tail. She was a fast animal, but if old Chief Pocatello came through, and Sam felt confident that he would, Sam thought his odds of being the first into the Great Salt Lake City were rather good.

The *Liahona* was enormous. Giant, rattling metal tracks snapped and ground in an approximately rectangular polyhedron around each of her sides, higher in front than in the back, flattening anything they rode over under tons of steel. Her body was shaped like a sailing ship's, but more square, and the sides bulked out above the grinding tracks, making them visible before, behind, and from the side, but not from above. She had a wheelhouse like the *Jim Smiley*'s, but where Sam's wheelhouse might squeeze in a fourth man in a pinch, if that man were willing to stand, the *Liahona*'s could easily accommodate a platoon of marines. Its deck, too, was vast, and though it was all dusty and weather-stained, the surface was sprinkled with dozens of wooden benches and parasols from the relative comfort of which its passengers could observe the passing scenery. Many of the benches and parasols were close enough to the rail to be visible from Sam's lower observation point.

Fifteen miles an hour, Sam thought, *Pocatello had better come through for me.* He chewed the stub of a cigar. *For me and the United States taxpayer.*

During the night, one of the Pinkertons had disappeared and the other had been found dead. The dead one presented a relatively minor mystery; someone had cut his face up pretty bad, and no one the bouncers asked about it had cared to 'fess up to anything. They'd done the obvious thing and thrown the body into the icehouse until the next U.S. Marshal happened through and could investigate. By which time, Sam had intimated wryly to the bouncers when they inquired as to his whereabouts, the trail was likely to be cold.

O'Shaughnessy had stayed hidden in the *Jim Smiley* and the bouncers, in their role of makeshift police, hadn't tried to suggest that they had the authority to board and search her. Sam had been careful not to do anything to give them the idea that they did and they'd all gotten along famously.

The missing Pinkerton was rather more of a mystery. His clothing had been found in the saloon's latrine, but no other trace of him; apparently the man had taken his wallet and his weapon and had gone running off alone into the wilderness in the middle of the night. Sam was as surprised as everyone else, and as little able to explain it. All in all, it was the sort of behavior he associated not with the Wyoming Territory but more with, say, Canada.

When the sun had cracked over the horizon, the last few passengers had loaded into the *Liahona*. Sam had stopped working on the boiler pipes to watch; he loved mighty moving machines and the *Liahona*, though she wasn't handsome, was as mighty as they came.

Her Captain, the Welshman Jones, had lowered a cargo door in back to march up a few crates and suitcases, and the passengers had come up the side by ladder. For those without the heart to make such a climb unaided, the crew had hung a pulley from a metal arm above the rungs and dropped a steel-and-leather harness. Several ladies and one man had come up that way, the ladies flashing various expressions of delight, relief, and disgruntlement at the heavy-armed truck-men who hoisted them. The fellow who had availed himself of the crew's assistance was the younger, whiter, and fussier of the two Englishmen.

Probably, Sam thought, watching him flap his arms like a turkey and cringe from contact with the side of the great steam-truck, *it had been the other Englishman who had punched the holes in the* Jim Smiley.

After the big steam-truck was loaded, some of the Fort's men climbed up onto the ramparts and walked the full circuit, scanning the horizon for threats with their spyglasses. The enclosure was designed to look like an old wooden stockade, with a jagged top like the shoulder-to-shoulder points of sharpened logs, but the wall was made of thick slabs of plascrete just like Bridger's Saloon and all its points were made of iron, as was the walkway that ran around the inside, giving the Fort's defenders a platform from which to watch and defend. The Fort sat squarely astride the road, with one huge tower-shouldered gate looking east, to the Platte and the Mississippi and beyond, and another gazing resolutely west, to New Russia, to California, and to the Kingdom of Deseret.

Once they had confirmed that the horizon was clear of hostiles, the Fort's people threw levers inside one of the west towers, and with a rush of steam into the center of the gate from both towers, the huge, interlocking steel fingers that comprised the gate itself groaned and withdrew into their plascrete housing, opening the way for outbound traffic.

Even idling, the *Liahona* coughed significant fumes into the air, and when Jones blasted the signal from the tin-peaked whistle at the corner of his wheelhouse and engaged the throttle, the black cloud that belched out of the rear of the stream-truck could have entirely covered any two Missouri counties or the entire state of Rhode Island. Steam hissed out, too, through various chinks in the beast's body, *pfffting* out past the gears that worked the tracks, from cracks in the hull and from a pipe that rose out the machine's back end, alongside the exhaust pipe, for the purpose.

Twenty-odd passengers on the *Liahona's* deck waved hands, hats and scarves at the Fort's staff lingering in the yard—none stupid enough to linger too close to the truck. The staff waved back, some with polite hats and some with less-polite single fingers and sneers. This was the edge of the United States of America, Sam was reminded; once the *Liahona* left Fort Bridger she entered the Kingdom of Deseret, and relations between the U.S. and the Kingdom were not always completely friendly.

Sam looked for the Englishmen and found them sitting by the rail and enjoying the sun. The dark one met his bold gaze, mustache for mustache, and when the Englishman raised his glass in salute, Sam toasted him right back. The pale one looked away.

Sam pulled his goggles down over his eyes and a scarf up over his mouth and nose.

To his surprise, as the *Liahona* thundered by and just before its cloud of dust enveloped him, he thought he saw the gypsy palm reader. So the vagabond showman was going to the Great Salt Lake City, was he? What had he said he was doing, something about a display of mummies? Sam hadn't really been paying attention, he'd been thinking about death. Death and Henry.

Well, fine, he'd have a good conversation with Mr. Brigham Young and then he'd go see the mummies. Maybe have his palm read again. For that matter, Young had something of a supernatural reputation. Sam tossed aside the last of his cigar and considered what questions he might ask the famous Prophet of the Rockies, if given the chance. *Is there an afterlife, Mr. President, and if so, where in its various parts is my brother Henry?* That about cut to the heart of the matter.

When the dust settled, Sam tugged his scarf down, shaking out the red-brown sand it had collected.

"O'Shaughnessy!" he roared, and then he saw the man waiting on the gravel at the foot of the ladder.

"What do you want, Sam Clemens, you bloody slave driver, you?" O'Shaughnessy roared back, stomping up out of the stairwell, but when he saw Sam frozen, staring down at the ground, he shut up. From ten feet away, Sam could smell the liquor on the Irishman.

"Good morning," Sam called to the stranger. "Can I help you?"

The man wasn't tall, but he was stocky, and he gave the impression of physical power. His hair and beard were long and streaked with gray and his body, the body of the horse he rode, and the body of the packhorse he led all bristled with guns and knives. He wore buckskins and furs and so did the animals. Sam peeled away his goggles for a more unobstructed view of this genuine Western curiosity.

"You're headed into Deseret!" the man growled.

O'Shaughnessy crept across the deck, avian head low, and pulled out a gun.

Sam glanced, not meaning to, and noticed that the pistol was unfamiliar and odd-looking, with a big metal bulb on the end of its muzzle and another where the cylinder should be. *Does it shoot gas?* Sam wondered. He prided himself on being a man who knew mechanicks, but guns were not his strong suit. *Where did O'Shaughnessy get such a thing?*

Sam took another sip of coffee out of habit and then spat the red mud out onto the deck. "Mercy!" he snapped. He poured the rest out to avoid repeating the mistake. "Is that some business of yours, mister?"

"Will it make you feel better about my intentions if I let your friend get the drop on me?" the mountain man called. "Hell, if I'd wanted you dead, you gotta figger, I'd a killed you in the night."

"I suppose I should count my lucky stars you're such a gentleman, then," Sam countered, but he nodded to O'Shaughnessy and the Irishman stood upright and showed his head. He kept the strange gun at his side, though, Sam noticed, and therefore out of sight.

"You aren't a Pinkerton, are you?" O'Shaughnessy asked.

"No!" The grizzled stranger barked a noise that might have been a laugh. "I'm a Deseret Marshal, though, if you're looking for a lawman. Name's Rockwell."

"Mostly, Mr. Deseret Marshal," the Irishman said, smirking at Sam, "it's the *lawmen* that come looking for *me*."

Idiot doesn't know when to shut his mouth. "What can we do for you, Mr. Rockwell?" Sam asked.

The mountain man hawked up a gob of phlegm and spat it into the dust settling around his horse's hocks. "You can turn this pretty little steam-truck of yours around and go home," he said gruffly. "It ain't safe for you in the Kingdom."

Sam ruminated on this communication for several long moments, but couldn't figure out what the fellow was up to. "This is a strange way to deliver a threat, sir," he finally countered. "We outnumber you and we have the higher ground."

"That's 'cause it ain't a threat," Rockwell objected. "I'm just stating a fact. I'm telling you that I am the law in the Great Salt Lake City and I can't guarantee your safety."

Sam scratched his head, a gesture that turned into a vigorous brushing off of dust. "Well, Mr. Rockwell," he finally said. "We haven't broken any laws of the Kingdom of Deseret, nor do we intend to. We have lawful business there, official business even, and as far as I can see, there's no reason we can't carry it out. Your dark intimations are very dramatic and I think you yourself would cut a fine buccaneerish figure on the stage, but I have things to do and I estimate that the curtain is about to close upon our conversation here."

"You ain't listening to me!" Rockwell snapped, swinging down from his horse. He reached for the *Jim Smiley*'s ladder, but as his hand grasped the first rung, O'Shaughnessy *tsk, tsked* at him, and Sam looked over to see his associate aiming the bulb-gun at the mountaineer.

"We'll stay better friends, Mr. Marshal," the Irishman smiled, "if you stay off our fookin' vessel."

Rockwell spat again, stared at both men like a hungry hawk, and then swung back into the saddle. "When you're lying on the red rock," he bellowed at them, "holding your guts in your hands and weeping out the last seconds of your lives, you remember this! You wanna call for your mamma in that moment, you can. You wanna call for Jesus, go right ahead. Just don't waste your damn time calling for Orrin Porter Rockwell!"

With a snort of indignation, Rockwell turned his horse's head and trotted towards Fort Bridger's westward-facing maw.

"Bloody hell, I hate these people already," O'Shaughnessy griped, holstering his fancy gun. The holster, Sam thought, reminded him of the ones he had seen tied to the Pinkertons' hips.

"Oh, I don't know," Sam disagreed, watching Rockwell turn north off the road into the sagebrush and scrub grass. "I kind of like a place that sends out a welcoming committee."

ᒪᛄᗯᎸᏅᎻᗯᒪ

"Mummies!" cried Edgar Allan Poe, flinging his hands up in a conjuror's wave before him. "Mummies, of both man and mysterious beast!"

He stalked the deck of the *Liahona*, the cool breeze snapping around his ears under the brim of his tall hat and blowing behind his smoked spectacles, threatening to dry out his eyeballs and his skin despite all the oil in his air. At least, between the *Liahona*'s speed and the height of its deck off the ground, the air was free of the reddish dust that the steam-truck's huge tracks churned up and spewed in its wake. He could barely keep from coughing as it was, and a lungful of dust would surely drag him down into paroxysms.

A little boy, dressed in overalls, a miniature sailor's jacket, and slouch hat and carrying a length of wire towards the wheelhouse, stopped to listen. Passengers' heads turned, including the heads of the two Englishmen … good.

"Mummies!" he cried again. "Mummies and other curious, fascinating, and even … *repellent* … evidences of the wisdom and high craft of ancient Egypt!"

From within his coat he produced one of Pratt's four canopic jars, the one with the baboon head, and spun on one heel in a slow pirouette with the little object held forward in his hands, showing it to the benches full of passengers. It hadn't been made to be used in this sort of a show, of course, but what Orson Pratt and Horace Hunley didn't know was unlikely to hurt them. He deliberately clicked to a stop facing the Englishmen, sitting on either side of a woman in a red dress, and assessed them carefully through his tinted lenses.

One man was younger, in his middle twenties, perhaps, and had the pale, flustered, and determined look of a privileged young fellow trying to make his way in the world. Something had carved a bite-shaped chunk out of the brim of his top hat, giving him a comical appearance, but he seemed delighted with Poe's theater, clapping vigorously as Poe tucked away the canopic jar and produced instead the cylinder of scarabs. *Absalom Fearnley-Standish*, Poe thought to himself, *who are you, really, and what are you doing here?*

His companion was older, nearing forty, and was hard, dark, scarred, and masculine. He was dressed in a frock coat and waistcoat like he might have worn on the streets of London, but he was hatless, and his clothing showed the dust and wear of many miles of road. Richard Burton, famous explorer, etcetera. *Well, Mr. Burton,* Poe mused, *let's assay you a little bit, test your mettle.*

Let's test you both.

"And magic!" he cried and, reaching into his canister, he pulled out a handful of the brass scarabs and scattered them across the laps of Burton, Fearnley-Standish, and their female companion.

"Aagh!" shrieked Fearnley-Standish. He would have jumped from his seat if Burton hadn't restrained him with a hand on his arm.

"Arjuna's bow, man, they won't eat you!" the explorer snorted.

Then Poe saw their female companion's face and froze. She was short and dark, all straight lines and grace, and though he would have recognized her through any disguise, she wore none.

It was Roxie.

Robert, you didn't mention ... but then, of course ...

She smiled at him, the polite and slightly flirtatious smile of a woman who is casually attached to another man but conceals within her a voracious, insatiable wolf. She didn't recognize him, obviously, but then it had been years, and Poe was proud of the verisimilitude of his false nose. Within his breast, a desire to seize her in his arms, sweep her to his chest and devour her mouth with his warred against an equally strong urge to pull his pistol from inside his jacket and blow out her vicious, wicked, conniving brains.

"Well, man!" Burton snapped. "Get on with it!"

He felt stunned, his vision out of focus. He floated, lost. Then, in the sea of passengers' faces under flapping parasols, he saw the physiognomy of his accomplice, the haggard dwarf Jedediah Coltrane. Coltrane was mouthing something to Poe, a nervous look on his face; Poe's professionalism reasserted itself and he tore his eyes away from Roxie's.

Stepping back, he raised both hands about his head, one of them holding the cylinder by its lid, and cried out in a loud voice, to be sure that the entire deck could hear him. "Behold the incantations of Thoth! Behold the power of Hermes, Thrice-Greatest! Behold the might of the Egyptian priests, able to reach through the curtain of death itself and command the obedience of the inanimate and the damned!"

When he was sure they were all watching him, he waved his empty hand in a great circular flourish over the scarabs, carefully thumbing the *recall* button inside the canister's lid. "Nebenkaure, panjandrum, Isis kai Osiris!" he shouted.

The clocksprung beetles sprang instantly to life. With a great *chittering* and *clacking*, each metal bug rolled upright, oriented itself, and then began its trek. From the laps and boots of Roxie and the Englishmen, from the bench they sat on and the floor beneath them, the brass beetles swarmed in a great mass toward Poe.

He raised his hands, stood still, and laughed as diabolically and mysteriously as he could as the bugs climbed his clothing, laughed when he felt the first brass legs touch the bare skin of his neck, laughed with his whole chest and belly as the scarabs detoured around his head and crawled up his left arm, kept laughing as they swarmed ticklishly about his fist and dropped one by one into their native canister, and then, for effect, stopped laughing at the exact moment in which he slammed the canister shut.

The spectators went wild.

"That wasn't Egyptian," Burton said sourly, but the passengers all about him applauded, and a few whistled or whooped in excitement.

Coltrane clapped along with the crowd, shooting shrewd appraising looks at the people around him. *Sizing up the marks,* Poe thought. The man had the ingrained instincts of an inveterate carny. The little boy with the loop of wire stood stiff as a statue, his eyes so wide they threatened to swallow his face.

"They're scarab beetles, Dick," Fearnley-Standish pointed out.

"I meant the words," the darker man growled. "Pure higgledy-piggledy. Nonsense. Arrant balderdash."

"My name is Doctor Jamison Archibald!" Poe announced. "Tonight, at seven o'clock by the Captain's watch, in the stateroom, for the very reasonable sum of two copper pennies, any passenger may see exhibited and explained these and other marvels, visual and auditory. See the uncanny hypnotic hypocephalus in action, stealing the souls of men! Witness the muscular terror of the dire Seth-Beast!"

"Will children be admitted free of charge?" inquired a plain-faced, reedy-voiced, gray-wrapped matron in a blue prairie bonnet, clutching under her bony wings a trio of similarly undernourished-looking brats.

"My dear madam," Poe stage-whispered, meeting her eyes over the rims of his spectacles, "the things I have to display are dark and terrifying apparitions; the stuff of nightmares. Children will not be admitted *at all.*"

The little boy with the loop of wire shuddered.

"There's nothing hypnotic about a hypocephalus," Burton huffed to Roxie. "It's just a damned pillow!" He glared at Poe. "The Geographical Society would cut you to pieces, you knave!"

Burton was the genuine article, then, and not some impostor. He also seemed to be a tough customer, and his fuse was none too long. Poe decided he would have to be careful around the explorer. On top of everything else, the man seemed very attached to Roxie. Was he playing her?

Was *she* playing *him?*

Poe felt uneasy. "For an additional three cents," he quipped with a bow in Burton's direction, "you may join me at the lectern tonight and share your commentary."

Burton's jaw went rigid and his face began slowly turning purple. "As for the Seth-Beast, you humbug, there's no such animal! It is a mere symbol of chaos, and the Egyptians made it up!"

Coltrane *woofed!* raucously in the ear of the little boy, who jumped nearly out of his skin and went scuttling on to the wheelhouse to complete his errand. The dwarf laughed heartily at his own prank.

Poe bowed again, deeply, and raised the canister to incite another round of applause. He turned and walked away, upstaging Burton and not letting him finish.

"It's just a jackal!" Burton shouted after him across the deck. "With the ears and tail of a jackass!"

ᒪᴇᗺᴡᕁᓍᕝᴡ

Absalom cleared his throat. Annie didn't look up.

He felt ridiculous, leaning slightly into the wind to keep his hat on his head, coattails flapping behind him, a mint-spiked lemonade in each hand. What if she thought he was an idiot? She had looked so happy talking to the Brute the night before—maybe he was actually the sort of man she *liked*.

Absalom was uncomfortably conscious of his smoothness, his refinement, his lack of facial hair, the humiliating look of his damaged hat. He didn't think he could bear it if she mocked him, not in front of all the other passengers.

But then, he thought to steel himself, a man who would dare to court an Angel must needs risk a terrible fall.

He cleared his throat again. Still she didn't look up. Her nose was buried in a book of some sort, a cheap-looking print with a soft cover that appeared to be profusely illustrated with dreadful pictures of gunmen and wild animals.

"Pardon me, miss," he said. "I thought you might enjoy taking some refreshment."

The Angel looked up and smiled. "Aw," she said, "that's so sweet of you." Absalom smiled and handed her the lemonade. "Thank you," she said, took the drink, and returned to her novel.

Absalom stood by her side for a few seconds. When he couldn't think of anything to say, he turned and lurched away.

Lᴇᴡᵠᴏʜᴎ

Burton's head hurt and he badly wanted to stab someone. Anyone.

He'd woken up in discomfort and had immediately been saddened to see Roxie sitting at his cabin's dresser, fully dressed and finishing up with her coiffure.

"You are one hell of a woman."

Roxie had stood, smiled, and then stooped to kiss his cheek. "Remember that," she had said simply, and then she was gone. He was left with the salt-creamy smell of her body and astonishing memories.

He shivered.

At least he had slept soundly—that in itself was a luxury for Burton, who was a terrible insomniac. He had luxuriated in the rest, lying in the little bunk as long as her smell and the warmth of her body lingered, eventually forcing himself to shave, dress, and rejoin human society.

His head-butting with the gypsy circus-man calling himself *Archibald* on deck had been pointless, the fruit of Burton's irritability and a further aggravation to it. After the showman had announced his schedule and disappeared below decks, Burton had begged to take leave of Roxie for an hour or two to handle some personal business and had come back to his cabin.

He sat at the tiny wooden table that folded down on a hinge from the wall, a blank page before him and a Robinson's Patent Metal Self-Inking Stylus clutched in his fist like a spear. *You're a man of letters, damn you,* he told himself, *you can write this.*

Dear Isabel, he scratched out at the top of the sheet, and then ran out of words.

A drink would fortify him. His glass and Roxie's from the night before still sat on the dresser. He could tell which was which because hers was marked at the lip with smudges of lipstick, and he instinctively reached for the smudged one—but he stopped himself.

He must be fair to Isabel. He, Dick Burton, had made a mistake. Men made mistakes, but this one, he resolved, was a mistake that needn't affect his engagement in any way, that Isabel needn't ever know of. He could carry this guilty cross alone, but he must break off his fling with Roxie before it went any further. Certainly before Isabel learned of it.

He took the other tumbler, his glass from the night before, and the square bottle of gin. About to pour the liquor, however, he paused. There were crystals in the bottom of his glass, fine and few, like a little crusted sugar or salt, maybe, but nothing that the gin could have left behind.

He sniffed the glass—the crystals were odorless. He looked at Roxie's glass; no crystals.

Hmmn.

He pushed away the glass with crystals, poured half a shot of gin into Roxie's tumbler and took a sip.

I am well into the Rockies and the American West is everything I expected it to be, he continued, the Stylus pouring its black ink out smoothly as he wrote. *I have seen mountain men, red Indians, and wild animals, not to mention vistas to match or exceed anything I ever witnessed in Goa or the Horn. Still,* he lied, *without you I find it sterile, uninviting and dead. I wish you were here, my darling.*

He looked at what he had written and snorted in disgust. "Dick Burton, you faithless worm," he rebuked himself, and he crumpled the sheet into a ball and threw it into the corner of the room.

He looked at his glass again.

What were those crystals? He didn't remember adding anything to his drink, though, frankly, his memory of the night before had become a little hazy. He must not have slept well, he thought, but he didn't remember waking during the night.

He finished the drink, and on a hunch he pulled out his attaché case.

The case was where he kept the three documents that were at the core of his mission: his own commission letter from Her Majesty (personal to him and making no mention of Fearnley-Standish), the letter credentialing him as an Ambassador from the Court of St. James (not a word in that letter, either, of Fearnley-Standish or what his role might be) and a sealed letter, addressed to President Young. Burton had not read the letter to Young, but he thought he knew its contents—Her Britannic Majesty expressed a willingness to negotiate with the President towards ceding certain assets to the Kingdom of Deseret in exchange for an appropriate posture *vis-à-vis* the emerging American conflict and the government of the Confederate States to be.

The assets, which Burton was instructed to identify only verbally, were large stretches of Alberta and British Columbia, all the territory bordering the northern edge of the Kingdom and running to the Pacific Ocean. Brigham Young would gain wheat fields, coal mines, and a major port—Burton didn't see how Deseret could turn the offer down, as it needed to feed its people and power its machines just like any other nation did, and he expected his mission to be over within forty-eight hours. Upon boarding the *Liahona* he had hidden the slim black case underneath his bunk, locked its combination, and, as an alarm to warn him of tampering, he had closed the case with one of his own hairs pinched in it.

Now the hair was gone.

Burton stared at the case.

He checked the combination lock, finding it locked and the dials in the 0-0-0, 0-0-0 position he'd left them in. But the hair was gone.

Roxie. His mind rebelled at the accusation, but it must be her.

No, you idiot, he thought. *You feel guilty because you have broken your troth, but that is no reason to suppose that Roxie is a thief or a spy. She's only a woman, after all, beautiful and clever, and oh so dangerous and sweet in the way she moves, beneath that red crinoline or without its veiling*—he cut off that train of thought.

No, it could have been anyone. The cabin had been locked, but Captain Jones or someone in his crew must have another copy of the key, and someone could have stolen it. Or simply picked the lock.

It could have been Fearnley-Standish, the little weasel. He was the reason Burton had put a hair in the attaché case in the first place—he hadn't wanted his ostensible colleague to steal the letter to Brigham Young and cut Burton out of the mission, as he seemed constantly to be trying to do with his bizarre pretensions to authority.

That must be it; Fearnley-Standish had bribed a truck-man to give him the key, he had let himself in at some moment while Burton had been away, and he had opened the case.

Though whoever had done it had also been able to open the combination locks on the attaché case. That was no mean feat; Burton was certain his combination was a safe secret, not a birthday or some obvious number, but 8-5-3, 0-9-1, which, reordered into 09/1853, made September 1853, the month Burton had entered the Kaaba, the first kaffir, he believed, ever to have done so, and almost the first European. No one would think to try those digits as a combination, surely, so whoever had opened the case had done so by some other means—had picked the lock.

Was Fearnley-Standish capable of such a thing?

Burton's eyes flickered to the crystals in his tumbler. He stifled the doubts in his heart as he choked back the memory of white ankles. *No,* he told himself again. *Not Roxie.*

He opened the case. Inside, everything looked all in order. The three letters were there, inside a large, flat, leather wallet, and nothing unexpected had been added.

Or had it? He picked up the sealed envelope addressed to *Mr. Brigham Young, President of the Kingdom of Deseret* and hefted it. It looked like the same envelope, but whoever had opened the case might have switched envelopes or might have steamed the envelope open and switched out its contents. *Might have,* he considered, *but to what end?*

He might be played like Rosencrantz and Guildenstern, from Shakespeare's play. Hamlet had swapped their sealed letter for another, hadn't he? And where the original letter instructed the king to kill Hamlet, the substitute instructed him instead to kill Rosencrantz and Guildenstern.

Bad way to go, that. Embarrassing.

"Bhishma's buttocks!" Burton cursed darkly. He was going to have to open the letter. It wasn't contrary to any explicit direction he had received, but it definitely went beyond his affirmative instructions and it smacked of underhandedness and shady ethics. Burton had no qualms about raiding the enemy by stealth, but sneaking about to get around his allies, or worse, his superiors, was unmanly and dishonorable.

On the other hand, he could not risk the possibility that the Yankee Clemens was somehow responsible and was sending Burton in to meet Brigham Young bearing a letter that read *Dear Sir, please commence aerial raids on Richmond and Savannah at your earliest convenience. Sincerely, Victoria. P.S., have the bearer of this letter staked to the ground in front of the nearest coyote den.*

The tools that he and Fearnley-Standish had removed (that *he* had removed, he corrected himself with a rueful grin, Fearnley-Standish hadn't done a damned thing) from the *Jim Smiley* the previous night and stowed in the hold of the *Liahona* hadn't been here this morning, when Burton had made a point of checking. If Clemens hadn't got his tools back, then someone else had got them.

Burton sighed. There was no good way around it; he would have to look.

It was easy to steam the letter open using a jet from the convenience steam hose (usually used to make scalding hot tea or iron clothes or clean filthy boots) below the hot spigot in the cabin's little brass sink. Burton unfolded the letter inside with trepidation, sitting again at the table to read it. He knew that he was doing what he had to do, for the sake of the mission, but he still felt like a thief, a trespasser, a blasphemer.

It didn't look as official as he had expected, nothing like the credentials—no seal, no formalities, just a simple note on the Palace's headed paper with a signature—but then, Burton reflected, it wouldn't. The official mission was his; the note was a personal communication, an assurance of personal interest and sincerity from one head of state to another. He read the note with fear in his heart and a mounting paranoia in his aching brain.

Dear President Young,

To the formal documents credentialing my envoy, I wish to add my personal statement of confidence. Captain Burton is a man of proven merit in many extraordinary circumstances and I trust you will find him as capable, as bold, and as interesting as I do.

I trust also that we will be able to reach agreement. All parties declare themselves to be against the outbreak of hostilities, but you and I mean it sincerely, and I believe that between us, your Kingdom and mine can ensure that the American squabbles regarding membership and secession are resolved in a way that does not compromise our nations' prosperity. Captain Burton is authorised to make certain promises to you in order to clarify that our interests are aligned; I will honour those promises.

Cordially Yours, VRI

Post-Script. Captain Burton is a man of action. If you have need of him in that capacity, please show him this letter as my instruction to him that he is to cooperate fully with your requests.

Ha! Burton thought. Again no mention of the tiresome little Foreign Office man, and the Queen's note was all about *Captain Burton* and his mission. So Fearnley-Standish was a liar, just as he'd thought.

But what in blazes did that post-script mean?

He closely scanned the letter again, not for meaning this time, but to look at the letters and the paper for any sign of inauthenticity. Forgery and its detection were not his métier, but he thought of himself as an astute and perceptive man and the letter passed his smell test. The sheet's heading and watermark looked official, and the handwriting throughout looked consistent. Before the gum on the flap could dry, he refolded the note, replaced it, and re-sealed the envelope.

He held it in his hands and considered what to do. Someone, he thought, had likely read the letter, and he couldn't know who. Possibly, though he thought it unlikely, someone had *tampered* with the letter.

Still, its contents were consistent with what Burton knew of his own mission, although he wondered what Her Majesty could mean, suggesting that Brigham Young call upon his services as a *man of action*. Well, he *harrumphed* to an imaginary audience, he *was* a man of action, after all, and if President Young needed to call on his assistance in some matter, Burton would do what was necessary, for Queen and country.

On reflection, Burton decided that this episode had given him a salutary warning. It seemed likely that some rival, some enemy even, had looked into the official correspondence of which he was the appointed bearer, but there was nothing compromising in those letters, nothing that would give away Burton's bargaining position or weaken him or make him vulnerable in any other way.

The true core of Burton's mission was locked away in his own memory, unassailable. And because it could have been worse, Burton was now duly warned that his attaché case, even locked in his cabin and sealed behind a combination lock, was not a sufficiently safe place for the letters.

He'd have to carry them on his person. Burton tested his frock coat and found that, by tearing only a couple of stitches to either side of the mouth of its inside breast pocket, he could make the pocket wide enough to swallow the document wallet. He put all the letters into his coat and was about to put his coat on when his eye caught the loose sheets of paper and the Self-Inking Stylus on the folding table.

He sighed, sat, and took up the Stylus.

My Dearest Isabel, he wrote after dating a clean sheet. *I am a terrible correspondent and though I know that you deserve a thousand times better, I find that all I can do is write to say that I think of you daily, that I consider myself pledged to you, and that I shall do my utmost to serve out this commission for Her Majesty in a fashion that will bring honour and respect to you and your family.*

Vishnu's hairy belly, he thought, setting the Stylus down and grinding the heels of his palms into his eyes. Could Roxie have drugged him?

"Behold the hypocephalus!" Poe cried, and Jed Coltrane, leaning against the wall near the rear door of the stateroom, resisted snorting out loud. *At least,* he thought, *the poor bastard isn't coughing up a lung.* He wondered how much time the Richmond doctors had given Poe to live—he didn't think it could have been very long.

It was a bally, in the end, a free show. At least it was free from Jed's point of view—the entire price of admission was two cents, and Captain Dan Jones took both of them. But a free show now would mean better word of mouth for the paid show later. Even a carnival without a secret mission put on ballies from time to time.

The hypocephalus, which to the dwarf sounded like the name of a particularly nasty strain of a soldiers' disease, was pinned against an upright display board. It was a complicated circular diagram, full of little drawings of stick figures, thrones, animal-headed people, stars, and squiggles, all inked onto a tattered piece of yellow cloth that might have been linen, or something really old, anyway.

It looked Egyptian. Like the scarabs, though, it was bunkum, and Jed knew it. Some Richmond clever-dick had painted it. Poe always called it the *hypnotic hypocephalus*, but Hunley and his boys were geniuses and Jed figured you could probably wear the thing over your face and it would let you breathe underwater or spit flame or deflect bullets. Poe probably knew, but he'd never told Jed. Still, bunkum aside, he did his best to look fascinated and attentive, to encourage the audience be fascinated and attentive, too.

Poe stood to one side of the hypocephalus in his full carnival-gypsy-snake oil-doctor costume on a low platform that looked improvised out of a wooden pallet; for that matter, Jed reflected, he hadn't seen his boss out of costume since they'd left Richmond. He hadn't even taken off the fake nose and beard, unless he'd done so out of the dwarf's sight. To the other side of the hypocephalus stood the Englishman Burton, jaw resolutely clenched and eyes burning like his stare alone could punch through the walls of the steam-truck.

"Behold," Burton called out his stubborn counter-introduction, "Doctor Archibald's famous ancient Egyptian pillow!"

The old carny in Jed almost laughed at the big explorer—he'd done such a good job increasing interest, and therefore attendance, Jed doubted any shill could have done any better. The stateroom of the *Liahona* looked like it might have been built to seat twenty for dinner. Whatever table usually filled its floor was gone, though, and in thirty-odd folding wooden chairs, paying passengers sat and stared. Burton's associate, the diplomat Absalom Fearnley-Standish, was one of them. He sat beside a pair of empty seats, looking lonely and forlorn as he protected them with a battered top hat that was missing part of its brim.

No sign of the woman Jed was waiting for, though. That was a shame; it wouldn't hurt to collect a little cash from the evening's show, but really, of course, it was supposed to be a distraction. Oh, well, maybe he'd have to be satisfied with just dealing with the Englishmen.

Poe smiled at Burton's jab and continued. Even in the weak electric light of the stateroom (pulsing blue from glass globes pegged in two rows to the room's ceiling), he wore his smoked spectacles. If pressed, he would claim that his eyes were weak, but of course the glasses were an important component of his disguise.

As was the show.

"My colleague would describe the great pyramids of Giza as mere tombs," Poe said with a wise and condescending smile. "The sorcerer-priests of Memphis and of Thebes have long had the practice, handed down to them by their forefathers, who learned the dark arts at the feet of Hermes Trismegistos, the great Ibis-headed Thoth himself, of sleeping with their heads upon cloths such as this."

He locked his eyes upon a pair of spinsterly women in the front row and proceeded to talk to them intimately, as if giving a private lecture, switching his gaze exclusively back and forth between the two.

"You observe the great throne at the center, the rightways upper section and the inverted underworld, the stars and the symbols of the great expanse of earth. The hypocephalus is nothing less than a map of the universe, as known to the ancients, and dreaming Egyptian sorcerers drew from it the power to control their dreams ... and the minds of their fellows."

The two ladies gasped a prim objection and a murmur crept through the audience.

"Rubbish!" roared Burton, his face turning purple. "Poppycock! Nonsense of the highest order, and reeking of base deceit and fraud! This man owes you all a refund! There is no basis for any of this hogwash, these explanations are not scientific! What kind of *doctor* are you, man?"

The front stateroom door opened and the woman Jed was waiting for slipped in, dark hair, red dress, on the plain-looking side. He let no expression cross his face, but felt a satisfying mixture of pride in the success of their distraction and anticipation of the crimes he was about to commit. He discreetly patted the bulges in his jacket to reassure himself that he was appropriately armed.

The woman sat by the diplomat, as Poe had suggested she likely would, and Jed continued to wait. He'd give her a minute to settle in before he exited the show, just in case.

The pale Englishman looked disappointed at her arrival—or maybe he was disappointed that he was still holding an empty seat.

Poe bowed in mock deference. "I'm sure we would all be eager to hear a proper *scientific* explanation of the hypocephalus, sir," he said in a wheedling, groveling way that again almost made Jed laugh.

"There is none!" Burton barked loudly, his fists clenched and punching at the air. "We don't know what they're for!"

Poe affected a look of pitying disappointment. "No?" he said.

"No," Burton growled. He punched his forehead and jaw forward, like a bull glaring at a matador. "They've been found under the heads of a few mummies, priestly mummies, and there is no scientific explanation for them."

Poe let his spectacles wander out over the breathless crowd in the stateroom. "They lay under the heads of priestly mummies," he repeated, "and science cannot explain what they were for!"

He smiled puckishly.

The audience laughed.

"Yet!" Burton roared. "Science has no explanation *yet*, but it will have!" He looked like he might bite the heads off the two ladies in the front row; they shook their heads disappointedly and clucked at him.

The audience laughed louder, and Jed let himself out the door. Just as he shut it behind him, the quiet semi-darkness of the blue-lit iron hallway erupted into explosive racket.

"Shoshone! Shoshone! Beat to quarters!" A crewman of the *Liahona* burst past the dwarf, shouting at the top of his lungs, and banged at the door of the stateroom he had just left behind.

A bugle squealed out its *tantara-tantara-ta!* into the night.

Jed didn't know what *beat to quarters* meant, but it didn't sound good. He picked up his pace to a trot, heading for the first of the cabins.

He heard the soft *hum* behind him of a Brunel gun's engine warming up, and he threw himself around a corner just in time. With a sharp whine the rifle fired and he felt the rush of air on his shoulder blades as its projectile whizzed past him and heard the *foomp!* of the bullet punching a hole in the iron wall where it struck.

"Dammit," grumbled Jed as he tucked himself low against the wall, ready to surprise his pursuer. "You can't go three steps in this country without rubbing eyeballs with crazy people."

He heard a new whine, louder and sharper, and the pounding of booted feet, and he coiled his body into a tight, tensed spring. When the Shoshone brave ripped around the corner at full tilt he was majestic, iron plates and finger bones rattling about his chest, streaked paint turning his face into a terrifying apparition. In his hand he waved a vibro-blade cutlass, two-edged, a nasty piece of work that Sam Colt's factories had started turning out alongside their revolver, trying to compete with the steam- and magnet-powered guns that everyone wanted these days, not to mention the Maxims coming out of Maine. The vibro-blade ran on electricks and, for the fifteen or twenty minutes that its charge lasted, the razor-sharp serrated weapon *hummed* back and forth with an intensity that let it cut through metal plate like butter.

The Indian warrior ran proud and furious and, most of all, he ran tall. He never saw the dwarf squatting low in the shadow, had no warning, and when Jed cannonballed into his knees he tumbled to the ground, sinking his humming sword straight down into the floor.

Jed rolled right past the hollering Shoshone and kept running. He hated to leave a dangerous man at his back, but he had a job to do.

CHAPTER FOUR

his was the lady's cabin, Jed reflected as he eased the tumblers into place with his steel picks. He was still breathing hard from his tussle with the Shoshone.

A double cabin, though Poe had said he thought the lady was traveling alone. Or was that what Poe had said, after all?

Jed wasn't always one hundred percent sure he understood what Poe said. Shame to have to kill a woman, anyway, but life was hard and she'd be dead sooner or later of something, whatever Jed did. Hell, it's not like she'd be his first, and why should he care more about killing a woman than a man?

Besides, Poe had been insistent—he *really* wanted this woman dead.

The last pin *clicked* into position and the lock opened. The tramping of boots overhead and the muffled gunshots made the dwarf a little hesitant, but a moment's reflection convinced him that all the chaos would provide further distraction for his errand. He checked the narrow hallway in both directions and then slipped into the cabin.

The room was dark. Jed groped at the wall and found the metal switch, but toggling it didn't turn on any lights. *Have the electricks gone out?* he wondered. Maybe the Shoshone had damaged the truck somehow.

No matter. Jed Coltrane was nothing if not resourceful. He crept by touch around the edges of the room, guessing that the cabins were more or less standard and he ought to find a cot against either wall, a few feet from the door. When he bumped into the first cot, he stopped moving and leaned his hip against it.

Jed pulled the scarab canister from inside his coat and popped open the lid. It took an effort of will—he kept envisioning the dead Pinkerton in the squatpot stall, devoured in seconds by the beetle swarm—but he shoved his hand inside the cylinder and scooped out a clump of the brass bugs, which he scattered underneath the cot.

"Don't be so chickenshit, Jed," he muttered to himself, feeling the cold sweat on his forehead.

Boots pounded outside the door and he waited, hand on his knife hilt, until they had passed. For a moment, he thought he heard the hushed wheeze of another person breathing, but that was crazy; no, it must be the sound of air circulating through the truck's vents, or metal slowly settling.

He stepped forward cautiously, in a line perpendicular to the cot behind him, feeling in front of him with his extended foot and fingers, until he found the other cot. "Here we go, you fraidy-cat," he cursed at himself, "almost done." He dug out another handful of insects and tossed them beneath the second bed, listening to the metallic rattle as they bounced into place.

He closed the canister, already breathing easier. He was turning to make for the door in the darkness when the thought caught him that he should really take a look, just to be sure that the bugs were reasonably hidden from view, and he hadn't tossed them into a mousetrap, for instance.

He clambered down into a kneeling position between the two bunks and dug for a box of lucifers in his pocket. With a practiced twitch of the wrist, he snapped a match along the outside of the box and it sputtered into flame—

A hard-toed boot kicked Jed Coltrane in the face, and his vision exploded into stars.

"The *hell*?" he yelled as he tried to roll away.

For his trouble, another kick crashed into his ribs and he spun through the air, slamming hard into the iron door of the cabin.

Forget the knife. Jed pulled the Pinkerton's gun from under his arm and squeezed the trigger. *Zing! Zing!* The odd weapon only flared slightly in the pitch black cabin, but the bullets *clanged* off the room's walls and bit their way into the furniture. They threw up sparks, enough for Jed to see a shadowy form looming up in front of him.

Damn thing didn't seem to have legs—

—*zing!*—

—the boot, or maybe it wasn't a boot after all, smashed Jed's gun hand and his lost his grip on the pistol, which disappeared into the gloom.

"Damn you—" he shouted, and then a strong hand with long nails, almost like claws, grabbed his throat and threw him bodily to the floor, a knee on his chest and something cold and hard against his cheek.

He smelled lavender. And soap. Some sort of cloak fell around him, covering his chest and legs.

"Hold still, shorty, or I'll cut out your eyeball." The voice was so incongruously sweet that it took him a few seconds to realize that it was feminine.

Coltrane, you just got beat down by a woman.

The hand—the soft, sweet-scented hand—came away from his throat and he heard a *click*. A blue light sprang into being a few inches above his face, a glimmering globe held in the palm of a woman who was graceful, fierce, freckle-faced, cute as a button, and kneeling on Jed's sternum. She wore dark goggles on her eyes and held a curving, vicious-looking knife to his face.

Not a woman, dammit. A girl. *Poe's gonna kill me.*

"What's that?" he asked.

"Fireless Darklantern." The girl squinted suspiciously at Jed. "I thought you boys worked for Hunley, or doesn't he give you the nice toys?"

Jed involuntary shot a glance under one of the cots and then felt like an idiot. "Hell!" he growled.

"Don't worry," she reassured him with a perky grin, tapping the Darklantern against her goggles, "I saw it all. The Darklantern is for *your* benefit."

Feet pounded again in the hall, but Jed hesitated to call for help—it might be that Shoshone with the vibro-blade, and he was likely happy as a cat in the crick with Jed Coltrane. Before he could decide whether to yell or make any move to try to distract his combatant, she pressed her blade tighter against his cheek, arching eyebrows at him.

He bit his tongue.

The pounding died down.

"What are the bugs?" she asked. "I mean, besides being part of the medicine show?"

Jed did his best to grimace fiercely. *I probably look like an idiot, though,* he realized, *pinned under the skirts of a girl.* "What are you, fifteen years old?" he asked her. "Your mamma know you're doing this?"

She slammed the Darklantern down onto his face like a lightning bolt and he cried out in pain. Again and again she punched him and when the room swam in and out of view and whirled around him, she slid him across the floor, jerked the canister from inside his coat, and rolled him face down on top of a dozen scarabs. They pushed into his face, cold and metallic, like studs protruding from the metal floor, and one pressed against the soft flesh at the corner of his mouth.

He heard a soft *pop*. Twisting his head, he could see that the girl, keeping him pinned with her knee and one hand, had opened the canister with the other. He wondered where she had put the knife and if he could make a grab for it, but his head was spinning and he felt like he was on the verge of throwing up.

.J. Butler

"You got more bugs in here, I see," she said, eyeing the contents. "This some kind of weapon?"

"I ain't talking," Jed said doggedly.

"Right," she said. "Well, I guess I'll just start pushing these buttons and see what happens."

Jed squirmed, his mind flooded with visions of himself, consumed to nothing by the scarab plague. He wasn't dazed anymore, but he was starting to feel scared. "Don't!" he barked through clenched teeth.

"Oh, but why ever not?" she asked. Out of the corner of his eye Jed saw her reaching with her thumb, pantomime-like, towards the buttons inside the canister's lid.

Bang!

The cabin door crashed open and the gap was immediately filled with a man's body. The *hum* of the vibro-blade came with him and the dwarf's entire body tensed in nervous fear of being stuck with it.

The girl sighed, sounding more irritated than afraid, and she spun away—

—releasing Jed and leaving the canister sitting on the floor—

—and punched the intruder in his stomach.

The man grunted and stepped back and Jed rolled to his feet, shaking himself and slapping bugs away from his skin in a sort of chicken-like dance even as he lunged for the cylinder.

The man swung his cutlass at the girl and she stepped under the blow with amazing nonchalance, punching him once more. She lashed him again and again and he staggered back, his sword snarling as it chewed chunks out of the walls with his erratic, unaimed swings.

Jed scooped up the canister and tried to sprint around the whirling skirts of the goggled girl.

"No, you don't!" she snapped. Her curved knife reappeared in her hand and she slashed at Jed.

His circus training and experience saved him. As the blade swooped down, he hurled himself sideways into the shadowed corner of the cabin, tumbling, then leaping up, and feeling the blade *swooshing* through the space at his shoulders. He bounced against the two walls of the corner, throwing himself back at his attacker—

—she turned away, batting aside the cutlass—

—Jed sprinted for the door, grateful to be small as he slipped past the whirling skirt and thrashing buckskins—

—she gripped the attacking Indian by his elbow and threw him over her hip, planting him heavily on his back and disarming him at the same time, the cutlass suddenly switching into her hand, where it loomed incongruously huge and deadly.

Jed saw the Pinkerton's stolen gun lying just inside the door, at the fierce Valkyrie's heel, and he scooped it up at a run.

Then he slammed his thumb down on the *attack* button inside the canister lid, snapped the lid shut and burst out into the hall, running as fast as his legs could carry him.

"Aaaaaagh!" A scream echoed after him down the corridor. A man's, he thought, and he imagined the redskin being devoured by Hunley's brass beetles. He hoped they might also get the girl, or at least slow her down, but he couldn't wait around to find out.

He slammed the lid of the cylinder shut just as the beetles within it began to swarm and shoved the gun back into its shoulder holster. He needed to find a place to hide, somewhere sheltered from the fray. He ducked under two men wrestling on a staircase, one a *Liahona* crewman and the other an Indian, and rattled up toward the hatch.

Jed popped out into the chaos on the deck to find it brightly lit, all electricks blazing blue. Men struggled hand to hand with sticks, knives, axes, and improvised clubs made by swinging rifles, grunting and cursing each other as each man tried to throw his opponent to the deck or, better still, to the ground. The breeze told him that the steam-truck was still rolling, but a knot of armed men thrashed each other back and forth at the wheelhouse and he feared it would shortly stop. Stopping meant capture and the dwarf knew he couldn't let Hunley's scarabs falls into the hands of a bunch of Wyoming Territory redskins. The Seth-Beast was harder to operate and the hypocephalus, hell, Jed didn't even know if it did anything at all, but the beetles were easy to figure out and they were deadly.

He had to hide them.

Could he hide the canister in his room? No, if they were stopped, the whole point would surely be to rob the passengers, and the cabins would all be looted. He needed a place up here on deck where he could stash the cylinder, preferably a place where he could hunker down with it.

He looked around frantically, seeing no sign of Poe, nor for that matter of Burton, among the many combatants; maybe they were fighting down in the stateroom, too.

His eye fell on the wheelhouse. It was flat and low-roofed, and if he could get on top of it he could lie down and be unseen.

He ducked low as he ran, scurrying like a bug among the benches and parasols and short Franklin Poles that made an obstacle course of the *Liahona*'s deck. He held the canister in his hand, afraid to stop the beetle swarm just yet because he wanted to make sure that both his assailants in the cabin were devoured, and afraid to put it into his coat pocket, in case the canister opened on accident before the beetles were done swarming.

He ran past the fighting in the wheelhouse and saw that the truck's crew was losing ground. Only the Welsh Captain Jones and one other man still resisted and surrender must now be inevitable and only moments away.

Jed ducked around the front of the wheelhouse and saw what he was looking for; the wheelhouse was close enough to the front that the railing, together with the ridges and gaps formed by the metal-plate construction of the wheelhouse itself, gave ready footholds to any climber, even a short one, to get up the ten feet comfortably. He leaped to the railing and then scrambled up the front of the wheelhouse, hoping no one looked through its windows in the moment he passed before them, and then he set the canister upright on the rooftop—still closed, mercifully—and hauled himself up on top, kneeling at the edge of the space with his toes dangling over behind him.

To Jed's surprise, he wasn't alone.

The little boy with the slouch hat sat there, huddled in the shadow against some kind of speaking horn and staring at Jed with fearful eyes.

"Shoot, kid, I ain't gonna hurt you," Jed barked gruffly. He wondered what the boy would think at the sight of the returning beetles and then shrugged to himself; if he saw them at all, there'd be no reason to connect the scarabs to any passenger disappearances, especially during an attack by local savages. No, best just to keep the kid calm. "Here, maybe I got a chocolate bar." He patted his jacket pocket, trying to find a Cadbury's Cocoa Wand he thought he'd squirreled away—

—something grabbed his ankles and jerked him off the roof.

Jed Coltrane the circus midget fell, well, like the professional that he was. He kept his head, and grabbed with his hands. Both hands gripped the edge of the rooftop and he caught himself, arresting his downward plunge. He felt his body *thump* against the windows of the wheelhouse, but they held, and whatever it was that had grabbed him fell away.

He snatched with one hand at the canister above him—whatever happened, he couldn't let that fall into anyone else's hands—then looked down.

Below him, a beaded-shirt Indian jumped, grabbing for Jed's ankle again. Hanging by just his left hand now, he skittered up the wall with his feet, dodging out of the way of the redskin's leap. He tried to continue skittering and get up onto the roof again, but his left hand alone wasn't strong enough for the job and he slipped down, still hanging.

Above him, the little boy burst into tears. "Shh!" the dwarf urged him. What was the boy's name? *Jesus or* something.

The Indian lunged again and again Jed Coltrane squirmed up and out of reach. How often could he do this? He needed a better solution.

John Moses, that was it. "You got a gun, John Moses?" he asked. The little boy shook his head no, weeping.

The red man jumped and Jed dodged, almost losing his grip this time.

Dammit, Coltrane, you've got a gun, right in your coat. And knives to spare. Only you don't have a free hand. He looked at the cylinder; he could set it down on the roof, just for a minute.

"Don't touch this, kid!" he grunted. He reached up to set the canister down, when he saw the Indian pull an ax from his belt.

"Hell!" he yelled, out of time. The red man stepped forward, ax raised—

—and before he could swing, Jed whacked him with the scarab cylinder.

He hit the man on his upraised forearm and the lid popped open. Brass bugs spilled down like a waterfall of metallic death, *chittering* horribly as they cascaded over the Indian's face, into his eyes and his open mouth, and poured hungrily about the soft flesh of his neck and down into his beaded leather shirt. His screams came out choked and muffled by his mouthful of death and were lost in the general clamor.

Mercifully, Jed kept hold of the cylinder.

"Look away, John Moses," he urged the little boy as he laid the open canister onto the rooftop and clambered up beside it. It came out sounding like concern for the boy, but that wasn't how he meant it; the scarabs were a secret military technology and he couldn't let just anyone watch them in action.

Damn it, was he going to have to kill the child? He didn't like kids, but he didn't like the idea of killing one, either.

The boy had stopped crying, though, or at least he had calmed himself down to hushed sniffling. Well, if he had to kill him, he'd rather the child weren't sobbing at the time. Jed tried his friendliest grimace on the kid and it seemed to help; John Moses smiled back at him.

He looked back down at the swarming beetles and saw that the flesh and bone were gone, and the beetles still swarmed. They'd look for new targets unless he stopped them and, for that matter, the scarabs below must have finished their work.

Jed pressed the *recall* button and sat back to watch the cylinder fill as the beetles all returned to their case. It took a minute or two, and he listened to the sounds of fighting dying down and looked at the boy John Moses, wondering what to do.

John Moses looked back at him. "I'm brave," he said finally, lips trembling. That didn't help.

"Yeah," Jed agreed, "you're brave." He couldn't turn the scarabs on the boy at this close range safely, but he could shoot him with the silenced gun, or just break his neck, and dispose of the body later using the beetles. He found thinking about it nauseating. *Dammit, Coltrane, what's wrong with you?*

The metallic rustling stopped as the last of the scarabs nestled away inside the cylinder and fell still. With a heavy heart, Jed closed the lid. *Decision time,* he thought. It had to be done with a knife; that would be quieter, even quieter than the Husher. He slowly reached inside his coat …

"You saved me!" John Moses whispered. He lurched forward to grab the dwarf in an awkward hug. "I'm brave, but you saved me!"

Jed felt a thickness in his throat he hadn't felt in a long time. He found himself reaching past the hilt of his knife and the butt of the Pinkerton's pistol and digging into his pocket, finally locating the Cadbury Wand, which he pressed into the boy's hands. "Yeah," he admitted hoarsely, "I guess I did."

Bang!

A gun went off on the deck and other sounds of scuffle ceased.

With a great shuddering jerk, the *Liahona* rumbled to a halt.

"Shh!" Jed urged, pulling John Moses flat onto the rooftop with him. The boy followed readily, half the Wand already stuffed into his eager mouth.

"This is your Captain!" Dan Jones shouted. He was held by two of the Indians and a third waved a pistol over his head, firing a second time for effect.

Bang!

"This is Captain Jones speaking!" the Welshman shouted again. "I am surrendering the *Liahona* to these men, who are Shoshone under the command of Chief Pocatello. Chief Pocatello is a friend of the Kingdom of Deseret, so I'm certain that this is all a misunderstanding. Do not be afraid. Please cooperate with these men and we will sort this out. All property will be returned, please be patient and no one will be hurt."

Bang!

As if to emphasize as ironically as possible this last claim, the pistol-holder fired a third time into the air, and then the Shoshone swept Captain Jones and two other crewmen into the wheelhouse. As they began the process of herding passengers back below decks, Jed crept away from the edge and pressed himself as flat as possible.

They wouldn't find the body of either of the two Shoshone warriors he'd killed, of course—they'd been consumed. Still, they would find their clothing and they might be suspicious, especially if they connected the disappearances with that of the Pinkerton the previous night.

Just to be on the safe side, Jed Coltrane drew his stolen pistol.

LEⱯꟼOᖷⱯ

Burton endured the indignity with all the grace he could muster, gritting his teeth against the bile that threatened to rise up in his throat at the thought of it. Being captured was one thing—Burton had resisted, as was his manly duty, and had only been taken prisoner after felling three of the Shoshone, two with one of the *Liahona*'s iron chairs and the third with a traditional punch to the teeth—but being held prisoner in the company of the snake oil salesman was entirely unacceptable.

They sat on the deck in the night's chill, three to a bench, as the *Liahona* thundered away from the main road on some side track, under the alert glare of several Shoshone braves. The Indians were armed like desperadoes with a miscellany of powerful personal weapons.

Burton saw several electro-knives and at least one vibro-blade cutlass, Maxim pistols as well as the more usual Colts, tomahawks, clubs and brass knuckles, and one repeating cross-bow, the vicious head of its loaded bolt staring cruelly at the passengers under guard and reminding them to sit very, very still. One or two of them carried a Henry or a Remington, but their standard issue weapon seemed to be the Brunel rifle, long and heavy, which they leaned on like staves or spears, heavy coiled-magnet-engine-end down. They didn't use bayonets, but in the squabble he'd seen more than one brave use his Brunel like a quarterstaff; the heavy guns were highly adaptable to this purpose and had proven effective, as a welt on Burton's own forehead told him eloquently.

A number of the Indians wore dark goggles over their eyes and Burton wondered at their purpose—did they confer some sort of darkness-penetrating vision? He'd never seen their like. A few wore metal breastplates, though most covered their chests with leather, bead, and bone. They wore their hair long down their backs, decorated with feathers and strips of brightly-colored cloth.

To Burton's left sat Roxie, elegant, cool and collected, and he wished they were alone. He would have liked to ask her, indirectly and cleverly, of course, about the contents of his glass, and whether she had drugged him or tampered with his official correspondence, and just who she really was.

Also, he would have liked to throw her to the deck and make passionate love to her, body and soul, and damn any watching eyes, like the savage that his enemies accused him of being. Like the savage that, with half his heart, he wanted to be. Like the savage he knew he could never be with Isabel.

At least, he thought, he should compliment her on her work in the stateroom fray.

"You have an impressive right hook, for a woman," he told her, and though he meant it as an ungrudging compliment, she looked amused and underwhelmed.

"You did well enough against the Shoshone yourself, Dick," she returned the compliment. "You might do nicely for yourself in the Rocky Mountains. You could prospect or trap or be a bounty hunter."

Oh, yes? he wanted to shout. *Is that because I am a* man of action?

But he refrained and said nothing and threw no one to the deck for passionate lovemaking. Instead he just *harrumphed* a not-quite-polite acceptance and felt a lesser man for his own emotional stinginess.

D.J. Butler

"If you learned a little needlework," she added, "who knows how many exciting careers might open up to you?"

"I find myself in agreement with the lady," said the charlatan Archibald, who sat to the other side of Burton. He seemed to shrink, to melt into himself, to rest small and unobtrusive in Burton's own shadow. Burton wondered if Roxie could even see the man. "I hope there are no hard feelings on the subject of the antiquities, and in particular the use of the hypocephalus. I wouldn't want to offend a man of your stature and known talents."

A man of action? Burton wanted to gripe, and then caught himself. Hanuman's thumbs, must he suspect everyone?

Of course not. Roxie is as innocent as the gypsy, he thought, and then he remembered the mysterious crystals in his glass. *However innocent* that *was.* And how did the snake oil Egyptianeer recognize him? Stature and known talents, *indeed.* He snorted. Vicious maneaters, all of them, and he'd do well not to forget it.

"I'm a showman, of course, and I know it," Archibald continued, and then suddenly his words were cut off by a hard, wet coughing fit that ended by being stifled into a white handkerchief. "But *hypnotic hypocephalus* sounds much more impressive than *pillow for mummies,* don't you think? And wouldn't you rather have people interested and looking at the antiquities, even with silly ideas in their heads, than bored and looking away?" He looked weaker for the coughing, thin and bed linen-white.

"Eh," Burton muttered abstractly, feeling guilty for his own suspicions. "It's nothing. I'm not offended."

The charlatan might even be right.

He felt the *Liahona* slow down and snapped himself out of the quagmire of his own thoughts to look ahead; they were arriving.

A ring of thirty-foot-tall Franklin Poles, like the ones in front of Bridger's Saloon except that a queer green spark showed in the blue light of these pillars, surrounded a low, rocky hill. Dark, nearly invisible filaments hung between each set of adjacent poles like a web; Burton might have missed them entirely except that the filaments, too, occasionally crackled with blue electricity. The dry earth was scorched free of vegetation for a few feet on either side of the wires and the burnt air stank of ozone. Behind the filaments, clustering all over the top of and around the bluff, sprouted a riot of skin- and bark-covered teepees.

The explorer in Burton noted the teepees with interest—this far from the Great Plains, he'd expected a different kind of dwelling, something more in the lines of a hogan or a wigwam or even a house. Also, the incongruity of teepees protected by a wall of electricks intrigued and amused him; he hadn't seen defenses like this in Egypt or in the Horn.

He thought he could spot hints of riflemen lying among the rocks of the bluff, too. Assuming they were also armed with Brunels, that height

70

would give them a range of miles and make them devastating to any encroaching force. Anyone approaching who was delayed by the sparking fence would be exposed and likely shot to pieces in no time. Burton had seen the damage that the Brunel's magnet-driven bullets could do, even at shockingly long ranges.

"Astounding," Jamison Archibald murmured.

A sparking, sizzling metal gate hung between two extra-thick pylons, across the road in front of the *Liahona*, barring forward progress. Burton watched in fascination as a brave stepped from the *Liahona*'s wheelhouse and yelled in the direction of the compound ahead, whooping and waving an arm until the pylons hissed out a thick emission of steam and smoke and the gate swung sideways on steel cables, opening to admit the captured steam-truck.

The *Liahona* coughed and ground forward again. Watching the electricks fence pass by, Burton suddenly became aware that Roxie, still sitting at his side, was talking to someone, and not in English.

The man was Shoshone, and dressed like all the other Indian warriors, though he was older than most of them. He had a smile on his face but Roxie was furious. Burton had been studying Shoshone, along with Ute and Navajo, since his departure from London, and though his skills were still rudimentary, they were enough to understand this conversation once he focused on it. After all, he thought, allowing himself a moment of pride, he was quite simply damn good with languages.

"Big Beard Chief Brigham will be big angry with you!" Roxie snapped. Her Shoshone was fast, but heavily accented. "Big Beard Chief Brigham always friend to the Shoshone!"

The older man scratched himself calmly and answered in smooth, articulate, native Shoshone. "Captain Jones will get his truck back, don't worry. And I will personally come down to the Great Salt Lake City on my best horse and drink a lager with Brigham to make friends again. I've had worse losses today on my side—two of my men are missing." His eyes narrowed. "In strange ways. What is my Brother Orson doing these days that he is not sharing with his Brother Pocatello?"

Burton tried not to give any indication that he understood the conversation. *Orson,* that must be Orson Pratt, the great inventor—some said *madman*—of the Kingdom, the man behind the mighty airships, the man whose genius drove Burton's mission. But how could any Shoshone be missing *strangely*? He thought of the Pinkerton who had disappeared from Fort Bridger, leaving his clothing behind; was that some new and exotic weapon of Pratt's, and if so, what could it be? A flesh-disintegrating ray?

He shook his head, baffled.

And who was Roxie? She seemed to be some sort of agent of the Kingdom, or at least of its President. He wished now that he had investigated her a little better, at least asked her a few more questions. *You're an idiot, Burton,* he told himself. *You're a fool for nice legs in a skirt.* He noticed then that the gypsy was looking at him curiously.

"What?" he snarled, and immediately looked away, communicating disinterest in any answer.

Archibald only chuckled, until his chuckle ended in a soft wet cough.

Roxie was talking again. "If bad things in Kingdom because of you delay, I self make Shoshone forever unhappy!" The fox yip of her voice was fierce enough to make Burton feel nervous and he forced his eyes to wander around the teepees, the tethered horses, and the banked fires as the *Liahona* ground again to a halt. "I make all ladies in Kingdom wear Shoshone skin hat, eat Shoshone testicles!"

Burton shivered involuntarily. Who *was* this woman? His spike of fear was seasoned with sharp pangs of attraction.

The old Shoshone, though, was calm. "I don't know what bad things might happen in the Kingdom because you arrive a day late," he said urbanely, "but I'll take the risk." He turned away and headed for the ladder.

Roxie hissed in exasperation and glared at Burton. "Well?" she snapped in English.

Burton shrugged defensively. "Nothing. It pleases me to see that you have friends among these savages. Maybe you can talk them into letting us go."

"Savages, indeed!" Roxie snorted, rising to her feet to join a line of passengers being dragged and Brunel-prodded towards the ladder by the Shoshone. "Savages, indeed!"

LE⅃NꟼOⅣⅥ

Absalom hadn't come west expecting to be imprisoned and much less had he come expecting to be imprisoned in a cave. Well, perhaps it wasn't truly a *cave*, he thought, but it was at least a *pit*.

Blue electricks snapped and sparked here and there in the walls, but they lit the cavern only dimly. Further light, even dimmer over the artificial illumination with which it competed, filtered down from the blue-grey circle of open sky above. Most of the illumination in the pit, though, was orange-yellow and was thrown by several pole-length torches, jammed into the soft ground at irregular intervals and adding a smoky, woody note to the human reek that assailed Absalom's nostrils. The latrine trench in the corner, complete with unsmoothed, barky log seat, didn't help. He resolved to hold off using it as long as he possibly could.

Some of the *Liahona*'s other passengers seemed perfectly at ease with the situation. Burton was one of them. Shortly after the Shoshone had thrown them into this chamber, sealing the entrance behind them with a coal-powered, fume-spewing portcullis, Ruffian Dick had stomped once around the big cell and then slumped down against one wall and gone straight to sleep. Other passengers had joined him in dozing, as had the steam-truck's crew, not to mention Absalom's Angel, who proved to be surprisingly rugged. Absalom was one of those who were unable to sleep and he paced about the pit, wondering what he had gotten himself into. Also pacing in circles was the *Liahona*'s captain, who looked supremely indignant and muttered to himself with every step.

He had to save Abigail. That's what he was doing here and that was worth any amount of standing in a pit, or of being subjected to the bullying arrogance of Dick Burton, or even of having to use a log-hewn latrine. Also, if he could manage it, there were Foreign Office objectives to achieve (Absalom's real commission letter, issued after he called in several favors and got several fellow-Harrovians roaring drunk, simply said *assist Captain Richard Burton*) and the dignity of the Empire to maintain. The dignity of the British Empire, of course, had survived all manner of primitive latrines.

The portcullis puffed steam and black smoke and jerked up into its rock-carved housing. The older Indian warrior whom Absalom had seen on the *Liahona*'s deck entered and in his wake, to Absalom's surprise, came the two men who had surprised him the night before, behind Bridger's Saloon. Despite his disorientation, panic, and anger, Foreign Office mnemonics training kicked in and he remembered their names: Lee and Hickman. The three men stopped inside the gate, surveying the prisoners.

Absalom stormed across the pit to the three men, but Captain Dan Jones got there first.

"This is bloody nonsense, Pocatello, aye, and you know it! When President Young hears what you've done—Hickman! Lee!" He looked astonished. "What are you doing here? Tell the Chief he can't keep us locked up!"

Chief Pocatello raised a restraining hand and smiled wryly. "Spare me," he said, "I already got the whole speech from Sister Eliza."

Lee grinned. "I guess you did, Chief."

Hickman thumped Chief Pocatello on the shoulder with enthusiasm. "Sometimes even an Injun can be a poor dumb unlucky son of a bitch, can't he?" he shrilled in his high-pitched voice.

Jones looked from one face to the next, puzzled. "Will you not get us out of here, then?"

"Don't worry, Brother Daniel," Lee reassured him, "the Shoshone'll let you go in the morning. None of your passengers will be any the worse for wear."

D.J. Butler

"Did you Danites arrange this?" Jones demanded to know, and then he frowned. "This isn't something Brother Brigham ordered, is it? If he wanted to change my schedule or my route, he could have simply told me so."

Hickman snickered. "Naw, we ain't done this. I guess Pocatello ain't such a tame Injun as you thought, is all."

"Why are you laughing?" Jones demanded. His face was turning red with rage and frustration. "Deseret's premier land-ferry from the Wyoming Territory has been waylaid by former allies with all passengers and crew. Is that funny to you, Hickman? Are you amused that the *Liahona* was attacked?"

Hickman shrugged. "I got an eclectic sense of humor, I guess. I can laugh at jokes other men tell almost as easy as I can laugh at my own."

"Don't worry, it would take a railgun the size of a piñon pine to put a scratch on the *Liahona*," Pocatello added. "And you must know that your Brother Brigham has not yet seen fit to sell me a railgun."

"I'm not worried about the *truck!*" the Welsh captain barked, his voice projecting like a foghorn. "I'm worried about John Moses! I can't find the little fellow and Jonathan Browning will kill me first and then die of grief himself if I lose his son!"

Pocatello's expression seemed compassionate. "I'll have my men check the truck again," he told the *Liahona*'s captain. "Maybe he's hiding. A boy that size, he might be under a chair and we just missed him."

Jones nodded stiffly, his face still a mask of fury and fear, and walked away, throwing himself to a seated position in the sand. The others seemed to finally see Absalom and he cleared his throat by way of annoyed greeting. Perhaps these men could help him.

"Why look, it's the Englishman," Bill Hickman squeaked, and then walked past Absalom with no further salutation.

"We've already seen this one," Lee added to the Shoshone Chief. He too walked on, leaving Absalom floundering alone.

Chief Pocatello shrugged and followed the two white men. The three of them paced around the pit, examining the *Liahona*'s passengers and crew. Absalom trailed them at a short distance, feeling ineffectual but unable to think of anything to say that would get their attention and respect. Some of the crew seemed to recognize the two white men and glared at them, but Hickman and Lee reserved their interest for certain of the passengers. They whispered to each other about Burton, and Hickman even bent to toss a small dirt clod at the man, like you might test a wild animal, but Ruffian Dick lay still, breathing deeply and giving no signs of anything but restful slumber.

They smirked at Burton's lady friend Roxie, too, and separately at Absalom's Angel, who sat with the older woman; the former spit on their boots and the latter looked away, bored. Hickman and Lee continued on, then stopped for a long time staring at the Egyptian antiquities showman Archibald. He sat quietly on the dirt and looked back, gently. Absalom positioned himself by the two ladies and tried desperately to think of something to say to confront their captors.

"That ain't a natural beard, is it?" Hickman asked, squinted. He pulled up one of the torches and held it over the other man.

"No," Archibald agreed, "it isn't. I'm a showman. My show is a serious one and requires the gravitas of a beard. Lamentably, I myself do not grow a good one, so this beard is … borrowed."

He smiled.

"Didn't you have a helper of some kind, back at the Fort?" Lee inquired. "A short man, a dwarf?"

"I did," the exhibitor agreed. "Tell me if you find him—he's disappeared, along with some of my tools."

"Lots of folks are vamoosing all of the sudden around here. Maybe," Hickman suggested, eyes glinting cruelly as he planted the torch, stepped closer and pulled a long knife from his belt, "the little bugger's hiding in that haystack on your chin."

He lashed out quickly, like a snake, and grabbed the carnival man by his neck. Lee stepped back a pace and put his hands on the butt of the pistols on his belt, as if warning bystanders not to intervene. Doctor Archibald made no move to resist or flee, but lay limply in the other man's grip while his false beard was shaved down to gum and stubble.

"There, now," Hickman said as he finished the rough shave and re-sheathed the knife. "You look presentable, much more like your picture. I guess Brother Brigham'll be happy to see you now."

Like his picture? What was Hickman talking about? And why did he think the traveling presenter of Egyptian antiquities would be interested in an audience with Brigham Young? Absalom trembled, feeling out of his depth. He turned to the ladies, meaning to offer them a reassuring glance, and was surprised to see, for just a split second before she reasserted control, an expression of shock and surprise on Roxie's face.

"Yes, but did you find my dwarf?" the showman quipped.

Hickman didn't take the joke well. "No, Mr. Poe, I didn't," he squeaked, and pulled a battered revolver from a holster low on his hip, cocking it ominously with one thumb. "Maybe I didn't search you closely enough."

Absalom didn't want to intervene. In his heart he knew that he was not a brave man and he desperately wanted Doctor Archibald, or *Poe*, if that was his name, to fight his own battles. He apparently had a history with Lee and Hickman.

But watching these frontier bullies threaten and intimidate a harmless old man reminded him too much of Abigail, of her being abducted by the notorious Rockwell—Rockwell, whom Absalom had met the night before and to whom he had done nothing, though the man richly deserved any thrashing that any person at all might be able to give him—and something in him pushed him to act.

Also, he couldn't let his Angel watch him stand by any longer.

"Excuse me, gentlemen," he intruded, forcing his legs, by an effort of will, to carry him forward. "We were never able to finish our conversation last night, and I was unable to ask you a question I had meant to pose." He almost stumbled to a stop, conscious of eyes on him. "I'm coming to the Kingdom of Deseret on official business, on business, in fact, of Her Majesty Victoria, Queen of the United Kingdom of Great Britain and Ireland," he hoped that a little title-waving might help defuse the situation, "but I have personal affairs to see to as well."

"Yes?" Lee prompted him slowly.

"My sister," Absalom said, then cleared his throat. "I've come looking for my sister. Her name is Abigail Fearnley-Standish, though it's possible ..." he trailed off, mustering his strength so as to be able to speak the unspeakable, "it's possible that she goes by the name of *Rockwell* now."

Hickman paused and squinted in Absalom's direction, pistol cocked and pointed at the sky, the lapels of Archibald's coat clenched in his free hand. "Funny," he grumbled, "I thought our conversation last night went on plenty long, and I didn't hear nothing about no sister then."

Lee looked surprised and amused. "I don't think I know your sister," he said. "Are you suggesting that she might be married to *Orrin Porter Rockwell?*" He and Hickman shared a look that was both knowing and surprised.

Absalom felt very conspicuous now, very vulnerable, and very alone. He also felt the gaze of his Angel upon him like a mantle of lead. Unsure if he could speak without bursting into tears or fainting, he nodded and thrust forth his jaw in that same stoic, ape-like expression he'd seen on Dick Burton's face every day now for months.

"Well, ain't that peculiar?" Hickman drawled, tossing Archibald to the dirt and turning his attention to Absalom. "'Cause as I recollect it, last night we asked you if you'd seen our friend Orrin Porter Rockwell, and you allowed as you hadn't."

I hadn't, Absalom wanted to say, even though it would have been a lie, but he couldn't force the words out. He managed to shake his head, and thought he kept his hands from trembling too terribly much.

"Not only that," Lee remembered, his baritone becoming a menacing growl, "you suggested that you didn't even know who Porter Rockwell *was.*"

"I don't know him," Absalom gulped out, and he put up his hands, palms forward, in a non-threatening gesture. "Please be calm, I don't know Mr. Rockwell."

"I'm inclined to think that you're lying to us," Hickman said, and he leveled his pistol at Absalom's forehead. "And if you don't come clean now, I'm inclined to shoot you."

CHAPTER
FIVE

J ed Coltrane spent the night lying on the rooftop of the *Liahona*'s wheelhouse with the boy, John Moses. After the Shoshone had disarmed and unloaded the steam-truck's passengers and crew they'd turned the boiler down and idled all the electricks and in the blue-firefly-dotted darkness that followed Jed had slipped down briefly to collect a few items to make the night a little more bearable: a pea coat from the wheelhouse, a couple of wool blankets from one of the cabins, a large tin of chocolate cookies and a bottle of milk from the galley, and a flask of brandy from his own room. He'd stuffed the big-eyed boy into the pea coat and then wrapped each of them inside a wool blanket and they'd munched cookies together in silence in Jed's little stick joint on the wheelhouse roof.

He'd taken one other thing from the wheelhouse, which was a long, telescoping spyglass, of steel-bound brass construction and providing an impressive degree of magnification when fully telescoped. Jed had let John Moses look through the spyglass briefly, but then the boy had fallen asleep in his puddle of wool. Jed had spent a couple of hours alone, examining the Shoshone camp carefully and trying to figure out his next move.

Not far behind the *Liahona*, a couple of clocksprung horses had galloped up to the gate of the encampment and been admitted. Jed had seen plenty of clocksprung animals in Eli Whitney's South; clocksprung men planted and harvested cotton, clocksprung mules pulled every domestic load imaginable, and soldiers and cavaliers rode around the roads of the country, roads so bad for the most part that only the ruggedest trucks could have survived them, on the backs of clocksprung horses. These two mechanical animals *clop-clop-hissed* through the welcoming Shoshone braves and he thought about stealing them, but they too quickly disappeared with their riders, two white men in long coats, in the direction of the central bluff.

Jed snapped his spyglass shut in frustration.

So much for that idea, Coltrane, he thought. *Only a real mark would work at how to sneak deeper into the camp in order to steal his means out. What are you, Coltrane, new?* The dwarf sat back and returned to considering his other options.

If the steam-truck were smaller—*much* smaller—he might be able to operate it himself and try to break out of the compound that way. He might be able to steal a horse, he thought, but he didn't know how to get the gate open. He considered flight, tunneling, disguise, and everything else he could think of, watching the Shoshone sentinels drift occasionally through the witch-lit camp, and had finally reached the point of surrendering to the inevitable and settling in to wait, when the Shoshone opened their gate and a second truck rolled in.

"Good hell," he muttered to himself. It was the *Jim Smiley.*

He trained the pilfered spyglass on the smaller truck and wished he had a better way to listen. Even without being able to hear the words that passed between them, though, there was no mistaking the friendliness of the greeting that Sam Clemens and his skinny, porkpie hat-wearing Irishman got from the old Shoshone and his braves who ambled up to receive them. With the telescope, too, Jed could clearly see the nut change hands—Clemens carefully counted out a series of gold coins and passed them over to the Shoshone, who whooped in gleeful appreciation.

"I'll be damned," he said. "What's going on here?"

Clemens and the Indians walked together, chatting and grinning and slapping each other on the back, on toward the bluff in the center of the encampment. As Jed watched through his spyglass, they disappeared into the tunnel mouth into which all the *Liahona*'s crew and passengers had been taken.

Leaving the *Jim Smiley* unattended; thin twists of steam and coal smoke jetting from its pipes.

Jed looked again at the compound's gate. It was an electricks work, so Jed would be afraid to touch it with his hands, but he knew enough about the subject to believe that rubber protected you from electricks, and the *Jim Smiley* was a steel capsule surrounded by walls of rubber—big India-rubber tires and an inflated black rubber belt most of the way around. That ought to be enough, he thought. He could sneak aboard the *Jim Smiley*, bring her out of her idle and simply charge out the gate. How hard could it be? And by the time anyone wised up to him, he'd be halfway back to Fort Bridger. There he'd ...

He faltered. He'd what, exactly?

Would he tell the locals that he was a secret agent for a covert leadership faction of the southern States, men who were illegally organizing a shadow government in preparation for an expected civil war, and ask for volunteers to come help rescue his fellow secret agent from wild Indians? Jeez, if he had cash, he might be able to hire some muscle, but he didn't even have that, and even if he went door to door in the *Liahona* and burgled all its rooms, he doubted, from the look of the passengers, that they'd have enough wealth all together to hire a single one-eyed gunman and a spavined nag.

He could jump into the *Jim Smiley* and ride jock down the mysterious tunnel, but that seemed like suicide for a lot of reasons.

He gnawed his knuckles and schemed. He knew that Poe was carrying something that Brigham Young wanted, though Jed wasn't sure what it was. Not that it mattered; he couldn't pack all of Poe's Egyptian knicks-knacks off the *Liahona* and onto the *Jim Smiley*—it was too bulky for him to do it alone, and even if he had help, he couldn't manage it without being seen.

If he could get a message to Young, though, then the man might send Deseret troops, or some of his feared Danite assassins, out to rescue Poe and retrieve whatever it was he and Poe were negotiating about. But Jed had never before been west of the Mississippi and he wasn't sure of the way to the Great Salt Lake City.

But Clemens knew the route. That was where he was headed.

And Jed could stow away.

He checked his shoulder holster and big jacket pocket; the gun and the scarab cylinder were secure. He could hide in the *Jim Smiley*'s lockers and kill the two Federal men before they got to Deseret, just to be sure. The boy, of course, he'd leave here.

He looked down at John Moses, asleep with a cherubic smile on his face.

He shivered. The night was getting cold. The boy was wrapped in a pea coat and a blanket, but he still might feel the chill. Plus, when he woke up alone, he might be afraid. And if the Indians found him, who knew what they'd do?

Jed shook himself.

"What the hell are you thinking, Coltrane?" he demanded out loud. The boy was warm and sleeping like a log, and if he woke up, there were cookies and milk to finish. Sooner or later, someone would find him, and he'd be taken care of. If he got too nervous he could always let himself down.

He scooted to the lip of the rooftop, then paused. *Aw, hell,* he thought. *The boy might talk.* He might talk to the Shoshone, tell them he'd been up here, and they might figure out Jed killed their braves. They might even figure out he'd stowed away on the *Jim Smiley* and come after him. Worse, they could figure it out while the *Jim Smiley* was still sitting in the compound, *and then it would be all over, Jed Coltrane, you miserable little dwarf.*

He'd have to kill the boy.

No time to have qualms about it; Jed forced himself to grab the Pinkerton's gun and jerk it from its holster. He pointed it at John Moses's head. He felt freezing cold sweat running down his own face and he blinked stinging salt out of his eyes.

John Moses snored, softly.

What if he needed someone to show him the way to the Great Salt Lake City?

What if things went wrong on the *Jim Smiley* and he had to kill the two Federals early? He'd need someone like the little midshipman to show him which turns to take.

Damn you, Coltrane, you're fooling yourself.

But in his heart he knew he wanted to be fooled.

Jed re-holstered the gun and shook John Moses gently. "Come on, you little shit, nap's over. We got to get moving before the sun comes up."

ᒪᛂᘺᛉ0ᔈᘺ

The antiquities exhibitor began to cough. Hard, loud, wet coughs racked his chest and his entire body jerked in obvious spastic pain. He doubled over, elbows digging into his knees, hacking and coughing and making retching sounds as he spat into the dirt.

"Damn, old man," Hickman drawled through his nose, "you don't sound good." He turned his head to look at the showman, whose false beard he'd shaved off.

A Shoshone warrior shouted an objection, jumping forward—

—but there was Absalom's Angel, spinning improbably in the air like a beskirted top, the heel of her boot slamming into the brave's breastbone, impelling him backwards and to the earth—

—and Burton was standing at Absalom's side, revolver cocked and pointed at Hickman's jaw. Lee and Hickman both started, taken by surprise, and then froze.

There was a moment of uncomfortable silence during which Absalom focused on willing his bladder not to betray him.

"He stole my gun," one of the Shoshone grumbled sullenly.

"Well then, I reckon this is a standoff," Hickman suggested.

"I disagree," Burton answered in a deep deadpan.

Absently, Absalom noticed that the gypsy had stopped coughing. He now stood upright and was holding a cloth to his mouth.

"I might could shoot your boy, here," the Deseret man pointed out.

"You do me a favor if you shoot him," Burton snarled. "And then I shoot you, so I've done my duty to the Queen and am doubly happy. Not only that, but I go to the Geographical Society and regale my colleagues with tales of my adventure killing genuine Western outlaws. I take your bullet-punched skull along as an exhibit, and then I put you on my mantel. I win three times over. From my point of view, the best thing you could possibly do right now would be to shoot Abby here."

"Abigail!" Absalom cried out indignantly, and then realized what he'd said. "I mean *Absalom*! My name is Absalom Fearnley-Standish, blast you all!" He was torn between feeling gratitude for Burton's intervention and fear that Burton might mean exactly what he said.

"My friend might could shoot *you*, though," Hickman continued, nodding in Lee's direction. Lee kept his hands clearly off his pistol grips, but they were close enough, Absalom thought nervously, that he could grab them and shoot quickly. He wondered if he were about to see a real display of Western quick-draw gunfighting. He might enjoy that, he thought idiotically, if it didn't result in his own death.

Lee, though, wasn't focusing on the confrontation in front of him. Instead, he seemed frozen in place, his hands hovering in place, his gaze fixed on Doctor Archibald, who still held his handkerchief before his mouth with one hand and with the other seemed to be making circular gestures in front of the cloth.

Burton, in any case, paid not the slightest attention to Lee.

The explorer shrugged. "I'll take the risk."

Hickman squinted, his face twitching slightly.

"You got my back, ain't you, John?" he called out.

To Absalom's surprise, Lee didn't answer. He swayed slightly on his feet and Absalom wondered if he'd been drinking. He still stood staring at the man called Poe and his white handkerchief.

"Lee?" Hickman risked a split-second glance in his friend's direction.

Lee fell forward headlong, crashing full-length into the dirt.

"Lee!" Hickman shouted. The slight trembling of his pistol hand made Absalom feel very nervous.

"Your friend's unwell," Burton observed with a sneer.

Absalom was beginning to take heart and felt enough bravado to pile on.

"Perhaps he's been drinking," he suggested.

"No," Poe corrected them, carefully folding the white cloth—which, Absalom now thought, looked rather large for a handkerchief, and wasn't there writing on it?—and putting it away in his coat pocket. "He's fallen asleep. The excitement was too much for him."

"Helldammit!" shouted Hickman. His nostrils flared, he bared yellow-brown teeth, and his eyes jumped back and forth between Burton and Absalom.

"It isn't my first choice, but I'm willing to lower my gun if you lower yours," Burton suggested in a cold, gravelly tone. "And I suspect that Her Majesty would prefer that outcome, all in all."

"You first," said Hickman.

"Like hell."

"I ain't gonna lower my gun," Hickman insisted.

"Sure you will," interjected a new voice. "You both will, or my Irishman here will plug you full of holes."

Absalom turned, and nearly jumped out of his skin. It was the brush-mustachioed Brute who spoke, chewing his words out around the stub of an unlit, partly-smoked cigar. To his side was a bony, red-haired, beak-nosed man in a long coat and porkpie hat, who held a long brass repeater rifle to his shoulder in shooting position, aimed straight at Hickman. Behind them, with long Brunel rifles pointed forward, came four Shoshone braves. To the side stood Chief Pocatello, looking relaxed with his arms folded over his chest.

"We'll all shoot you, Bill," Pocatello said, his eyes twinkling merrily. "Put it back in the holster."

Burton immediately complied, his movement crisp and salute-like. The man was an ape, but to his credit and Absalom's relief, he was an East India Company ape.

Hickman dawdled and looked sulky as he put his gun away.

"It ain't like you to abandon a friend, Chief," he whined. "You shouldn't ought to turn your back on a man."

"Or a snake," Burton added.

"I just don't want any shooting, Bill," Chief Pocatello said. "We'll put Lee over his saddle for you. Why don't you take him back to the Fort?"

Bill Hickman whimpered like a kicked dog and he shot Absalom a venomous glare, but he took the offered help and trudged for the gate with a couple of Shoshone braves, dragging John Lee between them.

"That was some luck, wasn't it?" Absalom commented to the mysterious Poe, who only arched his eyebrows and pursed his lips in return.

"You're Sam Clemens," Burton said to the brush-faced Brute. Absalom could have kicked himself for not recognizing the man in the Saloon.

"And you're the skunk that punched holes in my boiler pipes," Clemens batted back. "Name's Burton, I understand."

"True," Burton acknowledged, "and yes."

Absalom felt his throat constricting. "I ... I ..." he stammered.

"Don't you worry your pretty girlish Etonian head about it, you bloody toff." Clemens's Henry-armed companion spoke in an Irish brogue. "We know it wasn't you."

"Harrovian," Absalom murmured defensively.

"Same fookin' thing." The Irishman spat on the ground.

"What do you want?" Burton pressed Sam Clemens, his face hard.

Clemens sighed and looked wistful. "Mostly," he said, "I want to gloat. Will it ease your feelings if I dress my gloating up in homespun philosophy?"

"It might," Burton allowed.

Clemens gnawed on his stub and reflected. "I could tell you that *cheaters never prosper*," he said, "but if you know anything about the United States Congress, you'll know that's a crock of manure."

"What goes around, comes around," Burton offered coolly.

Clemens shook his head dismissively. "Too Eastern, too much symmetry, too much yin-this-and-yang-the-other-thing. What if I just leave it at *never go up against a riverboat man when his smokestack is on the line?* It isn't exactly pithy, but it's got a certain sly innuendo about it and it resonates."

"I suppose your Shoshone friends will hold us here while you get a head start," Burton said grimly, and Absalom's heart sank at the prospect of the mission's failure. *Well*, he thought, *at least he could still find his sister.*

"Of course," Clemens admitted. "Also, I'm going to steal all your coal."

ᒪᕮᘺᖌᓍᚻᘺ

Not long after the gray pre-dawn sky over the pit transitioned to a bright morning blue, the Shoshone raised the portcullis and let out the crew and passengers of the *Liahona*. Braves stood at the mouth of the tunnel to meet their former prisoners as they were disgorged, cheerfully returning weapons and making assurances that nothing on board the truck had been disturbed. Captain Jones stormed out first, yelling "John Moses! John Moses!" before he was halfway across the compound towards his idling vehicle.

Poe let himself drift at the back of the crowd. He exercised all his considerable powers of inconspicuousness and stealth, but he knew it was wasted effort. Roxie had seen him without his beard and surely she had recognized him as easily as he had recognized her. His only hope, and it was a slim one, was that she still believed him to be dead and that her belief was strong enough to trump the evidence of her own eyes. She had tried to kill him in Baltimore, after all—trickster, liar, seductress, poisoner—and, at the Army's instruction—at *Robert's* instruction—he had let her believe she had succeeded. She almost *had*. He had died to the world, then, had ceased to be *Edgar Allan Poe* or *Edgar* or *Ed* to almost every human being he talked to, had assumed a series of false identities, many even nameless, in pursuit of the various missions the Army had given him.

For many years at a stretch, the only human being who had known he was alive and known his real name, Poe's only source of genuine human contact, much less kindness, had been his case officer, Robert Lee.

No, he could hope she thought he was dead, but he knew better. He had seen the surprise register on her face when that thug Hickman had pierced his disguise and he had noted how thoroughly she had avoided him thereafter. She was too good to ever give the *appearance* of avoiding him, but the fact remained that Hickman had shouted his name and she hadn't met his eyes or stood close to him since. Perhaps she didn't trust herself not to reveal her knowledge or perhaps she was simply afraid that Poe might seek an opportunity to take his well-deserved revenge.

Either way, she knew, and that put him and all his objectives at risk.

For that matter, Hickman and Lee knew. Who were they and where did they get their information?

As he let Roxie and other passengers flush out through the tunnel ahead of him, he pondered again the questions that had been running through his head for hours. What did Brigham Young want? What did Orson Pratt want? What did *Roxie* want? Did her presence on the *Liahona* indicate that Young knew of Poe's mission and wanted it thwarted? Or did it mean that Roxie knew Poe was alive and was after him again? Or was it mere coincidence? Was she still Young's agent? Was she Pratt's?

And where was Coltrane? Obviously, the dwarf had failed in his errand, since Roxie was alive and well. Had she killed or disabled him somehow? But she had been at the show, and then on the *Liahona*'s deck. Was the young high-kicking woman a professional associate of Roxie's— might *she* have defeated Poe's dwarf?

He watched the young woman now, careful not to drift too close to her. The English diplomat, Fearnley-Standish, was chattering to her frantically, spewing out a torrent of words. She tolerated his walking beside her and when he reached out to hold her hand, she squeezed his fingers once, briefly, before letting them go. Her face was the iron visage of a nymph and she looked very much in command of the conversation and strong, and Poe could imagine her possessing undisclosed and dangerous skills. She might very well have done Coltrane in.

Poe could carry out his mission without the dwarf, assuming Hunley's devices were all still intact, and in particular the ones he had to consign to the Madman. He patted the whistle around his neck to be sure he still had that, at least. He couldn't be so conspicuous as to rush out to the *Liahona* first, but he did need to assure himself that he still had his other tools.

And he had to get to the Great Salt Lake City as fast as possible.

Damn Samuel Clemens.

When Poe reached the *Liahona* he could see its Captain and crew on board, on the deck, and through the few portholes, searching furiously for their missing midshipman. "John Moses!" Poe heard the Welshman shout, over and over but to no avail.

A crowd of the truck's passengers mobbed beside one of its enormous tracks, facing off against the old Shoshone chief. Pocatello stood to face their irate stares with his arms crossed over his chest in casual unconcern. The mob carried weapons and if Pocatello had been a lone man he might have had to fear for his life, but half a dozen braves stood about him, all armed to the teeth, and of course the rocky bluff above the compound was a glowering hedgehog of snipers. Roxie was not in sight—likely she had slipped aboard the *Liahona*, to avoid Poe's presence yet again, and now her young companion followed her.

"Did you leave us enough coal to get to the Great Salt Lake City?" cried out a long-faced Swede, despair in his voice.

Pocatello shrugged. "I gave Sam Clemens a free run at the truck's coal room. I don't know how much he took, but he seemed anxious to be sure he got there ahead of you, so my guess is that he didn't leave you nearly enough."

"Have you no shame, sir?" demanded one of the spinsters to whom Poe had paid special attention during the previous night's show.

"No, ma'am," Pocatello acknowledged, "I do not. I have a people to lead and feed and protect and this was purely a business transaction in my people's interest. Don't worry, ma'am, your Captain Jones is a resourceful man and I expect you'll make it down into the Valley soon enough. In the meantime, if you're hungry, we have food we can share … for a reasonable price."

He grinned.

Poe thought he saw where this conversation was going, and wanted to cut it short. He had seen the *Jim Smiley* and he doubted that it was large enough to carry away all the *Liahona*'s coal, even if it had stuffed its every compartment full to overflowing.

With another quick glance around to be sure he saw neither Roxie nor the young woman he suspected of being her assistant, he raised his voice to pose a question to the Shoshone chief. "I see that you're a commercially sophisticated man, Chief," he said. "Is there anything else you might condescend to let us have for a price? Anything necessary for the operation of a steam-truck, say?"

The Chief batted his eyes innocently and Poe knew he had guessed correctly. "I suppose I might," he conceded. "Did you have anything specific in mind?"

"Coal, for instance?"

Chief Pocatello's grin broadened. "Why yes," he said, "I believe I do have some coal I might be able to sell to you. And I'm no expert, but I guess it's probably just the right kind for the *Liahona*'s boiler."

LƐꓺꟼOꓦꟺ

"Hell and begorra," Tam exclaimed under his breath, inaudible over the rumble of the steam-truck's operation and the faint rattle of the strapped-down dishes in their various shelves and cupboards, "there's a kid aboard."

He stared at the child, a round-faced little boy overwhelmed by a man's large pea coat, spilling out of the pots and pans cabinet beneath the galley counter. The boy stared back, with big eyes—and didn't every one of Mother O'Shaughnessy's children have big eyes, didn't all kids have big eyes? *Don't get all sentimental, me boy.*

"I only wanted a fresh bottle," Tam muttered, "and Brigit help me if there isn't a three-year-old kid where the whisky's supposed to be."

"Four," said the boy, and then his eyes flickered to the space behind Tam.

Tam hadn't survived his life of dedicated misbehavior by being slow or even by mere good luck. He saw the flick of the boy's eyes and heard a very faint creaking sound, without consciously formulating any idea of what it might mean, he spun about and threw himself backward, at the same time whipping from its holster, the strange gun he'd stolen from the dead Pinkerton and pointing it at whatever might be behind his back—and found himself staring down the barrel of an identical pistol, aimed by a grimacing, hairy-knuckled, downright monkeylike bastard of a dwarf (*and isn't every midget half a monkey, really?*) who hung by the strength of one arm out of the china cupboard.

Tam saw realization dawn in the dwarf's eyes at the same moment that he himself understood what had happened to the second Pinkerton.

"Jebus!" barked the dwarf.

"I hope you wiped your tiny little arse before you climbed in there," Tam sneered. "Sam's particular about liking all of his food *without* monkey shite in it."

They both jumped—

—both fired—

—*zing! zing!*—

—both missed.

They both kept moving. Tam whirled clockwise on his good leg in the small galley and the bloody-damn-hell monkeydwarf sprang from one cupboard to another and then onto the covered (and therefore not unbearably hot) steam heater that served as cooker of all meals served aboard the *Jim Smiley*, both of them firing all the while.

The damned little monkey moved like a butterfly, flitting back and forth like he knew just where each bullet was going to go, and Tam could barely see him move, much less hit him. Like some surreal dream, the guns only *zinged!* demurely, but crockery burst in fountains of ceramic splinters and bullets whined off the iron walls of the galley, chewing through the wooden cabinets and cupboards like termites pumped full of coffee.

The air filled with dust.

"Brigit!" The Irishman choked as a bullet hit him in his left arm. That was the second bullet he'd taken in forty-eight hours. His booted feet slipped, scrabbled for a grip among the rubble on the galley floor, and then brought him down with a heavy *thud!*

The midget slammed his shoulder blades against a corner of the galley, his little feet on a varnished sideboard, and raised his silenced gun to take aim at Tam again.

"I'll kill the boy!" Tam roared, and the dwarf stopped. Tam lay on his back, bleeding and battered, and he pointed his pistol at the little boy. It was a bluff and a gamble and the dwarf might call it, but Tam had no other choice. If the dwarf and the boy were together and the dwarf cared about the boy, Tam just might survive.

The midget hesitated.

"I'll fookin' do it!" Tam insisted, cursing and shaking the pistol for emphasis. "I killed the Pinkerton, you know I did, and I'll by damn kill the boy, too!"

The dwarf raised his gun, but slowly, hesitating.

The little boy burst into tears.

Saint Anthony help me, this is it, Tam thought desperately. "Drop the bloody gun, monkey!" he shouted, trying to keep the fear out of his voice.

The dwarf gritted his teeth, looked at the sobbing child, and tossed his pistol to the floor.

Tam felt a wave of relief flow through his whole body.

He stood up slowly, keeping his pistol carefully trained on the boy as he shook dust and china chips out of his clothing. He kept his eyes on the dwarf, still perched on the countertop, as he crouched to pick up the second Pinkerton gun, tucking it into his belt.

"Praise Judas Iscariot and all the bloody saints," he sighed, "you're a reasonable little gargoyle. I thought for a moment there that I'd robbed my last bank."

Squinting down the barrel of his gun at the weeping boy, he pulled the trigger.

Click.

"See that?" he laughed. "Empty. I'se just about shitting my trousers that you were going to shoot me again."

The dwarf jumped.

He flew straight at Tam, knobby, hairy fists extended over his head like clubs, like the flailing orangutanish mitts of a charging ape.

"Shite!" Tam ducked and the dwarf crashed into his shoulders, bowling him down and hurling both of them out into the *Jim Smiley*'s short hall. Ape fists pulled Tam's porkpie hat down over his face to blind him and an ape thumb gouged into the tender bloody bullet wound in his arm.

Tam screamed in pain and pulled the trigger of his pistol twice before he remembered that the gun was now empty. He felt little feet pad past him, but he could pay them no attention for the little fists, little fingers, and little teeth that assailed him.

The gun was empty, but it wasn't useless. He clubbed the dwarf, rolled, and got his knees between the two of them. Just as he felt little teeth sink into his ear, he kicked his legs—

—hurling the dwarf against the iron wall—

—and ripping off his own ear.

"Aaagh!" he screamed.

He slapped the hat from his face and clapped one hand over his bleeding ear. "You fookin' *animal!*" he roared at the midget, who was bouncing to his feet again, like the little bastard was cast out of India rubber—and then Tam saw the gun lying on the floor of the hallway between them.

The *loaded* Pinkerton pistol.

"Shite!"

The dwarf jumped for the gun, but Tam kicked faster, hitting the pistol and sending it skittering away down the hall and out of reach of both men. Missing the pistol, the dwarf landed instead on Tam's leg, and he brought his elbow down like a hammer on the Irishman's knee. The pain almost blinded him.

"Bloody *mite!*" Tam shouted. He dug the fingers of his good arm into the dwarf's hair. The dwarf resisted, but by throwing his own body weight to the side and heaving with all his might, Tam managed to twist his assailant aside, pin him against the wall with one hand, and scramble again in the direction of the lost weapon.

But the little boy had picked it up and was pointing it at the Irishman.

Tam paused, lying on his belly, looking up past the bulbous muzzle of the pistol at the four-year-old holding it.

"Nice lad, good lad," he panted. "Give your uncle Tam his gun back now."

The dwarf struggled, clawing at Tam's wounded arm. Tam gritted his teeth against the pain.

"John Moses!" the dwarf shouted, and Tam closed his fist down over the dwarf's mouth, silencing him.

The little boy raised the pistol doubtfully.

"Easy, son," said a man's voice.

Through the pain and adrenalin it took Tam a moment to recognize Sam Clemens, but there he was, standing behind the boy with his queer rubber-soled shoes and his crotchful of rivets, talking to him nice and gentle like he was the kid's own dad. "Easy, son. Let me have the pistol and I'll make them both stop fighting. How does that sound to you? Isn't that what you want?"

Tam squinted up and through the sweat and blood in his eyes he saw that Sam was unarmed and smiling. The boy hesitated only a moment, and then handed the Pinkerton's pistol over to Sam Clemens.

"Thanks, son," Sam said to the boy. "You did the right thing." Then he pointed the gun at the two men struggling on the floor.

"I'm no expert in these things," he said, flapping his bushy eyebrows at them, "but I believe I know which end bites. The next one of you to strike the other, move towards me, or do anything other than just lie still, I'll shoot him."

Tam collapsed, exhausted, and felt the dwarf do the same. *Good old Sam Clemens*, he thought. *Good old Missouri Sam.*

LƐⱮⰘ0ꟼꟼⰘⱮ

"I regret the barbarism," Sam Clemens said, nearly shouting to be heard over the rumble of the *Jim Smiley* and the wind that ruffled his hair and tried to rip all his words away.

He'd like to have lit a Partagás to celebrate his impending victory, or at least his manifest lead over the gargantuan *Liahona*, but that would have required him to shut the wheelhouse windows and he liked the breeze too much. "Which is not quite the same thing as an apology, because I'd do the same thing again if I had to."

The dwarf grunted an acknowledgement that made no concessions. He was tied to the second of the wheelhouse's chairs, bound hand and foot but left with his mouth free. If Sam had been smoking, he'd have given the little man his own cigar. Or at least, Sam thought, considering how low his store of good Partagás cigars was dwindling, a few puffs off Sam's.

The boy John Moses sat in the third chair, free and munching on a flat square of ship's biscuit. Crumbs from the biscuit fell and spotted the black rubber matting that covered the floor of the wheelhouse, matching the rubber that encased the wheel itself and the soles of Sam's shoes and the head of each control.

"You gonna kill me, Clemens?" the midget growled.

Sam considered the question as he drove, goggle-protected eyes drinking in the glorious mountains, pine woods, and tall grasses surrounding the trail ahead. Off to one side, a great swath of trees had been burnt into spent matchsticks, utterly consumed along with the grasses around them, leaving nothing but a long, straight streak of blackened earth and stone. Sam wondered if that might be the result of a phlogiston gun being fired from the air and then shook off the thought. Speculation was pointless; he had a mission. Besides, the burning was almost certainly the result of some perfectly natural cause, like a lightning strike.

The road from Fort Bridger down into the Great Salt Lake City was a wide track, hammered flat by the passage of many horses, wagons, steam-trucks and, if the tales were to be believed, even handcarts, back in the old days. Some day in the not-too-distant future, the railroad would reach from the Atlantic to the Pacific. That railroad might belong to American companies or it might, if he wanted it, belong to Brigham Young and the Kingdom of Deseret. Either way, when it did connect, it would no doubt absorb a lot of the traffic to and from the Kingdom of Deseret.

That would be fine by Sam, he estimated. Less traffic meant higher speeds and faster winds and fewer people to mar the scenery. Not that he wasn't going full speed now, with his steam valves opened all the way and O'Shaughnessy down below, swearing and shoveling coal into the furnace as fast as the old girl would take it.

Old girl, my skinny white Mississippi backside, he smiled at his own affectation. As if the *Jim Smiley* weren't state of the art, built new this year by the United States Army to the specifications of its own agent, Samuel Clemens. She was reasonably fast, not as fast as the *Liahona*, but faster than most trucks, and her big knobbly wheels sent her flying over obstructions that would completely stymie lesser craft. That made her perfect for the whole great wide territory west of the Mississippi, or, for that matter, just about any territory in the world. Except for outright tropical forest, Sam guessed, and if it came to that, he'd fix a blade on the front of her and slice right through any jungle he came to.

And, of course, she could float, that was Sam's ace in the hole, should the *Liahona* look likely to overtake them. He glanced down at his charts and guessed that he might be within a quarter of an hour of the Bear River.

He wished no one aboard the *Liahona* any harm, naturally. He just wished them abject failure, confusion, and ignominious defeat. Turning to look over his shoulder, he quickly scanned the wide road behind and still saw nothing of the Welshman's hulking land-ship with its hieroglyphic name on the bow.

"Well, mister," he finally said to the dwarf. "I can't say just yet. You won't tell me who you are or what you were doing playing hide-and-go-seek in my saucers. You might be someone I ought to shoot, you might be someone I ought to trade for pemmican to the next Shoshone I meet or you might be someone who needs to pay me for a ticket, but I have no way of knowing until you explain yourself."

The dwarf grunted again. "I might be someone that can tell you something useful."

"Oh, yeah?" Sam asked. "Like what?"

The dwarf had a sullen, calculating look on his face. "Like who punched holes in your boiler pipes night before last."

Sam grinned. "Now, that might have been a poor tactical move on your part, my friend. If I didn't know better, that offer might make me suspect that you yourself were the culprit and that would put you squarely in the *malefactors needing to walk the plank* category. At near ten miles an hour, I suppose you'd survive, but I don't think you'd enjoy the experience."

"Don't care who done it, huh?"

"Of course I care." Sam gestured expansively at the wheelhouse and the deck of the *Jim Smiley*. "I love this old girl. That's why I had that rascal Dick Burton imprisoned by the Shoshone and then went out of my way to meet him and laugh in his face at his failure." Sam pulled a cigar from his jacket pocket and shoved it into the corner of his mouth. Even unlit, he could taste the victory puff. "Got anything else to trade?"

The dwarf glowered and hunched down in his chair.

"His name is Coltrane," the little boy suddenly offered around a mouthful of biscuit.

"The hell?" the dwarf snarled, taken by surprise.

"Don't hurt him," the boy added. "He's nice."

"Well, well." Sam almost laughed. "Is he now? Do you know who Mr. Coltrane works for, John Moses?"

The little boy screwed up his eyes in concentration. "Arbishaw," he said, and Sam saw that it was a guess or a half-recollected name at best. "Archibarch."

The gypsy? That was interesting.

"Thank you, John Moses."

Coltrane glared at Sam.

"I suppose to be on the safe side, and as a matter of policy, I should toss you overboard now," Sam told the dwarf.

"He saved me," John Moses objected.

Sam turned a sharp eye on the little boy, who seemed to melt beneath his gaze, shrinking to mouse-sized in the wooden chair.

"Did he?"

John Moses nodded timidly.

"Stay out of this, John Moses," Coltrane urged the little boy. There was an incongruously gentle note in his voice.

"Tell me about that," Sam said.

"Coltrane is a scary boy, but he saved me from the Injuns," John Moses averred. "Also the ugly skinny-faced man with the red hair."

That would be O'Shaughnessy; Sam laughed out loud.

"Just for that, John Moses," he told the boy, "I won't throw Coltrane overboard."

He was still laughing when he looked again behind and saw, dark and small against the yellow grasses of the horizon, a blocky smudge. It was coming his direction, and it was big enough that it could only be one thing.

The *Liahona* was overtaking them.

Sam pulled the funnel-tipped speaking tube from the dashboard and held it to his mouth. "Pack her as tight as she'll take it and get up here, O'Shaughnessy!" he barked. "We have company and they won't be happy to see us!"

He slammed the tube back into its slot, pawed at his charts and stared at the road ahead. *Where, oh where, was that Bear River?*

LᴇᴎꟿOᴎ

The Welshman Jones was angry and Burton didn't blame him.

Roxie seemed perturbed, too.

Not only had Sam Clemens stolen all the *Liahona*'s coal, he had apparently kidnapped its mascot, a little boy named John Moses. The Shoshone, at least, denied any knowledge of the boy's whereabouts and there was no sign of him on the truck, which had been turned inside out twice.

As long as he thought the little boy might be in the Shoshone camp, Jones had been impossible to pry away from the place, no matter how much Burton and others had cajoled. The passengers and crew had bought Pocatello's coal and reloaded the bins of the boiler room without their Captain. The moment Chief Pocatello persuaded him that John Moses must be with Sam Clemens, however, like some capricious storm god, he performed a complete *volte-face* and was impossible to restrain. Within minutes, the *Liahona* was underway and Jones was in his wheelhouse, shouting into speaking tubes. As soon as they'd reached the main track and turned southwest, Jones left the big spoked wheel in the hands of one of his men and attached himself by the eye to a roving spyglass.

The steam-truck roared through the high mountain country at a shockingly fast clip, and Burton realized that Jones had been sparing the engines earlier. "Rama's teeth, we must be going twenty miles an hour!" he exclaimed to Roxie, who stood at his side at the railing, her hair snapping like a banner in the breeze.

"Out the way, pal!" shouted a burly crewman as he pushed them both aside. He and two mates dragged a length of reinforced pipe of some kind, complete with bolt-fittings, and, with hex-wrenches the size of Burton's arm, began fastening it to the deck. Burton stepped back, keeping Roxie on his arm, where he could keep an eye on her, and stared in awe.

The thing was clearly a gun, and a railgun at that. He'd seen similar weapons on ships many times and years before; they were the large-scale prototype of which the Brunel rifle was the small-scale second generation. He'd never seen one mounted on a steam-truck, though.

"What is it?" he asked Roxie, and watched her face from the corner of his eye as she answered.

"Mr. Clemens is about to find out that in the Rocky Mountains we know how to play the game," she said darkly, her eyes glued to the road ahead. "And we play for keeps."

Her guard was down, Burton thought, she was emotional. He considered confronting her right then and there, demanding to know who she was and what was her scheme, but decided against it. She was *too* wound up; who knew what she might be capable of when this angry?

"There he is!" Jones roared, and Burton felt Roxie's grip on his arm tighten. He looked ahead and saw, across an open stretch of yellow grass, a silver-blue ribbon of water cutting across the far end of a long meadow. A flat, wide, heavy wood bridge with a staunch toll-gate in the middle carried the trail over the river, and, just this side of the bridge, Burton spotted the *Jim Smiley*. He saw it first by the plume of dirt that it kicked up, but once he'd noticed it, there was no mistaking it for any other steam-truck on the road, not with all that black India rubber wrapped around it and the big riverboat-like paddlewheel on the back.

There seemed to be a light on the small truck, the orange light of a fire, and it wasn't making for the bridge—it had turned off to the side and was rolling directly at the river.

"What's he doing?" Burton wondered.

"Gun ready, sir!" shouted one of the crew.

"Load!" came the Captain's answer. Jones pried himself away from the telescope to rush out and check the lay of the long gun, squinting along its barrel and then scuttling back and forth between it and the wheelhouse to compare lines of sight.

The *Jim Smiley* hit the river and, amazingly, kept going. Burton snatched the Captain's telescope, momentarily forgotten in his enthusiasm for the gun, and took a closer look. The big rear paddlewheel of Clemens's truck churned up a white foam, pushing it through the river water like a steam ship. Through the spyglass he saw that the orange light was fire, a brazier of some sort, on the deck of the *Jim Smiley*, and a man stood beside it to tend it. He was holding something in the fire …

something that suddenly burst into flame itself.

The man hurled the flaming object at the bridge, where a gout of flame burst up at the point of contact.

Then he did it again. And again.

"He's burning the bridge!" Burton shouted.

The tollhouse crew, two white-bearded men in overalls, made the realization at the same moment, and Burton saw them hurl themselves into the river to escape.

Then the *Jim Smiley* was across the river, its heavy wheels dragging it up the bank on the far side and toward the line of pines at the end of the meadow. Fire licked hungrily from multiple spots along the wooden bridge.

"Full speed! More coal!" Jones shouted into a speaking tube, shouldering his pilot aside and seizing the wheel. "Load and prepare to fire!"

The *Liahona* roared straight at the flaming bridge, its Captain squinting past its bow, through the flames at his disappearing competitor. The truck rattled from side to side and the bitter taste of smoke began to stain the breeze whipping past Burton's face. Crewmen snapped open a compartment at the base of the gun and laid in a long steel shell, pointy-tipped and the length of Burton's forearm.

"Hold on!" he shouted, and dragged Roxie, half-resisting, to one of the deck's benches. He whipped off his own belt and, over an inarticulate mewl of objection, strapped her to the seat. She twisted at the waist and looked ahead to see what was going on.

Burton rushed into the wheelhouse. Jones squinted through the window at the fast-approaching inferno of the bridge and Burton grabbed his shoulder.

"Don't shoot!" he yelled. "The child may be on that truck!"

Jones shrugged him off. "Do you think I'm an idiot, boyo?" he snarled, and pushed the explorer away. He squinted again, hunching down over the wheel and scrutinizing the long meadow. "Fire!" he yelled.

With a great *whoosh* and a sharp humming whine, the gun fired.

Some fifty feet to the side of the *Jim Smiley* a small stand of trees, the hillock of earth beneath them, and the gray boulders in their midst all exploded into a mist of dust and splinters.

"Load!" Jones shouted again, and the *Liahona*'s nose plunged onto the burning bridge. The strained timbers groaned ominously; at the best of times, Burton thought, it must struggle to bear the weight of this monstrous Behemoth. Would it be able to do so while it burned?

They sprinted toward the tollhouse, full-tilt.

Burton whipped the borrowed spyglass to his eye again and found the *Jim Smiley*. Clemens's man must be steering her now, because Clemens himself stood at the back of the truck, to the side of the paddlewheel, watching the *Liahona* with a cigar clenched in his teeth. At this distance it had to be his imagination, but Burton would have sworn that Clemens was grinning at him.

"Fire!" Jones bellowed again, and the earth to the other side of the *Jim Smiley* erupted in a volcano of dirt.

The bridge sagged, fire whipping all about the fringes of the *Liahona*'s deck.

"Load!" Jones yelled again.

"Captain Jones, we're not going to make it!" Burton snapped uselessly, then wedged his body into the corner of the wheelhouse, behind a chair bolted to the floor, preparing for impact. He took a last glance at the *Jim Smiley* just in time to see it disappear into the trees.

This river can't be that deep, he told himself. *The bridge will collapse and the steam-truck will be delayed, but we'll be able to drive out directly.* He told himself these things as persuasively as he could, but in his heart he doubted and prepared for the worst.

The prow of the *Liahona* shattered the wooden toll-gate like matchsticks.

"Hold on!" Burton yelled, to no one and to everyone.

Then the bridge snapped and the *Liahona* fell into the river below.

PART THE SECOND

𐐐𐑉𐐀𐐁𐐮𐐻𐐯

DESERET

CHAPTER SIX

exican Stridermen evacuated the *Liahona*'s passengers so the crew could pump out its furnace and restart it. They had just happened along a few hours after the big steam-truck had shattered the bridge, bound for the Salt Lake Valley, and by then the passengers clustered on the truck's deck were bored, restless, and ready to be helped ashore. Other than the showman, Archibald, or Poe, or whatever his real name was, who seemed to be keeping out of sight.

Dick Burton looked furious, like a bear in a pit, snapping at anyone and anything that got in his way, and he stuck to the steam-truck's captain like glue. Absalom made sure to steer clear of both of them. Captain Jones, if anything, looked even angrier than Burton, so Absalom was happy to get off the *Liahona* for a little while.

Absalom rode across to the west bank of the river in the folding back rumble seat of a Strider with a long-faced woman he didn't know and her two children. He had tried to maneuver to get into the same Strider as Annie, but when passengers had lined up to board he hadn't been able to find her. He was polite, though, doffing his damaged hat and smiling at the children even when one of them kicked him in the shin. Some of the baggage had floated away with the flooding of the *Liahona*'s belly and the Stridermen chased that down too in their jerky, long-legged vehicles.

Absalom had never before seen a real live Mexican or one of their Striders, and he found them fascinating. They looked vaguely chivalrous, like knights of the trash heap, with smoked-glass visors on their bulky helmets, cup-like padding on knees and elbows and shoulders, high riding boots and many-buckled leather harnesses belted about their hips and chests. They behaved like knights, too, deferential and helpful and modest, though they kept their visors down. With their rifle-fired suction harpoons they had quickly snared the larger pieces of luggage. One of the Striders had knelt down and disgorged a Striderman, who had waded into waist-high water with a long pole like a boathook and dragged in the last of the passengers' drifting things.

One of the final items recovered was a smallish trunk that Absalom recognized as his own and he had rushed over to the Striderman as he dragged it up onto the bank.

"Thank you!" he cried. "Thank you, er, officer! Sir!"

The Striderman pulled off his helmet and shook out long curling black hair, down past her padded shoulders.

"I am not a *sir*," she said in a rich Mexican accent.

She was beautiful. Her skin was cinnamon-dark, her eyes were coal, her lips were full, and she looked like she might just punch Absalom in the face. He swallowed hard.

"Ma'am," he corrected himself.

"No, cabrón," she insisted slowly. She talked to him like she was talking to a backward child. *"Si yo fuera un oficial* ... if I were an officer, I would be a *sir*. Man or woman makes no difference, all officers are *sir*. But I am not an officer, I am a Master Sergeant." She edged one shoulder in his direction, as if the chevrons stitched onto it were supposed to mean something to him. "And Master Sergeant is as high as I go. The Ejército Nacional has a policy of *not* promoting its best gunners out from behind their guns."

"Yes, ah, I see," Absalom lied. "How shall I address you, then?"

She turned partly away from him and mounted the bent leg of her Strider. The vehicle reminded Absalom of the tales of Baba Yaga and her chicken-legged hut that his Russian grandmother had told him when he was a small boy. It consisted of a cockpit the size of a couple of sofas jammed together, protected from the elements by a glass windscreen and a leather membrane on an accordion skeleton that could be pulled over to protect the Stridermen from inclement weather.

Inside the cockpit were two chairs and the folding rumble seat, and around the outside of it were built-in compartments, like steel saddlebags and holsters. A swiveling platform with several cannons protruding from its nose rose at the back of the carriage, but the entire thing was studded with tubes like guns of unknown make and power. Absalom had seen the Mexicans shoot harpoons out of some of the tubes, but at least one big one in front seemed to have a spring-loaded hammer on the top of its many-chambered cylinder, and Absalom had seen an open pouch full of things that might be bullets, built into shiny brass jackets. Two legs sprouted from the right and left sides, or shoulders, of the carriage. Each leg dropped through two powerful pistons and a large, flexible ball joint to terminate in a crude four-toed claw. The Striders *hissed* and *clanked* when they moved and emitted a constant puff of thin black fumes out their tail. They looked like giant, menacing chickens.

"*No creo que sea necesario.* I don't really see that joo will need to talk to me again at all, *inglés*," she said, sounding completely indifferent. "*Peró en caso que tenga ocasión,* joo can call me Master Sergeant." She hopped with practiced nonchalance up the bent leg of her Strider and vaulted into the carriage. Now that he knew she was a woman, he wondered how on earth he had missed it before. Even through her padding and bodysuit, he could see now that she was curvaceous and very feminine. "Master Sergeant *Jackson*, if joo need to tell me apart from Ortiz *allá*."

Absalom wondered if Ortiz was also a beautiful woman. Maybe they all were, though he thought if President Tubman's Ejército Nacional consisted entirely of ebony-skinned Amazons, Mexico City would have been a more desirable Foreign Office posting than it was.

Pffffffft-ankkkh! The Strider rose smoothly to its feet, pistons sliding, steam hissing from its joints, and fumes chugging out its tail. Master Sergeant Jackson dropped her smoked glass faceplate back into place and said something to her companion in the carriage. She didn't wave to Absalom as the Strider turned its back on him and crunched off through the tall grass to join its fellows, resuming their collective trek into the Kingdom of Deseret.

She didn't look back to see *him* wave, either.

𐤀𐤉𐤂𐤄𐤉𐤀𐤉

"You're being real brave, boy," Jed told the big-eyed youngster. "Keep it up, we'll be outta here in no time at all."

What the hell are you doing, Coltrane? he wondered. *Ten years ago you would have killed that kid the minute you saw him on top of the* Liahona*'s wheelhouse; killed him with your bare hands and then fed him to the beetles. Of course, it would have been crocodiles back then, you hadn't ever met Horace Hunley or any of the crew that the Richmond set like to call* Whitney*'s boys, and you were doing flips on the circuit with a shit-eating grin on your face, catching nickels they threw at you with your toes, or working the Ikey Heyman with one eye out for Johnny Law, in case the patch money didn't hold. Hell, how long has it been since you wrestled an alligator? Or even saw one?*

Government work's making you soft.

That was a real problem, since it wasn't a government he was working for. Not yet, anyway. Right now it was just a bunch of men. They *wanted* to be a government, Jed thought that someday they *might* be a government, but right now they were traitors and hard men and desperadoes in the halls of power. He couldn't really afford to get crosswise with his bosses, especially not over some damn kid.

Jed sighed. He wriggled and twisted, the ropes that the beak-nosed Irishman had used to tie him chafing at his wrists and forearms and ankles. He and John Moses—also tied hand and foot—sat in a big bathtub like two wiggling peas in a porcelain pod, with a white curtain, three shut doors, and most likely a *Do Not Disturb* sign between them and the hall.

"We could yell for help," John Moses suggested.

Of course that seems like a good idea to him, Jed realized. *He lives here, he's innocent, he's just a kid. Me, I yell for help and even if someone does hear me through all the doors and the hissing of the pipes in the walls, I gotta start answering questions I'd rather not, like for starters probably "What's a cracker dwarf from Shitsville, Arkansas doing hog-tied in a bathtub in the Deseret Hotel?" and eventually maybe even "Hey, midget, what do you know about the disappearance of a Pinkerton detective from a honeypot stall in Bridger's Saloon in the Wyoming Territory night before last?"*

It hardly mattered, anyway. If there were any chance of their being heard, the Irishman would have gagged them. Or cut their tongues out. "You go ahead and give it a try, John Moses," Jed suggested, jerking one shoulder to try to dislocate it on purpose. Not Sam Clemens, though. Sam seemed to be, what? Merciful? Fair? Aloof? Undecided? Ironic? The dwarf wasn't sure, but he knew if their places had been switched, he'd have killed the Union man and thrown him off the steam-truck.

Or maybe not, given that Jed Coltrane seemed to have become a complete sissy.

The Irishman, now, he'd have killed Jed for sure, if Clemens hadn't interfered. The little man stopped his writhing long enough to shudder. As soon as they had checked in, the evil-looking red-head had spent all of three minutes experimenting and had figured out how to work Hunley's scarab cylinder.

It wasn't any great trick; the thing only had two buttons. But the way O'Shaughnessy had gone about it took a certain determination and a dark bent of mind. After shaking both his tied up prisoners out of the steamer trunk in which they'd come up to the hotel room, he'd said nothing. Instead, he'd made a show of pouring the scarabs out over the little boy. Then he'd pantomimed pressing the buttons.

"No!" Jed Coltrane had shouted, and the Irishman knew then what he had in his hands, or at least he could guess. Two destroyed seat cushions later, he'd packed the cylinder back into his greatcoat pocket and when the two Yankees had left, the scarabs had gone with them, along with both the Maxim Hushers. The Irishman was going out among the Mormons dressed to kill.

Jed had expected John Moses to be hollering now, but the boy just stared at him with patient, observant eyes. He stared back, a little fiercer than he needed to, to make a point.

"What?" he wanted to know.

"You're brave," John Moses said. "You're the bravest kid I know."
Jed Coltrane's effort to dislocate his own shoulder fell apart in the paroxysms of his own laughter. "Oh, that's good," he laughed. "That's really rich." He sighed, some of the tension shaking out of him, and then he scrunched up onto his knees and tried to poke his head through the tub's curtain. "Let's try some tumbling." He'd never been good at the contortionist stuff, anyway. He curled forward as he let himself roll out of the tub, so he completed half a somersault and landed on his own shoulder, relatively painlessly. His falling body jerked the curtain open and it stayed.

John Moses was puzzled. "What's so funny?" he asked.

Jed wormed his way across the floor on his belly. The boy's voice, resounding from behind the curtain and within the tub's recessed niche, echoed and bounced as if far away. He hoisted himself to his feet by pushing off against the wall with his head. The doorknob was too big for his teeth, but he thought if he hit it just right with his head—*crack!*

Nope.

"Look, John Moses," Jed grunted, not really sure why he was bothering to explain, "you ain't ever seen a kid like me before. You ain't seen a kid as hairy as me, as ugly as I am, as foul-mouthed, or as drinks as much. That's 'cause there ain't no such kid, not in this whole wide world."

Crack!

Still nothing. His head hurt a bit, but not so much that he wouldn't try it again.

"There's *you*," John Moses objected.

"I ain't a kid. I'm a midget. That's a grown man, only shorter and more ornery."

Crack!

The third time, the door popped open.

John Moses's eyes were saucers.

"Stay here a minute," Jed told him, and it only took a little more than the promised minute before he managed to knock over a dark wooden correspondence desk, wrangle a letter opener from its drawer, and saw himself free. He liberated the boy, then threw aside the letter opener. The Irishman had the guns and all Jed's knives and his piano wire and the scarabs, so a letter opener was worse than pointless; it would only tempt Jed into rash action, as if he had a real weapon in his hands.

He'd settle for his knives back, but what he really wanted was a gun. Something big, that would punch holes in a man. Jed had a specific man in mind for the punching.

"You're still brave," John Moses said defiantly. His slouch cap lay in the corner of the suite's front room and John Moses retrieved it with

D.J. Butler

dignity unnatural in such a small boy, pulling it down onto his head. "I wish I was brave."

Jed knew he was going to have to leave the boy here. He'd leave the boy, go get himself armed, somehow, and go after the Irishman. He needed the scarabs back and then he needed to find out what had happened to Poe and if there was still a mission. He didn't want the boy screaming for help as soon as Jed left, of course. He decided he'd better try to inspire the kid. "Sure, you're brave," he agreed.

"I cry a lot," the boy said.

Jed shrugged. "So do I," he lied. Hell, he couldn't remember if he'd ever cried, not even as a boy. Crying would just get you a whipping from Pa, especially if you were the runt and no good around the farm, except to wrestle with the hens for their eggs and milk the little nanny three times a week. Jed had left that dump behind as soon as he possibly could. He'd never looked back, and he sure as hell had never cried about leaving. "That ain't neither here nor there. Being brave is not running away when people need you."

"Oh, yeah?" the boy asked.

"Yeah," Jed repeated, "and that means I ain't so brave. I've been running all my life, from one damn thing or another." He rubbed his wrists, enjoyed the tingle of feeling that returned to them with the renewed blood flow. It was a line of bullshit he was selling the boy and he knew it, but at least it was a line of bullshit that he wished was true. "You got a Pa, don't you? And he sticks around, does right by you and your Ma?"

John Moses nodded solemnly.

"See now, that there is a brave man."

Jed was just about ready to leave the little boy. He considered taking him down to the street and leaving him there, but he didn't want to be seen abandoning the kid. No, he'd get the boy to use the toilet and sneak off while the door was shut. He still had to figure out how to get himself armed. At least the Irishman hadn't taken his money, but Jed had precious little cash. Maybe enough to buy one puny knife and that hardly gave him any comfort.

He wondered where Poe was.

He had to deal with the Irishman first—he couldn't risk the mission getting knocked into the dust, much less getting hanged, because one vicious red-head nursed a grudge—and then he needed to get back with his boss and get the mission on track. "And he's got a job too, don't he? What's your Pa do for a living, John Moses?"

John Moses smiled with pride and stuck out his little chest. "He makes guns. He owns his own shop."

Jed Coltrane almost laughed out loud. "Does he now?" he asked. "That sounds like a fine and noble occupation. And is your Pa's shop somewhere in the Great Salt Lake City, by any chance?"

106

"No." John Moses shook his head. "But it's real close, and the train will take you there."

Jed had visions of riding the blinds under some Deseret train. He could do it, he'd done it often as a carny, but he didn't like the idea of doing it with such a small kid as a companion. He knew his luck couldn't have been that good. "I'm afraid I ain't got the money for a ticket, kid," he said with a wistful grimace, patting down his nearly empty pockets. "You got any cash?"

"You don't need money, silly," John Moses answered. "This is the Great Salt Lake City. Only I don't know where the train station is from here."

Jed felt like he was beginning to see light at the end of his personal tunnel and he grinned. "That's what the guy behind the front desk is *for*."

ᏗᏝᏋᏝᏉᏝᎩ

The Great Salt Lake City made Sam Clemens feel *alive*, despite the bow tie he'd wrapped around his neck.

The whole thing—the whole swarming, ticking, crazy thing—was one big device, everything tightly knitted together and pumping in sync. There were footpaths, clean plascrete strips for walking that were open to the early evening air on the ground level, cutting in and among the columns and towers, and bordered all along with orange trees and rosebushes. There were footpaths overhead, too, undergirded with steel and encased in glass and running from building to building over carriages, horses, steam-trucks, and other pedestrians.

The vehicular traffic flowed along shockingly wide streets. There were various other tubes whose use he couldn't surmise, radiating out from each building like irregular wheel spokes. Some were large enough that a man might crawl through and had grates on the side. A few vented steam. Some were tighter in radius and made entirely of glass, and Sam thought he saw small, blurred objects shooting through them from one building to the next. They looked like high-speed aerial trains for pixies, he mused.

Iron lampposts dotted the footpaths, topped with glass bulbs that at night, Sam presumed, would cast some sort of light on their surroundings. Franklin Poles, and a prodigiously large number of them. In the daylight they were swallowed up and invisible against the grandiosity all around them.

Even the open air lot where he had left the *Jim Smiley* had been fenced in by plascrete walls and lit with Franklin Poles and criss-crossed with walkways. It had felt more like a room than a field.

D.J. Butler

In the center of it all was a huge dome, sitting nestled among streets named South Tabernacle, North Tabernacle, East Tabernacle and West Tabernacle—Sam admired the mechanick's sensibility embodied in the names of the streets. Radiating out beyond the Tabernacle streets, the other streets weren't even named, just numbered. The sheer effronterous modernity of it cheered Sam's heart.

Only it wasn't a dome, Sam decided, not really. It was an egg. A big, rounded, bulbous tower of plascrete, steel, and glass, textured with windows and balconies and staircases and shorter, octagonal towers jutting even higher out of its sloping sides. Plants grew all over it, bright and dark green and rose-red and orange and blue, an explosion of color that was unnatural against the dusty green-brown backdrop of the Wasatch Mountains behind it. That was the Tabernacle, Sam knew, the spiritual and administrative heart of the City and the Kingdom, and right next to it sat the Lion House, where President Young lived and had his office.

The Lion House was where Sam was headed.

Salt Lake City's great advantage over American cities was its newness, Sam thought. It had been built from scratch in the last ten years, and its builders could incorporate every advance they wanted from the works of men like Brunel, Whitney, Maxim, and Hunley, and in doing so they didn't have to work around what had been built before. There were no old streets to dig up in order to lay down pipes for plumbing, steam, or electricks. There were no old property lines to contend with, no ancient by-laws, no rights-of-way, nothing. The bees had come to an empty desert and been able to build exactly the hive they had wanted.

The Tabernacle looked like a beehive, too, and reinforced Sam's impression that he was himself shrunk and among the honey makers. *It's a Hive of Men*, he corrected himself, *a hive built and run by men of industry and surely, necessarily, designed and led by men of vision*. Men like the President of the Kingdom of Deseret, Brigham Young, whom Sam was on his way to meet now, strolling among the towers on an open path.

Sam lit a Partagás to celebrate.

If only he didn't have to have the Irishman with him. The red-headed sourpuss slunk in his wake like a bad smell. Specifically, like the smell of cheap liquor.

He didn't need O'Shaughnessy for the mission, of course, not this part, not for a short stroll through a more or less civilized city and a first diplomatic contact, but Sam was afraid that if he left Tamerlane O'Shaughnessy in the hotel with two prisoners he'd come back and find the Irishman with two corpses and a story.

It'd probably be a good story, though.

Just not worth the death of the little boy.

Sam didn't have a hat and he regretted it. The women he passed *en route* to the Lion House nodded, and the men all raised their hats to him.

1

Some of the men had the rough, unshaven look of Hannibal or St. Louis or Kansas City about them, but many of them and, Sam thought, nearly all of the ladies, had some polish. Maybe not the polish of a Richmond or a New Orleans or a Boston, but they looked at least as sophisticated and elegant as, say, the burghers of Chicago. The men were also all armed; Sam had never seen so many pistols. He wondered if the ladies might be carrying guns, too, in their handbags.

He noticed that they all carried pocket watches, and seemed to look at them frequently. He'd never seen a crowd that looked more intent on being punctual.

He also noticed, idly and without thinking too much of it, that the distribution of ladies was uneven. Some men, especially older men, had two or even three women on their arms and he saw a lot of younger, less-bearded gents alone or in each other's strictly manly company. There were more women than were usual in a frontier society, he thought, but they seemed to travel in clusters.

Lacking an apparatus of salutation equivalent to the bouncing hats, he took to plucking his cigar out of his mouth and swishing it in friendly circles at the passersby. O'Shaughnessy just grunted suspiciously and kept his porkpie screwed on tight.

A steam-truck passed, blue, armor-plated, and slow-moving, with Old Glory crisply flapping from a pole to the right of its wheelhouse and the flag bearing the blue and gold arms of the Commonwealth of Massachusetts offsetting it to the left. Behind it came a second, and then a third. Soldiers, Sam thought. A Northern regiment. They sat on the decks of the trucks and others might have been inside, a couple of dozen on each vehicle, with carbines and pistols and the well-worn boots and uniforms of men who knew their job. Sam waved his cigar at the soldiers too, doing his best to look like he wasn't trying to appear nonchalant. *I might not really be cut out for this secret agent stuff,* he thought.

None of the soldiers waved back.

"Poor bastards," Tamerlane O'Shaughnessy muttered bitterly. "Tomorrow could be war and them all blown to bloody bits."

"Indeed," Sam agreed, biting his cigar again. "Them or the other fellas."

"Jesus and Brigit love 'em all."

The Lion House was a large grey-painted building with white trim and dark green shutters on the windows to match the tall dark green junipers standing guard around it. Sam ran fingers through his thick hair, and examined it from the footpath for a minute. The building might have been a dormitory or a barracks or a boarding school, and in itself wasn't remarkable. Its name came, Sam presumed, from a brass lion that crouched over a crenellated entrance hall on the south side of the building, where Sam now stood. It looked conspicuously like an official entrance.

In the garden between the Lion House and the Tabernacle squatted half a dozen installations. They looked like brass-bound glass bells resting among the azaleas, cherries, and plum trees, with wheezing accordion-like bellows inside each and wisps of steam curling from their bases at every *whoomphing* squeeze. The mechanick in Sam wondered what the glass bells did; they looked like they moved air, or maybe they built up pressure in some invisible system, something buried under the garden.

A crystalline lattice of the narrow glass tubes ran above the garden, connecting the Tabernacle to the Lion House, and the bells were connected by more glass tubes to the trellis overhead. From here, it looked like the network existed to shoot squirrel-sized bullets back and forth between the Tabernacle and the Lion House. The bells moved something, maybe.

"Is it true, then, that it's full of the old man's wives?" O'Shaughnessy asked in a titillated whisper.

The question seemed tawdry and trivial in the face of this gigantic puffing machinery, but Sam hadn't recruited the Irishman for his sage perspective or his powers of incisive reasoning. "I hope so," Sam ruminated out loud. "I quite like the idea that old Brigham's man enough to attract twenty women."

"Or thirty or forty," O'Shaughnessy corrected him with rumored numbers.

"Or a hundred," Sam agreed, "*and* that he's civilized enough that he actually *married* them all."

"Hell and begorra," O'Shaughnessy swore. Sam didn't know if that was meant to signify agreement or not.

"I'm also amused to think that in this case," Sam continued, "as I find is only rarely so in the affairs of men, vice must be its own punishment."

Under the lion and beyond the entrance stretched a long hall. Bulbs perched along the walls between the many doors.

Looking at the inside of the building, Sam could imagine that it might house a dozen of the patriarch's famous wives, along with their concomitant children, but at the moment the movement he saw was muted and infrequent. Deep in the hall a woman in sturdy pioneer dress crossed from one side to the other without looking up.

The nearest door was open.

"Come in," called a man's voice, and they did.

The largest wall of the office they entered was entirely occupied by circular cubbyholes. They were made of brass-bound glass, with brass trap doors closing them, and in a constant, nearly steady, *thump-thump-rat-a-tat*, the cubbies were filled with objects flying in from elsewhere, through the wall. Three men worked the device, opening the cubby doors and extracting cylindrical cases from the full ones, which they twisted open to extract strips of paper. They collated and examined the strips in light from floor-to-ceiling windows on a long, narrow table that ran parallel to the wall down its entire length. They then generated new strips with hand-printed messages on them, screwed them into empty cylinders, and then slammed them back into the cubbies. When the brass door shut on a cylinder-loaded cubby, it *hissed* sharply and the cylinder disappeared, sucked away into the ether.

This was one terminus, Sam realized, of the network of glass tubes he had seen above the City. It was some kind of communication system. O'Shaughnessy took a step back and shuddered.

A fourth man oversaw the frenzied beavering of the three clerks. He was short and stocky, with a rounded face, strong nose and high forehead that combined to give him an intense and classical look. A square beard jutted off his chin only, trimmed and neat. His suit and waistcoat were sturdy but of fine wool, inclining slightly to the dandy in physical appearance.

He wheeled on one heel and dragged Sam in with a handclasp and a fierce grin. "Mr. Samuel Clemens," he snapped. "We've been expecting you. I hope you haven't had too much trouble on the road." He spoke with an English accent. Northern English, Sam thought. Maybe Liverpudlian. "However much civilization we've brought to the Valley, the roads connecting us to the rest of the world remain rough and dangerous routes."

"No trouble at all. You'll find I'm duly credentialed," Sam drawled, taking a wallet of official documents from his jacket pocket and pressing into the man's hands. The man took them and set them aside on the long table without looking at them. "And now you have the advantage of me twice over."

"George Cannon," the other man presented himself. "I'm President Young's Secretary. I know you'd like a meeting with the President, but he's out of the office and—" Cannon gestured at the wall of tubes, "not otherwise reachable."

"This is a communications network," Sam observed. He nodded, admiring the tubes and the message slips, and Cannon nodded with him.

"And a good one," Cannon agreed. "Only sometimes President Young is too big a man for the system. I understand you're staying at the Deseret Hotel."

"I was told it had the best bar," Sam quipped. Of course the government had instructed him to stay at the biggest, fanciest hotel in town. He might be a spy, a saboteur, or even a thief by the end of this venture, but he was also a diplomat.

"It has the finest," Cannon agreed. "Those looking for local color sometimes prefer the Hot Springs Hotel and Brewery at the Point of the Mountain. Rockwell's place. But Brother Rockwell is further away and he won't let us install a message tube, so you'll be easier to reach at the Deseret."

Sam cast another glance at Cannon's three clerks, who hadn't slowed or even looked up from their work since his arrival. "I see you're a busy man. I take it you'll inform the President of my arrival and send word to the Deseret when I can meet him? I hope I don't need to impress upon you that the President of the United States regards my mission as critical."

George Cannon smiled. "Rest assured, Mr. Clemens, that President Young feels the same."

Then the interview was over and without further formalities Cannon turned around and dove back into the labors of his clerks. Sam and O'Shaughnessy showed themselves out.

"Jesus and all the bloody saints," the Irishman muttered on the walkway outside the Lion House. "It isn't human. It's like insects, it's like a herd of sheep, it's like … something, but it isn't human."

Sam dug out a double eagle and pressed it into his aide's hand. "You'll feel better about everything with some whisky inside you. While you're at it, check on the dwarf and the little boy. Mind you, though, O'Shaughnessy," he said in his stern a voice as he could muster, "I'll be right behind you and I aim to return that child to his family. Don't cause me any trouble on that account."

"Hell and begorra," O'Shaughnessy objected, "when have I ever caused you any trouble, Sam Clemens?" The Irishman had enough self-awareness to wink at his own joke, but he didn't wait around for further instructions.

Sam watched the other man go. He was right, of course, it was inhuman. The whole thing was like a device. Standing inside George Cannon's office had been like sitting inside the clocksprung brain of one of Eli Whitney's famous machines, a cotton harvester or a mechanical mule.

Only half the cogs were people.

When Tam had disappeared from sight, he turned to head out across the Great Salt Lake City in a different direction, away from the Hotel. He pulled out a Partagás as he went, but he didn't light it; the real reason he put his hand in his pocket, under cover of retrieving a new cigar, was to check the lining of his coat.

The rubies were still there, safe and sound.

"Well, Mr. Pratt," he muttered under his breath. "Here I come."

ᎯᏞᎶᏞᏇᏞᎢ

The gate to the Kingdom of Deseret punched through a mighty wall built by the hand of God himself, Burton thought. *How appropriate.*

From the Bear River crossing, the mountains had risen around them and eventually they had found themselves barreling down a narrow canyon at the speed of Captain Dan Jones's inexorable wrath. Burton was aware of that wrath keenly, because having got himself into Jones's shadow at the collapse of the Bear River bridge, he had been careful not to leave it. The wheelhouse gave absolutely the best view of the entire journey and Burton wasn't about to give it up unprompted. He didn't know where Fearnley-Standish was and he didn't much care. He was probably lying in a faint in their cabin, mooning over that Mormon girl he was daft for.

He didn't know where Roxie was either. He told himself he also didn't care about *her* whereabouts, but he knew in his heart that was a lie.

At a bend in the canyon, when Burton estimated that they must be within a few miles of the Great Salt Lake City, grey granite cliffs shot toward the sky on both sides of the road, creating a narrow stone gullet.

Just inside the near entrance to the narrow neck of land, men in buckskins and flannel shirts flagged the *Liahona* down. Near its far end, Burton saw a bank of earth and a glaring row of mismatched heavy artillery pieces. Above the canyon rifle muzzles peeped from among thick, dark green pine.

And this, he thought, *is the welcome that a* known *craft receives. One of their own, even.* The Mormons were as crazed and paranoid and dangerously violent as any Afghan tribe, even apart from the Madman Pratt and his flying ships.

A rangy young man in buckskins and a shapeless felt hat, apparently unarmed, came up the side of the *Liahona* and clasped arms with Captain Jones. His lean face bore the long, wispy beard of a young man who had never shaved but had no natural gift for the growing of facial hair.

"Come back around to the Cottonwood Fourth Ward Elders Quorum again, has it, boyo?"

The newcomer chuckled. "Yeah, Brother Cannon sent an inspector in disguise and he caught the High Priests napping. No more gate duty for the old boys, I'm afraid."

"Shame, that. Some of the old boys, you know, Swenson, can shoot the whiskers off a squirrel."

"Absolutely," Swenson agreed. "And I feel greatly reassured that the Kingdom is safe from an incursion of squirrels, be it ever so large or be-whiskered. Just so long as the invasion ain't planned for naptime. You got a manifest for me?"

"Aye." Jones handed over a big logbook together with a single sheet of paper. "Original and a copy."

Swenson reviewed them quickly. "Looks fine. Anything we need to go talk about in the wheelhouse?" He shot a quick sidelong glance at Burton, and Burton felt appraised.

"We were waylaid," Jones growled, "but that's a matter for Brother Brigham's ears. Did you stop a fellow by the name of Clemens by any chance?"

Burton took that as his cue and stepped closer.

Swenson shook his head. "He passed through. I didn't know to stop him."

Burton cleared his throat. "He would have had diplomatic papers, anyway," he said, injecting himself into the conversation.

"Never yet saw diplomatic papers that'd stop the bullet out of a Henry." Swenson shrugged. "Hell, I don't care that he was driving that fancy new steam-truck, even. If I'd known the Captain here wanted the man stopped, he'd have been stopped." He leveled frank blue eyes at Burton. "Who are you that I oughtta wind the crank on my give-a-damn machine?"

"He's alright," Jones muttered.

Burton extended a hand and smiled a rugged, manly grin. "Richard Burton," he introduced himself. "That is to say, *ahem*, Captain Richard Burton, special envoy of Her Britannic Majesty Queen Victoria."

Swenson shook it confidently. "Jerry Swenson, second counselor, Elders Quorum, Cottonwood Fourth Ward. President Williams is back up there with the artillery—he's an old Battalion man and knows his big guns. First counselor's fishing."

"*Fishing?*" Jones spat, dismissive. "And war coming and all?"

Swenson shrugged. "He's taken to shaving every day, too. He might be bucking for a release."

Burton heard a sharp whistle. Swenson turned and sloped to the railing of the *Liahona* and Burton and Captain Jones trailed in his wake.

Below stood another buckskin-clad youth, his fingers in his mouth to whistle. Stretching beyond him, standing at still attention in faint curling jets of steam, was a brigade of American soldiers mounted on clocksprung horses. They had come up behind the *Liahona*—like Burton, they were entering the Kingdom.

The animals were majestic. Burton had seen clocksprung beasts before, in ones and twos and even, in the possession of one of England's great peers, a team of four of them, perfectly matched and pulling a carriage together. But here he saw a couple of hundred. They shone like a dull sun through smoke, polished bronze cared for by soldiers and buffed to a high sheen to make an impressive entrance.

They looked like real horses, only larger, especially in the shoulders and the hindquarters. The animal's back, overly narrow by comparison, was devised in the shape of a saddle. They even had short clubbed tails and stylized curly manes, both hammered out of bronze, at least in the case of the rank and file. A parade of real animals would have twitched and swished collectively at flies and shaken its many heads, but the metallic column stood stock still. At this distance, Burton told himself, it must be his imagination, but he thought he could hear a faint *whir* and the grinding of tiny clockwork cogs. Even standing still, the faintest traces of steam clung to the beasts'—*No*, Burton thought, *they aren't animals*—to the *vehicles'* legs.

The train of soldiers wore the blue uniforms of the United States Army, and they sat astride their mounts two abreast and, Burton guessed, a hundred deep. They were cavalrymen, with sabers and rifles and pistols bristling about them and a confident swagger showing in the way they sat their mounts. At their head rode two officers. Both the officers' horses were marked out by steel-shining trim in their manes, tails, hooves, and saddle. One of the men, whom Burton guessed to be a Captain or better by his brass shoulder scales and broad-brimmed cavalry hat with crossed brass sabers above the forehead, raised his hand in a sharp salute to Swenson. The other, with similar scales but a stubby-brimmed cap like a blue fez, sat on a mount whose two shoulders bore holsters for flagpoles.

One holster held a flagpole from which snapped a blue flag. Burton could make out its details by squinting: a toga-clad woman stomped victoriously on the chest of a fallen man whose crown lay nearby. Words stitched into the banner proclaimed *SIC SEMPER TYRANNIS* and identified the flag as belonging to *VIRGINIA*.

The other holster, ominously, was empty.

"Great Lakshmi's lotus," Burton murmured, "has it begun already?"

"Captain Everett Morgan, Third Virginia Cavalry!" the Captain shouted.

"A Welshman!" Captain Jones called. His voice sounded hopeful and a little playful.

"A Virginian!" Captain Morgan shouted back. "Is one of you gentlemen in charge here?"

"That's a pity," Jones muttered, and Burton felt he had to agree. The Virginian Captain's standard bearer wasn't showing the Flag of the United States. Was this a sign that Virginia was already in revolt? If it was, what was his duty? Should he approach Captain Morgan and propose a joint conversation with Brigham Young? That seemed premature. He should get closer to the Captain and find out more, he decided.

"I'm in charge, Captain," Swenson called, and shimmied quickly down the ladder to meet the soldiers.

Burton observed the Captain. He was a paunchy man, but had the sort of hard paunch that one sees on a man of action who is also a horseman; he looked hard and fierce and dangerous. His chin and upper lip were scraped meticulously clean, but curly russet hair covered his ears and the angles of his jaw and sprouted above his squinting eyes like an angry thicket. He had two pistols, six-shooters, on his belt, grips pointing forward in the cavalry style, and two more on his steel saddlehorn, and all four holsters looked well-oiled and worn.

Burton had just resolved to climb down and talk to the man when the *Liahona* jolted again into forward motion. He drifted back along the deck through chatting and scenery-ogling fellow passengers and sat down on one of the last benches so he could watch Swenson and Morgan negotiate the Third Virginia Cavalry's entrance into the Kingdom of Deseret over the back end of the *Liahona*. Swenson was business-like, competent, and unconcerned, reviewing papers and talking with the Virginians' Captain. Burton wished he could hear what they were saying and though after peace, his instructions were to seek alliance with and the benefit of the Southern states, he more than half hoped that young Jerry Swenson would bar entry to Captain Morgan and his Third Virginia.

Then Captain Jones passed the artillery bank and turned a corner, and the mounted soldiers were lost from sight.

Burton heard a loud collective gasp and several cries of alarm. He shifted in his seat to look forward and nearly fell out of his seat.

Above the *Liahona*, something hung in the sky. His first impression was that it *filled* the sky, but then he decided that that was only because the sky over the canyon was narrow.

But no, he recovered himself. The sky wasn't all that narrow.

The *thing*—could it be a *vessel?*—was *huge*.

From beneath, it looked like a sailing ship might look to a fish, complete with copper-sheathed, though flattened, hull. Four cups were affixed to the corners of the craft, turned down, like the four shoulders of a great crawling beast, and the insides of the cups pulsated with golden light. Burton could barely guess from his vantage point what the upper side of the vessel might look like, but it seemed to curve up at its front and back, like an exaggerated Viking ship, or an ancient Sumerian Magur-boat, and some sort of shimmering sail stretched up above it.

Like some mythical beast, some weird Rocky Mountain *bakunawa* or *vârcolac*, it rose through the air and blocked out the sun.

And it was immense.

He'd seen his share of montgolfières, big silk bulbs of hot air that Her Majesty's military forces, like all civilized nations, used for reconnaissance and weather observation. This was something else.

It was impossible to tell its exact size, but Burton realized from their straight wings and soaring flight that the birds passing in front of the … thing … were raptors, hawks or maybe even eagles of some kind. And though he saw their outlines clearly, they were dwarfed by the flying ship. He wished he could see a human figure on board to get a more precise notion of scale, but he guessed roughly that the cups must be ten or fifteen feet across each, and the thing was, more or less, the size of an actual Viking ship.

But it flew.

"Sweet Siduri's ankles!" Burton cursed softly. It was true, then. This was why Victoria, if there was to be a war, didn't want Brigham Young and his wild mountain Mormohammedans fighting against her. Flying ships. Put a hundred trained riflemen on her, and they'd be a deadly striking force, especially for raiding.

And what about the rumors of phlogiston guns, then?

The ship turned. It pushed forward slowly, sail bellying out and turning to make the ship tack, though Burton had the uneasy suspicion that the craft's movements were undetermined and unaffected by the currents of the air. The cups continued to pulse, the light emanating from them intense, but leaving the canyon below unmarked by shadow, as if it were light that an observer could *see*, but not light any observer could *see by*. With the splatter of illumination, the vessel pushed off the mountains and flitted away out of sight.

"Yudhisthira's dice!" he swore again.

"Oh yes, boyo," he heard Captain Jones say. He shook himself out of his trance and saw that the Welshman stood nearby, watching him with an amused smile on his face. "And that's the *old* one. He's built four of them now and if you think the *Captain Moroni* is something, wait until you get a glimpse of the *Teancum*."

ᗺᒋᎶᒐᕁᒐᑫ

It was good healthy criminal habits that saved Tamerlane O'Shaughnessy from the Pinkertons when he went back to the Deseret Hotel. If he'd still been with Sam Clemens, he might have had no good choice but to follow Sam, right in through the big shiny glass front doors just as he'd come out of them, but since he was alone, he took a less direct route, away from the stinking masses of ordinary law-abiding citizens.

Tam slunk past the Deseret on the opposite side of the street, trying not to limp too much on his injured leg, porkpie pulled down over his brow. There again, on the front of the Hotel, as on the front of the other buildings he looked at, was a scrawl of that ugly wiggly Indian-looking writing he'd seen on the side of the *Liahona*. What was wrong with these people? Latin characters had worked fine for fifteen hundred years of Irishmen, what on earth made the Mormons think they had to go and start meddling with the alphabet God made? *If Jesus and all his bloody-damn-hell apostles could use A, B, and C, who are the Mormons to go and make up some other shite?*

The streets of the Great Salt Lake City were mastodontic; enormous, wide, and flat and coated with tar. So huge, Tam could see in his mind's eye a pack of these clean and pressed Mormons chasing a bison herd right down the middle of any one of them. All that was missing was a cliff to drive the bison off of and, queer as this place was, Tam wasn't so sure that he wasn't about to turn a corner and find that very thing. Or a herd of bison themselves, for that matter. The width of the street meant that Tam had to really squint hard out of the corners of his eyes and that at the far end of a parabolic sweep of his birdlike skull, to get a good look at the Deseret's doors.

And there, sure enough, was a Pinkerton.

Tam recognized the man personally—Harris … Harolds … Harlow … Harrow … something, the name didn't matter, he'd seen the man in Pennsylvania more than once and knew who he was—but even if he hadn't, the funny mix of stealth and obviousness would have given him away. It was like the cock-of-the-walk trying to sneak a bite of cookie dough from the kitchen. That was how the bloody-damn-hell Pinkertons always looked. They were just too full of themselves to be really sneaky (and wasn't it like them to stick a man to follow Tam who was so instantly recognizable?)

No wonder the Mollies and others always cottoned on to them so fast.

It was probably also the width of the street that prevented Harris, or whatever his name was, from seeing Tam. That or the Sunday Picnic girls. The Pinkerton loitered in the door smoking a cigarette and reading a newspaper, but the paper was held at the level of his chest rather than his face and his eyes scanned the street over the top of it.

He scanned the street and especially he scanned a trio of pretty girls, thirty feet ahead of Tam. The girls giggled and chattered and beamed in that way that only girls who are absolutely convinced of their own unblemished and bouncing perfection can. Tam didn't know if they were really going to a picnic, but they were too pretty and too silly to be doing anything else. Harris the smoking Pinkerton, though, seemed to feel differently. He watched the flibbertigibbets carefully for any signs of criminal action.

He scanned the girls closely and he missed Tam. *Brigit bless poor Mother Harrison for bringing such an idjit into this cold, hard world.*

Tam walked around the block and entered the Deseret's bar by a side door, a little service entrance with no sign, either in or out. He'd known there was a side door—he'd looked for it—before he'd been willing to go in the front the first time. A hot, grimy, humid little hall let him, after a short trot, into the cool, airy bar, chilled by overhead fans. The bar was huge, all marble and dark woods with a high ceiling and stone columns like a cathedral and busier than the number of its guests warranted.

Tam eased into a seat at a tiny booth and slipped out a Husher under the table. Fumbling through instructions printed on a plaque in the center of the table, he wrote a drink order and his room number on a card chit, stuffed it into a glass cylinder, and shoved the cylinder into a tube in the wall. The systems reminded him of the Lion House and made him feel vaguely uneasy. With a soft *whumph!* the tube sucked the cylinder away and three minutes later his drink jogged around to the table in the hands of a fresh-faced young blonde girl wearing yellow and black stripes. Tam smiled and ogled her once (*Doesn't a man have a duty to affirm their prettiness to all the pretty girls? Otherwise, who do they make themselves pretty for?*), but shooed her away to continue his watch on the lobby.

He saw three Pinkertons. One paced back and forth just inside the door and watched the lobby (Tam kept his head well down, like a serious drinker or a man reading over his whisky) and two spoke with the concierge. He was fully prepared to shoot any Pinkerton that came up to him with one of their bloody-damn-hell cheap calotypes, but none did. They must have searched the bar patrons before he'd arrived.

When the Pinkertons finished their conversation, they left by the front door. Tam waited ten careful minutes before putting the gun back into its holster and tossing down the last of his drink. *No point in wasting good whisky, me boy.*

The Deseret Hotel had a lift and it was a good one. He and Sam Clemens had ridden it up and down earlier, Clemens looking all nonchalant and impressed with his own sophistication, but Tam had barely been able to keep his mouth from either dropping open or spewing out curse words. The lift was smooth and cool, with no jerking in its action and no steam leaking into the carriage. It was a work of genius, ultra-modern and perfect, not like the herky-jerk affairs that shifted men up and down inside the mine shafts of Pennsylvania.

And Tam ignored it. If there were any Pinkertons still lurking around, for sure they'd have their beady little eyes on the lift. Instead, he limped up the Hotel's stairs, cursing to himself with every twinging step.

His wounded arm and leg ached and so did his ear where it had lost a piece to the midget. He itched to rough the dwarf up, but he had promised Clemens he wouldn't. He could scare the little bastard, though. He could put the fear of God and all His angels and Tamerlane O'Shaughnessy into the little bugger and if the moment arose when it became necessary to break his word to Clemens, he wouldn't mind it so much, so long as he was able to explain why he'd had to do it.

No Pinkertons in the stairwell.

Tam kept one hand on the grip of a Husher and the other ready to whip out his spring-loaded stiletto.

Maybe he ought to kill him after all, necessity or not, and just apologize to Sam when the deed was done. Maybe that would be wisdom. What would Mother O'Shaughnessy do if she were in Tam's position? The Pinkertons were nosing after him, after all, and the dwarf knew that he had killed their man in Fort Bridger.

No Pinkertons in the hall upstairs, either.

But the dwarf had killed the other one. Maybe he could turn the little fellow into the Pinkertons and blame him somehow for both deaths? Or kill him and leave both Hushers on his body somewhere the Pinkertons would find it?

Tam listened at the hotel room door; no sounds of Pinkertons inside.

But even framing the midget wouldn't make the Pinkertons his friends. He'd still killed their precious little Taffy Bevan and they knew it. There was nothing for it; he had to kill the dwarf.

Tam opened the door.

"Hell and begorra!" he cursed.

Loops of cut rope lay on the floor. He knew even before he ran into the bathroom to check, pistol in hand, that the dwarf was gone.

The boy was gone, too.

In a reflex action he checked his own pocket, and of course the cylinder with its cargo of manic everything-eating beetles was safely stowed away. *Bloody idjit*, he mocked himself. As if the dwarf might have snuck up on him on the street and picked his pocket.

No, but he might have snuck up to the Pinkertons on the street and turned Tamerlane O'Shaughnessy in. It was a good bloody-damn-hell job that Tam had kept out of sight in the hotel, and no wonder Pinkerton Harvard was standing outside the front doors.

Tam slunk back to the Hotel's lobby, waiting in obscure shadows and watching to be sure it was Pinkerton-free before he approached the concierge. The man was little and square and clean and the brass nameplate on his chest said *SORENSON*. This was the same fellow who had just been talking to the Pinkertons, he was sure of it.

"Ah, good afternoon to you, Mr. Sorenson," Tam started.

"And to you, Mr. O'Shaughnessy," the desk clerk returned.

Tam grabbed the grip of his Husher and almost drew it. At the same time, he looked involuntarily at his chest and was almost surprised to see that he wasn't also wearing a nametag. *Ah, but he knows you because you're a hotel guest, me boy*, Tam thought. *Calm yourself, he's done nothing to you, and you can always kill him later.*

But it wasn't good that Sorenson knew him. That meant that if the Pinkertons showed the man a calotype, he would have recognized it, even if they called it something bloody stupid like *Seamus McNamara*.

Or do they finally know my real name? Did they show him a calotype and say Here's Tam O'Shaughnessy, call us when you see him if you want a little bit of that reward money? *Maybe that's how he knows my name now....*

The calotype ... suddenly he remembered that he was still carrying it around, in the pocket of his coat. It felt like it burned him. He should get rid of it, somewhere, but the lobby of the biggest hotel in the city was not the right place.

"Ah ..." Tam hesitated. *Where in bloody-damn-hell is my share of the famous Irish smooth talking now that I need it?* The lobby was far too busy with people or he might have shot Sorenson on the spot, out of sheer embarrassment. Or knifed the bastard.

"Some gentlemen were looking for you, Mr. O'Shaughnessy," Sorenson continued blandly, as if Tam weren't standing there stammering and drooling like an idjit with his heart all full of murder. "Some *foreign* gentlemen."

Foreign? Yes, of course, because this was the Kingdom of Deseret and nothing to do with the United States of America at all. But Sorenson didn't talk like someone who had just turned Tam in to the Pinkertons. "Oh, ah …"

"I had no instructions from you or Mr. Clemens, so of course I told them I didn't know you."

"Jesus, thank you," Tam blurted out. In his relief, he almost squeezed the Husher's trigger.

"You can call me Sorenson," the clerk smiled mildly. "*Mister* or *Brother*, depending. Some of our Mexican brothers and sisters are named Jesus, but I was born in Copenhagen and my parents named me Anders."

"I see." Tam adjusted his hat on his head and realized he was sweating, silly fool that he was. He had dodged a bullet, and through no clever maneuvering of his own. Still, the Pinkertons were out there somewhere and it would pay to keep that clearly in mind from now on. "Sorry, Mr. Sorenson."

"I asked where you might contact them in case I did see you," Sorenson continued, "but the gentlemen declined to give me any further information."

"Brigit's dugs, I bet they did, ha!" Tam couldn't help himself. *Stop acting like an amateur and a dunderhead, Tamerlane O'Shaughnessy,* he told himself. He straightened up his posture and his coat and felt better for it. He'd have felt even better if he could have kicked the Harris right in his balls at that moment and then stabbed the man in the face.

The clerk only smiled mildly at him, but Tam saw that the little man's hands both rested on the counter, palms down. Tam coughed and dug out the double eagle Sam had given him by the Lion House. It was one of the few gold coins he had. Sam Clemens was a good egg and could be counted on, but if Tam had one complaint it was that his boss did have a tendency to keep all the money to himself.

Tam plunked the coin down on the counter and it immediately disappeared, whisked away by the little clerk's fingers. "And how else can I help you today, Mr. O'Shaughnessy?" Sorenson asked.

Excellent question. "Have you seen a dwarf in the lobby this afternoon?" he asked. "The little fellow might conceivably have been in the company of a small boy."

"In fact, he was." The concierge smiled. "I gave them directions to the train station just before the foreign gentlemen arrived."

CHAPTER SEVEN

I could kill you where you stand, Edgar."

The voice came from behind him and it was Roxie's. Since it was Roxie talking, the words might be complete and utter lies, a bluff.

Then again, it was Roxie, and she probably *could* kill him where he stood.

Poe turned around slowly, grateful his pockets were empty.

"Shall I call you *Reynolds*?" he asked.

He had just put on his biggest overcoat, the one with all the pockets inside. He had put it on intending to carry away, in the coat's pockets, Hunley's four canopic jars, designed to specification of the Madman, Orson Pratt. For all his rumination on the subject, Poe had no idea what the jars did, and knew only that the designs had left Hunley's smartest men scratching their heads and wondering.

But he had seen some of Hunley's other Egyptiana at work and if he was going to be shot in the body, he didn't want some pestilential plague of death accidentally unleashed against his own flesh. Years of training and experience kept him from shuddering as his imagination was invaded by a vision of himself thrashing out death throes in the grip of a brass scarab swarm, or melting in a puddle of acid, or bursting into flame.

Roxie sat on Jed's bunk. He hadn't seen her because she'd been behind the door, and it had been dark. He kicked himself for moving so quickly. She held something in her hands that looked like a small glass globe, full of sizzling blue light.

"We both know that's not my name," she said quietly.

D.J. Butler

"You have an accomplice," he inferred. If he was going to die, at least he'd know how. Besides, talking might buy him time.

Roxie nodded. "She replaced the hair you'd left in the door after I came in."

"I was reckless."

"You always were."

"Not since Baltimore," Poe said, and he meant it. "I learned my lesson, and I've been very careful."

"It only takes one mistake."

For years he had dreamed of this moment. He thought he had seen it in every possible configuration, the final confrontation between himself and Eliza Roxcy Snow. He had seen himself poisoned, stabbed, strangled, and burned in acid, because that was an outcome he feared and half-expected on a daily basis. Mostly he had seen himself as the one doing the killing, by gun, by knife, by throwing her hated, beautiful body under the wheels of a train, by shoving her head into the clocksprung jaws of a cotton thresher, but always by some means that was satisfyingly physical and violent. And always he imagined himself first delivering a final oration, telling Roxie that she was evil, that she had a heart of stone, that whatever Satan there might be, in whatever hell he could muster, would surely delight in adding her to the infinite ranks of his gibbering minions.

Now here he was, and he didn't have the will for any of that. "You were my mistake," he said simply.

"And you were mine." She looked so sincere that he couldn't laugh, no matter how outrageous her words were. He wondered what game she was playing.

He considered his weapons. They were virtually none. The Seth-Beast was locked away in the hold of the *Liahona*. He didn't carry a gun. He had the hypocephalus tucked into a pocket of his vest—he would have to try to get it out and use it on her. He doubted it would have any effect, though, not with her training and her iron will.

To set up his play, he hazarded a fake cough. It came out a little more forcefully than he meant it and brought several more in its wake, involuntary, before he managed to stop it.

"Consumption?" Roxie asked. She did an excellent job of feigning an expression of heartfelt concern, the straight lines of her face melting into compassion. Poe wanted to applaud and invite her to take a bow for her theatrics.

Instead he nodded. "It hardly matters now. I assume you'll kill me with that device you're holding."

"You know me so well."

"Poison? That would be appropriate and typical. What is it, a gas?"

"I don't want to kill you, Edgar," she said.

124

"You've had a change of heart since Baltimore, then," he quipped, and he faked another cough, smaller this time, and this time it didn't trigger anything further.

He wondered if she had seen him hypnotize Lee in the Shoshone stockade. She might not let him get the handkerchief. If he went for the hypocephalus and she attacked, he must be prepared to defend himself. He moved, relaxed, into a more centered and balanced position, a basic and inconspicuous defensive stance of baritsu. For the thousandth time, he thanked Robert in his heart for the years of training and discipline.

Roxie hesitated. "That wasn't me," she finally said.

"You probably expect me to believe that," he rejected her claim of innocence.

She stood up. "I expect you to be shrewd enough to know that sometimes, in our business, the dagger doesn't know that it's the dagger."

Well, that rang true, but then, verisimilitude was the strength of the best lies told by the best liars. And Roxie was the very best.

"And the dagger," she added, "never *wants* to be the dagger."

He coughed and then reached for his vest.

Roxie raised the glass ball over her head.

"Don't move!" she snapped.

He froze.

"You would deny a dying man a handkerchief into which to cough up fragments of his lung?"

"This is Wyoming; spit it on the floor," she told him, her voice the perfect mixture of cold steel and tortured pity. "I don't know which is worse, Edgar. That you might truly be dying, or that you might be faking your own death to take advantage of my feelings."

So much for the hypocephalus.

It was to be a desperate physical attack, then. Poe braced himself, looked at the way she stood and thought about how he would try to grab her and which direction he would throw her when he did. Would the gas kill both of them? Of course not. It would be something to which she had already taken the antidote, or to which she was immune. Or maybe the Madman had fitted her with a device in her mouth or her throat, which would filter out the toxins.

If Pratt could save her body, his mind lurched desperately and counter to its discipline, couldn't he save mine? He wrenched his attention back to the moment.

"It's worse than either of those, my dear," he mocked her. "I *am* truly dying *and* I want to take advantage of your feelings. Sadly for me, you have none."

Suddenly Roxie backed away, turning and retreating towards the door. "My associate is outside."

"The pretty young dilettante," Poe guessed. "The brunette with the freckles, who kicks so high."

"Even if you survived this," Roxie brandished the sparkling globe, "she'd kill you with her bare hands. She's a champion of the Eastern fighting arts and a stone-hearted killer."

"She's your protégée. How else could she be?"

Roxie opened the door with a hand behind her. "Remember this," she told him.

Then she threw the globe down to the floor—

—it shattered into a thousand pieces in a sparkle of light and a dying *pfizzt!*—

—she disappeared into the hallway of the *Liahona*—

—and shut the door behind her.

Poe took a gulp of air and jumped for the door. As he grabbed the knob, he heard a loud *click* outside. *She's locked the door,* he thought. *Don't panic. Just open the lock from the inside.*

He thumbed the latch that should have unlocked his cabin door; the latch didn't budge. Poe felt his own heart beat faster.

He didn't have a gun. He needed something to smash the door with. He scrambled, fumbled with the combination, lungs bursting, opened his big steamer trunk, and pulled out one of the four canopic jars. It was a little stone thing the size of a pickle jar, pinkish, and with a monkey's head.

He spun and smashed it against the doorknob, using the monkey end like the head of a hammer.

Crack!

No effect. His lungs were bursting.

Please, don't let this jar burst open and spill out something evil. He imagined it sprouting octopoid tentacles, a swarm of wasps, a cloud of burning acid.

He swung again.

Crack!

The door and the jar held firm. His body trembled, he desperately needed to cough. She was a devil, to torture him this way, to force him to hold his breath.

Was it some kind of test, to see if he was really consumptive? No, that was both too diabolical and also idiotic. His head was beginning to spin and the room around him was bathed in unnatural white light.

He swung a third time.

Crack!

The door stood steady. The canopic jar was unmarred.

His lungs betrayed him. Poe dropped the jar and sank to his knees in the puddle of glass fragments. He coughed violently, hacking up bloody phlegm onto the carpet, gasping and sucking in air between coughs. The air was canned and stale. Was he being poisoned?

He spat blood onto his own hands and the floor and the glass, blood and phlegm, and he expected to fall over and die.

But he coughed and spat again, drew in a deep breath …

And lived.

The canned air was just the regular stale air of the interior of the big steam-truck.

The poison hadn't worked.

He looked at the glass fragments, at the little filament inside it, and realized that he'd been a fool. It wasn't that the poison hadn't worked.

The little bulb had never had poison inside it at all. It had been an electricks device, some sort of hand-held light.

A bluff.

He laughed, but only for a moment, before sobering up.

What, then, had Roxie wanted?

Poe tore off his false nose and threw it into the corner of the room.

ᎠᏦᎶᏓᏫᏑᎢ

John Moses had been a little bit too confident about their ability to ride the train for free. He told his name and his father's name and that he needed to go home—to some place called *Ogden*—and, sure enough, the conductor with the stylized bumblebee on the front of his cap let him on board the shiny brass and steel train. He even gave the boy a warm smile and a pat on his little head.

Jed, though, got a hard stare.

He coughed awkwardly once or twice and scratched at the plascrete with his toes, hoping the conductor would have a heart and usher him aboard as John Moses's friend. Meanwhile, he looked around the station. Half a dozen platforms lay side by side, linked by parallel catwalks overhead, steel with wheel-and-compass designs alternating in their balustrades with smiling steel suns. Jed knew for certain that no train connected from anywhere in the United States to the Kingdom. If there had been one, he and Poe would have taken it. Did Deseret connect to Mexico, somehow? Or to the Republic of California? Or New Russia?

The conductor didn't budge and finally Jed gave in. He dug deep for a little cash, the last of his rectangular California pieces, got a return ticket, and was at last allowed onto the same carriage as the boy. The inside of the train was leather and wood and brass, with sliding glass windows and clean red carpet with gold bees woven into it and a restaurant car and everything. It was the nicest train Jed had ever ridden, not that he was a train man.

They took a seat just before the porter reached them.

"Standard English or Deseret?" he asked.

"Deseret," Jed said, just for kicks, and produced a nickel. It was a mistake—whatever *Deseret* was, it wasn't English and the dwarf couldn't read it. The pages were covered with strange squiggly characters he couldn't make out. The same kind of incomprehensible gibberish, he realized, as was painted on the side of the *Liahona*. "Why didn't anybody tell me they speak Chinese here?" he grumbled.

Only it wasn't true. They spoke perfectly good English, as good as any American and better than half the people in Arkansas.

So what in hell was all this garbage in the paper?

"Choo, choo!" John Moses yelled as the train lurched forward and pulled out of the station.

His excitement was so infectious that the dwarf felt compelled to holler with him. "Choo, choo!" He knew he was drawing stares from everyone on the car. Secret agent or not, for just one moment, he didn't care.

Jed wasn't one hundred percent sure, but looking out his window as the train pulled away, he thought he saw a man in a porkpie hat, jumping onto the very back of the train.

ⱭⱵ6ⱵⱷⱵⱵ

Sam checked the handwritten note he'd been carrying in his alligator-skin billfold twice to be sure. The numbers he'd written down matched the address of a windowless brick building set back inside a city block, away from the Great Salt Lake City's wide streets and crowded on all sides by the uncaring backs of warehouses. Pipes, including glass message channels, ran out from the brick building in all directions, into and around and above its neighbors. The building *hummed* with a low, pulsating throb like the distant playing of Indian drums.

"By the shores of Gitchee-Gumee," Sam found himself chanting. "By the shining Big-Sea-Water."

This was the place, all right.

Sam was no spy, not in his heart, but he'd been given very precise directions by men who really, truly *were* spies. He circled the block to be sure he wasn't followed. Then he found the door. He didn't knock and he didn't look around to see if anyone was watching him; if anyone *was*, that gesture would surely mark him as a trespasser.

He just turned the knob, walked in like he owned the place, and shut the door behind him.

Inside the throbbing got louder and was joined by the steady tumbling sound of falling water.

There were windows to the outside, he now saw, but they were like arrow slits, high on the walls, long and narrow, and the strips of light they cast were brilliant but thin. Sam waited a minute and let his eyes adjust. He stood on a catwalk of plascrete and after a moment he was able to see well enough to realize that only a waist-high iron railing separated him from a serious fall. Below, he heard and smelled churning waters and he felt a faint humid spray on his face and hands, but even when his eyes had grown accustomed to the gloom he could see nothing in the abyss. Mixed in with the cool green smell of the water, he detected the comforting tang of engine oil.

Pipes, brass pipes big enough that if they were lying flat a man could have walked inside them, shot up out of the unseen watery depths below and exploded over his head, radiating outward like flower petals or the spokes of a wheel. The pipes were the immense boles of trees in this strange jungle, and the flowers were a profusion of gauges, dials, wheels, clamps, levers, hanging chains, pulleys, switches, and other paraphernalia. In the dull light it all loomed huge and glowed like old bronze. Staircases climbed up and down.

Sam was curious what the waters below looked like. He imagined an egg yolk hell full of dead sailors and blind, translucent sharks, or the slimy blue seas of creation and a gate to a secret inner world, or at least a vaulted and columned lake like he'd read about under the Hagia Sophia in Istanbul.

But Sam Clemens had his instructions and left the itch of his curiosity unsatisfied.

Instead, he found the nearest staircase and began to climb.

He had just set foot on the third and uppermost catwalk, grateful that it was too dark inside the water station to really see down to the ground below him, when a second person entered the building. A brilliant square of light opened without warning ahead and slammed shut again with a *clang!* and then he heard the slow pacing of feet as a man walked towards him.

The catwalk was narrow and Sam fought down a momentary fear that he had been betrayed for the fortune he carried in his pocket. After all, if he were thrown over the catwalk here, he knew he would surely die. On the other hand, his murderer would lose the rubies, too. Still, the plascrete ledge felt humid, clammy, and every-so-slightly slippery under his feet. He rested a hand on the iron railing to reassure himself.

A blue light snapped into being, chest height, in the darkness. The fizzling will-o-the-wisp electricks illuminated the face of an old man, bearded and crag-browed, with goggles over his eyes. He wore a simple dark wool suit, and the white hair on the back of his head was swept straight up behind him to make a kind of crest or cock's comb that caught the blue crackling light and reflected it like an off-kilter halo.

"The light is for your benefit," the old man growled. "I can see fine without it."

"Thanks," Sam said dryly. "I suppose you must be the—"

"You first!" snapped the old man. "Didn't you get instructions?" He sounded like a northerner, Sam thought, like a New York or a Vermont man.

"I did," Sam admitted, "and I apologize. I am neither a cloak and dagger man nor a Freemason, so I find this all a little ..." He stopped himself before saying anything insulting and cleared his throat. "I am the Boatman," he declaimed, trying to imagine that he was in a school play and everyone else was just as embarrassed as he was. He'd felt like an idiot memorizing these lines, but sure enough, this old fellow was going to insist on them. "I come seeking the knowledge of the air. Are you Pratt, by the way?" It had never been made clear to him whom exactly he was supposed to meet.

"Shh!" the old man chastised him. "I am the Seer, keeper of the knowledge of the air. By what token shall I know thee, Boatman?"

Sam felt like a fool. "I have the rubies, dammit!" he snapped. "Do you want them or not?" He pulled the bag from inside his jacket and held it up in the blue light. It was a fortune, he knew. More than once, he told himself that a smarter man than he was would have simply taken the rubies and fled the country. For that matter, it wasn't too late for him.

He was out of the country already.

"Yes!" the old man yelled, his voice echoing over the rumble of the waters below. "And yes, I'm Pratt!" The blue light winked out and Pratt snatched the bag out of Sam's hands in the darkness. So he really *could* see; Sam assumed it had something to do with the goggles the old man was wearing and was duly impressed. "Have you no respect for my need for secrecy? How was I to know I was dealing with the right man? Don't you understand how dangerous this is? Do you think we're playing a game, you and I? Do you want the whole thing to collapse around our ears and all of them to come down on us?"

The old man's voice dropped in volume at the end of his speech and Sam heard his feet shuffling away in the darkness.

"Wait!" he called. "Wait a minute! Don't you owe me something, Mr. Pratt?"

The shuffling stopped and Orson Pratt laughed, a high cackle in the gloom. "Yes I do, Mr. United States, yes I do. Meet me tomorrow morning. Tomorrow morning at eight o'clock at ... at the north doors of the Tabernacle. I'll bring all the plans."

Creak.

The square of light appeared again, searing Sam's eyes. He held his hands up to shield them and Pratt slammed the door shut.

Boom!

The echo of the door banged back and forth for a long time in the darkness and Sam felt vaguely defeated. Pratt had sounded like he was making up the rendezvous time and place on the spot and Sam wondered if the inventor had any intention at all of holding up his end of the bargain.

Well, if Orson Pratt wouldn't sell the plans for his flying ships to the United States, Sam would just have to succeed in his primary objective. He would persuade Brigham Young to join with the United States government in preventing war.

And if that failed too, well, Sam had come prepared do bad things.

𐐔𐐆𐐘𐐆𐐙𐐆𐐤

Ogden was a railroad station in the center of a tiny town surrounded by farms—Jed saw it all from the window as they rolled in, less than an hour after leaving the Great Salt Lake City. The station here was smaller, just two platforms for two lines. He and the boy spilled out in a wave of hayseed farmers and small-town businessmen and a couple of ladies with shopping bags and were swept along almost instantly in the street. It felt like a thousand small towns Jed had ridden into as a carny in his youth and his eyes instinctively raced up and down the street in search of policemen.

"Where's the loc?" he muttered. "I mean, where do you live, kid?"

"Come on," John Moses said, pointing up a broad hillside. "My house is just up there."

Jed shot a suspicious eye over his shoulder several times before they lost sight of the station, but never saw a porkpie hat.

Trudging up a graded gravel road in the warm shadows of black walnuts and elm trees, Jed Coltrane suddenly became conscious of the fact that he smelled bad. He probably smelled bad most of the time, he thought, only most of the time he just didn't give a rat's ass. Now, for some reason, it bothered him. He was rumpled, too, disheveled and beat up and chafed, and generally unfit for human company.

He laughed out loud. *Coltrane, you idiot,* he thought, *you're acting like you're about to meet the parents of your sweetheart. Cut it out.*

"This is it," John Moses said.

The dwarf looked up and down the street. The buildings were red brick bungalows, each on a small farm or orchard lot, and half of them looked like they belonged to some kind of tradesman. Jed saw a smithy, a dry goods store, and a tailor. And John Moses's parents' house had a wooden signboard out front like an old tavern, with a pair of crossed six-shooters painted on it.

Out behind the bungalow were rows of cherry trees, and a big brass pump station, quietly emitting a faint coal-smoke tail as it humped up and down and up and down, trickling water out of a cone-shaped spout into a maze of irrigation ditches swirling out in a circle from the center where it stood. Off to the side was a brick outbuilding with doors and window trim painted a bright fresh white, to match the bungalow.

No porkpie hats in sight.

"Let's go in, then, kid."

There was a knocker on the front of the bungalow's door, but no amount of hammering brought any result. "My mammas might be running errands." John Moses adjusted his slouch hat, a little nervous. "I guess we should go talk to my poppa."

Mammas?

Jed's scarred knuckles rapped on the door of the outbuilding and produced an immediate result. "Coming!" called a man's voice, and then the top half of the door swung open and inward, leaving the bottom half shut with a sort of built in shelf at its top like a little business counter.

The man who answered the door had no hair right up to the very top of his head, nor on his face, but thick brown sprouts of the stuff all around his ears, behind his skull, and under his jaw. Someone who liked the man might have suggested he looked like a lion. An observer in a less flattering frame of mind could have commented that he looked like a color-inverted black-eyed Susan, with a white bud of a face poking out in front of a dark curly bed of petals. Jed Coltrane didn't care either way—he'd seen uglier.

Time was, he saw uglier all day, every day.

The thing that struck him was the apparatus on the man's face. It looked like a shiny brass lobster, wrapped halfway around his head, front and back. One thin claw curled up along his bony cheek, forming a loop over his right eye, inside of which was wedged a convex lens of shiny glass.

The man looked over both their heads for a moment, and Jed cleared his throat.

"Hello," the man said. He looked down at them and blinked. His right eye was gigantic, seen through the lens. "John Moses. And a short person." He squinted through the monocle. "An adult."

"Midget," Jed said gruffly. "Dwarf. Pygmy. Runt. Tom Thumb. Did I miss any, professor?"

"Homunculus?" The man suggested. "Lilliputian? Bantam?"

"I guess that about covers it," Jed growled. His ears felt hot and his hands twitched involuntarily at spots about his body where, by rights, knives should have been hanging.

"Poppa," John Moses interrupted in a pleading tone, "this is my *friend.*"

"Ah." The boy's father swung the bottom half of the door open. "In that case, I am Jonathan Browning, and it is a pleasure to meet you. Will you be one of the crewmen of the *Liahona*, then? Brother Dan usually brings John Moses home himself."

He invited Jed into the outbuilding and onto one of the three plush chairs, slightly frayed but comfortable, that crouched around a low circular table in the nearest corner of the room. Jed sat, but his eyes roamed the walls. "Jed Coltrane," he murmured distractedly. They were covered with some kind of thin white board, pegged full of holes in a close grid. Into the holes were poked steel hooks, and on the steel hooks hung guns.

All kinds of guns.

Over all four walls of the building. More guns were stacked, more or less neatly, on the three large tables in the center of the room. Still more lay disassembled, or pinned in vises, or had important pieces that had been removed and inserted into obscure tooling machines. Jed didn't consider himself a lover of guns—knives were more his thing—but the sheer overwhelming number of weapons on the wall made him whistle. He'd come to the right place. In his mind's eye, he saw the underhanded Irishman shot to pieces in a thousand different ways, Jed at the trigger every time.

The two Brownings sat in the other two chairs.

"No, I ain't one of the crew," Jed said distractedly. He wondered for a moment how he could steal a few of these weapons, then felt guilty for having the thought, then felt ashamed of himself for the guilt.

Coltrane, you damn crybaby, he told himself. *You need a gun. You* came here *for a gun.*

Of course, you could buy one. But with the cash you've got left, it'd be one cheap piece of shit.

Maybe you could borrow *one.* Of course, that would mean returning it, which would imply coming back to a place Coltrane had been before, which wasn't something Coltrane had done very often in his life.

"Poppa, Injuns took the *Liahona*!" John Moses peeped.

Jonathan Browning's magnified eye popped open even wider and Jed Coltrane flinched. "Was it the Shoshone? Has anyone been told? Does Brother Brigham know?"

Aw, hell. "Look, I jest … yeah, I reckon it was the Shoshone. But look, the boy and I escaped, he ain't hurt, and he wanted to come home, that's all."

"Yes, well," Browning huffed. "Yes, thank you very much. Has Brother Brigham been told? If not, I should get down to the train station or the sheriff's office and get a message sent immediately. Tell me how I can repay you."

D.J. Butler

Uh oh. Can't have that much attention, Jed thought. Besides, the *Liahona* wasn't his problem. "Yeah, I'm pretty sure. Yeah, now that I think of it, of course he knows. Look, it's all under control, I jest wanted to bring the boy back."

"Yes." Blink. "Thank you." Blink, blink. Jed really wished Jonathan Browning would take off his eyepiece. The dwarf found it unnerving. It made the man look like a machine. "Tell me how I can thank you. Please."

Jed chased a fist into his pocket after his precious few remaining coins. Poe had always had all the real money, and after buying the train ticket, Jed found himself running lower than he'd like, even aside from his need to get armed. Precious few coins and all of them Mexican. He sighed. "Well, Mr. Browning, as it happens, in our escape we had to leave my guns behind. I'm used to being around rough customers, as they say, so I've always gone armed, and I'd hate to change that habit now that I'm on the frontier. I see you're a gunsmith. Maybe you could sell me something. Something on the inexpensive side." He cleared his throat. "And I mean *really* inexpensive."

Browning's face broke into an indulgent smile. "This isn't the frontier, Mr. Coltrane. This is the Kingdom." He turned and gestured at the entire shop. "Please, I beg you. Take any one of them, as a gift from me."

"*Any* one?" Jed wondered, stunned at the man's generosity. There were guns as small as wrist-concealed derringers on the walls, but there were cannons too, big guns that would require horses to drag them around.

"Good heavens, you're right, I'm ashamed of myself. You've restored my son to me. Take any *two*. Take *what you need*. I'll fill a pack with ammunition too, and I'll see what one of my two Elizabeths might have in the way of a loaf of bread or a pie." Jonathan Browning stripped the eyepiece away from his face as he launched himself to his feet and strode purposefully from the shop.

"One'll do very nicely, thanks," Jed found himself mumbling in something that resembled polite manners. He saw himself holding a pistol to the Irishman's temple and pulling the trigger. "One is all I'll need."

John Moses was grinning.

"What does he mean, *one of his two* Elizabeths?" Jed asked the boy as he started to browse through the weapons on the walls. He found a nice long-barreled pistol he liked, spun the cylinder, sighted along it experimentally, and set it on the table.

"There's Elizabeth my mamma," John Moses explained, like it was the most natural thing in all the world, "and Elizabeth his first wife, my other mamma."

That accounted for his *mammas*. Jed grunted. He'd seen weirder, among the Chickasaw and the Creek and in the Ozarks. "You got two

134

mammas," was all he said, not a question and not a judgment.

"Yeah," the little boy agreed. "And twenty-one brothers and sisters."

"Holy shit!" Jed spat out, then checked himself. "Sorry, boy, I don't mean nothing by it. I jest ain't ever seen such a big family."

"I know," John Moses said. "Sometimes *holy shit* is what I think, too."

Jed Coltrane laughed. "You're alright, kid," he said, and his eye fell on another gun he liked. It was bigger than a pistol but shorter than a shotgun or a rifle. It looked like a rifle, but built really short in the barrel and with a boxy round metal drum hanging underneath it.

John Moses looked. "That's a sort of rifle," he said. "Poppa calls it a *'gas-powered, drum-fed, rapid-fire repeater'* to customers."

Jed pulled the gun off the wall and hefted it. The stock felt good tucked under his arm. The gun was heavy, but then Jed Coltrane had strong carny arms. "It feels good," he said. "It feels like a killer. Is it accurate?"

John Moses shook his head *no*. "But it shoots a thousand rounds a minute."

Jed whistled. "No kidding?"

John Moses nodded. "When he's talking to me, Poppa likes to call it his *machine-gun.*"

The dwarf looked at the weapon and its bulky drum. "How does it work?" he asked.

John Moses showed him. "It takes paper cartridges. You have to load up a whole drum ahead of time and that takes a good long while. When you shoot, though, it all comes out fast. You can really chew through targets."

Targets. "You ever shot at anybody, kid?" Jed asked. "I mean, at a real live person?"

"Not yet." The little boy chewed his lip and looked down at the machine-gun. "But I guess I could do it if I had to. I could be brave. But I think it'd have to be for a real good reason."

"Like family, kid," Jed suggested.

"Yeah, like family," John Moses agreed.

Jed imagined himself firing a thousand rounds into the Irishman. A thousand rounds a minute was a whole lot of death. "That'll do," he said.

Time to get back to the Deseret Hotel. Death and hell to any porkpie hat he spotted on the way.

ᏗᎫᎬᏗᎿᎫᏋ

The message paper curled up at the edges as the bellboy took his tip and retreated. Sam automatically smoothed back the paper with his thumb, and to his surprise he smudged the ink. "That's fast," he muttered. The message was hand-printed in a lovely copperplate, all in capital letters like a telegram.

To: Mr. Samuel Clemens

In Care of the Deseret Hotel

Sir:

    President Young informs me that he is presently working in the office of the Beehive House and that you may find him there for the next several hours. He welcomes your visit at your earliest convenience.

    You will find the Beehive House adjacent to the Lion House, where you and I met. I trust I will not strain your powers of discrimination if I observe that it is the large residence with balconies and a beehive on top and not the adjacent Tabernacle.

Regards,

Geo. Cannon

Sam crumpled the sheet up, lit it with his smoldering Partagás, and tossed it into the grate. Other men's sarcasm made him feel like his territory had been trespassed upon. Well, his *earliest convenience* was right now, he calculated, so gripping the cigar in his teeth he pulled his jacket off the back of a chair and shrugged into it, heading for the door.

He'd just been sitting around, anyway, wondering.

He wondered where in tarnation his criminal Irishman had gotten to.

He wondered if his Irishman had made off with the dwarf and the boy, or vice versa. He hoped the boy was unharmed.

But most of all, because the Irishman and his vendetta with the Appalachian midget seemed like a sideshow in more ways than one, he wondered what was going to happen with Orson Pratt.

As Sam pushed his way out of the big front doors of the Deseret Hotel, he thought he saw, just for a moment, a reflection in the glass windows across the street. He would have sworn, in that moment, that he was seeing the midget Coltrane and that the man must be off to Sam's left, fifty feet or so.

He jerked his head around to see, though, and the dwarf wasn't there.

Trick of the mind, he thought. *Illusion, self-deception.* He was wondering where the dwarf was and his brain produced an image of the man. He spun around to his right and paced in the direction of the Beehive House.

Sam's mission objectives were clear, though he'd expected from the start that things on the ground would get considerably foggier. His superiors had expected it too, he thought; that's why they'd sent a man of judgment and perception.

"Ha!" he barked a single peal of laughter at his own vanity and spat the stub of his cigar into the sparkling clean gutter. As the next headgear-doffing couple passed, Sam twinkled empty fingers at them in a way that made him feel like a bawdy house flirt.

First, persuade Brigham Young to visibly ally with the United States in deploring the secession of any individual State or association of States. Get him to put pressure, with the threat of his famous airship fleet, on the so-called Confederate leadership, head off the secession, get them back to the table to keep talking about tariffs and railroads and all the other nonsense that was threatening to split the United States apart. He was on his way to pursue that objective this very instant.

Second, and right under Brigham Young's nose, secretly deliver rubies (a negotiated *quid pro quo*) to an agent of the famous Orson "Madman" Pratt (and in the event, it had been Pratt himself, and not an agent, to take delivery), in exchange for comprehensive schematics of Pratt's, and Deseret's, airship technology, including designs of its individual airships. Sam had delivered the *quid*, the rubies. Pratt had given him an appointment to deliver the *quo*, which would be a pile of papers in some shape, but the spurious, off-hand manner of the appointment's making led Sam to consider the possibility that Pratt had no intention of following through. Sam would be at the appointed place at the appointed time anyway, of course, but if Pratt didn't show, Sam would have to think seriously about the remainder of his objectives.

Third—and this was where Sam's instructions foresaw real possibilities of confusion on the ground, not to mention disaster, mayhem, and even crime—do whatever he could to aid the United States in the coming war. This might mean, he'd been told, stealing Pratt's airships, or stealing the schematics, or acts of sabotage against the Deseret aerial fleet or against the Kingdom on other fronts. He'd likely have to figure it out for himself in the moment. Sam wasn't a diplomat and he was even less a spy, but he *really* wasn't a thief or a saboteur. He was prepared to do his duty, but he sincerely hoped it wouldn't come to that.

Or if it did, he wanted to be able to unleash Tamerlane O'Shaughnessy and wash his hands of the consequences. Really, that was what the crazy Irishman was for. Sam didn't need a bodyguard against these—he twinkled his fingers again at a woman-old man-woman trio of passersby—harmless, eccentric, mechanically-minded Deseret Mormons. They were no threat to him or to the United States, however strange it was that their old men snapped up all their most attractive women.

He kind of—almost—liked them.

The Beehive House was built in a style that Sam thought was current, and that those who concerned themselves with fashions in the houses of the wealthy liked to call *Greek revival*. Tall white columns rose up above a wraparound porch and supported a white-railed wraparound balcony at the second story. Above that a mansard roof climbed to a widow's walk (*or maybe a widows' walk*, Sam thought merrily, wondering exactly how many women would mourn President Young if he ever failed to come back from sea) that in turn surrounded something that looked like a big pedestal, or maybe a pulpit. On top of the pulpit, preaching to all the architectural splendor below, perched a little beehive. In the shadow of the gigantic Tabernacle, it was an acorn lying beside an oak tree.

It was hard to be sure from the outside, but it looked to Sam like a suite or a wing of some sort actually linked the Beehive House and the Lion House together. One big, happy family, then. Really big, if the stories contained even an ounce of truth.

And it was a rare story that didn't contain at least an ounce.

Sam badly wanted to light a cigar, but in the interest of diplomatic decorum, he refrained. He straightened up his bow tie, paced up the walk, and encountered a double-wide white door with no knocker. An engraved plate beside an elegant brass chain read *PULL.*

He pulled: *ding-ding-dong.*

The door opened and Sam found himself smiling stupidly into the face of a clean, pressed, pretty young woman.

"Good afternoon," she said sweetly.

"Yes." He smiled, caught a little off guard. For a moment, he couldn't remember what he was doing here, so he reached into his jacket and produced a Partagás. He waved it at her in a polite hello.

She frowned.

He put the cigar back, abashed.

"If you're looking for President Young, my father's not taking visitors at the moment," the young woman said.

"Your father?" Sam was amused, though of course if the man had thirty wives, he probably had a daughter or two out of the bargain. He knew from calotypes that Young was a serious-looking old goat, but then it was a universal rule that half the world's women, including the pretty ones, had fathers who were less handsome than average. He suppressed an impulse to ask her about her family life and instead cleared his throat officiously and gave his most charming smile. "Your father's expecting me. My name's Clemens, and I'm a U.S. government man."

The girl grinned back at him. "Be careful, Mr. Clemens. Words like that frighten some folks around here."

She led him down a long hall and around a corner and brought him to a door where two big, broad-shouldered men in dark suits, long coats, and hats stood guard. One held a rifle, but they both wore pistols on their hips.

"Mr. Clemens is here to see my father," she told them. "He has an appointment."

They squinted and bared yellow teeth, fierce as any Mississippi keelboat man or logger from the Great North Woods, but they let him in.

Brigham Young's office was bigger than the communications room in which Sam had seen his man George Cannon, earlier in the day. Here, too, there were glass and brass message tubes and a sorting table, but there were only half a dozen of the tubes and the table was a small one, unobtrusively out of the way.

Cannon's room had struck Sam as the working center of a great socio-mechanical brain. Young's looked like the den of a lion. Its walls were painted the confident, masculine red of a hunting lodge, its three large sofas were a brilliant gold, and all the wood, most conspicuous being a deep, broad and tall desk, absolutely clean on top, was stained dark and well-polished. There was a globe in one corner of the room and full bookshelves and that surprised Sam. Hadn't Young been a cabinetmaker, or some similar sort of tradesman in his Yankee, pre-Mormon career?

Two more tall, stone-faced gunmen stood inside the door. A fifth stood by a tall, yellow-draped window, and as Sam coolly looked him over, he thought he saw, just flickering in the corner of the window, a face. He wasn't sure, but he thought, again, that it might be the face of the midget Coltrane.

He fought back a spasm of astonishment.

Should he say something?

Best not to, he decided quickly. He didn't want to take responsibility for anything the midget might do and besides, Young's security guards would certainly catch him any moment.

If he was even really out there, after all.

Two men stood up at the sofas from a tray of tea and Sam crossed the office to shake hands. President Brigham Young wasn't tall, but he wasn't short either, and he was powerfully built. With his curly hair, the beard around his jaw and chin but clean-shaven upper lip, and ox-like shoulders, he looked like a man who knew how to use a plane and chisel.

"Fornication pants!" Young snorted.

Sam froze, unsure he'd heard the man correctly, thinking maybe he was witnessing some rough Mormon attempt at humor.

"He is a modern man, Señor Presidente," the other man said. He was a heavy black gentleman, completely bald and clean-shaven but for a little sharp spike of graying hair beneath his lower lip, and he wore a careful smile on his face.

"That doesn't give him liberty to seduce my daughters," Young barked, "no matter how convenient he, or they, might find the unbuttoning of his pants!"

"I … I …" Sam found himself stuttering, an affliction from which he hadn't realized he suffered. He swallowed hard, to get rid of the fragmented sentences, and tried again. "I hadn't realized that Mr. Levi-Strauss's trousers were so potent," he essayed a disarming joke. "Will it put you more at your ease if I remove them?"

"Mr. Clemens." It wasn't a question, and it was growled. They shook hands. "This is Mr. Juan Jermaine Tomás Salvador María Zerubbabel Armstrong, Ambassador Plenipotentiary to the Kingdom of Deseret from the Republica de los Estados Reunidos de México." He grinned. "Give or take a name or two."

"Joo have no missed one yet," Armstrong said. He radiated gravitas. He and Young both did. If not for the fact that Armstrong also exuded a certain easygoing humor and charm, Sam would have felt daunted by Young's bear-like assault on Sam and his innocent Levi-Strauss pants. Sam shook Ambassador Armstrong's hand, too. "Mr. Clemens. Joo are the United States man, aren't joo?"

"Yes I am," Sam admitted. "The way people talk about me around here, I'm starting to imagine that my arrival was expected."

Crash!

The glass of the tall window exploded inward in a fury of tiny splinters, stinging Sam's cheek and lodging into his curly hair. Sam stumbled back and away from the window as he turned, his eye barely able to follow the blur of action.

There was a man, short but built like a bull, and he had a sword in his hand. No, not a sword, the long fighting knife they called the Arkansas Toothpick. Long hair and beard and buckskins flapped behind the newcomer as he charged.

The bodyguard standing by the window moved, but not fast enough. The intruder threw his body at the bigger man. Before anyone could react he had a forearm around the man's throat and his long, wicked knife pointing directly into his eye.

The other guards froze.

"You're not the midget!" Sam exclaimed in surprise. "You're Rockwell!"

"What?!" Young bellowed.

The Deseret lawman from Fort Bridger stared at Sam with piercing blue eyes in a scarred and weatherbeaten face. "You's expectin' a midget?" he asked.

The Ambassador pivoted to look at Sam with concern. "That is a good question, Señor Clemens. Were joo expecting a midget to come through the window?"

Sam laughed out loud. *Oops.* "No, Ambassador, no, Mr. President, I wasn't. I just … I …"

"I dunno what they told you, Brother Brigham!" Rockwell howled, "And I don't know nothin' about no midgets!" His voice was rough and raw and he smelled like a mountain man from ten feet away. "I don't know what Lee said, but I'm loyal to you like I always been."

"You're holding a knife to my bodyguard's face, Port!" Young roared. He looked like he was about to paw the floor and charge.

The mountain man backed his knife away half an inch. "But you know I'm loyal, don't you? You'll treat me right? You won't listen to whisperin' voices and throw me to the wolves without me gettin' a fair hearin'?"

"Have I ever been unfair to you, Porter?" Veins stood out in Young's neck. "Have I ever been unfair to *anyone*?"

"There's things I gotta tell you, Brother Brigham, there's men as are disloyal, as are plottin'." The blue eyes danced wildly from each of Young's bodyguards to the next. "You ain't listened to Eliza, you gotta listen to me!"

"Put down the knife!"

Rockwell nodded and dropped the weapon to the carpet.

Sam breathed a sigh of relief as Young's bodyguards swarmed him, pulling multiple pistols and blades away from his body and out of his reach. His shoulders slumped like a defeated man, but he had a childlike expression on his face. An expression of hope, Sam thought, and trust, which seemed incredible in light of the affronted, raging irritation clouding the face of Brigham Young.

The door opened and five armed men barged in. At their head stumped a lean, bent man, with a stubbled face and aimlessly drifting eyes. Sam recognized him from Chief Pocatello's corral. Now he openly held a pistol in his hand.

"Hickman!" the mountain man snarled. He tensed and strained like he wanted to jump to the attack, but two of the big bodyguards held him firm.

"Orrin Porter Rockwell," Hickman acknowledged in a nasal drawl. "More fool me, wasting all that time looking for you in Injun territory, and I coulda just sat right here and waited."

He raised his pistol, pointed it at Rockwell's chest and fired.

CHAPTER EIGHT

Sweet Hildegard, that's a lot of guns," Tamerlane O'Shaughnessy whispered to himself.

Another man might have been tempted by the store of weapons. They were shiny and new and some of them looked downright powerful. Tam, though, was already carrying two Maxim Hushers (*What better weapon could there be for a man with a need for discretion and privacy than a gun that killed with a whisper? And to have two of them? An embarrassment of riches, me boy.*) as well as the box of little brass murder beetles. Tam was not a man who collected toys; he was a man who picked up a tool when he needed it to get the job done. Mostly the job was killing someone that bloody deserved it and Tam at the moment found himself well stocked with tools.

He watched the dwarf leave, heading back down the hill to the train station. He might have killed the man then, only the little bastard was carrying that thing the boy called a *machine-gun*. Besides, once lead started to fly, other armed men on the scene inevitably felt it was their business to get involved, so Tam didn't want to start a gunfight right next to a gun *shop* with a gun*smith* in it.

He was looking for an attack situation with a little less risk. He scanned the area around the gun shop and its neighboring farms, noticing the gigantastic looming mountains above, each one the bloody-damn-hell size of Ireland herself, it seemed, and empty as a whore's heart. That's where he needed to get the dwarf, out of town and into the wilderness, or else back into the city and in a blind alley.

He was about to turn to follow the wee circus monkey back down the hill when the gunsmith left his shop and went back into his brick cottage. That left the little boy, sitting all alone in the workshop.

"Curious fellow," Tam muttered, and he stopped to watch. The little boy in the slouch hat pushed a stool over to a workbench and climbed up onto it. There was a vise at the corner of the bench with a long brass gun barrel in it and a magnifying lens poised over it on a mechanical clamping arm. The boy stood on the stool so that he could get a good view down through the lens and crouched there, examining the barrel.

"Weird little freak," Tam muttered. "Thinks he's a fookin' gunsmith, he does." He didn't know why the midget was so in love with the kid.

But he was. And that thought gave Tam an idea.

Some shite about Mohammed and mountains, but he couldn't remember what, exactly.

He pulled one of the Hushers from its holster and checked the bungalow to be sure no one was looking out the windows.

ᏗᏦᎦᏗᏫᏗᏁ

Bang!

A red flower of blood spouted from the mountain man's shoulder and he rocked back in the grip of the big bodyguards.

"Hickman!" President Young shouted, his voice taut with command and anger. "Porter was restrained."

"Yeah, I reckon so," Hickman agreed. "And so are you." He gestured with his pistol at Young, Armstrong, and Clemens and instructed the other thugs: "Tie 'em all up and get 'em on the truck."

"What are joo doing?" demanded the Ambassador. He drew himself up to his full impressive height, like a cat arching its back to hiss or a cobra flaring its hood. Sam thought he would have been intimidated in Hickman's place and envied the Ambassador his charisma.

But Hickman was unimpressed. "I'm takin' you prisoner, fat man," he drawled. "Don't bother threatenin' me with the wounded sentiments of President Tubman. She's far away and the only troops you got local are a couple of them shitbucket Striders, and they ain't even in town."

Clemens didn't resist as a big man roped his hands tightly together behind his back.

"*I* have forces in town." Young's voice was a rattling lid of calm over a well of fury, but the veins on his neck and temple were thick as ropes and his skin had gone the color of a beet.

Hickman grinned. "Only they ain't *your* forces no more, Brigham."

"You're yellow, Hick," Orrin Porter Rockwell coughed. He looked surprisingly vital for a man who had just been shot, but he wasn't struggling against the two men who held him. "You're lily-livered. You're chicken. You shoot me when I can't fight back and then you walk around tall like you done something impressive."

"Helldammit, yes," Hickman agreed with a yellow-toothed leer. "I'd shoot you again right now, blow out your dirty damn brains, only I ain't sure I want you dead quite just yet. I might need you alive for trading. Or for a threat. Or maybe I'll just shoot off your fingers one at a time when I'm bored."

"Traitor!" Young shouted.

"Shut your mouth," Hickman tittered.

Sam heard the rumble of an engine outside and then twin jets of coal exhaust and steam plumed into the room through the shattered window, announcing the arrival of the back end of a smallish steam-truck. It was a boxy cargo vehicle and its tin back gate clattered into the Beehive House's flower beds, unloading two more large, grim-looking men.

"Hoods on the prisoners," Hickman ordered, and one of his captors jammed a bag down over Sam's head. It smelled like apples and burlap, but he could breathe through it well enough. The same man started pushing him—in the direction of the steam-truck, he guessed.

"I guess Lee gave you the dirty work, didn't he?" Rockwell taunted Hickman. "Watch out, Hick. He might have to kill you when it's over, make sure you can't cause him trouble later."

"Shut up, Port," Hickman retorted.

"Porter," Young rumbled.

Sam tripped up some sort of ramp and was thrown to the ground. More apple smell.

"Or what?" Rockwell pressed, ignoring both his captor and his President. "You gonna kill me? You think I care? I suppose it was Lee that had the *balls* to try to pull this off. I just can't figure out where the two of you got the *brains*. Pooled together, you might just have enough smarts to play noughts and crosses against a mule. *Play*, mind you. I ain't sure you could *win*."

"Porter!"

Sam heard footsteps and scuffling on the gangplank behind him.

"No, I don't reckon you care if you live or die, Port," Hickman admitted. "That's always been your charm. But you'll care if I shoot *Brigham*. Hell, that was my instructions when I come here and I got half a mind to do it anyway."

Rockwell said nothing. Sam heard thuds and grunts around him as other men were tossed into the steam-truck with him and then the *clank* of the truck's gate being shut again.

D.J. Butler

Absalom Fearnley-Standish sat on a bench on the deck of the *Liahona*, sipping a lemonade alone.

He wasn't moping, no, he was made of stronger stuff than that, he tried to tell himself, but he was in a reflective mood. He'd felt reflective since Annie had rejected him.

He knew her name was Annie because he'd asked her. He'd been a little out of sorts since he'd met the Mexican Striderman ... Striderwoman ... *Master Sergeant Jackson*, and he'd thought he could use some pleasant diversion. He'd found her below decks, standing outside a cabin door and listening at it. That didn't seem like very ladylike behavior, he told himself in retrospect, but it was cardinal that a gentleman didn't dwell on the unladylike or ungentlemanly behaviors of others, and frankly, at the time he hadn't even noticed it. At the time he'd just been happy to see her.

"I wonder if you would enjoy another lemonade, Annie," he'd said, and then, to avoid any misunderstanding, he'd added, "I mean, with me, on the deck, and perhaps together with a little conversation. I'm not just a man of action, you know." That should have reminded her of his courage in standing up to Lee and Hickman. Then he'd given her his best Harrovian smile. "I think you'll find I can be quite charming."

She had looked him in the eye in the sputtering light of the hallway electricks and said, without missing a beat, "If you don't get out of here right now, Absalom Fearnley-Standish, I'll stick my boot so far up your backside you'll be picking leather out from between your teeth for a week."

He liked to think he had reacted decisively.

It was not a situation his father had prepared him for, nor the Foreign Office. Competing norms milled about in his head and collided. *A real lady doesn't talk like a sailor,* he remembered his mother saying to him, preparing him to meet a female second cousin who was decidedly not an acceptable match. *A gentleman doesn't strike a lady,* he'd heard from a schoolteacher when as a young man he'd been badly beaten by a larger, older girl, and was silently congratulating himself on landing at least one good blow to her nose. *A man never backs down from a fight,* they'd told him at Harrow. More than once. His professional training won out over the lessons of his childhood traumas and, though it seemed to him that a stuttering eternity might have passed, he was reasonably certain that it had only been a moment or two. *A Foreign Office man always practices discretion.* He knew when he wasn't wanted.

He'd turned on his heel and left her to her eavesdropping in the corridor.

Rotten little tease, he reflected, nursing his solitary lemonade in the afternoon sunshine. Well, this was the Great Salt Lake City, anyway, and really, he had no time for women. They could only distract him from his mission. From his two missions, he reminded himself.

146

A cavalcade of American soldiers overtook them and continued on ahead. Their horses were clocksprung, which in itself was fascinating; clockwork was still a relatively new technology, and very exciting. Absalom had seen clocksprung curiosities in London—a clocksprung rector and church choir at a fair in the little London borough of Wetwick, and a clocksprung violinist in a private salon exhibition one evening— but it was in the American South that the technology had flowered. First under Eli Whitney, and then driven by Horace Hunley and his team, southern inventors and engineers had revolutionized their agriculture on its basis.

Absalom had a desire to see the horses. He wondered for a moment whether he should care about their presence from a professional point of view or observe it very carefully, but he let it drop when he saw Dick Burton glued to the rail, staring at the cavalrymen. On the one hand, he knew Burton would properly observe and note anything that mattered to the success of their joint diplomatic mission—Burton's mission, really, though Absalom would never tell *him* that. On the other hand, he resented Burton's overbearing manner and his presence generally and he didn't want to be seen paying attention to anything Burton was interested in.

He let the horses pass and sipped his lemonade.

Burton turned away from his observation and saw him. "Be careful of the sun, Abigail," he growled. "You may get wrinkles."

"Ambassador Fearnley-Standish, blast you!" Absalom snapped. He dug into his jacket pocket to pull out his Patent Metallic Note-Paper-Book and then felt a little foolish for it. His notes for future memoranda of reprimand seemed petty in light of all the drawn guns and knives he'd seen in the last twenty-four hours. "Look, if you must know, I have a sister. Her name is Abigail, as it happens. Last night I ... I was excited ..."

Burton sneered at him. The scars running up both sides of his face looked like horns, giving his face a devilish aspect to it that frightened Absalom—just a bit—even in the noonday sun. "Yes," he said, "I saw just how *excited* you were, Abby!"

Absalom knocked over his lemonade in his haste to start scribbling in his Note-Paper-Book and Burton stomped away. *Impertinence. Insubordination. Woman's name.* His pencil shattered and Absalom snorted in impotent rage as he threw it over the side of the steam-truck.

The *Liahona* burst out of the canyon like a mouse racing out of a hole in the wall. The mountains fell away in cliffs, dropping thousands of sheer, snow-mantled feet into short, rolling foothills. Ahead, beginning already in the foothills, lay a gleaming city of brass and glass and sparkling plascrete broken only by the green of parks and plazas, and beyond it all a vast lake the same color as the sky.

It was pretty. It was all pretty, it was huge and impressive and shiny and new and it all worked, clean white steam rising up into the pale blue sky rather than the thick black murk that hung like a rag over central London. There was something about the plascrete here as well that made it prettier, Absalom thought, even prettier than what he'd seen in London or Paris or New York. It sparkled, like it had bits of china ground up into it or something. Maybe it was the mountain air.

The big steam-truck wheezed to a stop at a crossroads, right at the edge where the foothills flattened into valley floor. He didn't think they could have arrived yet and, out of curiosity, Absalom stood and walked to the rail. To the left and right, tar-paved roads curled around the circumference of the enormous valley, punctuated by brass towers, brick farmhouses, and irrigated fruit orchards. Ahead, the road plunged directly into the city, swallowed immediately by the steel, brick, brass and plascrete of tall buildings. In the center of the crossroads stood a small hut with a man hanging out of its doorway, waving a little red flag at the *Liahona*.

"What is it? Don't you know I'm badly behind schedule as it is?" Captain Dan Jones bellowed from the rail at the man. Burton stuck to the man like his own shadow. Absalom kept his distance, but stayed within earshot.

"You're diverted!" the semaphorist yelled back, and he waved something in his other hand that looked like it might be a glass tube with a bit of paper inside. "Everyone is, they even sent riders around to the farms!"

"Is it Indians?" Jones roared. He looked like he didn't care if it was Indians or not, and if the flag-waver told him that the Great Salt Lake City was being invaded by the Ute, Paiute, Gosiute, Shoshone, Navajo, Blackfoot, Crow, and Apache peoples simultaneously, he still wasn't going to change his course. "Fire? Crickets?"

"I don't know!" The gateman tossed his flag inside the little booth and shut the door. "All I know is it's got something to do with the Twelve and you're the last traffic I'm expecting down the Canyon. Can I get a ride to the Tabernacle?"

The *Liahona* crawled to the center of the Great Salt Lake City. The problem was that all the traffic—or very nearly all of it, anyway—was going the same direction. Horse-drawn carriages and wagons competed with steam-trucks and even the occasional clocksprung beast for the same space on the tar and Absalom thought that the pedestrians walking (again, in the same direction) on the sparkling plascrete walkways would arrive before he did. They walked with a sense of urgency and constantly looked at pocket watches.

He looked ahead for the brigade of American cavalrymen, but they were nowhere in sight. A slow tide of top hats, frock coats, buckskin jackets, boots, wheels, buckles, horseshoes, and gears seeped along, bearing him with it, disappearing into something that looked like a giant plascrete egg, a vast bald genius skull sprouting patches of green vegetable hair in zigzagging rows and propped up with a wild whirl of pipes running straight out from it in every direction. He looked down side streets and saw that all the traffic everywhere was bound for the same place.

Good, he thought. *No,* excellent. *If everyone in the Great Salt Lake City is in the same place, it should be very easy to find Abigail, or at least figure out how to find her.* And her husband, that scoundrel Orrin Porter Rockwell, was a famous man.

Unexpectedly, the *Liahona* lumbered right, dropped down a steep ramp, and went underground. Absalom, along with all the other passengers on the deck other than that obstinate ruffian Dick Burton, ducked, but the top of the entrance was several feet over the top of the wheelhouse and the sudden collective cringe was unnecessary. It was an enormous gate, and the space it opened into was a mammoth Avernian shed full of steam-trucks of every size and description.

The *Liahona* shuddered to a slow halt. "Get everybody off!" Captain Jones shouted to crewmen on the deck and then he was first down the ladder. *Anxious to find the little boy,* Absalom thought, and he admired the man's doggedness and integrity.

The big steam-truck had come to rest in a vast plascrete hangar, surrounded by smaller craft. A gleaming brass arch gave egress, two lines of inlaid brass text pounded into the stone above it presumably both identifying the same place. *SALT LAKE CITY TABERNACLE,* said the line in English. Above it, about the same length, was a row of squiggly gibberish that Absalom couldn't decipher.

Burton went over the side close on the Captain's heels. Absalom waited until Burton had disappeared into the building, before he, too, joined the trickling migration off the ship and into the bowels of the Great Salt Lake City. He had clambered down awkwardly, reminding himself that the fact that he didn't climb like a monkey was evidence of progress in his family tree, and nodding and smiling patiently at the stopped and frustrated flow of exiting persons waiting for him to finish and get out of the way.

He was still among the earlier of the departing passengers; none of them had any idea why they had been diverted from the station they expected to arrive at and the crew couldn't seem to explain it to them. Absalom worried for a moment for Annie's safety in the event of a passenger riot, until he remembered her promise to fill the gaps in his teeth with boot leather. He decided he was sure she could take care of herself, straightened his hat and his dignity, and headed for the Tabernacle.

Down and then up, past some heavily-trafficked side corridors, and then Absalom stepped out onto a plascrete landing and froze, astonished. The Tabernacle was immense.

The building must consist almost entirely of a single room. It was a vast auditorium: an amphitheater with a dozen—no, thirty—no, fifty?—rows of seating in wide, scalloped brass alcoves, climbing up into dark shadows out of view, all looking down on a large stage. Around the rim of the stage were a dozen brass Franklin Poles, each sprouting up into a blue-shimmering globe of electricks. Three further Poles, of the same shape only taller, rose up on the center of the stage itself, over a row of fine-looking stuffed chairs and a tall, stair-mounted pulpit.

Absalom's heart sank. There must be thirty thousand people in the room, crawling along plascrete ledges, greeting each other calmly, moving serenely into seats. He saw Captain Jones a hundred feet away, plowing with strong arms through the crowd, calling out queries whether anyone had seen his midshipman, John Moses.

Even if Abigail were here, and he had no idea if she would be, he'd never be able to find her.

"Absalom!" a female voice shouted.

He whirled, half-hoping it might be Annie, half hoping it might be Master Sergeant Jackson—

—and was astonished to see that it was his sister Abigail. She was dressed in a man's waistcoat, a voluminous skirt and pointy-toed leather boots like a vaquero might wear. He almost laughed out loud at the incongruous sight of her.

"Abby!" he shouted. He tried to embrace her despite her clownish appearance and his sister slapped him in the face.

"Didn't Port find you on the trail?" she demanded. She looked furious.

"Port?" He felt flushed, his cheek stung. "Porter? Do you mean Rockwell, the man who abducted you?"

"You poor fool," she said, and she really seemed to pity him, "don't you know you're in danger?" She grabbed Absalom's elbow and tried to drag him back in the direction from which he'd come, but he resisted. He'd been pushed around by enough women in the last twenty-four hours; he was going to take a stand. "I only came to check the passengers of the *Liahona* just in case. Port was supposed to stop you from ever getting this far."

"Yes, I know I'm in danger!" he hissed. He wanted to yell, but he was conscious of the crowd all around him, farmers and tradesmen and merchants, all dressed like they'd put down their occupation at a moment's notice and come to the Tabernacle, all asking each other what was going on and all denying any knowledge. He was an outsider here and this was not the time or place to make a figure of himself. "I've had a knife at my throat—that was your Port, I'd like to add—and I've had guns pointed at me and been kidnapped by red Indians and … and … threatened with a boot in my posterior!" He cringed inwardly, feeling that he had organized his rant poorly, from a rhetorical point of view. He should have kept his list to three, and should have saved the most impressive of his complaints for last … he realized he'd run out of steam and stopped talking. "Yes," he said. "You're in danger, too. I've come to rescue you."

His sister looked puzzled and a little annoyed. She was younger than he was and they shared a naturally fair complexion, but the sun had darkened and hardened and aged her, and her furrowed eyebrows shot out the hard, angry stare of a frontier woman. He tried not to cringe under it.

"Port said you were a diplomat." Her accent was changing, too. She still sounded English, but a little less so—her vowels were flattening out, her voice was hardening. "He said the Queen was sending you with that explorer, Captain Burton."

"Yes," Absalom agreed. "Your Mr. Rockwell tried to frighten me off, but I came, anyway. He did this." He pointed to the ruined brim of his hat. "I had to call in every favor I was owed and promise more than one favor myself, but I arranged to have the Foreign Office send me, so I could take you away." He faltered a bit under the stare. "Take you back … home. Back home to England."

"I don't want to go back."

"But … you were kidnapped." This was not how he had imagined the conversation going. He felt a little indignant at her resistance.

"No, I wasn't."

"I went to a lot of trouble, you know."

"That's not my fault."

"You disappeared. You had been seen with that scoundrel, that wild man Rockwell, and then you disappeared and you said nothing at all to anyone in the family, and nothing to any young lady of our acquaintance. I know because I asked them all."

She shrugged, an unladylike, American, and vaguely vulgar gesture. "I eloped. Are you armed?"

"Eloped?" He could scarcely credit the idea. This was not the girl he had grown up with. "Were you mad? Are you mad *now*?"

She shrugged again. "It seemed romantic at the time and besides, no one in the family was going to approve my marriage to a wild mountain man. Least of all Father." She squinted at him. "You should be armed."

"Why should I be armed?" Absalom felt off-balance, surprised, stranded. "You used to be a very reserved young woman, I remember. What happened to you?"

Abby laughed. "Life happened, dear brother. Marriage happened. I came West, I learned to run a tavern, I grew up."

"You run a tavern?"

"A hotel and saloon. One of the most famous in the Kingdom." Her face relaxed for a moment into happiness and pride, then hardened again. "Now you must leave." She pulled a dull, long-barreled six-shooter from under her skirt and pressed it into his hands. It was a much bigger gun than his, less sophisticated, less delicate, more likely, he knew, to kill a man.

"What are you afraid of?" he asked, refusing the gun. "I already have a gun, thank you very much. And I can't go. I am an emissary of Her Majesty." He sighed. "I suppose I should be grateful it isn't a brothel."

"Yes, dear brother," she said, and forced the heavy pistol into his hand, wrapping his fingers around its smooth grip. "You should be grateful. And you should take a second gun—it can't hurt to be too well armed in this country. And yes, I know you have a mission. That's the problem. Port thinks you're being set up. Port thinks something terrible is going to happen and you're going to be blamed for it."

ＵＪＧＪＰＪＩ

"Brothers and Sisters, thank you very much for your attendance. I'm afraid it is my duty to burden you with the weight of a terrible announcement."

The speaker was a burly fellow, with a round face, a square little chin-beard, and the accent of a man from the English industrial midlands. He held a speaking tube pulled up to his mouth that threw his words out through enormous brass cones hanging high in the ceiling, and his voice was calm but strained. He was dwarfed by the pulpit at which he stood, but any man would have been and Poe couldn't tell whether he was tall or broad or a midget from his vantage point up in the scalloped terraces of the Tabernacle.

Thinking of midgets, he wondered again where Jedediah Coltrane had ended up. He hadn't seen the little man since the hypocephalus debate aboard the *Liahona*. That in itself was troubling. Coltrane could be dead, somewhere out on the sandy soil of the Wyoming Territory with an electro-blade in his back. Add to that the fact that the scarab beetles had disappeared with him, that Poe had missed his scheduled meeting with the Madman Pratt, and that Poe's cover had been blown, he felt that, if disaster had not already struck, it was looming. Now he badly wanted to salvage whatever he could of it.

Also, he wanted to get away from Roxie.

"The news is distressing enough that in the interest of time, we will dispense with an opening hymn and prayer." The burly man almost cracked a smile, though the expression was fleeting. "And there will not be refreshments."

Poe looked over his shoulder and saw only the milling sheepskin jackets, waistcoats, and hats of the crowd. How to find Orson Pratt? He scanned the multitude. It was vast and he would never pick the needle of his man out of such a haystack. Was there any way to make Pratt come to him? He couldn't think of any, short of seizing the speaking tubes and asking for the fellow directly. Was there any way to calculate where in the building he might find his man?

Poe's eye fell on the stage in the center of the building. The stocky gentleman continued to talk and the plush chairs behind him were slowly filling with grave-faced men.

"President Young has been shot."

A hush fell over the entire enormous throng. Poe could hear men and women breathing around him and the here-and-there cries of small children, like seabirds wheeling above the gray vista of a lonely beach.

Poe recognized the men in the chairs from Robert's files. There was Wilford Woodruff, the obsessive diarist, and Lorenzo Snow, the vegetarian, and David Patten, bloody-handed victor of the Battle of Crooked River. These were the famous Twelve Apostles. They were taking chairs that, he now saw, must be reserved for them.

Orson Pratt was one of them. He wasn't on the stage yet, but if he came here, that's where he'd be headed. Poe found steps leading down to the bottom of the Tabernacle and took advantage of the stunned stillness of the crowd to push his way along them, greatcoat flapping heavy around him with the weight of the four canopic jars in its pockets.

"Good Danite men were on the scene," the Englishman continued. George Quayle Cannon, Poe realized who the man was as he headed for the floor, the so-called *Mormon Richelieu*, whatever that was supposed to mean. "I have been told that Brother Orrin Porter Rockwell was also injured, defending President Young as he has done for so long, and as he defended Brother Joseph before that. The Danites removed President Young from his office to give him into the care of a physician but he could not be saved. I do not know the fate of Brother Rockwell. I understand that our men have, however, apprehended the shooter."

Poe reached the bottom of the stair and found his way blocked. Around him, a crowd of bereft faces stared up at the stage that now loomed over his head. Two steps forward would put Poe on the lowest floor of the Tabernacle, and another six would put him at the short staircase that climbed onto the stage itself. He couldn't take those steps, though, because a tall, heavy man in a coat and cravat, with a long pistol at his hip, barred the way with a glower.

Poe could see more of the Apostles now, the thin-lipped Orson Hyde with unruly hair and the clear-browed Heber Kimball with no hair at all, whispering solemnly to each other as they mounted the stairs to take their seats. "Excuse me, brother," he said politely to the staring guard, "but I must speak with Apostle Pratt. May I pass?"

"Why don't you take a seat ... brother?" the big man grunted back. His voice sounded like he was one-half Danish and the other half bear.

"I regret to say," Cannon continued from the pulpit, "that the First Presidency is therefore dissolved. The Quorum of the Twelve Apostles, I have been informed, will meet, along with other leaders, to deliberate how to reconstitute the Presidency. I understand that those meetings will begin tomorrow morning at seven, at the Lion House ... so if any of the Twelve or the Seventy are in the Tabernacle and haven't yet been informed, please join us at that hour. The Deseret Hotel has already agreed to make accommodations for those coming from out of town to participate."

Pratt moved into view in the well of the Tabernacle, drifting from some unseen entrance towards the stage. He was bald and bearded and frayed and rumpled, looking every inch the *Madman* he was named. He walked with his head bowed and twitching, lips mumbling some soundless litany.

"Look," Poe pointed him out to the Dane, "there he is. If you will just let me past—"

The Dane snorted and grabbed Poe by the front of his coat.

Poe didn't want to hurt the big man. He also didn't want to attract attention. But he felt his mission objectives all slipping out of his grasp, he was frustrated and desperate. So when the guard grabbed him by his coat Poe seized the big man by his thumbs and thrust them backwards without mercy.

The Dane gasped and lurched to his knees. Poe looked around quickly to see if anyone had noticed what he was doing, but the crowd was rapt, unable to take its attention off the pulpit.

The big man whimpered.

Pratt was at the foot of the stairs.

Poe was out of time.

He threw the Dane sideways, trying to get him out of the way without hurting him more than was necessary, and rushed forward.

He crossed the open floor in three long steps—

—Pratt moved up the staircase—

—Poe heard the guard scramble back to his feet, cursing, and come after him—

—Poe grabbed the Madman by the elbow, coughing. He knew he looked like a crazed gypsy himself, with his hat and his greasy hair and smoked glasses and fingerless gloves and bulky coat. He had only one chance.

"I am the Egyptian," he hissed desperately into the Apostle's ear as the man turned and stared at him indignantly. He tried to hold his lungs together by sheer force of will. "I come seeking the knowledge of the air."

"You're coming with me, you crazy beggar!" Poe felt the Dane's big hands grab him and jerk him away.

Pratt stared, confused, uncertain.

Poe couldn't let it end this way. He stepped backwards, close into his attacker, got a leg under the man's instep and his body under the man's weight—and threw him forward over his shoulder, onto the ground.

Thud!

Poe tossed his man away from the stage, planting him close in against the base of the wall, so that the angle would hide any more scuffling from most of the audience. Hopefully the distraction of the speech and the setting would do the rest.

The big man writhed as he flipped, and as he hit the plascrete the Dane was already pulling his pistol, thumbing back the hammer.

"Stop it!" Pratt commanded, and Poe and the guard both froze.

Orson Pratt scuttled forward, off the stage and back into the well. "This man is with me," he hissed to the big guard. "Thank you … er, brother, for your caution. As we … as we heard today," he gestured vaguely to the pulpit and George Cannon, "your care is … is valuable. Thank you."

The big man looked dubious.

Poe braced himself to be shot.

"Please return to your post," Pratt continued. "This man is not a danger, but … but the next one might be."

"We profoundly regret to tell you one more thing," Cannon continued, "but we feel that we must." His voice echoed loud and brassy from the ceiling cones. "The man who shot President Young has been identified. His name is Samuel Clemens."

As if this news had freed him, the Dane backed away. He glared one last time at Poe, uncocked his pistol and returned to his station. Further around the base of the stage, other guards, whose attention had been briefly caught, now looked away. The crowd above appeared not to have noticed.

Poe sighed with relief and adjusted his glasses.

Cannon wasn't finished. "Mr. Clemens is an agent in the pay of the United States government."

He paused.

If a silence could be thunderingly loud, Poe thought, *this is it.*

"Come on," Pratt whispered, and grabbed Poe by the sleeve. He dragged the younger man down a plascrete hallway that cut underneath the lower tiers of seating, the entrance by which the Apostles had all come into the building. "Say it again," he said. There was an excited light in his eyes, as if he were thrilled.

Poe didn't feel thrilled. He felt off-balance, discombobulated, entirely outside of the foreseeable strands of his web of planning. *Could Sam Clemens really have shot Brigham Young? What would have been the point of that?* If the American government assassinated the President of the Kingdom on the eve of the outbreak of hostilities, what could that do but precipitate Deseret into the war, and on the side of the seceding Southern states?

"What?" he asked. It made no sense.

"Start over," the Madman insisted. "Who are you?"

Are we playing a game? Poe thought, but he complied. "I am the Egyptian," he repeated. "I come seeking the knowledge of the air."

The old man beamed. "I am the Seer, keeper of the knowledge of the air. By what token shall I know thee, Boatman?"

"Boatman?" Poe asked. *What?*

"I mean, *Egyptian*. By what token shall I know thee, Egyptian?" Pratt blushed.

Who was the Boatman? What kind of double game was going on here? Did Robert know there was a Boatman? "You shall know me by the four sons of Horus, which I bear," he answered, according to the script.

"Very good." The Madman quivered with excitement. "Do you have them here?"

Poe nodded. "Do you want them now?" *What had the Boatman brought, or what was he supposed to bring—are there more mysterious canopic jars out there?*

"Yes! Give them to me." Pratt held out his hands, which trembled as if he were a drunkard with a bad case of the shakes.

"And now," George Cannon finished, "I will turn the time over to better speakers than I am. Most of you, I suppose, know Brother John Lee, especially those of you from the southern valleys. I know that all of you know who he is."

Poe shrugged out of his heavy coat and handed it over to Orson Pratt. The Apostle grinned to feel the weight in his hands and positively danced into the garment, smiling from ear to ear. "Thank you," he said, patting down the bulky pockets and visibly counting them *one-two-three-four.* "Thanks to your Mr. Jefferson Davis, to whatever extent he knows what is going on, and to your Mr. Robert Lee, Colonel Lee, that is, and especially to your Mr. Horace Hunley and his mechanicks!"

Oh, Robert, Poe thought. *What insanity have you gotten me involved in? Who is this Madman Pratt, and what is he up to?*

And what infernal devices did Whitney's boys build for him?

"You will not have forgotten that you owe me some papers as well," he reminded Pratt.

"Schematics!" snapped the Apostle. "Of course I haven't forgotten." He looked around him as if suspecting eavesdroppers, then leaned in close to whisper into Poe's ear. "Tomorrow morning at eight," he said. "Come to the north entrance to this building. You'll get what's coming to you then."

He turned to go and Poe grabbed his lapel. "You'll understand, sir, that this makes me nervous. I expected you to give me the documents *today*."

"And *I* expected *you*," Pratt grunted fiercely, "at the *water station!* It's late, do you understand? I am out of time, I could not possibly have gotten these any later! Do you imagine that I carry around airship plans in my pockets at all times, waiting for tardy secret agents, dressed all to catch the eye like Harlequin in some Italian comedy? Ha!" He snorted like a horse, shook himself free of Poe's grasp, and shuffled away, back down the hallway and out of the Tabernacle.

Poe leaned against the cool plascrete wall, wondering what was next. *Could Sam Clemens be the Boatman?* he wondered. His craft, the *Jim Smiley*, was amphibious, as he had neatly demonstrated at the crossing of the Bear River. And if he was the Boatman, had he traded with Pratt for the same schematics Poe sought? What had he offered in trade?

Had Sam Clemens shot Brigham Young in exchange for airship schematics?

But how would that make any sense? Was it worth deliberately getting the Kingdom of Deseret into the war on the side of the seceding states, just to be able to have the schematics of weapons now in the hands of one's enemies? It didn't hold together.

But Cannon had said something about the leadership succession. What had it been? He had said that the Quorum of the Twelve Apostles would meet to decide who the next President would be.

Could that be it? Clemens had killed Young to clear the way so that Orson Pratt could become President of the Kingdom of Deseret. In which case, maybe the Boatman's trade was entirely different from Poe's. Maybe Clemens wasn't going to get the schematics; maybe what he got in trade was the promise of the new President to enter the war on the side of the Union and the North.

And then what? Clemens gets executed, a sacrificed pawn? He's pardoned, or surreptitiously freed and allowed to escape in the night by the new President?

Poe shook his head. Not enough information.

"You all likely know that Brother Lee is one of the chieftains among our Danite brothers," the speaker at the pulpit went on. "What you may not realize is that he is also the adopted son of President Young." Cannon paused and looked down, as if struggling with emotion. "At his request, Brother Lee will now say a few words to the congregation about his father."

George Cannon stepped back and took a seat. He sat behind the row of Apostles, Poe noticed, but three of them immediately turned back and held a brief, whispered conversation with the man.

Have we played into their hands? Poe wondered. Perhaps Whitney's boys had devised some terrible weapon, and he, Poe, had just delivered it to the Madman, who as the Kingdom's next President would turn that same weapon against the defenseless troops of Virginia, Alabama and South Carolina.

Perhaps if he showed up at eight o'clock the next morning, Pratt would have him killed. Perhaps Clemens would pull the trigger himself as his last act before he fled the Kingdom. Clemens or his Irish thug with the Henry rifle.

Another man took the pulpit. He had a weary smile between protruding jug ears and hadn't shaved for a day or two. He wore a long brown overcoat, yellow waistcoat, and a red bowtie. Compared to all the long beards behind him and in the stands, he looked like an eastern dandy, but he had an animal air about him, something in his step that gave him away to Poe as a fighter and a man of action.

Poe had already seen the man; Lee and his scraggly, whiny-voiced henchman, Bill Hickman, had found Poe in the Shoshone stockade only the night before and had threatened him before being faced down by a combination of various men, including the two Englishmen and the Yankee Sam Clemens.

Lee gripped the edges of the podium firmly, as if he or it or both might collapse without the mutual support. Then he opened his mouth and spoke in a pleasant, tired baritone.

"Brothers and Sisters, everything is going to be all right."

There was a collective sigh in the gigantic building and then the hum of murmured conversation, as if tens of thousands of bees had been holding their breaths and now, at the signal of their queen, they could again begin to buzz.

The doors through which Orson Pratt had exited were kicked open, and in walked a handful of soldiers. They wore the hats, insignia, and pistols of Virginia cavalrymen and at their head strode a paunchy man with gnarled and ludicrously overgrown reddish-brown hair climbing both jaws but stopping short of his chin and upper lip. He wore a Captain's star and brass scales on both shoulders and as he walked his hand rode on the hilt of a long cavalry saber swinging from his belt.

Poe hesitated. The soldier was a Virginian and for a moment Poe wrestled with an impulse to approach the man, reveal his own rank and demand to know what the Captain's instructions were.

But of course that was silly.

Poe looked down deferentially, scraped backwards, and got out of the soldiers' path.

"Brothers and sisters," the man Lee said again, "I do not know why the United States government decided it had to murder my father ... *our* father ... our *prophet*."

Poe crept out of the hallway and looked around at the filled seats. His audience hung on Lee's every word.

"But I know this." He raised a warning, instructive finger, his face was stern and impassioned and patriotic. "They shall not get away with this foul crime. I will not permit it. *We* will not permit it."

The soldiers marched up the stairs and onto the platform.

"*Our friends* will not permit it."

He fell silent and let the import of his words sink in. The murmurs rose to a high pitch and he waited for them to fade.

The soldiers came to attention in front of the seated Apostles. Poe looked at the faces of the Kingdom's leaders. Some of them looked stricken, some fearful, some resolute. None of them seemed surprised by the presence of the soldiers.

"Brothers and sisters," John Lee continued. "Allow me to introduce one of our friends. This is Captain Everett Morgan of the Third Virginia Cavalry and these are some of his men. Captain Morgan will be assisting us to maintain order in this confusing time."

Lee stepped slightly to one side and Morgan joined him, pulling up a speaking tube and talking into it. "Good people of the Kingdom of Deseret," he said gruffly, "the great State of Virginia greets you. At the request of your leadership, the men of my unit will be deployed in the Great Salt Lake City to keep the peace."

Robert, Poe thought, *is this your doing? Plots within plots. Is this a countermove to the Union plot of which I am unaware? Did Robert learn of Clemens's mission after he had sent me and send in the cavalry to assist? Will Everett Morgan and his men arrest Orson Pratt along with the Union soldiers?*

Or is there some other game going on here?

Not enough, not enough information. Poe banged one fist into the cup of his other hand in frustration.

"In addition," the cavalryman continued, "please be aware that there is a regiment of Massachusetts infantry at large in the city. If you see them, please do not render them any assistance and inform your leaders of their location. You are likely to see gunfire this afternoon and maybe tonight, between us and the men of Massachusetts. Whatever you see, or think you see, I ask that you remain indoors. Defend yourself against the Massachusetts men if you are compelled, but do not attempt to render assistance to the Third Virginia or otherwise become involved in any way. Thank you."

The Captain handed the speaking tube back to Lee and stepped away again. Murmurs rose again.

Poe wondered who could give him more information. Clemens, if he could find the man, but he must certainly be in custody. Or if not, if Cannon was lying about that, then the Union man would be in hiding.

"In order to avoid confusion," Lee added, "immediately following this meeting, I will ensure that Captain Morgan and his men are dressed in *gray* uniforms. If you see men in blue military uniforms, you should assume that they are soldiers of the United States military and you should report them to your Elders or High Priests as soon as possible. I must add my voice to the urging of Captain Morgan. Brothers and sisters, I am sorry to say it, but there will be shooting tonight on the streets of the Great Salt Lake City. I must insist that you protect yourselves and your young ones. If possible, if you do not need to be in town for tomorrow morning's meetings, I suggest that you go out to your farms, or visit family in Ogden or Provo, if you must."

Poe left the hallway and started back the way he had come. The Danish guard didn't even notice as he passed, too intent on watching what was happening on the stage.

"Brothers and sisters," Lee finished, "for now, please go back to your homes and your shops. Pack some necessaries to get out of Salt Lake for a day or two, collect your children. Pray for President Young's soul and for the Twelve and the Seventy, but please don't be worried. The situation is entirely under our control."

Burton, Poe decided. Surely the Englishman must be an ally and maybe he would even be a source of information.

CHAPTER NINE

I gather at least some of you gentlemen know each other," Sam said dryly.

He would have liked a lit Partagás between his teeth, but his hands were tied behind him, there was a burlap sack over his head, and his body bounced along in the cargo space of a steam-truck that, he thought, could only be generating that many bumps by driving over a mountain-sized pile of armadillos.

First things first.

He felt a wall against the small of his back and he began inching his way up it into sitting position.

"The sons of bitches're probably listenin', so be careful, but hell, yeah, I know President Young." It was Rockwell's voice, hard and twangy like dried gut, but muffled. Sam guessed he was hearing it not only through the sack over his own head, but probably through a sack covering Rockwell's head, too. "I thought he knew me, too, but I guess he musta figured old Bill Hickman and John Lee were more trustworthy. Was it the saloon, Brigham? Was that what turned you against me?"

"Peace, Brother Porter." Remarkably, Sam thought, Young's voice did sound peaceful, though moments earlier Sam would have been unsurprised to see the man rip off human heads with his bare hands. Peaceful, with a little truck-caused vibrato. "I see that I've made a mistake."

Sam was sitting up now and he turned his attention to his hood. He shook his head vigorously—the sack was loose and he thought it might come off easily, but for his own thick, curly hair, which caught at it and held it in place.

"I ain't worried about *me*, Brother Brigham, I'm worried about *you*. 'Cut not thy hair,' Brother Joseph told me, 'and no bullet or blade can harm thee.' I ain't scared of dying."

"I do not wish to quibble," Ambassador Armstrong intoned in his deep voice, "but I saw joo take a bullet only a few minutes ago."

"I'm *shot*," Rockwell admitted sullenly. "I ain't *harmed*."

Sam kept shaking his head. His nostrils were full of the smell of apples and started to tickle.

"There's no reason to fear dying, regardless," Young said, and now something of the gruff tone returned. "God's great work will roll on, His mighty machine will continue to pump and churn and perform its great and mysterious marvels. If four little, nondescript cogs such as the four of us are taken from one slot and put into another to perform a different task for a while, it matters not at all in the eternal scheme of things."

"*Achoo!*" Sam sneezed on a downward shake of his head and the sacking flew off, hitting the truck floor in a cloud of dust.

"*Salud,*" the Ambassador offered.

Sam looked around. The back of the steam-truck was just a big empty box, dimly illuminated by slices of daylight cutting around the back door that doubled as a gangplank. The other three men had all also managed to struggle into sitting position, Sam now saw. Their captors might be sitting up front, but wherever they were, Sam couldn't see them.

"Thank you," Sam said.

Rockwell's head snapped up. "I can hear you better now, Clemens. Someone take the sack off your face?"

Sam laughed. "I sneezed it off. Just an everyday marvel performed by one of God's nondescript little cogs."

"Can joo see the men? Are they watching us?"

"No," Sam told them. "We're alone in some kind of cargo space. I assume you all can smell the stink of apples just as well as I can. Our captor-cogs must be performing *their* share of the Lord's marvels by driving the truck."

"Fools mock, but they shall mourn," Brigham Young said grimly.

"I don't recognize the reference," Sam admitted, "and I thought I was familiar with the Bible." He looked at Rockwell. The man's buckskin shirt was soaked in blood, but the floor wasn't. He seemed to have bled for a while and then stopped. "For a man who's been shot, Mr. Rockwell, you look like you're doing alright to me."

"No bullet or blade," Rockwell repeated, nodding his sack-shrouded head.

"It's from the Book of Ether," Young sniffed, as if he were repeating something that every idiot knew.

"Ether." Sam didn't recognize the name. "Is that the stuff in outer space or the stuff that puts you to sleep?"

"Both!" Rockwell guffawed.

"Porter!"

Rockwell hung his head. "Sorry, Brother Brigham."

"It is good that joo mock, a little," Ambassador Armstrong offered. Sam almost laughed. The combination of the Ambassador's accent and the sight of three men with sacks over their heads made him feel like he was in some sort of comic medicine show. "Mockery is the health of a democracy. But joo must not mock too much and joo must not mock to hurt. Joo mock to tell the truth."

"I don't intend to hurt, Mr. Ambassador," Sam deferred to the other man. "I just don't understand. I don't see how it is that Mr. Young can know that he's a cog in God's great machine and that if he dies, God will just move him somewhere else and give him another job. I can't even imagine what that would be. Personally, if this little jaunt ends in my death, I hope the good Lord reassigns me to the haunting of Mr. Hickman. But how does Mr. Young know, one way or the other? It's the certainty that I feel I have to mock. I poke fun at it in order to deflate it."

"The question you want to ask me isn't *how does Mr. Young know*," Young asserted. He had an almost-angry edge to his voice and a disturbing amount of dignity, for a man with an apple sack over his head.

"No?" Sam asked. He hadn't really thought that he was asking any question at all.

"The question you want to ask me is *how can Mr. Clemens know*."

Sam had no answer to that and they bounced along a while in silence.

⌂⌐⏚⌂⏚⌐⌐

Burton nodded to the gypsy Egyptianeer, Archibald, on the way down. The purveyor of circus-ring Egyptology raised a finger like he wanted to get Burton's attention, but Burton had no time for the man and kept walking. If he waited, he'd lose his opportunity.

A big man stood at the bottom of the stairs like a sentinel, but he was distracted, staring up at the pulpit over his head with tears in his blue eyes. Burton pushed past him and aimed for the small knot of military men crossing the plascrete well of the Tabernacle, heading for a discreet exit.

"Captain Everett Morgan!" he called out, straightening his own back and shoulders to a self-consciously military bearing. "Sir!"

Morgan turned.

Close up, his facial hair made him look bellicose and dangerous. Burton smiled at the man, grateful that his own scars gave him a certain ugly masculine charisma as a counterpoise.

"Yes, suh," Morgan said. His voice was heavy with a sort of sardonic skepticism.

"I am Captain Richard Burton," Burton identified himself, extending a hand, "Special Envoy of Her Britannic Majesty, Queen Victoria."

"You hear that, boys?" Morgan drawled over his shoulder. "Even the Queen is taking an interest." He didn't take Burton's hand.

"Yes," Burton snapped sternly. "Yes, by Indra's thundering chariots, she is! What kind of military officer are you, that so cavalierly dismisses the envoy of a valued and valuable ally, and that on the brink of war!"

"Brink?" Morgan asked, slyly. "I'm afraid I must correct you, suh. The brink, exciting as it was, was yesterday. Today is rather more humdrum and ordinary. Today is merely another day of war."

"All the more reason!" Burton snarled through grinding teeth.

"As for alliances, suh, do you imagine that a mere officer in the field makes decisions as to what nations are and are not his allies?"

"No sir, I do not!" Burton raged. "I also do not imagine that such a man, if he wishes to remain in the field and an officer, may with impunity ignore the decisions of his government as to who his allies are!"

One of the cavalrymen surged forward as if he wanted to punch Burton. Burton welcomed the attack, longed for a chance to prove himself to these men, but Captain Morgan held his soldier back with a half-raised fist. He met Burton's fierce gaze with a sly look and seemed to think for a moment.

"Tell me then, suh," Morgan finally said. "Your Queen. Whose ally is she? Is she the ally of the United States? Or is she the ally of some other party?"

Burton had no patience for this fiddle-faddle and for a moment he almost wished Fearnley-Standish were here. Just for a moment, though. He bit back the bitter thought and organized some careful words, words such as he thought a true diplomat might conjure with. "Her Majesty is a friend of the American people," he said, "and their various governments, and a friend of peace. I am her Special Envoy with a mission to the Kingdom of Deseret—"

"Yes, suh!" Morgan clapped as if applauding some point he himself had won. "And I am a humble officer of the Third Virginia Cavalry. If you wish to discuss the affairs of the Kingdom of Deseret—" he pointed up at the stage, at John Lee "—you should talk to that man."

"I have a mission," Burton ground out each word slowly and distinctly, "and I had hoped to be able to discuss it with my ally. Perhaps I have mistaken you."

"Perhaps you have," the Captain agreed lightly. "Perhaps, if you find yourself at such a loss, it means that your mission, as you refer to it, is finished. I certainly have no instructions for you, no instructions regarding you, and no interest in further conversation. I have my own orders, my own men to take care of, enemies to pursue, and reinforcements for whose arrival I must prepare. Good day, suh."

Captain Morgan tipped his hat sarcastically and disappeared into the exit.

Burton was so mad he almost spit on the floor.

ᘓᒧᎶᒧᗱᒧᑊ

"Hell and begorra!"

Tam's head hurt for want of a drink. It had been hours and Mother O'Shaughnessy had never let him go that long without at least a nip, even as a boy.

The midget disappeared, out through the gates of the train station and into the Great Salt Lake City. He still carried the *machine-gun* case like he was a dance hall fiddler and the pack full of ammunition and loaded extra drums slung over one shoulder. Even heavily laden as he was, he was hard to track in the crowd.

It hadn't been easy following him with the little kid in tow. Tam had switched his hat and coat for a big, dirty duster and a broad-brimmed cattleman's hat he'd found in Browning's shop and he'd made the boy wear his own porkpie. He'd put on a kerchief and tucked his long scarf in his pocket and wished he had a pair of dark glasses.

"Keep your eyes down and your mouth shut, boy," he'd warned the kid, "or I'll by-Brigit shoot you and leave you for the buzzards."

"I ain't afraid of you," the boy John Moses had said at once, but then he'd shut up and done as he'd been told. Tam had kept a hand on the grip of one of his Hushers the entire time, but he hadn't had to draw the gun.

The midget was a suspicious little bastard, though, always looking around him and sometimes doubling back on his own tracks. Tam wondered what he was afraid of (though in this fallen world, wasn't it the honest and prudent man who was always afraid of everything, and always looking out for his own interests?) and stayed on his toes so the little man never got a good look at his face.

Was it the Pinkertons he feared? It might be. There'd been two at the Great Salt Lake City train station, on the very platform, when Tam had disembarked, poking around with their calotypes and asking questions. Tam had tightened his grip on the boy's hand, but the Pinkertons hadn't approached him and there hadn't been any trouble. Lucky for him, the Mormons didn't seem all that interested in being forthcoming with the Pinkertons. The cold shoulder he saw them giving the lawmen was almost enough to endear the Kingdom of Deseret to him forever. Coltrane had gone one way, right in front of one of the detectives, so cool butter wouldn't melt in his mouth, and Tam had dragged the boy with him in the other direction. They'd crossed over the tracks below on parallel catwalks, Tam careful not to overtake the smaller man with his longer steps.

He almost lost the dwarf at the exit, and he almost lost him again outside the train station. The little man crossed one of Deseret's exaggeratedly wide boulevards there and immediately on his heels the street filled with American military steam-trucks, barreling past at full steam. It was the Massachusetts squaddies again, the same ones he and Sam Clemens had seen earlier. Before, they had had the practical, slightly underslept, getting-about-one's-business look that soldiers everywhere always seemed to have when not in action or suffering through some drill or actually asleep.

Now, they looked frightened. The steam-trucks bellowed and groaned and squealed like enormous bellyaching hippopotami as they rushed past and the soldiers on their decks clutched their carbines and looked about them like they feared being shot at from every window they passed, or even by the birds of the air.

What Brigit-blessed nonsense had happened in the short hours while he'd been gone? Tam stepped up his pace, easily gaining ground on the little man with his longer strides, and dragging the boy along, as often as not lifting him off the ground by the wrist. *Not too much, Tamerlane O'Shaughnessy me boy*, he warned himself. *Don't want to completely overtake the little goblin.*

The dwarf crossed the half mile or so of the city center to the Deseret Hotel. Tam and his hostage watched from around corners as Coltrane took the lift up (presumably up to the suite that Tam shared with Sam Clemens, but what in Brigit's name could he be doing up there, up to no good, but at least it was Tam who had the beetles of doom), returned promptly, had a brief word with the desk clerk (it was still that helpful fellow Sorenson, Tam saw), and then idled on the street outside.

After half an hour of idling, at some prompt Tam didn't detect, the dwarf started moving again, back toward the giant beehive in the center of the city. He stayed in public, visible places and Tam was beginning to feel like a whore in church from all the eyes on him. If the dwarf wasn't going to go into any dark alleys of his own free will and choice, Tam might just have to show him the boy and force his hand.

Then things took a turn that was surprisingly … sneaky.

Tam and the boy sat on a brass and plascrete bench across the wide street from the big egg the Mormons called their Tabernacle. The bench was sculpted on its sides with the image of an angel blowing a long straight trump, with the two trumps extending along the sides of the brass-slatted seat, and honeybees flying out the ends of the horn. There was an open space around and before the bench, a green and planted square, and the dwarf moved around on the far side of it, so Tam could watch him comfortably from where he sat. He tried to ignore the spiderweb of glass piping over his head and the whizzing of objects being shot through it, the pumping up and down of glass and brass bellows off in the corner of his eye, and all the glittering surfaces of plascrete and metal and glass, and pay attention to where the action was.

The dwarf didn't go to into the egg. He went to one of the buildings across the square from it. It was a house, a big fancy house, a lords and ladies house, and it looked really strange here in the Great Salt Lake City, surrounded by plascrete and brass pipes and weird fey things scooting around inside glass tubes. The other building was the Lion House that he had already gone into with Clemens, and the two looked like they might even be joined at one corner, but this building looked totally different. It had tall columns and a beehive on the top of it like a cake decoration and under the second-story balcony held up by the long white columns, some of its windows were very tall. The dwarf knocked. A young woman came to the door and listened to him politely but didn't let him in.

The dwarf Coltrane made as if to leave, but once the door was shut he sneaked around in the shrubbery, peering in windows.

"Dirty little bugger," Tam muttered.

He was good, quick, and quiet, and little, of course, and Tam already knew that he was as agile as any squirrel. Tam had sharp eyes, but if he hadn't been following the little man in the first place, he never would have been able to spot him creeping about the house with the beehive top.

Then Coltrane ducked, like he was hiding from someone Tam couldn't see.

Other men came to the front door of the house and were admitted. Tam didn't pay them much attention, except to notice that there were four or five of them and they were armed. But then everyone in this bloody-damn-hell place carried a gun.

Then a man, a full-sized man, detached himself from the bushes not far from the dwarf and hurled himself in through one of the windows. He was a crazy-looking bastard, with a long beard, a knife in one hand, and dressed head to toe in leather, like some character out of a penny dreadful.

Crash!

Tam was no fool, to grab his gun and go rushing into a fight that was clearly none of his business. Still, he kept his hand on the weapon, just in case.

Bang!

The little boy sat bolt upright like a bullet had hit him. Tam tightened his grip on the Husher, but stayed put.

"Did Jed get shot?" John Moses asked, eyes big and round.

"Shut up!" Tam hissed. "No, he didn't!"

A steam-truck, small and boxy and ugly, smashed through a hedge to Tam's left and surged up onto the green grass surrounding the beehive-cake house. Tam was so surprised he nearly jumped out of his seat, but quick motion wouldn't do. He kept his nerve, and as the truck pulled up in front of the shattered window, he crept from the bench with all the rat-like stealth and grace he could muster (and if prosperity was a sign of God's grace, what more blessed creature was there, anyway, than the lowly rat? no doubt it was due to his fervid adherence to the first commandment, *be fruitful and multiply*). Tam dragged the boy with him, and squatted down behind a row of rosebushes to watch what was happening.

From his new vantage point he could see in through the window and the first thing he saw was Sam Clemens. Clemens's hands were tied behind his back and a big man, one of the armed men Tam had just seen come into the building, maybe, pulled a sack over his head.

"Jesus, Brigit, and the Duke of Wellington!" Tam cursed. He didn't love the man, but he liked him, and by any fair calculus he probably was in Clemens's debt. Besides, in any scenario where armed thugs were tying up a man to take him prisoner, Tam's natural sympathy was with the prisoner.

Almost any scenario.

Then the men with guns dragged Clemens out the shattered window and threw him into the back of the truck.

The kidnappers had other prisoners too, and Tam saw their faces as they were bagged and then tossed on board. There was a big black fellow in a very fancy suit and cravat and there was the crazy-looking bastard with beard and buckskins and then there was another face he recognized, at least from calotypes.

"Fookin' hell," he muttered. "The bastards're kidnapping Brigham Young."

What now? Tam wondered. He didn't have time to plan, he knew, he had to act. He needed to follow the truck, but if it left the city, any pursuit would instantly be visible.

He needed to get *on* the steam-truck.

He could let the boy go—he'd just have to go after the dwarf later.

Except no, wait a minute, Coltrane was still there in the bushes, and Tam couldn't have the little bugger shooting him in the back while he was trying to mount a rescue for good old Sam Clemens. *Bloody-damn-hell.*

The steam-truck was a wheeled platform with two metal sheds on it, one shed being the glass-windowed wheelhouse and the second being a cargo space. Between the two was an iron furnace beneath a boiler and beside it a tender with a short-handled shovel strapped to its trapdoor lid. The wheelhouse was empty and no one else was about the truck—all the men were inside, wrestling with the prisoners, and now was the moment to act.

Tam dragged the boy with him, across the garden space and toward the truck. As he approached it with long steps, Jedediah Coltrane stepped out of the bushes. He had unboxed his machine-gun and now he raised the hateful thing in Tam's direction.

Tam drew a Husher and pressed its muzzle against the boy's temple. *Don't even try it, you stupid little fooker,* he mouthed at the dwarf, and then he clambered up the short iron rungs to the front platform of the steam-truck, by its squatty little wheelhouse. The boy cooperated.

Coltrane glared at him with desperation and shifted his grip on the stubby rifle.

"I'm brave," John Moses called out softly to the dwarf, "don't worry."

"Don't worry, you dumb fookin' midget," Tam hissed, "he's brave." He grinned threateningly at the dwarf. "I'll come back for you later, you hear?"

He holstered the Husher, grabbed the boy tight under one arm, and climbed up a second ladder that took him to the roof of the truck's cargo compartment. He was careful to hold the boy in front of his own body, in case the dwarf decided to risk a shot.

The dwarf's indecision ended when the truck gate slammed shut and the armed men came walking out toward the wheelhouse end of the truck again. He faded back into the shrubbery but Tam felt his hard, piggy little eyes still staring in his direction as he yanked the boy flat on the truck's roof. It was a wide, flat space and there were mooring rings to hold on to. Just to be on the safe side, he unbuckled the boy's belt and re-buckled it again through one of the rings. *No sense losing your hostage, is there, whether to escape or the accidents of an overzealous turn?*

"The safehouse?" a rough voice asked. "Or the ranch?"

Boots *thudded* dully on metal as men climbed aboard.

"Nah, Hatch, I got a better idea," answered a whiny, nasal voice. "Lee's gonna find out we ain't followed his instructions precisely to the letter and we need to get somewhere he won't expect to find us. And helldammitall, we know Rockwell ain't home, so I reckon we ought to go to his place."

There was the harsh laughter of men and then the *groan* of the steam-truck shifting into gear.

"Give me back my hat," Tam snapped, and took his porkpie back from the little kid.

ᗿ⅃Ꮆ⅃ᖚᗿ⅃

"I think it's time to lay our cards on the table, Captain Burton," Poe said.

The two of them stood in the plascrete well, under tens of thousands of staring eyes but alone. The Apostles huddled on the stage with Lee and Cannon, the Virginians had filed out, and in the aisles it was a slow, somber, but still chatting, every-man-for-himself of Saints filing out the doors.

Burton crossed his arms, looking every inch the muscular and demonic defier of convention, the flouter of taste, the explorer who would go where he willed, and damn the consequences. What did Queen Victoria think of the Kingdom of Deseret that she had sent such a man? What did she think of Americans generally? "Agreed," the Englishman said. "Start with your real name."

"Edgar Allan Poe," Poe said.

Burton furrowed his brow in doubt. Poe removed his smoked glasses and his hat, and smoothed his hair down. Burton cocked an eyebrow.

"Poe," he murmured. "By the Sapta Rishis, I think you might be telling the truth. I see your nose has shrunk."

"I am and it has."

"Nevermore!" Burton shouted, then laughed at his own joke. Poe smiled weakly. "But you're dead."

"The rumors of my death are greatly exaggerated," Poe said. "Deliberately so. I am in United States Army Intelligence. When … enemies … attempted to kill me, and very nearly did so, with no small amount of public spectacle, my superiors and I simply let them think they had succeeded."

"Shame to end such a writing career," Burton tut-tutted. He was taking the revelation well, Poe thought. "Ten years ago, wasn't it? And I thought the Hajj was a long time to be in disguise."

Poe shrugged. "No one reads fiction, anyway."

Burton considered this. "So why tell me who you are now? What are you doing here and what is it you want from me?"

"You are Her Britannic Majesty's special envoy to the Kingdom of Deseret, are you not? Surely your task here relates to the looming secession crisis? If the southern states secede, Brigham Young—the Kingdom—will have a decision to make and Her Majesty must care about the outcome." Poe didn't need the confirmation, but he waited for Burton's slow nod anyway, as an indication that the man was following and anticipating his train of thought and willing to engage in an open discussion.

"Yes," Burton drawled.

"The secession is a fact," Poe continued, satisfied. "The South will secede, not willy-nilly but *en masse*, as a new and separate unity. Maybe it already *has* seceded. War may or may not be in the offing. It is very likely,

I think, that it is. English cotton mills, the mills that grind out prosperity for her entire Kingdom, take in cotton from the southern states. Victoria cannot want war and if there is war, she must enter on the side of the states with which her mill owners are economically aligned. The question, then, becomes, what will Deseret do?"

"That isn't *my* question," Burton growled.

Poe hesitated. "What's *your* question?" he asked.

"I don't need a lecture about the economy of the United Kingdom of Great Britain and Northern Ireland. I want to know what game you're playing. My question is: whose side are *you* on, Mr. Edgar Allan Poe?"

"Quite." Poe sighed. "I never would have approached you, Captain Burton, except that my cover is blown. The Mormons know who I am. Specifically, their agent, your lady friend, Roxie, has recognized me."

"Roxie!" Burton looked surprised, but even more, he looked disappointed.

"I guess you may have already had your suspicions about the woman."

"Quite." Burton's face settled into a glare sandwiched between beetling brows and a jutting granite jaw. With his scars, he looked like a real goblin.

"You *should* suspect her. It was she who poisoned me, nearly killed me and ended my writing career, a decade ago in Baltimore." He omitted to mention that his putative murder had also scuttled his then-impending marriage, turning his fiancée, a perfectly decent and happy woman, instantly into a grieving widow. Poe felt a slight twinge of regret, like he was betraying a confidence to Roxie in telling Burton these things.

But that was insane. He owed her no confidence. If anything, he owed her a bullet in the forehead.

Only he kept thinking of their meeting in his cabin in the *Liahona* that morning, when Roxie had had him at her mercy and hadn't killed him. *Remember this,* she'd said.

Surely, she was playing him. Again.

"Are you Sam Clemens's man?" Burton asked, shaking him from his reverie.

"No," Poe said. "Clemens and I are both in Army Intelligence, but he and I never worked together and I don't believe he even knows I am alive. He remains, as far as I know, a loyal Union man."

"And you are a secessionist."

"I'm a Virginian. Like other Virginians, I will serve my state when its leaders feel they must withdraw from a union that is noxious to its interests, that will tariff it and vote it into submission and poverty. Like all Virginians." Like Robert.

"Your mission was secret. Your cover is blown. Now you join with me … why?" Burton looked genuinely puzzled as he wrestled with the situation. "To jointly persuade the new leadership of the Kingdom of Deseret to enter the war on the side of the South? But they seem amply persuaded of that course of action already. Clemens with his single bullet appears to have accomplished more than you and I together ever could, whatever blandishments we might have had to offer."

Poe shook his head, wondering what blandishments the Englishman had been sent to offer to Brigham Young. "I'm not persuaded. There are … plots … here. Men are machinating and I fear they are machinating for war. There is a rush to blame the United States. I am a Virginian, Captain, but like you … like all reasonable men, I hope … I would have peace rather than war. I reveal myself to you because I need an ally and because I hope that you may possess information I do not. Secret things are being done here, terrible secret things, and I don't know what they are."

Burton shook his head. "I have no information," he said somberly. "But Sam Clemens doesn't strike me as a murderer."

"Brigham Young isn't dead."

It was Roxie's voice, it came from behind him and it caught Poe off guard. Again.

He whirled, prepared to defend himself, but Roxie stood relaxed, casual, non-threatening. With her was her younger companion, the girlish young woman with the curly brown hair and the freckles.

"Do you mean he unexpectedly survived the shooting?" Burton asked.

"Someone was shot all right, but I don't think it was Brigham," the younger woman said. "I had to kiss two of Brigham's sons and beat hell out of one of his house Danites to get the information, but they all said the same thing. He was in his office with the Mexican Ambassador and the Yankee. There was a shot and then some of the Danites, including some pretty senior fellows, came in, and disappeared with Brigham. There was blood on the carpet, but no body left behind."

"So Cannon's version of events might be true …" Poe pondered.

"Danites are … as they are painted in the penny dreadfuls?" Burton was hesitant, for once. "Tarring and feathering newspapermen? Stuffing ballot boxes at the Gallatin County elections? Gunning down Governor Boggs in a dry goods store in broad daylight? Massacring Indian tribes to remove them from fertile farmland? Robbing wagon trains of emigrants bound for Novy Moskva or California? Hanging federal agents? Slitting the throats of the wounded Missouri men at Crooked River?"

"The degree of exaggeration," Roxie answered him, "is not as great as you might think."

"They're President Young's bodyguards?" Burton continued.

"Roughly," Roxie said, with a hint of a smile at the ambiguity in her answer.

"So this information is completely inconclusive," Burton said. "It could be that Clemens made an attempt and his bodyguard whisked the President away. Perhaps it was Clemens who was shot."

Poe shook his head. "Then we wouldn't have had this emergency meeting and the announcement of Young's death. If Young is alive, then this is a *coup d'état*, Captain Burton, and you are in the uncomfortable position of the ally on the scene at the time."

"You and I both." There was a gleam in Burton's eye that seemed to say that he wasn't entirely unhappy to be in the situation.

Poe laughed. "True." He turned to Roxie, loath to trust her but unwilling to discount her information. "Do you know which … Danite … took President Young?"

"*You* know him, as it happens," she informed them. "It was Bill Hickman, with some of his boys." She nodded to Burton. "You may remember him as the low-life, backstabbing snake who almost shot your friend."

Poe shuddered. He remembered Hickman, and it made a dark sense. Hickman and Lee plotted to take power. They anticipated the arrival of the Yankee Clemens, they arranged to kill or kidnap Young and blame it on the United States. Then in the moment of the Kingdom's bereavement Lee stepped forward to reassure the Mormons that everything would be alright, he and the Third Virginia Cavalry would protect Deseret and its Saints from the nasty evil Yankees.

The next President of the Kingdom of Deseret wouldn't be Orson Pratt.

It would be John Lee.

And his first act would be to take the Kingdom to war.

"Fearnley-Standish isn't my friend," Burton muttered, a little grimly "Arguably, he may be my colleague."

"What do you want, Eliza?" Poe hardened himself, chased out the strange, almost-forgotten feelings of vulnerability and need.

"I think you're right, Edgar." Her voice was soft, warm, encouraging, gentle. He willed himself to keep his eyes open and his focus tight on her, his mind tough. "Annie and I are inconvenient to the new overlords and we will soon be rendered harmless. We need your help to find and rescue Brother Brigham, to overturn this coup, and to avert the war."

"I'm appalled the Kingdom could get itself into this state of affairs," Poe said. It was an unfair comment, but he saw that the knife was in and part of him wanted to give it a hard twist. "Aren't you its top spy, Eliza? Have you been asleep while this revolution has been building under your very nose?"

"That isn't fair!" Roxie's protégée snapped.

"Hush, Annie," the older woman told her.

D.J. Butler

"I will *not* hush!" the girl objected. "The only reason I haven't already kicked his teeth from here to his precious Baltimore is because you're sweet on the pucker-faced little cogitator!" Poe flinched and prepared himself for a kung fu kick.

"Enough!" Roxie ordered, but her companion charged on.

"Listen, you!" She jabbed a finger in Poe's direction, her crinoline crackling slightly with the energy of her motion. "Just because Brigham Young gets good advice doesn't mean he's going to take it! He's President of the Kingdom, not the all-seeing and almighty God Himself! Roxie warned him Lee and Hickman were up to no good, Porter Rockwell warned him, too, but he just liked and trusted John D. Lee way too much to believe us!"

Poe felt duly abashed, though he wasn't sure that he should. "Is that true?" he asked Roxie.

"It's true." She cracked a crooked smile. "Brigham Young is not the all-seeing and almighty God."

Poe felt mollified, but Burton showed the proper masculine hardness that Poe wanted to evince. "And why should I help you, Roxie? Why should *we* help you?" Poe met his gaze and they nodded to each other, each reinforcing the other's resolve. "This is a mess and it may be a crime, perhaps a *coup d'état*, but I don't see that it's my problem."

Roxie nodded humbly, though the brown-haired Valkyrie behind her looked stubborn and almost angry, as if she might at any moment explode into action and make good on her threat to kick Poe to Baltimore. "I had hoped that you would do it for your Queen, Captain Burton," she said, and then she turned to look at Poe. They locked eyes, and her lip trembled. "And as for you, Edgar ..." Tears pooled above her lower lashes, and one slipped free, cascading mournfully over her high, austere cheek. "You have no reason to do it. No reason at all. And yet, I hope you will."

What a consummate actress she is, he thought. *A very devil in a corset. And what a consummate fool am I.*

"Yes," he said, "I'll help. My mission is to treat with President Young." He smiled ironically. "And I have no taste for plotters."

Burton looked suspicious. Perhaps he had private reservations, but he kept them to himself. "Fine," he harrumphed. "Where do we start? Hickman? The Danites?"

Orson Pratt? Poe wondered, but he said nothing.

As if prompted by Burton's question, Burton's diplomat colleague materialized. Another observer might have laughed at Absalom Fearnley-Standish in his long coat, waistcoat, cravat, and top hat, especially given that a crescent-shaped piece of the top hat's brim had been sliced neatly out of it, giving him a nibbled-upon appearance. Poe, though, saw his erect posture and his fussily-maintained outfit and admired the young

174

man's ongoing struggle to maintain civilization and manners, despite his coarse environment. He hoped Fearnley-Standish persisted. In his right hand, pointed at the floor but obviously loaded and capped, he carried a long, worn revolver.

Fearnley-Standish was fair and pale and at his shoulder came a woman who was brown as a chestnut, and who looked like she had completely traded civilization for practicality. She wore a man's vest and cowboy boots and her dress swished loose and comfortable. At first blush they looked like opposites, like chalk and cheese, Poe thought the Englishman himself might say, but then something caught his attention and he saw them differently. Squinting, he looked again.

Strip away the dirt, the tanned skin and general weathering from the woman, and they could be twins.

Certainly siblings.

Poe searched his memory for Robert's files and what they might have said about a Miss Fearnley-Standish. Disappeared, he recalled. No police investigation, no newspaper articles, no further mention. Strange for a girl from a good family like the Fearnley-Standishes to just vanish without a trace.

It reeked of scandal and mystery and family honor, and suddenly Poe realized what Absalom Fearnley-Standish was doing in the Kingdom of Deseret.

"Captain Burton," the fair Englishman said, breathing hard from the exertion of descending down into the well of the Tabernacle. He spoke with a crisp educated accent, the precise vowels of a public school man. Eton or Harrow, Poe guessed. "And Mrs. Snow. Annie." This last greeting was more than a little stiff, Poe thought. "And, er, you, sir, however you are calling yourself today "

"Poe," Poe said.

Fearnley-Standish nodded. "Fine," he agreed. "Mr. Poe. This is Mrs. Abigail Rockwell." Mrs. Rockwell curtseyed, a gesture utterly inconsistent with her clothing but showing glimpses of a good upper middle class upbringing in greater London. Fearnley-Standish shot Burton a look under his eyebrows, a look that might have been sheepish. "Née Fearnley-Standish," he said, barely louder than a mumble.

"Ha!" Burton barked. His eyes gleamed with triumph and holier-than-thou reproach. Fearnley-Standish looked like he wanted to crumple and disappear under Burton's glare, but the explorer didn't press his advantage and just bowed to his colleague's sister. "Captain Richard Burton, madam," he said to her. "Your servant."

"Sir," she acknowledged him.

There followed a flurry of bows and curtseys and the exchange of names, but to one side Absalom Fearnley-Standish approached Burton and cleared his throat.

"Yes, Absalom?" Burton asked. He was the shorter man, but he pointed his chin at the ceiling and the cast of his eye made him look like he was gazing down on the diplomat. Poe looked away, nodded at the ladies, and listened sharply.

"Dick … er, rather, Captain Burton," Fearnley-Standish began. "We must compare schedules and organize ourselves. I must make a … er, a small detour. Regarding a personal matter."

Richard Burton threw back his head and laughed.

ᎠᏧᏪᏫᎠᏁ

Jed Coltrane ran.

It wasn't easy and he wasn't fast. He had short legs in the first place, and in the second he carried the long case of the machine gun in one hand and a heavy pack of ammunition bouncing on his back.

The Irishman had John Moses.

The … somebody … the Mormons? … somebody named *Hick* … had Brigham Young, and also Clemens and some very fancy-looking Mexican man.

All of them were in a steam-truck, going somewhere, and the only clue Jed had as to their destination was the name *Rockwell. Rockwell's place*, that's where the thugs had said they were headed.

He had to find Poe.

Just minutes, it seemed, after the steam-truck with its kidnap victim cargo had pulled out, crowds had descended on the gigantic egg-shaped building. They came on foot, by horse, and in all manner of vehicle, hitching their animals to convenient posts and leaving trucks and clocksprung mules standing idle beside plascrete curbs, but it was like a switch had been thrown on a giant battery and the traffic that had used to flow in all directions around the egg suddenly all fell into it.

If the *Liahona* was in town, Jed guessed, Poe might end up inside the egg, too. And if it wasn't, hell, he had absolutely no idea how to get hold of his boss. He felt a little conspicuous with the machine gun, but he looked around and saw that just about everyone else was armed too. The observation calmed him down.

He cut his pace to a walk and went inside the egg, under a sign that said *SALT LAKE CITY TABERNACLE* above a line of that silly-looking gibberish writing, the same crap that had filled the newspaper. What was wrong with these people?

He cut across a crowded circular hall that he guessed must ring the entire building, then through a wide, people-stuffed plascrete gullet and suddenly found himself spat out into the abyss.

Jed Coltrane was not afraid of heights. Jed Coltrane was not afraid of crowds, either. Hell, he'd tumbled from heights in front of crowds in more small towns on the Chitlin' Circuit, the Sawdust Circuit, and even the Borscht Belt than he could ever hope to remember.

But the inside of the Tabernacle daunted him anyway. It was huge, the biggest open space Jed had ever seen that wasn't God's own great out-of-doors, like a palace for human-sized bees, or something bored and decadent Martians might build, or a node of the Sea King's stronghold from the bottom of the ocean. It was gigantic, and it shone like polished brass, and it swarmed with people. Seats climbed up above his head in rows and met somewhere up there behind giant brass trumpets like amplifying cones. Seats climbed down and piled onto a smooth plascrete space, in the center of which was a stage with chairs and a pulpit and a thicket of Franklin Poles.

"Jebus," he muttered.

Down on the floor, beside the stage, stood Poe. His boss was talking with the Englishmen, some tall Mexican drink of water and, if Jed's eyes hadn't failed him due to age, exhaustion, or sheer fatigue from having seen so much weirdness in the past forty-eight hours, the two ladies from the *Liahona*.

The one Jed had tried to kill and the one who had tried to kill Jed.

They were all talking like friends.

"Okay, Poe," he mumbled as he rolled down the plascrete steps. "You're the boss." Besides, he needed Poe's resourcefulness, his powerful brain, to help him find John Moses and get the boy back.

The Mexican wore a leather outfit that covered her from head to toe and was spangled with buckles, straps, and small protective shells. She held a helmet with a smoked visor under one arm and wore a big old handgun on her hip, and if Jed hadn't forgotten his military lore, she had sergeant's stripes on her shoulder. She was talking as he arrived at the floor.

"Joo may do as joo wish," she said, in a voice like smoked honey and bullets, "but *mi responsabilidad es el* Ambassador Armstrong. I only thought that joo might be potential allies *para mi* and Sergeant Ortiz."

"We might indeed, Sergeant Jackson." Poe noticed Jed's arrival. "And this is my associate, Jed Coltrane," he introduced the dwarf to the others.

"Uh … okay, boss." This sudden friendliness made Jed uneasy. It made him want to throw scarabs on all these Englishmen and Mormons, frankly, and the painful recollection that the Irishman had the scarabs too didn't help.

"They know my name," Poe said, smiling.

Poe looked at his boss and at the others. Was this a test? His boss was such a devious thinker, with a brain that explored all the twists and turns of every possible outcome before ever committing to a plan of action, it didn't seem possible that he had just up and told these people his real name.

Hell, Jed wasn't even sure that *Poe* really *was* his real name.

"Okay." He nodded, trying to look serious. "Fine."

"Poe," Poe added, looking irritated. "Edgar Allan Poe."

"Yeah, I know it, I just … jebus, Poe, how do I know what you expect outta me?"

"What I should have learned to expect from you by now," Poe snapped, looking exasperated, "is piscine acuity and porcine tact!"

"Boss," Jed said, feeling very tired and very stupid, "I'll tack up all the signs you want, pie signs and poor signs and cuties and whatever the hell else you jest said, but first you gotta help me find a guy named Rockwell."

CHAPTER TEN

hen the steam-truck finally rattled off the tail end of the armadillo mountain and slammed to a halt, it caught Sam by surprise and knocked him over.

"Damnation!" Orrin Porter Rockwell cursed.

"Port …"

"Sorry."

The gangplank fell open and Sam blinked for a moment in the sudden sunlight. He saw a dirt track through lanky yellow grass, scraping its way up a hill and ending at a rambling building that looked part hotel, part saloon and part ranch house. At its far end squatted a gigantic brass bulb, the size of another small building, with man-sized pipes elbowing out of its side and punching into the ground. Behind the building and the brass tank rose a high gravel ridge, and above that a sky so pale it was almost white. Off to one side was another building, one that might have been a stable.

"Yankee piece of trash," Bill Hickman berated him, and then the Danites pulled a sack over his head and Sam was blind again and drowning in the smell of apples. "Who told you you could take your hat off?"

They dragged him by his shoulders, so that his knees and feet bounced along in the dirt, Sam guessed for maybe a hundred feet. He heard the burble of water just before cold splashing on his ankles told him that he was at a stream, and then he was planted on his knees in chilly mud. On a hotter day, it might even have felt good, but this was shaping up to be a cool one, and the midday sun was barely warm.

"It's not too late, Hick," Sam heard Brigham Young say in a voice dripping with threat. He felt relieved to know he wasn't alone. The darkness and silence and being dragged along in solitude felt just a little too much like death for his comfort.

"Joo are making a very bad decision," Ambassador Armstrong weighed in gravely. "My President will not tolerate such treatment of her especial representatives."

Sam was unconvinced that such exhortations would help. "Set us free," he offered, "and I can see you get five hundred dollars."

"*Don't* set us free and I'll see scraps of your hide nailed to every damn tree between here and St. Louis," Rockwell spat, unhelpfully.

Clang! Thud.

Metal struck metal, then something heavy hit the earth and bounced off Sam's thigh.

"Whatever Lee has planned, nothing has been done that can't be undone." Sam found the sudden kindness in Brigham Young's voice unsettling after all the gruff ferocity. Young sounded stern, but Sam was a little bit irritated that the man didn't sound *angry* anymore. "You can still come home, Hick."

"Shut up," Bill Hickman said sourly. "*All* y'all."

Sam was dragged forward again, into a cold space, and then he was hurled against a wall. He collapsed onto what felt like a stack of smallish casks. The fact that his hands were still tied behind his back made it worse, because he couldn't catch himself or soften any of the blows. Splashing and scraping noises and three meaty *thuds* told him that his fellow-prisoners were being made to join him, and then a door shut.

Snap.

"Damn you!" Brigham Young yelled. "Set us free!"

No one answered him.

There was a long silence.

"Yankee?" Rockwell finally asked.

"I'm here," Sam said.

"Can you still see?"

"I'm afraid they've hooded me again," Sam informed the other men. "I'm as blind as Tiresias."

"Or Bartimaeus," Brigham Young suggested in a low rumble. "The man born blind in John nine, if you didn't learn that in your Gentile upbringing."

"I know who Bartimaeus is," Sam grumbled. "What do you mean, *Gentile*?"

"Be careful what joo say," the Ambassador warned them. "We are all in the dark and joo cannot be sure that our captors are not listening to us."

There was another pause. Sam still heard the running water and he felt cool air on his skin, so he guessed they must be in a springhouse.

"I reckon I count four men breathing," Rockwell whispered, "but I'll keep it down in case they got a guard at the door." He sniffed. "I smell venison, pepper, and butter. Didn't *anybody* see *anything*?"

"I did," Sam admitted. "Just a bit. I had my eyes free for a moment, just as they opened the back of the steam-truck and before they covered my head again."

"And?" Rockwell prompted him.

"I saw a house." Sam thought carefully about the glimpse he'd had and tried to be careful in his description. "It had a wrap-around porch, it was two stories tall, there were glass panes and white curtains in all the windows. The house was white, and it had blue-painted trim ... a lightning rod, I think ... two chimneys."

Rockwell laughed softly. "You notice anything ... funny ... about the house?"

Sam chuckled, too; in focusing on the trees, he'd almost forgotten the forest. "Yes, Mr. Rockwell, I did. There was an enormous brass tank at one end of it. Almost as big as a small house itself."

"Like a water tank?" Rockwell pressed.

"Could have been," Sam agreed. "It had pipes running into the ground."

Rockwell laughed again.

"You see?" Brigham Young asked in the darkness. "Cogs."

"What is it?" the Ambassador asked. "Do joo know where we are?"

"We're at *my* house," Orrin Porter Rockwell told him. "I reckon in my springhouse. I thought it smelled familiar. And delicious. And what that shit-for-brains Hickman don't know is that I keep a Colt and a Bowie knife in my food storage."

"What, in case the milk stampedes?" Sam actually felt glad that Rockwell knew where he was and had to hand the means of escape, but he couldn't help mocking the other man, just a little bit, for keeping weapons in his pantry. It was a reflex.

"In case bad men come for me while I'm getting out food for my supper," Rockwell said. "Or bears. I keep a pistol in the outhouse, too, for the same reason—you got a problem with that?"

Sam bit his tongue to hold back the obvious snappy answer: *Yes, I have a problem with the fact that you get food for your supper out of the outhouse.* "Actually," he told the mountain man, "I can see how it would be very inconvenient to not have a pistol and be caught with your trousers down. Though I'm not sure why you have an outhouse at all, if your hotel has modern plumbing."

"Just old-fashioned, I reckon."

"If you have trouble with your pants staying up," Young suggested in the darkness, "I'm sure I can find you a new pair."

ᑕᒍᎶᔑ�2ᒍᎥ

Tamerlane O'Shaughnessy watched Sam Clemens and his companions in misfortune get dragged out of the back of the steam-truck and tossed into a little log house straddling a spring at the bottom of a long hill. The Danites slammed a new padlock onto the door to replace the one they'd knocked off and left two *pistoleros* standing guard outside the springhouse (and shouldn't two be enough, in this empty wasteland?) while the rest of them trundled back up to the house in the steam-truck.

They parked beside the building and went inside. Afraid the truck might get back into gear and head out again if he waited, Tam quickly unbuckled the boy John Moses and the two of them stepped easily off the wheelhouse roof and onto the shingled slope over the top of the house's wrap-around porch.

The tar shingles were hot enough to bake bread in the afternoon sun. Tam shoved his pistol in the nearest window first, then poked his own beak in between the fluttering white curtains to be sure the room was unoccupied, then hauled himself and the gunsmith's son in and pulled them both to the floor.

"Stay down," he ordered the boy, then crawled over to check the door.

Locked, but he could open it from the inside.

The room was a bedroom and it looked like one that might be for rent. There was a single bed, with a cheap but cheerful iron frame and a flattened mattress and a chest of drawers with a cracked mirror and a side table and a pitcher of water beside a tin basin and a kerosene lantern. Tam didn't see anyone's personal effects anywhere in the room.

John Moses lay where he had been placed. He was quiet, but he had a cantankerous glint in his eye like he didn't really appreciate the genius of Tamerlane O'Shaughnessy's plans and didn't intend to fully cooperate in them. He'd looked sullen all the way from the Great Salt Lake City, a drive that had taken an hour. He hadn't made any noise or tried to escape, though, which was a good thing. Hushers or no Hushers, Tam didn't fancy his odds going up against half a dozen of these Deseret thugs, not unless he got to shoot first and from cover. Which, of course, is what Mother O'Shaughnessy had always taught him to do, in any case.

"I'm not going to hurt you," Tam said, then kicked himself for a stupid git. He tightened up his voice. "Unless you cross me, of course, you miserable little runt, or disobey me in anything at all."

John Moses said nothing.

"Right. Where are we, then? Is this Rockwell's?"

John Moses nodded.

"Rockwell's what? Is it a well? What's the big turtliffic tank nailed onto the side of the building? It looks like a saloon inside a big home. Is it a bor …" he had been about to say *bordello*, "boarding house?"

John Moses nodded.

"Talk, you little idjit," Tam gasped in exasperation. Out of reflex he pointed one of the Hushers at the little boy, but thought better of it and lowered the gun. *No point killing him, me boy. Not just yet.* "Talk. What the fook is this place?"

"This is the Hot Springs Hotel and Brewery," the boy said. "The tank is hot water, I think. You can get a hot bath here right out of the spigot, without even a boiler or a fire. But I don't know what a *fook* is."

Tam giggled. "A *fook's* not so different from an *idjit*. And what's a *Rockwell*, then?"

"Orrin Porter Rockwell. He's a man. He owns it. He's kind of famous. He's not a … fook, he's dangerous. He's a gunfighter."

"I've wet my breeches already." Tam chuckled. "You drink a lot, do you?" His own head hurt for whisky. A Guinness would do, or anything decent and Irish. He'd almost be willing to drink an English lager, at this point. "Come here often?"

"Sometimes with poppa. Or with Captain Jones." The little boy seemed to be relaxing a bit. "It's a good place to stop on a trip down to Provo or Nephi or St. George."

Tam brushed back one of the curtains and scanned the landscape around the hotel. "There's nothing around here for miles and miles but buffalo chips, lad," he disagreed. "This looks like a good place to get scalped by wild Indians."

"That, too," John Moses agreed. "But you can do that just about any place in the Kingdom, or in the Wyoming Territory."

"Smart aleck," Tam snorted, and restrained himself from cuffing the brat. "Look around and see if you can find anything in here to drink."

He settled in to squint out the window and think while John Moses opened and shut drawers and dug around under the bed. He could see a stable across the yard, with at least a couple of horses in it. Hanging offense or not, Tam didn't object to stealing a horse when he needed it; of course, Sam would probably insist on paying for the beasts and paying too much, if it was at all possible. Either way, once he got Clemens out of his cell, the horses would give them a way back to the Great Salt Lake City.

The springhouse was not quite out of sight at the bottom of the hill from where he watched. The two men in front of it stood alert, like they were used to standing watch or being bodyguards. He didn't think he could sneak up on them, and he'd rather not attempt a direct frontal assault when the odds were two to one against him.

"Nothing," John Moses reported. "I could go down and ask the kitchen for a glass of water."

"I'll wager you could, you little cog-rat," Tam snapped. An idea tickled his brain, and he chewed on it for a minute. "We'll go down together," he finally said. "Only first, we've got to arrange a wee bit of a distraction."

He led John Moses around the second story of the hotel. Thanks be to merciful Brigit, the floors didn't creak and Tam opened every door he found unlocked, collecting kerosene lanterns. In one room, he found a coat hanging from a wall peg and an unlocked valise.

Tam helped himself to the half-full fifth of gin he found in the valise. John Moses, who had followed dutifully in his wake the entire time, said nothing and stared bullets of reproach at the Irishman.

"Shut up, you," Tam muttered, and dragged the boy back into the room they'd left.

The steam-truck was still parked below them. It was a simple matter to slosh the kerosene from the bowls of all the lamps they'd collected over the wheelhouse and cargo hold of the truck, on the boiler and furnace in between and on both of its front tyres.

Then a single lucifer tossed out the window sent the whole pile of bolts and rubber straight to hell.

"Come on, then," Tam said to the boy. "Let's go downstairs and find ourselves a horse to borrow." He sucked out half the gin for emphasis and felt a little better for it.

"Okay." John Moses followed.

"Don't forget I'm armed," Tam reminded him. "And I'm a hard mean Irish fook, and Mother O'Shaughnessy taught me to hate brats."

�␣⊣6⊣⊕⊣⌐

"Good heavens, is it on *fire*?" Absalom hadn't meant to ask the question out loud, but he realized that he had.

Captain Dan Jones had looked positively murderous when the showman Poe had tugged at his elbow in the roiling crowds of the Tabernacle and asked for a ride south. He'd raised a big-knuckled fist like he might punch the Egyptiana peddler right in the face. Poe hadn't flinched, but violence had looked imminent.

But then Dick Burton had said, "We know where the boy John Moses is and we're going to get him."

Jones had spun one hundred eighty degrees and raced his passengers back into the steam-truck hangar. Crew not already aboard had been left behind, which seemed to leave the *Liahona* half-manned but functional.

The big steam-truck had chewed its way up the ramp and out onto the streets faster than Absalom would have thought possible. It helped that the entire population of the city seemed to be still inside the Tabernacle or milling about on its grounds.

For an hour, the *Liahona* had rumbled south as the sun climbed and the day grew warmer (Absalom was no backwoodsman, but he knew that the sun crossed the sky from east to west; once he realized that the nearer wall of dusty blue and white mountains was to the east of the Great Salt Lake City, it was impossible to get disoriented) on a broad highway paved with tar macadam. They had quickly left the urban center behind, passing into a maze of irrigation canals and furrowed patches that had shortly given way to sagebrush, wild grasses, and prairie dogs. As they rode, Captain Jones's truck-men had bolted the railguns to the *Liahona*'s deck again.

Absalom felt as if he were living a penny dreadful.

The valley narrowed to a broad bottleneck leading south into the next valley ("Provo," Captain Jones had managed to mutter in response to Absalom's query, "nothing to write home about.") At that point, responding to a flag from Captain Jones, Master Sergeant Jackson and her three fellow Mexican soldiers, riding two each to a Strider, had turned off the road.

Now as their vehicle nosed over the low, wide-shelving foothills supporting a tall gravel ridge, Absalom and others standing around the *Liahona*'s wheelhouse could finally see the Hot Springs Hotel and Brewery.

And the hotel was burning.

"'Tisn't the hotel," Abigail said at his shoulder, and for a moment he forgot that she was as brown and cracked as any Indian, not the milk-skinned girl he'd ridden ponies and played at conkers with as a child. "There's a steam-truck parked beside it and the truck is on fire. Look," she pointed. "There are men trying to put out the flames."

"That's the kidnappers' truck," the dwarf grumbled. "And I reckon it's the kidnappers as are playing fireman." He continued to hold at the ready his strange stubby rifle with the drum attached. Burton had asked the dwarf about it *en route*, and gotten a crotchety glare for his trouble.

"Stop the truck, Captain," Abigail told him. She touched Poe's dwarf gently on his arm. "And don't shoot. This is my home. We don't know for sure that those men are involved in the kidnapping. And there might be guests inside."

"Not to mention the boy," Jones grunted assent, and under the persuasion of his experienced fingers the *Liahona* ground to a halt, halfway down the bluff above the hotel.

"What should I do then, do you think?" the dwarf wanted to know. "Kiss the rotten dry gulchers?"

"We'll parley first. If we have to fight, we'll try to get the drop on them. Follow my lead." Absalom shuddered to hear Abigail talk so frankly and forcefully. She looked at Dan Jones. "Your men are armed?"

Jones nodded. He left the engine idling, stayed on the deck and started passing instructions to his crewmen.

Abigail slid down the ladder with a butterfly's grace, putting one hand on each side rail and apparently letting the rest of her simply fall. Absalom hesitated, embarrassed to follow because he knew he would make a much more awkward figure.

Burton pushed past him, and Poe, and the dwarf. They all seemed completely comfortable with the motion—the dwarf Coltrane only used one hand, since the other never relinquished the death grip it had on his strange firearm. The men all stalked across the sand towards the burning steam-truck in Abigail's wake.

Absalom noticed a second steam-truck parked behind the first and wondered just how many men there were at the Hot Springs Hotel and Brewery.

Just as Absalom had mustered the will to throw himself down the ladder, Roxie Snow stepped past him. Like Abigail, she held the sides of the *Liahona*'s ladder and slid down with practiced grace, her crinoline skirt filling and billowing like a mushroom cap.

Then Annie. At the top of the ladder she hesitated. "Maybe you should stay in the truck," she suggested softly.

Absalom's blood boiled. "Egad," he ground out stiffly. "What kind of man do you think I am?"

She shrugged as she levered herself over the edge of the *Liahona*. "I think you're cute."

Annie's skirt was of a lighter fabric than Roxie's, and it puffed up higher around her waist. If he'd already been on the ground, Absalom might have seen something scandalous. As it was, he saw the top side of a pretty pink bonnet, tied with ribbon, surrounded by the halo of a puffed-out pink skirt.

"I'm not a coward." Absalom gnashed his teeth, reached deep inside himself for something inspirational, and found the Harrow Song. "Follow up! Follow up! Follow up! Follow up!" he began.

He saw Annie pull a pistol from inside her skirt.

Singing, he grabbed the two rails of the ladder and threw himself over the edge and down, as the others had all done.

He dropped—

—it wasn't so bad, air rushing around his ears—

—his toe caught on a rung, halfway down—

—and Absalom tumbled to the ground, hard.

"*Unnh,*" he groaned.

Bang!

A shot. Absalom rolled to his feet and pulled his own gun from inside his frock coat, not the little four-shot derringer in his waistband, but the big revolver Abigail had given him at the Tabernacle. He heard Annie laughing and he resolved not to look at her. The action had begun, a fight was breaking out, his sister was in the thick of it, and he was going to save her. *And* show anyone who happened to be watching that he wasn't a coward.

He hoped Annie, in particular, was watching.

Absalom charged. Around the track of the *Liahona*, past its nose and toward the hotel.

"'Til the field ring again and again!" he sang.

"Thank you for your attention!" he heard Abigail yelling as she drifted into view. "Now kindly tell me what in hell are you snakes … you *gentlemen* … doing on my property?"

Absalom saw that she held her pistol overhead, pointed at the sky. He saw that there was no fighting, only Abigail yelling at the men in her home. But he saw those things just a moment too late, as he rushed past her and charged at the flaming steam-truck. He was already leveling his borrowed pistol at the nearest putative Danite, a heavy man in a wool jacket and shapeless felt hat, and he found he couldn't stop himself.

"And whose idea was it to light a truck on fire?" Annie demanded.

Bang!

Absalom had squeezed the trigger.

ᗡ⅃Ϭ⅃Ψ⅃Ͻ

The nincompoop Fearnley-Standish missed, of course. The heavy man he'd aimed at ducked, Fearnley-Standish didn't adjust his aim in the slightest, and his bullet shattered the windscreen of the flaming steam-truck.

Burton would have liked to have the luxury of time in which to throttle the whiny little weasel, but he didn't, as the Danite with the shapeless hat who'd just been shot at took objection to his treatment. He grabbed the hilt of a knife tied to his thigh and Burton had to step in to protect the resources—however impoverished, dysfunctional and unworthy—of Her Majesty's Foreign Office.

He punched the Danite right across the jaw, dropping him like a sack of grain.

Bang! Bang! Bang!

Guns went off all around Burton. Thank Krishna most people, even professional killers, were terrible shots. He drew his 1851 Navy and looked for an efficient target.

The Danites fired and withdrew into the house. Burton saw a lean, bent, lazy-eyed rogue who appeared to be shouting orders at the others and took aim at him. Hickman, wasn't that his name? Burton had already faced him down once, in the Shoshone stockade.

Bang! Bang!

"Helldammit!" The Danite grabbed at his arm where Burton had hit him and ducked out of sight into a doorway.

"Burton, get down!" Poe shouted.

Out of the corner of his eye, Burton saw that he was alone. Fearnley-Standish had flat-out turned and run, sprinting away into the desert. His other companions had retreated more modestly, into the hotel's stable. Poe was waving an arm to summon him.

"Like hell!" Burton shouted, and charged the porch. He knew it looked like recklessness but he didn't want to give the Danites a chance to settle in and get comfortable. If Fearnley-Standish's idiotic and premature assault had any virtue, it was that it had taken the enemy by surprise. To surrender that advantage now would be a foolish waste.

A Danite ran across the porch to meet him, raising a thick-knotted club. Burton ducked under the man's swing and pistol-whipped him across the face, sending him crashing onto the smooth boards.

He really wished he had his sword with him.

A man loomed into view through a window beside Burton, pumping a rifle in both hands. "Follow up!" Burton shouted. "I mean, follow *me*!"

He jumped into the window.

Crash!

A cloud of flying glass shards came with Burton into a small sitting room and together they pounded into the rifleman, banging his head against the hardwood back of a sofa and then knocking him to the floor.

"Get that animal!" Hickman yelled in a high-pitched, nasal voice, but his troops were in disarray. As Burton had hoped, surprise and initiative were still with him.

The downed rifleman grunted and tried to raise his weapon to shoot at Burton. Burton pinned his wrist to the floor with a sharp stab of his heel, happy to be wearing heavy boots. He felt the wrist shatter, but didn't hear it in the din.

Bang!

Burton spared a bullet for the Danite leader, forcing him to duck back again, out of the small parlor in which they stood. Three shots. Accounting for the empty chamber as well, Burton had two left. He'd be hard pressed to re-load under this fire.

Another Danite charged at Burton, this man waving a cavalry saber. Burton preferred a lighter sword for fencing, frankly, an épée or a rapier, but better a saber than nothing.

Bang!

The swordsman went down in a gush of blood and a cloud of gunpowder smoke. *Thank you, Mr. Sam Colt,* Burton thought.

Under his feet, the rifleman wiggled. Burton looked down in time to see the man swing with a short, ugly boot knife for Burton's pelvis. He twisted and stepped aside—

—and winced as the knife bit into his thigh.

Damned Danite.

The man lost his grip on the knife, stuck fast in Burton's leg, and moved to bring his rifle up again.

Bang!

The thirty-six caliber bullet from the 1851 Navy left a neat round hole in the man's forehead and a quickly spreading pool of blood under his skull.

Last bullet, Burton thought. *Just in time.*

He holstered his Colt and scooped up the rifle in one hand. It was a lever action rifle, a so-called Volcano, and an innovative weapon with which Burton was not very familiar. He knew it fired exotic bullets called Rocket Balls, each bullet with its own gunpowder charge built right in, which it chambered by the action of its famous lever. He had no idea how many shots it held, or how many he had left. Burton was a pistoleer and a swordsman and not much for rifles, other than for hunting game.

He heard shouting as he bent to pick up the saber. He was alone with two dead men in the little parlor, but two different hallways led out of the room and he heard boots and saw the shadowy shapes of men down both of them.

For a second, in a lit space at the far end of one of the hallways, he saw two faces he knew.

A less observant man might have missed them, but Burton had sharp eyes and a mind for detail. It came, he knew, from memorizing so many grammatical tables in so many different languages. He knew the man's face from the calotype that the Pinkerton detectives had been flashing around Bridger's Saloon, and also from the Shoshone stockade. He recognized the little boy, of course, from the *Liahona*.

They were Seamus McNamara, the wanted man, Sam Clemens's aide, and Captain Jones's little midshipman, John Moses.

In the split second in which Burton saw them, they disappeared from view. They were beyond the Danite mob, not part of the Danites, and they looked like they were headed outside. McNamara dragged the boy by the scruff of his neck.

"Kill that son of a bitch!" Burton heard Hickman squeal, and men charged into the room.

He didn't wait for their attack. He turned and threw himself out another window and back onto the porch. Glass fell around him and with him and he rolled to one side to get away from the window.

Bang! Bang! Bang!

Bullets flew out of the hotel in his direction, but the air was full of gunfire from all sides. Burton saw gunpowder plumes in the open doors of the stable and from the deck of the *Liahona* and here and there from behind trees and rocks.

Rama's teeth, his leg hurt, but Burton had no time for it. He set the sword beside him on the porch, pumped the Volcano, satisfied to hear the *snicker-snack* of a shell sliding into the chamber, and pointed it back the way he'd come.

The first Danite jumped out the window—

—*Bang!*

Burton shot him in the chest. As he flailed and staggered back, Burton pumped the lever and shot him again.

Bang!

Charming weapon, Burton thought. He could get used to a lever-action rifle.

Shoot to kill, that was the secret. Not to injure, or frighten. Don't imagine your enemy being hit or scared and surrendering because you shot *at* him—imagine him taking your bullet in his body and dying an instant death.

Most men were useless in a firefight because secretly they didn't want to kill the other fellow. In a war, most soldiers secretly fired over their enemies' heads for the same reason. In their heart of hearts, they objected to the killing. They weren't sissies or cowards, they were just civilized men.

Richard Burton was not really a civilized man and he had no such compunction. He'd survived a spear to the head and had himself circumcised as a grown man. He'd been in great pain and close to his own death so many times that the fear, pain, and death of other men were nothing extraordinary to him, or even troublesome.

He dragged himself to his feet.

An arm protruded out the window to shoot at him blind.

Bang!

Standing, he was easily able to step out of the way of the bullet and then smash the fingers of the gun hand with the butt of his stolen rifle.

"Dammit!" The attacker dropped his pistol and yanked his hand back inside. Burton was sure he'd broken at least two fingers, and hopefully more.

Burton heard footsteps on the porch roof overhead. He stooped, picked up the abandoned pistol, and emptied it into the roof. Yells of surprise and pain and the thud of a body hitting the shingles rewarded his efforts. Burton threw aside the empty pistol and retreated back around the porch, away from the parlor.

Once he had his back against some solid wood and a moment in which no one was shooting specifically at him, Burton began reloading his 1851 Navy. As his fingers went through the practiced motions of pouring in the powder and then thumbing in bullets and the little copper percussion caps, he looked for Captain Jones.

He spotted the man's blue hat on the *Liahona*'s deck. Jones and his truck-men lay on their bellies with rifles aimed and firing at the hotel. They were shielded from the Danites' return fire by the body of the big steam-truck and their elevated position made their shots devastating. Even the Danite sharpshooters in the second story windows had to fire upward to get at Jones and his men.

No wonder they'd had a hard time mounting an effective counterattack to Burton's charge. They were under serious pressure on other fronts.

"Jones!" Burton yelled.

Bang! Bang! Bang!

"Captain Jones!"

He wanted to tell Jones about the boy but he couldn't make himself heard over the gunfire. Burton considered briefly the possibility of running over to the steam-truck, but only briefly.

In the crossfire, he'd be cut to pieces.

Best to win the gunfight first.

Burton snapped in the final cap, holstered the 1851 Navy again and took a closer look at the Volcano. He thought the bullets were loaded into a magazine that was built into the gun's muzzle, somehow, but he wasn't sure and he didn't want to fiddle with it now. He'd just shoot until the rifle was empty, then switch weapons.

He slid the saber into his belt. It was awkward, but it would do.

Then Burton moved around the back of the hotel, looking for another window to jump through.

☐⌇Ꮆ⌇Ψ⌇⌇

"There's your Irishman," Poe said.

"Where?" Coltrane peered out the open stable door, keeping his head low to the ground. Clemens's Irish thug trotted down the slope on the far side of the hotel, dragging the little boy behind him. They didn't look like they were being pursued—the Danites in the hotel had all their attention focused on their attackers.

Coltrane lunged forward, like an involuntary reflex, and Poe caught him.

"He's got the kid," Coltrane objected.

The two of them crouched low in the stable, firing occasionally out the door with pistols they'd borrowed from Captain Jones. Coltrane hadn't yet fired his strange *machine-gun*, he'd said because it wasn't very accurate and he wanted to wait until he had a close shot. Elsewhere in the stable, the three women fired pistols at the big house into which Richard Burton had disappeared.

"You'll be diced," Poe told him, "puréed."

Coltrane squinted through the buzzing hail of bullets. "Yeah, it looks dicey, alright," he agreed. "What's the *pure-aid* you're talking about?"

"I mean you'll be mowed down instantly."

Bullets buzzed and snapped and whined about them, kicking up straw and dust and wood splinters where they hit.

Coltrane flared his nostrils and looked frustrated. "But the whole damn reason I came here was to save that kid."

"Also, we have a mission," Poe reminded him.

"Yeah?" Coltrane asked, squinting at Poe. "What's the mission now, boss? Far as I can tell, we're here to rescue the enemy, Sam Clemens."

"Brigham Young isn't the enemy," Poe pointed out, but he knew it was weak. "I'm not persuaded that Sam Clemens is necessarily the enemy, either. War may yet be avoided, and that is in everyone's interest."

"Jebus." Coltrane shook his head. "War's here, boss. Duck, before it gets you."

"Something nefarious is happening in the Kingdom," Poe agreed, "but the Union may yet be saved."

"How about Eliza Snow over there?" Coltrane jerked a shoulder in her direction. "Are you thinking that she's the enemy?"

Poe looked at Roxie. She leaned her beautiful body against a heavy timber and poured fire across the open yard at the Danites.

Bullets sang in a cloud all about them.

Poe sighed. He didn't know whether she was the enemy or not.

"I have an idea," he said. The whistle hanging around his neck felt like a saving crucifix.

"To end the firefight?" the dwarf asked. "Or to avoid the war?"

"To end the shooting and rescue the boy," Poe elaborated, ignoring the dwarf's pointed quip. "But I need to get to the *Liahona*. Can you lay down suppressing fire for me with that invention?"

Jed Coltrane laid aside his borrowed pistol and picked up Mr. Browning's machine-gun. "You want *some impressive fire*? I reckon I got the means to lay down some fire as impressive as anyone's ever seen in the Kingdom." He grinned.

"I'll count down from three," Poe instructed him. "On zero, you shoot." He tucked his own pistol into his coat pocket, shifted his posture a bit, and sighted out another door. The run to the *Liahona* wasn't far, maybe only a hundred feet, but it was a hundred feet of absolutely exposed bare earth and Poe didn't want to die at the hands of some vitamin-deficient desert-dwelling cretin for the sake of that stretch.

Fortunately, the *Liahona* was turned so that its ladder faced ever-so-slightly away from the hotel.

"Three," he said calmly. He said it a little louder than he'd meant to and the women's heads all turned in his direction. He breathed in deeply but gently, trying to fill his lungs with as much air as he could without setting off a coughing fit.

Coltrane checked the ammunition drum of his gun.

"What are you fools planning over there?" Roxie asked.

"Two."

Coltrane planted the gun's stock firmly under his arm and stood, ready to go. Bullets whined and snarled through the doors of the stable.

"Poe?" Roxie's voice sounded concerned. Damn her for the ambiguity, for the unsoundable, immeasurable, inextricably tangled mess she had made of his heart.

"One."

Coltrane spat on the floor. "Kidnapping sons of bitches," he muttered.

"Poe, I love you," Roxie said.

"Zero."

Poe hesitated a moment, deliberately.

Coltrane stepped into the open door and squeezed the trigger on his gun. Roxie's words and the sudden explosion of noise almost stunned Poe into immobility—

—*rat-rat-tat-tat-tat-tat-tat-tat-tat-tat!*—

—but not quite.

Poe sprinted.

He didn't waste time or effort looking to see what was happening to the hotel, but he heard Danites yelling, and their shooting ceased, and the air was shredded by the sound of every window in the big house shattering at the same moment. Coltrane's borrowed gun sounded like an army of roaring beavers *chewing* the hotel to pieces.

"Take that, you whoreson kid-stealers!" Coltrane shouted, and then Poe was safe, behind the *Liahona*.

The more normal gunfire resumed as he dragged his body up the ladder and threw himself onto his belly on its deck. Poe coughed deeply, almost choking on the thick ball of blood and phlegm that came up and that he spat over the side. He wiped his mouth on his coat sleeve like any barbarian and when he looked up he found himself staring into the face of Captain Dan Jones.

"Welcome aboard!" Jones shouted. "That's an impressive weapon your friend has, boyo, but I can't say I know what you're up to!"

Poe pointed to where he could just see the Irishman and the boy, disappearing into the weeds at the bottom of the hotel's long yard. "I've got something in the hold," he explained. "Something to put an end to the fight, so we can get the boy."

Captain Jones's face lit up into a snarl as he saw the child. "To hell with the hold, Mr. Jamison! I've got something in the wheelhouse." He gripped Poe's shoulder in solidarity. "Hold on!"

Jones scrambled on hands and knees into the *Liahona*'s wheelhouse, under the chest-high scythe of whizzing Danite bullets. Poe wondered if he was about to fire the railguns at the Danites, but they didn't seem to be very accurate, especially at short range. All he would do is punch holes in the hotel, which was already in bad shape.

Then Poe realized what Jones was up to, and wrapped his arms around the base of the nearest Franklin Pole.

The *Liahona* groaned as she shifted into gear, steam and coal smoke exploded out her tailpipes, and she lurched into forward motion—

—Poe held on—

—he heard a ragged cheer from the stable—

—then the *Liahona* plowed into the Hot Springs Hotel and Brewery.

The dusty blue sky above and around Poe exploded into timber fragments and shattered furniture. There was ceiling above him, and then there wasn't, and then there was again. Startled Danites on the second story of the hotel turned to shoot at the *Liahona* as it moved through them.

Poe drew his pistol and gamely returned fire, along with several of the truck-men, but the gun battle was brief. The Danites disappeared, flying away into oblivion as the hotel fell asunder under their feet. Poe felt tired and rattled and his lung felt like a stinking swamp of death. He struggled up the Franklin Pole to his feet, peering through the exploding and collapsing walls around him to try to see the Irishman and the boy.

Or Roxie.

Had she said "I love you" to him?

CLANG-NG-NG-NG!

The *Liahona* crashed to a stop and Poe fell to the deck, hard, and skidded.

His head spun. Steam billowed up around him. *Had the Liahona ruptured its boiler?* he wondered. But it seemed like there was too much steam for that.

Screaming.

Poe reeled to his feet, vision still swimming.

Half the hotel was gone, reduced to a pile of crushed matchsticks beneath the immense treads of Captain Dan Jones's steam-truck. The portion that still stood wobbled like a drunkard about to finish his evening badly. Jones and his sailors lay about on the deck of the vehicle, groaning, nursing injuries, and helping each other to their feet.

The *Liahona* puffed out steam and smoke, but it wasn't moving. Poe risked a look over the side, and saw that the treads were still. He looked at the ladder to make sure there weren't Danites coming up the side, then made his way forward to the wheelhouse.

"What happened?" he asked the truck's Captain.

Jones shook his head and staggered to his feet. He carefully armed himself with a long pistol from a rack above the inside of the wheelhouse door before answering. "I don't know, boyo. I'm pretty sure I was aimed straight when we hit the hotel, but once we were inside, the wheel jumped and everything got muddled."

Poe walked with Captain Jones to the front of the steam-truck. They moved carefully, watching for attackers, but the only living Danites they saw were running down, out, and away from the hotel. Around the front of the *Liahona* rose a veil of steam.

"The water tank," Jones realized. "I hit the water tank."

"I think your steam-truck may be in grave need of a little maintenance," Poe advised him.

Poe heard feet on the ladder and braced himself with his pistol. It was Roxie and he put his pistol away.

"Have you seen Burton?" he asked.

She wrapped her arms around him.

"I haven't seen him since he went into the hotel," he finished lamely.

"Burton will be fine," she assured him.

"He could be dead."

"Then Old Scratch and his minions have their hands full right now. Annie and the English girl are looking for the other Englishman now. And your dwarf is running down the hill after the little boy."

"I'd better go help him," Poe suggested, but he didn't move.

"Yes, you'd better," she agreed. She didn't move, either. She smiled elegantly, with poise and grace.

"Trouble," Poe heard Dan Jones mutter in his ear.

"Aren't they always?" Poe asked. He felt warm and calm and blissful. Somewhere in this bouquet of roses, he thought, there must be a thorn that would draw his blood. For the moment, he was content to smell the flowers.

"I don't mean *her*," Jones snorted. "I mean *them*."

Poe disengaged and looked up to see what Jones was pointing at.

Behind the *Liahona*, on the highway above the Hot Springs Hotel and Brewery, stood perhaps twenty-five dusty brass clocksprung horses. Their riders wore gray uniforms now and had pistols drawn.

They looked very serious.

The Third Virginia Cavalry.

"Dammit," Poe cursed. "The cavalry's here."

PART THE THIRD

ꙨꙄꙆꙡꙦꙨꙮꙶꙊ

TIMPANOGOS

CHAPTER ELEVEN

S houlda got a knife," Jed Coltrane grunted to himself as he sprinted.

A throwing knife in particular would have been perfect but anything with a blade would have been enough to kill Sam Clemens's thug. Even a pistol would have done nicely, or a carbine with decent aim. But the aim on the machine-gun wasn't good enough to hit the wiry Irishman. Not without hitting the boy, too.

Not without getting a lot closer.

When the hotel had collapsed, O'Shaughnessy had looked back, once. Jed had watched him assess the situation from his perch inside the stable door, then turn and shuffle quicker down the hill. Jed couldn't see where the Irishman was headed, other than toward the weeds and scrub oak at the bottom of the long yard. For once, he wished he were a taller man, with a taller man's vantage point on the situation.

No amount of wishing would make him grow an inch, though.

So he sprinted down the hill, trying his best not to be heard.

He knew there was a perfectly good question that was dying to be asked, which went something like, *Jed Coltrane, are you out of your damned mind? What are you doing risking your life for this kid, and he ain't even yours?*

He didn't ask the question, though. Once he started asking questions like that, it seemed to him that there wouldn't be any point to any of it. If he couldn't save an innocent little kid, what was the point of trying to stop wars anyway? Or win them, for that matter.

So he just ran.

Jed crested the slope of the yard enough to see the little two-roomed springhouse at the bottom of the hill just as the Irishman reached it. Two men in black coats stood before the building, holding rifles in front of their chests and looking nervous.

O'Shaughnessy looked up the hill and pointed at the hotel.

I'm spotted, Jed thought, but he kept running.

The two men looked up, saw Jed and raised their rifles. The dwarf threw himself onto his belly, fumbling to raise the machine-gun into attack position—

—but the Irishman drew his weapon first, the silent gun of the Pinkertons—

—and shot both the springhouse guards in the backs of their heads, *zip! zip!,* as neat as you please. They fell, pink clouds drifting around their faces.

Jed fired, aiming high.

Rat-tat-tat-tat-tat-tat!

A cloud of black smoke from the gun swallowed Jed, filling his nostrils with the brimstone reek of hell and death.

The bird-headed thug ducked, crouched, and picked up John Moses.

Jed stopped firing. "Damn!" he cursed, and scrambled forward down the hill, half crawling, half tumbling, fighting not to lose his grip on Jonathan Browning's gun.

The Irishman raised his firearm again and shot at the springhouse door.

Zip! Clang!

A shattered padlock fell to the ground.

O'Shaughnessy stepped around behind the corner of the springhouse, still holding John Moses in front of him like a shield. "Stay inside, Sam!" he shouted, and fired again at Jed.

Bullets whipped through the tall yellow grass around the dwarf. *So that's the way of it,* he thought. Well, if the Irishman was concerned about Sam Clemens, that gave Jed Coltrane a little lever to pull on.

He pointed the machine-gun at the springhouse and squeezed the trigger until the drum was empty and the hammer clicked on an empty chamber.

Rat-tat-tat-tat-tat-tat-tat-tat-tat-tat-click!

Smoke enveloped him as he fired. Wood chips and sawdust sprang off the rough log exterior of the springhouse like it was the inside of a sawmill.

"Die, Yankee!" Jed hollered. *There,* he thought smugly. *That ought to flush the ugly Irishman out.*

"No!" O'Shaughnessy screamed, and charged forward, knocking the boy John Moses aside as he did so.

Jed and O'Shaughnessy were ten yards apart and Jed realized his miscalculation—

—the Irish thug pointed his gun at the dwarf and squeezed the trigger—

—*click.*

Both men froze.

Jed's gun was empty, but O'Shaughnessy might not know it. He raised it to his chest, meaning to bluff—

—the Irishman dropped his pistol and slapped his hand down at his thigh—

—on an empty holster.

"Fookin' hell!" he shouted, and whirled around to face the boy John Moses.

John Moses stood calmly, holding the silenced pistol in both hands, pointing it at the Irishman.

"Good job, kid!" Jed shouted. "Give it up, you stupid Mick!"

O'Shaughnessy bolted.

He sprang across the stream, coat flapping out behind him like a peacock's tail, and crashed into a thicket of scrub oak trees.

"Shit," Jed grumbled. He sprinted to the springhouse. "Give me the gun, John Moses."

John Moses shook his head and pointed the Maxim at Jed.

"The hell? He might a got you killed, boy!"

"I don't want you to kill him," John Moses said stubbornly. "He's running away."

"Dammit—" Jed reached for the gun and John Moses raised its muzzle, aiming straight for the dwarf's forehead.

"No."

"Fine." Jed briefly considered reloading the machine-gun but that was a tedious, time-consuming task and the weapon was heavy, and the Irishman was getting away. He dropped the gun and shrugged out of the bag carrying ammunition. "Thanks for the loan," he said, and he rushed into the oak on O'Shaughnessy's trail.

ⵌⵕⵟⵡⵀⵔⵔⵕⵡⵒⵋⵌⵌ

Absalom stopped running in a grove of cottonwood trees.

Well, not a grove. Three trees standing together at the base of a long hill. He wasn't sure where he was exactly but, approximately, he thought he might be somewhere north of the Hot Springs Hotel & Brewery and downhill of the highway leading back to the Great Salt Lake City.

The mountains were on his right hand.

"Absalom, Absalom!" he heard behind him.

He threw himself in among the trees for protection, held his gun high, in as manly and determined a fashion as he could, conscious that in his effort to look the hero, he might instead have made himself the fool. When he felt appropriately composed, he looked back.

Abigail raced towards him through the little gulley down which he'd come. Right behind her came Annie, also running. Each woman held her skirt high with one hand and pointed a pistol at the sky with the other.

They looked silly and that made him feel a little calmer. He was careful not to laugh as they caught up to him.

"Absalom, stop!" Abigail shouted.

"I am stopped." His heart thundered in his chest as if it would never end. "I was looking for decent cover from which to continue the attack." He laughed his best baritone laugh. "I hadn't realized I'd come so far. Fog of war, uncertain terrain, all that."

"Are you wounded?" Abigail asked.

"That was an impressive charge, Mr. Fearnley-Standish," Annie added, catching up and stopping, but still clutching her skirt up over her ankles. Her *shapely* ankles, Absalom couldn't help noticing, even through her almost knee-high boots. "Only Mr. Burton charged with you, I saw. The rest of us took cover."

Absalom vaguely remembered Richard Burton running past him and into the building right in the teeth of the Danites and he realized that Annie must not have seen the events very clearly. He coughed with as much humility as he could muster. "Yes, well," he said. No one else was running down the gully, the gunfire had stopped, and he had no idea what was happening at the hotel at that moment. "Of course, after the initial charge, I thought I should take cover, as well. No sense running to meet a pointless death, is there?"

"You Brits are either the bravest men I've ever seen or you're stark raving lunatics in need of incarceration."

Abigail snorted.

"Yes," Absalom agreed, but then kicked himself for the insipidity of his answer. "Perhaps both." That wasn't quite right either, and he tried to make up for it by grinning his most piratical grin, but that just made him feel silly. He wanted to be a lunatic, stark raving mad from sheer courage, like the infernal Burton, so that Annie would like him. Sadly, he knew he wasn't cut from the right stuff.

"Are you wounded?" Abigail asked again. She dropped her skirt and balled her free hand into a fist on her hip. Her voice sounded dangerously flat and Absalom wasn't sure how to read that. Her question reminded him of the reason he'd come to Deseret in the first place.

"No," he admitted. "But the Danites appear to have occupied your hotel and all the shooting has probably destroyed the building. Will you come home with me now?"

She slapped him in the face.

"You idiot!" she snapped at him. "I've come back here for my husband, not for the damned building. Orrin Porter Rockwell is my man and I mean to stay with him!"

"Don't hit him!" Annie shouted. She looked surprisingly compassionate, so much so that Absalom half-hoped his sister *would* hit him again.

"No need to curse, ladies," he mumbled.

Pffffffft-ankkkh! Pffffffft-ankkkh! Pffffffft-ankkkh!

Absalom spun around, pistol pointing.

Behind him a big Strider crouched, lowering its carriage close to the ground. Absalom found himself staring down the barrels of large-bore guns and he raised his own pistol to shoot at the attackers, trying not to cringe too visibly. If he had to die, he didn't mind that it was a heroic death, defending two women—

"Stop!"

Annie spun like a top, throwing her leg surprisingly high into the air and kicking Absalom's borrowed pistol out of his hand.

Bang!

The shot went wide.

"Egad!" Absalom complained. He was about to ask *What did you do that for?* when the gunner snapped open the smoked visor of her helmet and revealed herself as Master Sergeant Jackson. "Thank you," he added, trying to recover his dignity. "Sometimes my reflexes are entirely *too* quick."

"Joo've got killer espirit, Meester Top Hat," Jackson called out over the chugging of her big machine. "But joo've got to get a little more control *de tu mismo.*"

Absalom was no Spanish speaker and the gunner's words baffled him slightly. Had she just advised him to control his detumescence? That didn't seem right. Anyway, she was smiling, so he smiled back.

"I've found control to be an overrated quality, myself," Annie responded. She stared fiercely at the Mexican Striderwoman and something about her stance made Absalom think she might jump up on the vehicle and kick Jackson.

He found the prospect surprisingly interesting.

"Joo'll find that it's more important, when joo have a bigger gun," Jackson shot back. She patted the barrel of the big weapon in front of her. "Wouldn't joo say, Top Hat?"

"Er …"

Abigail snorted again. "Get in," she told Absalom, hitching up her skirt and clambering up the Baba Yaga legs of the Strider. She climbed like a bear, Absalom thought, with muscle and purpose but no poise. Annie followed, more gracefully.

Absalom recovered his pistol and brought up the rear, trying not to embarrass himself in front of all the ladies. The driver, at least, he noted with some relief as he hoisted himself up into the carriage and dropped onto the rumble seat, was a man. His visor was up and he grinned at Absalom under an oiled mustache.

"Where are we going?" Absalom asked. He wasn't sure he cared very much. He had found Abigail and was still trying to persuade her to leave Deseret with him, and he wasn't in much of a hurry to accomplish anything else. Also, he found that he enjoyed being surrounded by women who were quarreling over him. "Back into the battle?"

"The battle is changing," Master Sergeant Jackson said. "Joo'll see. *Ándale!*" she barked at the pilot.

Both Mexicans snapped their visors into place and the Strider rose to its full height.

Pffffft-ankkkh!

1HƆ7ᴧЯ0ᗎᴧ8

Bullets buzzed through the wood and struck things inside the springhouse.

Thud! Thud! Snap!

"Ugh," someone grunted. *Clatter, foomph, splash.*

The bullets were hitting people too, Sam realized. Someone had taken a slug and slipped into the creek.

"I ain't hit," Orrin Porter Rockwell barked in the darkness.

"Nor I," echoed Ambassador Armstrong of the many names.

"Argh!" snapped a strangled, irascible voice.

"I expect that means President Young has taken the bullet," Sam concluded. "Mr. President, are you still with us?"

"I'm alive," Brigham Young chomped out the words.

"Good thing, too," Sam said. "I've seen the widow's walk of the Beehive House and I'm not sure it could take the weight of all your widows."

There was a moment of silence—Sam couldn't tell if it was shocked or awkward silence—and then Armstrong started to laugh, a dark rich sound reminiscent of smoked meat or chocolate or both. After a few seconds, Rockwell joined in with a surprisingly high-pitched snicker.

"Don't worry," Young answered, teeth in his voice. "Truman Angell built that house to my own specifications and I made sure he had that piece particularly reinforced."

There was a moment of silence and then Young chuckled.

Armstrong and Rockwell burst back into howls of laughter. Sam wished he had a Partagás. He had a craving for the taste and besides, telling a joke without a Partagás in his hand felt like doing a magic trick without a top hat and wand.

"I don't suppose they'd worry too much, though," he continued. "They'd just figure your cog had been repurposed to a higher level of the Great Machine." The laughter trailed off, a little uncertain.

"You're making a joke, Clemens," President Young snorted in the darkness, "but of course you're exactly right."

"Good to hear," Sam couldn't resist one last crack. "I can't abide any other outcome than being exactly right."

"Are joo badly injured, Meester President?" the Ambassador asked.

"I'm bleeding," Young said. "I've bled before. Let's get out of this place."

"Well, the gun's outta my reach," Rockwell explained, "seeing as it's up on a rafter and my hands are tied behind my back. Anybody else got the free use of their hands?"

They all muttered that they didn't.

"All right, then. The knife's in a barrel of beans, but it ain't very far down. All we gotta do is get the lid off it and dig down into the beans a little ways. I reckon we can do that even with our hands tied behind our backs."

"Which barrel is it?" Sam asked. "How do we find it?"

Rockwell hesitated slightly. "It's the one marked *red beans*," he said.

Armstrong started laughing again.

"Our hands being tied may not be the most daunting obstacle we face," Sam observed.

"Yeah, well, shoot me for an idiot, I guess," Rockwell grumbled. "I figured someday I'd be holed up in here with Injuns shooting at me, or a mountain lion. Never guessed I'd be blind and tied up, too."

⅄Ɔ⅂ᴧԀ0Ɣ8

CRASH!

Burton was racing through the upper story of the hotel, close on Hickman's heels and chasing the Danite leader through some sort of bedroom, when the *Liahona* plowed into the building. The force of it, and the surprise, knocked him to the floor and for several tense moments he thought he would die with Bill Hickman in a tangle of ruined house-carpentry and cheap furnishings.

When the shuddering was finished and the ruptured hot water tank had flooded the ground floor he was still on the upper storey, only one of the walls of the room had been ripped away, the bed had been torn right out of the room, and the cheap wallpaper was beginning to curl from the steam.

And Hickman was already scrambling to his feet.

Burton fired the Volcanic rifle at his man as the Danite slipped out the door.

Bang!

A miss, and though the bullet punched through the wall it still missed Hickman on the other side.

Burton pumped the rifle to fire again.

Click.

He tossed the Volcanic aside. He spared only a second's thought for the *Liahona*—it had passed by the room he was in, and was too far away for it or any of its passengers or crew to be of any help to Richard Burton.

Burton stood and drew the 1851 Navy from its holster. He left the knife in his leg. He'd pull it out when the shooting was over but he didn't want to do it yet, for fear that sudden blood loss would knock him unconscious.

He was already feeling a bit woozy.

Gun first, Burton staggered out of the room on Hickman's trail.

He saw Hickman squeezing out through one of the two windows in the next room just as he entered. One wall was torn away here too, and the air was wet and hot with steam.

Burton squeezed the trigger without hesitating, almost without aiming.

Click.

The gun misfired.

"Where's Brigham Young?" he shouted, pulling the trigger again.

Click.

"Rostam's mace!" he swore. The powder had gotten wet in the steam. He shoved the gun back into its holster and lurched across the room as fast as he could.

Hickman slipped out of sight, sliding down. Burton drew the saber, throwing himself towards the window.

Crash!

The bedroom's other window shattered and a man in a short coat and beaver hat piled through, knees and elbows first. He had one arm up in front of his face to protect it and a knife in each hand.

Burton aimed for the man's shoulder, hoping to incapacitate him and head off any fight. He was painfully aware that, outside the window, Hickman was scrambling down a short-shingled roof and headed for some surface that might be the top of a steam-truck.

He swung, expecting the man to land and lunge—

—his attacker dropped and rolled instead—

—and Burton missed.

The force of his swing carried him past the tumbling Danite and his wounded leg made him stumble and slide off-balance. Together, they put him out of position—which meant that the Danite's knife narrowly missed biting into Burton's belly and instead just cut through his coat.

Slicing open my official correspondence, Burton thought.

In return he kicked the Danite, to keep him rolling and move him further away so Burton could regain his balance. Teetering as he was, though, and kicking with a knife stuck in his thigh, Burton's kick was girlishly weak and ineffective.

The Danite's hat fell off but he sprang to his feet and charged Burton. He slashed with both knives, arms snapping back and forth in front of him like a willow tree whipping about in a high wind.

Burton longed for an épée, or a spear, or anything else with a point. A sharpened stick would have done nicely. The saber he had taken from the Danite was a chopping weapon only, a clumsy piece of work useful only to horsemen and hatcheteers. With a pointed weapon, he could keep the knife-wielder at bay. With this saber, he could only hack and slash, try not to expose himself too much and hope for a major hit on his opponent.

"Like I'm chopping down trees!" he grunted, not really realizing he was speaking out loud until he had done so. To emphasize his point, he swung for the knife fighter's throat, then quickly stepped aside as the other man lunged into the space vacated by the sword, slicing and stabbing in short, furious blows.

Thud! From outside. *That would be Hickman,* Burton thought, *landing on the steam-truck.* The Danite would get away if he didn't do something, and pretty quick.

He backed away in a circle from a flurry of blows. He felt the steam before he actually saw the missing wall out of the corner of his eye and turned sharply to avoid falling into hot water.

This was like a samurai sword; like the long, one-edged katana of the bushido warrior. Kendo, he knew the art of fighting with such swords was called. Gliding steps, long arcs of attack and powerful incapacitating blows.

Impressive to watch and effective against a similarly armed fighter.

Useless against a quick man with knives.

Burton backed away again under a rain of razor-sharp knife blades. The cuff of his coat sleeve lost two buttons to a slashing attack that he only barely avoided and his boot knocked aside the Danite's beaver hat.

Under the window a steam engine hissed into life, coughing vapor up into the curtains. Burton was out of time.

With his hurt leg his kicked up the hat, hurling it into his attacker's face.

The Danite kept coming, slash, slash—

—Burton sacrificed his left arm.

He thrust his arm in among the cutting blades. He felt the steel of one knife tear into the flesh of his upper arm. His heavy coat dulled the attack somewhat but not enough to prevent the searing pain entirely.

Burton grunted with pain—

—but he closed his hand around the wrist of the Danite's other arm, preventing that knife from stabbing him in the chest—

—and punched his foe in the nose with the heavy basket hilt of his stolen saber.

Hard.

The man stumbled back. Burton let him go and grinned a farewell as he tumbled through where a wall had once been, over the edge and into the steam and hot water below. He screamed as he fell, then hit the ground below with both a *splash* and a *thud*.

Burton had no time to waste on monitoring the man's fate, nor on removing the knives from his arm and leg. He threw himself through the window and bounced down the porch roof, just in time to flop onto the rooftop of the steam-truck's cargo compartment a split second before it pulled away.

"Rudabeh's blessed withers, but that smarts," he ground out through clenched teeth as the steam-truck turned and started bouncing down the field behind the hotel.

He saw the Third Virginia Cavalry, or at least a couple of dozen of them, arrayed beside the beached *Liahona* behind him and on the bluff above the steam-truck. They were talking to Poe and they didn't look friendly.

Burton tightened his grip on the cavalry saber.

⸮IƆ⅂ꟽЯ0ꟼꟽ⅃Ɔᓕ

Tamerlane O'Shaughnessy ran like the devil himself was after him. *Only it wasn't the devil, was it?* Because the devil was clearly the thieving little boy who had taken his gun just when he needed it most, not the ugly monkey whose own machine of death had apparently run empty or misfired or jammed at the crucial instant … the devil had better luck than that, didn't he?

Weeds whipped at his legs, but they were nothing. The branches of the bloody-damn-hell trees that poked at his eyes and scratched his cheeks, now those were things to worry about. What the hell did you call these things? Mother O'Shaughnessy never prepared him for trees like these. They had leaves like oak trees but they were midgets.

Tiny hell-spawned midgets like the circus freak on his tail.

Tam slapped at the last hedge of branches and broke through. His foot struck something invisible in the grass—

—pain scorched his ankle—

—he stumbled forward, tripped, caught himself on his good leg, kept hobbling.

If he couldn't run, he had to fight. He still had the stiletto on his wrist and the canister of weird brass beetles inside his coat … whatever they might do to flesh. *Of course, they certainly made a mess of some of the Deseret Hotel's upholstery, me boy,* he said to himself, *so you can likely guess what they'd do to a bit of tender meat.* They'd scared the shite out of the midget when Tam had pretended he was going to loose them on the child, anyway.

But the clearing wasn't empty; there was a little wooden hut in the center of it, a tiny shack with a hole shaped like a blazing sun carved into the door. *Is that a shithouse?* Tam wondered. *Who wants to run all the way down from the house, a quarter of a mile away, holding up the flap of his long woolens with every step, when he has a case of the trots?* A shithouse belonged right behind the house, not on the other side of the hill. These Mormons were idjits, all of them.

Tam shot a glance over his shoulder—the dwarf lagged behind, probably slowed down even worse than Tam by the fake oak trees because he was such a runty little thing. His head wasn't even visible above the trees' claws; Tam only knew generally where he was by the rustling of grass and the shaking of branches.

He had a few seconds' lead time but not much more.

Perfect.

Tam opened the canister. He cracked the outhouse door and lifted the plank seat worn smooth by years of straining Deseret buttocks, exposing a dark and reeking pit. He threw his scarf onto the edge of the hole—that'd catch the dwarf's attention and make him hesitate. Then he scattered brass beetles around the floor inside, over stones worn flat by use and the curling back half of a Sears Roebuck catalog, advertising hoop skirts and panacea tablets and wooden hobbyhorses and hunting rifles.

Leaving the door open a touch, he gimped as quickly as he could around and behind the outhouse to hide.

He looked at the canister while he listened for the dwarf's approach. There were two buttons inside the lid. He'd figured which button activated the bloody things back at the Deseret Hotel, turned them into unstoppable chewers and devourers of matter, but in all the excitement since he'd forgotten which it was. He let his imagination run wild for a few seconds, thinking about the irritating dwarf being chewed down to bones and buttons by a swarm of clicking brass beetles.

"Heh, heh," he chuckled. *You've got the little bastard now, me boy.*

But which button to press? He'd forgotten which was which and they weren't labeled or marked in any way.

He heard the soft *thud* and *swish* of little dwarf feet coming through the clearing.

To hell with it. He'd press both buttons and St. Brigit would do the rest. Mother O'Shaughnessy hadn't raised him to be a coward.

He held the canister in one hand and kept his knife hand free, just in case, but the stiletto still tight against his forearm, to keep one unpleasant little surprise in store for an appropriate moment. If he had a bit more of a head start, he reflected, he might have loaded the Maxim Husher, and that would have given the midget an entertaining jolt. Oh, well.

The door creaked open.

"The hell?" the midget muttered.

Tam jammed his thumb down over both the canister's buttons.

Click-clack-clatter, click-clack-clatter, he heard from the outhouse. He grinned, stood up, and limped two steps away from the outhouse.

"Shit!" the dwarf yelled, there was a *thump,* and the outhouse rattled, like the dwarf was wrestling someone inside. It was as good as a stage show, it was, all that shaking and noise and Tam bursting at the seams with laughter all the while. Tam imagined the little corn-pone-nibbler fighting all the beetles at once in there, maybe swarming together like a cloud into the shape of a fighting man, or maybe the beetles swarmed together into the shape of a bigger beetle.

It was like having a genie in a magic lamp.

He rubbed the canister fondly, feeling very satisfied and wishing he could have a nice drink of whisky to celebrate. Maybe the beetles could bring him some, if he rubbed their little brass bellies and asked nicely.

The outhouse stopped moving.

Then he saw a glistening brass carpet, edging out from under the outhouse door and swarming in his direction. It was the beetles.

And as they came, they devoured. He saw tiny brass bug-jaws tearing at grass and sticks on the ground and even little stones, shattering it all and ripping it to shreds.

Tam took a long step back.

Click-clack-clatter.

Surely, the little creatures were heading his way because they'd done their job, and now they were coming home to their jar to go nicely back to sleep again, weren't they? He'd jammed both buttons, and one was the *eat* button and one was the *go to sleep* button. They'd eaten, and now they were going to go to sleep.

The swarm kept coming. Behind it, the ground was gnawed clean.

Tam took another step back. "Easy, lads."

Could the dwarf have taken control of the bugs somehow, countermanded Tam's attack order? Tam shook his head, that notion made no bloody-damn-hell sense at all.

Click-clack-clatter.

Or did it? An ether device, a timer, a code of some kind only the bugs knew or could hear, a secret communication by vibration, Brigit's belly button, even telepathy? In a world in which flesh-eating metal bugs could be poured out of a can like so many oats, what *wasn't* possible? Tam's heart pounded like a railroad piston.

The swarm was almost on him.

Tam threw the canister away to his left, into the trees, and lurched away several steps to his right.

The metal bug swarm followed the canister.

Tam stopped and watched, realizing that he was sweating and shaking from nerves. Where the canister had landed he saw grass fall over as if it were mowing itself, and then a tree snapped and toppled to the ground, and then another.

He watched for thirty seconds or maybe a minute, until there was a circle of scoured earth around the canister and the beetles had crawled inside. No more *click-clack* and his heart was starting to slow down, but Tam didn't dare go pick the canister up.

Not yet. He'd let it lie a while.

Still, if the little bugs had done so much damage to the local flora, he had to imagine they'd made short work of the cracker midget. Tam chuckled, shook his head to clear out the adrenalin, and walked around to the front of the outhouse and its open door.

The seat was down again. There was no sign at all of the Sears Roebuck catalog, with its skirts and guns and toys and snake oil. *Shame, that,* Tam reflected, too late. The Sears Roebuck catalog made nice reading in idle moments, he should have kept it. No sign of the scarf or the dwarf, either, though.

"Bad luck, that," Tam chortled. "Shitty way to die." He laughed out loud, cackling like the vulture he resembled. "On the other hand, it seems I've lost my good scarf."

Click.

Tam froze.

"You lost more'n that, Irish."

Tam looked up. Above the outhouse door, on the inside, was a little shelf. The dwarf was perched up in the ceiling, wedged there with one hand on the little shelf and both feet against the far wall.

"Monkey!" Tam gasped.

"Proud of it," grunted the little man.

In his free hand, he held a long pistol, cocked and pointed at Tam O'Shaughnessy's birdlike head.

"Fookin' hell," Tam commented.

"Guess you forgot I could climb."

"You had another pistol?"

"Believe it or not, I found one in the crapper."

D.J. Butler

Tam slammed the door shut and threw himself to one side.

Bang! Bang!

Splintered holes erupted in the desiccated wood of the outhouse but the bullets missed Tam and he sprint-hobbled for the canister again.

The bloody-damn-hell metal beetles might eat him alive, but they might not, and the midget certainly would.

Thump!

Tam heard the door kicked open behind him and he knew the dwarf was only seconds from blasting him to oblivion. He staggered through grass, cutting across towards the artificial clearing where the bugs had *click-clack-clattered* everything right down to the ground like hyperactive sheep, or termites.

Bang!

Tam felt the bullet burn through his coat, narrowly missing his ribs.

He saw the canister and jumped, throwing himself headlong and grabbing for it like he was a drowning man it was a rope. He clenched his teeth and squinted at the thought that he might be throwing himself to his own death but he didn't see any of the little buggers on the ground—

—he hit, *oomph*, grabbed the canister—

—and rolled to his feet.

"Brigit!" he howled, pain lancing through his twisted ankle.

Miraculously, all the bugs stayed inside. They were quiet and still and Tam jammed down both buttons again.

Click-clack-clatter, click-clack-clatter, he heard in the canister as he raised it over his head.

The midget froze, gun pointed at Tam.

"They're activated, you little ape, do you hear me? They're turned on!"

The dwarf spat slowly on the ground. "I can hear 'em," he admitted.

"Shoot me and I throw the little buggers! Then we both die! Is that what you want?"

The midget seemed to be considering. "I want you to leave the boy alone," he said.

"I don't give a fook about the boy!" Tam felt hysterical.

"Then what the hell do you want?"

Tam considered, for a split second, the possibility of telling the dwarf. Maybe they could reach a deal. They could both agree not to talk to the Pinkertons, to lie low, and soon enough he and Sam Clemens would have finished this rotten mission and be out of the Kingdom. Tam could go off to California or Novy Moskva or somewhere else where the Pinkertons would never find him.

Hell, he might even be willing to go back to Ireland. Potato blight or not, he'd learned there were worse places to be.

Tam shook his head. No, he could never trust the midget. The man was crooked, he might turn Tam in for the reward money or worse. He might turn him in just because Tam was a Union man, and the dwarf was with the South. Or maybe he hated the Irish. The Southerners were notorious for that sort of ill-will and the little fellow had that horrible loping sound to his voice that marked him as a Mississippi monkey, or Louisiana, or something … Tam wasn't very good at telling those accents apart.

He had to bluff or threaten or fight.

Tam drew back the arm with the canister in it, like he was going to throw.

The dwarf cocked his pistol.

"Stop!"

The voice rang through the confusion of Tam's thoughts and over his thudding heartbeat like a bell. It came from somewhere over in the tall grass. Tam tried to split his eyes, send one poking around to look for the source of the voice while the other stayed fixed on his opponent. He could see the dwarf doing the same.

The voice belonged to the boy, John Moses.

He stepped out of the grass and into the clearing. "Stop fighting," he said. "It isn't nice."

"Oh, yeah?" Tam sneered.

"Yeah," John Moses said.

Then Tam noticed that the little boy held the strange rapid-shot gun. It looked gigantic in his childish hands. He struggled but he managed to lift it and hold the barrel more or less level. Level enough to mow Tam flat, judging by what he'd seen it do to the front of the hotel.

"I said stop fighting," John Moses repeated himself in his wee piping whistle of a voice. "And I mean it, you fooks."

"Shite," Tam said.

⅄HƆ⅂ꟽⱧOꝎ⅄⅊

"You're all under arrest," called one of the cavalrymen in a loud, trumpet-like voice. The men were out of their ordinary uniforms and wearing the strange gray outfits but the speaker had two chevrons on the sleeves of his jacket. Poe inferred that the chevrons marked him as a corporal.

"By what authority?" Poe demanded.

"On what charges?" Roxie chimed in.

"Who in blazes are you?" asked Captain Jones.

"Authority be damned," the Corporal drawled, "charges go to hell and I, you shiftless truck-gypsy, am the *government*. Haven't you heard?"

"We're armed," Poe called out. He very deliberately didn't raise his pistol—he didn't want to provoke an actual shooting match, outnumbered eight to one as he and his allies, if they really were allies, were—but it felt heavy and conspicuous in his hand. "You may not find us so easy to govern, Corporal."

The Corporal rode his horse-machine down the slope, and half his men followed his example. The rest stayed up on the slope, looking down on the *Liahona*, guns ready. The dozen cavalrymen stopped below the steam-truck's ladder and the Corporal looked up at the passengers and crew.

"Everyone is armed in this godforsaken country. But truthfully, sir," he said, "I care neither for you nor about you, so long as you stay where you are and do not interfere with the execution of my appointed tasks. I am looking for a Mr. William Hickman, who may go by the name *Bill*. He has been described to me in such terms that, homely though I find you to be, you are not nearly ugly enough to be the man I seek."

"I'm not Bill Hickman," Poe agreed. He was grateful for his smoked glasses, which let him survey the scene a little more than was obvious. The men who had ridden down to the hotel could be surprised and taken, he thought. The men still on the bluff, on the other hand, had a commanding vantage point. There would be no sneaking up on them, unless someone managed to creep around the *Liahona* itself.

He wondered where his allies were.

Hissssss!

An engine started with a loud squealing sound, somewhere inside or just on the other side of the hotel. Poe would never have heard it, except the house had been reduced to a tiny, shattered shadow of its former self.

"We came here looking for Hickman ourselves," Roxie added.

Gears whined, and a steam-truck suddenly spun into view around the ruined hulk of the Hot Springs Hotel & Brewery. It was a medium-sized cargo vehicle and it turned away as it emerged, rolling down the yard. Men in black coats with rifles, wet and bedraggled and not very cheerful, hung off the back.

"That might be him," Poe suggested. He was perfectly happy for the Virginian to capture or even kill Hickman. He wanted to rescue Brigham Young—he wanted to help Roxie—and that meant getting out from under the heel of these soldiers.

Pffffffft-ankkkh!

The sound was slightly muffled. He wondered what it could be. Maybe some part of the water tank was still grinding away at its usual task or finally breaking down.

"This way, gentlemen," the Corporal ordered his complement of a dozen and they trotted down the slope. The others remained behind, holding their high ground advantage.

Pffffffft-ankkkh!

"What's that sound, Captain?" Poe asked. "Please reassure me that the *Liahona* is not on the verge of exploding."

"No, boyo, she's solid," the Welshman ground his teeth. "But I'm pretty close to exploding myself, if I can't get off her back and find out what happened to the child."

He grabbed the top of the ladder.

Bang!

A single bullet ricocheted off the *Liahona*'s deck in a trail of sparks. Poe looked up to the cavalrymen on the bluff. One of them held a smoking carbine and smiled down calmly at the people stranded on the steam-truck. It was a Sharps Model 1853, Poe thought idly. A big gun, and one that would leave a big hole in a man.

Brrrrr-rap-ap-ap-ap-ap-ap!

A racket that sounded a little like thunder, a little like a belching giant and a lot like Jedediah Coltrane's machine-gun erupted behind the hotel. Poe jerked his head around to find the source of the sound and saw a Mexican Strider lurch into view. It had crept up slowly out of the trees and been hiding behind the hotel. Its guns now tore up the dry earth and grass around the cavalrymen in a surprise flank attack. The twelve Virginians broke formation, scattering out of the yard.

Bang! Bang!

The cavalrymen at the top of the hill fired and broke into a ragged charge down the bluff, rushing to the aid of their Corporal and comrades.

Pffffffft-ankkkh!

Over Poe's right shoulder, catching him completely by surprise, appeared the second Strider. It rose straight up, standing out of what must have been a carefully maintained crouch, in which it had crept up alongside the *Liahona*, staying out of view of the Third Virginia as well as of Poe.

Brrrrr-rap-ap-ap-ap-ap-ap!

The second Strider fired its guns at the flank of the cavalry coming down the bluff, catching them by surprise as well. Two horses went down, holed by the big Mexican guns, throwing their riders into the trees. Return fire was sporadic and half-hearted and the small arms bullets mostly *pinged!* harmlessly off the armored carriage of the Strider. Sitting behind the pilot and gunner in the second Strider Poe saw Absalom Fearnley-Standish, his sister, and young Annie Web.

"Hurrah!" Fearnley-Standing shouted, as if he were cheering on target-shooters or a fox hunt. He looked for all the world like he was enjoying a lovely summer picnic, though he did fire sporadic shots at the horsemen.

His sister Abigail leaned over the side of the Strider's carriage and poured hot lead out of a long-barreled pistol upon the scattering men of the Third Virginia.

Both halves of the cavalry unit were in disarray, falling back under fire from the Mexican guns. Poe turned back to Captain Jones to suggest that now would be a good time to continue the search for young John Moses Browning and discovered that the Captain was gone.

He was already down the ladder and racing to the bottom of the yard.

Poe followed, his lungs straining as he ran, and Roxie came with him. Behind them, he heard *bangs!* erupt as the crewmen of the *Liahona* opened fire on the already beleaguered Virginians.

He kept his eye fixed on the foot of the field, trying to ignore the very real possibility that a stray bullet might cut him down at any second. He saw the steam-truck stop by a springhouse straddling a creek at the bottom of the hill and its riders pile off. He saw them throw the door open, rush inside in numbers and drag out four prisoners with sacks over his head and hands behind their backs.

Poe's lungs gave out and he nearly fell over in a paroxysm of violent coughing. His running pace faltered and stopped.

Then Bill Hickman saw him and Jones and Roxie and the Striders.

The sour-faced, hunch-shouldered Danite drew a long-barreled pistol and clapped it to the temple of one of his prisoners. "Stop right there, helldammit!" he squealed as he yanked the sack away to reveal the threatened person.

His hostage was President Young. The man was bleeding and he looked as if he had been shot but he was alive.

Poe hacked up blood and phlegm onto the grass.

"Stop right there!" Bill Hickman yelled again. "Stop or I'll blow out his prophetic brains!"

CHAPTER TWELVE

Sam smelled apples and heard a ruckus and he wondered how he would know when to make his move. Probably, he thought, the first thing he'd hear clearly would be the Danites shooting Orrin Porter Rockwell full of holes, and then it would be too late. It was enough to make even a cheerful man despondent and Sam knew himself well enough to know that he was not a naturally cheerful man.

He was a joking man precisely because he wasn't cheerful. All humor, Sam thought, was gallows humor, because every man spent his whole life waiting for the drop. At that moment, the drop seemed imminent to Sam.

And then what?

"I'll kill your precious Ambassador, too!" Hickman shouted and Sam heard the *click* of a gun's hammer. The man's porker-squeal of a voice was, if it were possible, even more unpleasant when strained through burlap. "Now drop your guns, helldammit!"

Focus, Clemens, he told himself.

Sam heard the *thud* of weapons being thrown to the ground. Had he already waited too long?

"We've disarmed ourselves," Sam heard a man say, and the voice sounded familiar. The words ended in a lengthy fit of coughing. Sam racked his brains for a moment until he realized that it sounded like the gypsy at Bridger's Saloon, who had tried to warn him off his mission. He vaguely thought he'd seen the man again, at the Shoshone stockade.

Hadn't he been part of that face-off against Hickman?

Sam managed not to chuckle out loud. He should have known. And the swindler had had the impertinence to ask if Sam took him for a huckster!

"Let them go, Hick." This was a woman's voice, unfamiliar to Sam. He considered making his move right then—Hickman might be distracted by a pretty face. He held back, telling himself that it was because he didn't know the woman and he couldn't be sure she *had* a pretty face.

She might be homely and then her presence wouldn't be all that helpful to Sam.

She wasn't done talking, though. "You can tell Lee you were overpowered by the Mexicans," she suggested, "or you can just light out right now for California. Lee will never know."

Sam wondered if O'Shaughnessy was in California by now. He'd heard yelling outside the springhouse door that had sounded something like O'Shaughnessy's voice but the words were indistinct through the chinked logs and all the gunfire and Sam had convinced himself that the voice belonged to some Irish Danite. At least, surely, O'Shaughnessy would be on the road westbound, heading for the Pacific. Sam couldn't imagine the Irishman sticking around to complete their mission with Sam out of the picture. The man was hired muscle and a brute, a bruiser Sam had picked up in Chicago because he needed help and his bosses in Army Intelligence couldn't be sure that their own men were loyal.

Unless, of course, O'Shaughnessy had no idea that Sam had been kidnapped. The man could very well be lying dead drunk on the carpeted floor of the Hotel Deseret bar. Or just lying dead. Maybe he and Henry were having a drink on some heaven-sailing riverboat at that very moment.

Or maybe O'Shaughnessy was lying in the back of an eastbound steam-truck, wearing Pinkerton shackles on his wrists and ankles.

"I ain't letting nobody go," Hickman snarled, "and I ain't getting overpowered by no corn-eating Mexicans. Not so long as I've got a gun to the head of my portly gentleman friend here."

"Watch it!" yelled a voice Sam didn't know.

"England!" The voice was a man's, fierce and bellowing, and more familiar. It was hard to tell in two syllables, but it sounded English. It almost sounded like it might belong to Richard Burton.

Pow! Sam heard a sound like a heavy object falling, with a metal crack in the center of it.

"Where the hell'd *he* come from?!"

Bang! Bang!

"Rockwell's loose!"

Time to act.

Sam whipped the sack off his own head. Rockwell had cut the ropes on his wrists inside the springhouse, after digging through three barrels of dried beans and finally finding his Bowie knife by touch alone. Now armed with that same knife, the man charged splashing through the stream, racing straight at six Danites dripping with pistols. His opponents, in the middle of jumping off the back of a parked steam-truck, looked completely surprised by the attack. With his buckskin fringes and long beard snapping in the air, Rockwell seemed half-wild animal, half Old Testament prophet and one hundred percent American.

Sam was surprised at how cheered up he felt by the other man he saw in action. Richard Burton, the Queen's agent and sometime saboteur, knelt on Bill Hickman's chest on the creek bank and pounded him in the face repeatedly with the basket hilt of a cavalry sword. Burton's facial expression looked like that of a hungry cannibal in the early stages of preparing dinner, though he had a knife in his upper left arm and his punches were slow. Hickman must have been taken by surprise but he was groping for a pistol he'd dropped in the dirt and he looked like he was close to reaching it.

Sam wondered where Burton had come from but he had no time to dwell on the question.

Two men and a woman charged down the hill. They all held pistols. Sam recognized one of them as the gypsy, though his face looked a little different than Sam remembered. The others he was less sure about, though he thought he might have seen them in Chief Pocatello's stockade, too.

The President and the Ambassador knelt together in the middle of it all. Rockwell had correctly guessed they'd get the most attention from the Danites and had left their hands tied so as not to give the game away. Orrin Porter Rockwell was something of a savage but Sam found he was coming to respect the man.

Young and Armstrong might have been praying, for the serenity with which they sat still in the middle of the fracas, heads bowed and hands behind their backs. Young bled from his ribs where he'd been shot, though—they hadn't bound the injury inside the springhouse because it would have given away the fact that their hands were free—and he didn't look good.

Maybe they *were* praying, Sam thought. In their place, he might be.

Sam drew Rockwell's pistol, wondering where to shoot first.

The choice was made for him. Two Danites rushed around the front of the steam-truck, drawing long, straight knives from sheaths at their belts. They looked like they were rushing to join the dog pile on top of Orrin Porter Rockwell. Sam calmly pointed Rockwell's pistol at the man in front and squeezed the trigger.

Bang!

He missed. The two Danites cringed and faltered, then saw him.

Rockwell slashed like a dervish at the men surrounding him. He was too close for them to shoot back effectively but Sam saw that they had realized that too, and some of them were stabbing and cutting at the mountain man with knives instead.

Sam tried again.

Bang! Bang!

His shots missed and the bullets *whizzanged!* away into space off the side of the steam-truck.

The two men charged at *him* now.

It wasn't obvious to Sam that the change was an improvement. Confound it, he needed to start hitting what he aimed at.

Rockwell took a hit, a deep scratch on his hip. The bull-shouldered man staggered and kept fighting, stomping one Danite under the truck and kicking another in the belly, but Sam could see that he was bleeding and starting to slow down.

Burton had lost his grip on his sword and was punching Hickman in the face now with bare and bloody knuckles.

The gypsy and his companions were still running.

Sam raised the pistol again. Point blank now, he thought, even a child couldn't fail of *this* mark.

Bang!

He missed.

I'll be the shame of the entire town of Hannibal, Missouri, he thought, raising the pistol again and hoping he could get off at least one more shot as he was being knifed to death. *I'll be the laughingstock of the American West.*

Rockwell should have given the gun to someone else.

Rat-rat-tat-tat-tat-tat-tat-tat-tat-tat!

The two men charging him vanished, whipped off their feet, thrown to the ground, and stilled in a fraction of a second. Sam stood with his gun still raised for an uncomprehending moment, try to absorb the sudden evaporation of his attackers. It was as if Zeus himself had looked down from Olympus, decided that the Kingdom of Deseret had two men too many, and simply erased them. They were rag dolls before a scythe.

Rat-rat-tat-tat-tat-tat-tat-tat-tat-tat-BANG!

Sparks and ricocheting bullets flew off the top of the steam-truck like a lightning storm in a bottle, and the men clawing and biting and stabbing at Rockwell faltered.

The gypsy and his companions clapped guns to the heads of Danites. The men stopped fighting and threw their weapons to the ground.

Burton smashed Hickman one more time in the face with his fist. Hickman's hand, finally wrapped around the grip of his pistol, squeezed once.

Bang!

As a last shot, it was anticlimactic. The bullet disappeared into the deepening blue sky of the late afternoon.

Hickman collapsed and lay still.

Burton swayed, pale and drawn, and he glared at Sam with a reproachful eye. "You're the worst shot I've ever seen," he said through gritted teeth. "I've seen a ninety-year-old Armenian crone who shot straighter than you do."

"Sorry," Sam said, chastened. He had the presence of mind not to drop his gun, though only barely.

"She was missing half her fingers," the explorer added. "And she was blind in both eyes."

"Next you'll tell me she had a better mustache than I do, too," Sam guessed wearily.

"Agni's second head," Burton grunted. He swayed on his knees like a drunk man. "This country and its people are not what I was led to believe."

Then he collapsed on top of Hickman.

"You all right, Rockwell?" Sam called. His own voice sounded far away and muffled to him. "It looked like you took a few body blows."

"No bullet or blade!" Rockwell cackled, and kicked one of the downed Danites in the face.

Sam noticed that away, up the long hillside, two Mexican Striders were clanking in his direction. No one else seemed excited about their arrival, so he ignored them and turned to look for the source of the bullet-storm that had saved his life.

It was a midget. He was rumpled and dirty and unshaved, and Sam thought he kind of looked familiar, too, though he didn't remember where he'd seen the man. He stood holding a stubby-looking little rifle, the likes of which Sam had definitely never seen before, that had a bulky drum attached to its stock. Presumably to hold the cascade of bullets the gun was obviously capable of shooting. Sam was not a gun man but this little storm maker intrigued him.

The dwarf's face looked chagrined. He was examining the gun, and Sam now saw that its barrel was shredded and splayed open on one side, like a steel flower was sprouting from the weapon. "Jebus," the little man said.

A step behind and to the side of the dwarf stood Tamerlane O'Shaughnessy. The Irishman looked embarrassed too.

"It's a nice day." O'Shaughnessy shot Sam a rueful half-grin.

Sam nodded. He felt numb, and a little bit humiliated, himself. So it *had* been O'Shaughnessy outside the springhouse.

Behind the Irishman and the midget stood a little boy. He held a pistol—the same unknown gun Sam had first seen on the Pinkerton's hip and then in O'Shaughnessy's hands—pointed at the backs of the two men. It was a day for strange guns. No wonder the two men looked so shy, Sam thought. *What kind of self-respecting thug lets a little kid throw down on him?*

The child looked shocked. "I had to," he said. "I didn't want anybody to get shot. I only did it because I had to."

"You've been captured by a little boy, Coltrane," the gypsy said, apparently to the dwarf. "I hope he will condescend to parole you." Then he spoke to his unknown male comrade. "Isn't that your errant midshipman, Captain Jones?"

"Don't think I ain't embarrassed about it, boss," the midget grumbled. "He got the drop on me."

"Put the machine-gun down," the little boy said. He prodded the air with his pistol for emphasis. The dwarf did as he was told. O'Shaughnessy stared at the strange weapon like a starving man looks at cake but did nothing.

"I think it's busted, anyway," the dwarf said.

Captain Jones stomped through the creek, righteous rage playing across his square face. "It was you, wasn't it, boyo?" he demanded, staring hard at O'Shaughnessy. "It was you who kidnapped little John Moses there!"

The Irishman pulled out of his gun-lustful brooding and sneered. "Taffy was a Welshman," he chanted, "Taffy was a thief—"

Crunch!

Jones pistol-whipped O'Shaughnessy across the jaw with the gun in his hand, sending him sprawling into the tall, dry desert grass.

"Taffy came to my house," Jones finished the rhyme, "and he kicked out all my teeth."

"Muurrrmph," the Irishman groaned vaguely from the ground.

"I am reluctant to criticize another man's work," the gypsy called out, with a mischievous twinkle in his fatigued eye, "but you've spoiled the rhyme."

The quip snapped Sam out of his stunned reverie. He grinned. "True," he agreed. "Though I must say I find the *meaning* of the revised couplet reasonably congenial."

ᎭᏍᎯᏌᎯᎠᏫᏫᎳᏟᎢ

Burton awoke to find the knives removed and his arm and leg bandaged. He lay on a crackling bed of yellow grass beside his own coat and Roxie fussed over him.

Burton's mouth was dry and he felt weak as a newborn babe. He gazed coolly for several moments at the woman who had so stirred his passion in the Wyoming Territory and let strength and vitality ooze back into his limbs. When she noticed him looking, she met his gaze with something that was almost a smile.

"What's your full name?" he asked. "Your real name."

"Eliza Roxcy Snow," she said immediately. "Roxie isn't a pseudonym; it's just a nickname."

Burton gestured at his coat with his good hand. "My papers are in there," he told her.

She looked away. "Yes," she said after a moment. "I've read them."

"And *wrote*," he suggested.

"Wrote a little," she admitted. "Just a post-script."

"Why?"

Roxie couldn't meet his eyes. "We ... Rockwell and I, and Annie ... knew Lee and Hickman were going to move against Brigham, but Brigham didn't believe it. He wouldn't believe our evidence, and he wouldn't take action, so we ... well, we went against his orders. Rockwell tried to take out John Lee. And we tried to scare you foreigners away so the Danites wouldn't have the cover they wanted to move against Brigham. When you wouldn't leave I decided to try to recruit you instead. I knew Brigham would need friends who were ... men of action."

Burton chuckled. "I was hoist with the petard of my own vanity," he said ruefully. "You're very good. Scheherezade told me stories and I wanted to believe."

"No, Dick," she said, "yours isn't vanity. You really are a man of action."

"*Ruffian* Dick," he reminded her. "And you are more than just Brigham's agent, aren't you?"

She hesitated. Her dress was dirtied and disheveled and she smelled of gun smoke, but he thought her beautiful then, with the fine bones of her face framed against the blue sky above him. "I'm his wife," she admitted.

"Eliza Roxcy Snow Young," he chewed on the name. "One of ... fifty?" he hazarded a guess.

"It isn't a perfect arrangement," she admitted.

"No arrangement is."

"You're hard to shock."

"There are stranger things in life than sharing a man," Burton said. He prided himself on being hard to shock. "You forget that I've spent time in the Horn. In much of Africa polygamy is the norm. In places like Somaliland, where children are essential to a family's wealth, it's positively essential. Marriage customs are as often a function of economics as—"

"He doesn't know," she cut him off. "Brigham, I mean. He doesn't know I ... seduced you. He certainly didn't ask me to do it."

"Hmmn." Burton kept his reaction muted, but he was vaguely relieved to hear that their liaison had been Roxie's own idea.

"When did you puzzle it out?"

Burton sighed. "At the Tabernacle," he said. "You showed far too much emotion for a mere paid agent, especially a jaded and worldly spy. I thought you must either be Brigham's wife ..." he watched her closely, while trying not to look at her directly, "or else perhaps Poe's lover."

Roxie covered her reaction well, but lines appeared around her mouth as she tightened her lips.

Of course. He should have seen it before. Burton threw his head back and laughed, loud and long.

"I don't consider myself a comic figure," Roxie sniffed.

"You're not, Roxie," he agreed. "You're an adventure. You're epic. You're the *Chanson de Roland*, the *Odyssey*, and the *Mahabharata* all rolled into one razor-sharp poem and bound in crinoline."

"You of all men, Richard Burton," she said to him, "must find that adventure stories become tedious."

He laughed again. "Yes, I do, Eliza Snow," he agreed. "As a matter of fact, I believe I do."

ʇɟɔʇ ʍɥoⱴⱳ ⱳ8

Poe carefully dug out one scarab beetle and dropped it into a glass fruit jar, the only jar in the *Liahona*'s galley that had survived its wreck.

"Observe carefully," he said to Bill Hickman. He suppressed a powerful urge to cough. "The details are of utmost importance."

Hickman had no choice but to observe. He was tied to a hotel timber, arms apart and legs staked wide open into the dirt. Orrin Porter Rockwell held his bruised and puffy eyelids peeled back and his head fixed in place with one arm. In the other hand he held his Bowie knife, the blade of which he occasionally tapped against Hickman's cheek as a reminder of its existence and sharpness.

The rest of the audience, though, was more distracted.

The Danites, other than Hickman, had survived suggestions that they be drowned ignominiously and instead had all been tied up in a patch of scrub oak well out of sight of the highway; Young, Armstrong, the *Liahona*'s people, and three of the Mexican Stridermen stood watch or tended to each other's wounds, hunger, and thirst in the wreckage of the hotel's kitchens. Casual passersby on the highway were told that an accident had happened with the waterworks, all was under control and to keep moving—as of yet, there had been no passersby that weren't casual.

Everyone else stood in a semi-circle around Hickman. They were there to watch Poe's performance.

"Are you sure we have time for this?" Absalom Fearnley-Standish asked Ann Webb, Roxie's young protégée. "The cavalrymen might regroup, after all, or send reinforcements."

"We have to know everything he can tell us, whether or not we have the time," she answered. She held something in her hand that she had introduced as a Fireless Darklantern, which was a sort of glass globe that sparked full of blue electricity to light the night. The sun had set, so Poe worked by artificial light. He recognized the Darklantern as the device he had imagined to be full of poison.

"Don't joo worry," said the Mexican gunner Consuelo Jackson. "I took especial care to be sure that *cada uno de esos caballeros* left here on foot." She held a more traditional kerosene lamp. Depending upon where one stood in the competing circles of illumination, one looked shimmering-blue or greasy-yellow. "If he left at all, *por supuesto*."

"Pass me the mouse," Poe said to Jed Coltrane. The little man handed over his shapeless hat, which squeaked and twitched with the frantic motions of the doomed creature trapped inside. Coltrane and the Irishman O'Shaughnessy stood conspicuously apart and didn't look at each other.

"I suppose I have learned that what goes around comes around after all," Poe heard Sam Clemens say.

"Do not trifle with a man," Burton growled, "whose empire is in danger."

"You're a good fellow, Mr. Burton."

Poe shook the mouse into the jar. It squeaked, rushed around the sides looking for a way out, and then sniffed suspiciously at the brass beetle.

"I don't believe in the existence of *good fellows*, Mr. Clemens."

Sam Clemens laughed. "See? I knew we'd get along famously."

Richard Burton growled again. "Don't let the mustachios fool you. I am not an amiable man."

Poe set the jar on the ground, inches from Bill Hickman's crotch. "Quiet, everyone," he urged the others. "Mr. Hickman needs to be able to concentrate."

"What's that?" Hickman struggled not to look nervous.

Poe smiled. "It's a mouse."

This was a performance, a show like any other. He needed to build a little tension in his audience.

Hickman frowned. "I know it's a mouse, helldammit!" His forehead was sweating, though the sun had dropped below the horizon and the cool evening was rapidly sinking into what promised to be a cold night. "I mean the other thing."

The mouse squeaked.

"What does it look like, Mr. Hickman?" Poe asked. He held the jar up so the Danite could see it closely.

He squinted. "Shit, it's a …" Hickman screwed his face up in the effort of trying to guess. "It's a bug."

"Not quite." Poe set the jar back down, far enough from Hickman's crotch to leave his view unobscured. "It looks like an insect, but really it's a device for consuming. It's an eating machine. Would you like to see how it works?" He stood and picked up the open canister.

"What's it gonna eat?" Hickman wanted to know.

"First, the mouse," Poe told him. The others were all silent and he knew he had everyone's attention.

Hickman hesitated, then writhed in what might have been an attempt to shrug. Expressive body language was hard for the man, with Orrin Porter Rockwell gripping him tightly by the head. "I reckon I don't care one way or the other," he said. "You can show me if you want."

Poe smiled. "I *do* want to." He scanned the ground one more time to be sure he hadn't accidentally dropped a stray beetle somewhere, then pressed the *attack* button inside the canister lid.

The mouse squeaked once, sharply, and died under the murderous onslaught of a single set of brass mandibles. Poe heard a sharp gasp, he thought from Absalom Fearnley-Standish. Moments later, nothing was left of the mouse but the skull, a handful of the larger bones, and a stray bloody whisker.

The beetle continued to bite and tear at the bones for a few seconds, scurried in a circle once around the jar, and then shut down.

Poe shook the contents of the fruit jar out into his hand. He carefully laid the mouse skull on Bill Hickman's chest.

Hickman swallowed. "Pretty," he drawled, "but nothing you can't do with a knife and a little bit of free time."

Rockwell pricked his cheek with the tip of his blade.

"Ouch!"

"True," Poe admitted. He set the mouse's bones on the Danite's chest too, one by one, in a circle around the tiny skull. "It's easy to make the mistake of thinking that the solution with the most engineering incorporated into it is the best one. Sometimes, what is most effective is the simplest solution. The knife, the poisoned cup, the wire around the throat."

Hickman looked down at the bones. Uneasiness showed in his face, so Poe knew he was getting into the man's head. "So ... what do you want?"

Poe placed the brass beetle on Hickman's sternum. "Who says I want anything?" he asked.

Hickman grinned. "I know all kinds of good shit," he said. "I got information."

"How delightful for you," Poe told him. He dug a second beetle out of the canister and laid it on Hickman below the first.

"I ... hey! ... don't you want to know what's going on here? What, with the ... kidnapping and everything?"

Poe placed a third scarab over Hickman's belly button, and a fourth just below it. "Should I want to know?" he asked.

"Yeah!" Hickman struggled against his bonds and against Rockwell's iron grasp but he was pinned fast. "Hell yeah, you should!"

Poe placed a fifth and final scarab, balancing it carefully right on the crotch of Hickman's denim trousers. He stood, and held one finger conspicuously close to the *attack* button inside the canister's lid.

"You've almost found the man's chakras," Burton gruffed. "Not quite, but you're close."

"I can find his chakras easy enough, need be," Rockwell growled. "They hang the same place on a man as on a bear, more or less."

"So tell me," Poe said. "Tell me what you think I want to know so badly."

"Lee did it!"

"You mean John Lee," Poe prompted the Danite. "Brigham Young's adopted son, the Danite leader."

"Yeah. He's behind the kidnapping."

"That's interesting," Poe mused.

"Yeah? What's interesting about it?"

"What's interesting is that I happened to be in the Tabernacle when Mr. George Cannon introduced Lee to the congregation." Poe spoke slowly and deliberately and kept his eye fixed on Hickman. He let his words hang when he'd finished, to see what they would flush out of the prisoner's guilty conscience.

They flushed out nothing. "Yeah, that's him."

Poe kept a straight face. Was Hickman too clever to be baited, or too stupid? "As I recall, they both gave the distinct impression that President Young was dead."

Hickman's splayed eyes quivered. "I guess they was mistook," he suggested weakly.

"Perhaps," Poe agreed, "but I can think of other hypotheses."

Hickman sulked.

"Boss," Coltrane whispered loudly. "He may not know what *high posse trees* are. Just tell him you're going to hang him, if that's the point."

Poe nodded calmly, resisting both the Scylla of laughter and the Charybdis of irritation. "Let me propose this explanation," he said, watching Hickman closely. "Lee had you kidnap the President but then announced his death to all of Deseret. He is holding Brigham Young in reserve in case affairs go awry and then, if need be, he can resurrect the man at his convenience."

"Yeah, that sounds right." Hickman's answer was quick. Too quick.

"But then Lee has hung you out to dry," Poe probed.

Hickman shrugged.

"If he brings Brigham Young back to life," Poe continued, "someone will have to take the fall for the kidnapping. That can only be you, Mr. Hickman."

Hickman shrugged. He didn't seem very concerned, which must mean Poe was on the wrong track.

"There could be other explanations, of course," Poe thought out loud.

"The explanation is that John D. Lee figures it's about time he was made king over everybody," Hickman insisted. "I guess he musta been sick of everybody lording it over him all the time, just 'cause he was a frontier man and not some fancy English feller." He shot a look of resentment at Richard Burton. "And I reckon he's got the right idea."

"You're not a stupid man, Mr. Hickman," Poe lied. He coughed and the force of it in his lungs took him by surprise. The consumption was getting worse, he thought. He wondered how long he had. He spat into the dust at his feet.

"No, I ain't."

"You wouldn't let yourself be set up to take the fall for John Lee."

"I wouldn't," Hickman agreed. "And I ain't."

"You've got John Lee right where you want him."

"Yeah, I ... what? No, I'm Lee's man. He sent me to kidnap Brigham Young, and I done it."

"He sent you to *kill* Brigham Young, and you double-crossed him." Poe saw truth-induced hesitation in the other man's face, so he kept going. "You were supposed to kill Clemens, too, or at least capture him, but finding Rockwell and the Ambassador as well was entirely serendipitous."

Hickman stared sullenly at the line of scarabs.

"He means catching Rockwell and Armstrong was just plain dumb luck," Sam Clemens interpreted.

"Thank you, Mr. Clemens," Poe said.

"I was raised in Missouri." Clemens grinned. "I speak idiot."

"Of course, as long as you kept them all alive, you could release them later and minimize the damage. President Tubman might be angry but you calculated that if her Ambassador were alive, she couldn't be *too* angry." Hickman wouldn't meet Poe's gaze. "Maybe you could even take cover behind Lee, or get him blamed for it and say you were only taking orders. And in the meantime, you could hold them over Lee's head."

Hickman said nothing.

Rockwell held the blade of his knife against Hickman's belly, careful not to disturb the beetles. "'Fess up, you filthy little gutworm, or lose your chakras."

"I don't know what you're talking about." The words, and the shifty expression that accompanied them, were as good as a confession for Poe.

"And of course," Poe pressed on, "you kept the opportunity to play it the other way. You could free President Young. Maybe you could convince him that you had been acting under threat of violence when you kidnapped him, and that freeing him was a risky and heroic act. He'd reward you for your courage and sacrifice. Or you could convince him you'd been playing a double game all along, to flush Lee out. What kind of medals do the Danites give out for personal heroism, Mr. Hickman?"

"There ain't no medals," the Danite grumbled.

"Or maybe you were aiming for a more sordid sort of traffic, a simple dirty bargain. You could simply offer to betray Lee and free President Young, in exchange for whatever it is you hope to get out of all this."

Hickman sulked.

"So what is it that you're playing for, Hickman? How much of the pie do you want? Are you tired of being looked down on because you're the Jim Bridger type, and not the Daniel Webster sort, not a fancy Englishman?" Poe jerked his head at Absalom Fearnley-Standish, with his scalloped-brim hat. He coughed again and choked himself quickly before the coughs turned into a prolonged fit.

"I say," Fearnley-Standish objected mildly. He pulled a small metallic notebook from his pocket, then seemed to think better of whatever his intention had been and put the notebook back. "You make us sound like a nation of snuff-pinchers. We did stop Napoleon, you know. And settle America, if that's worth anything."

"Joo English weren't the first people to come to the *Nuevo Mundo*," Master Sergeant Jackson reminded him, with a grin that was both fierce and affectionate.

Hickman kept his mouth shut.

Poe waited, letting the Danite stew. He bent over to tidy the line of beetles, then straightened up and sighed.

"I'm not sure that it matters," he said, "but I admit to curiosity. Does *Lee* answer to Orson Pratt or do *you* answer to the Madman?"

Hickman's face surprised Poe with a look of pure astonishment. Even more surprising was the expression of complete discombobulation that passed over Sam Clemens's face before he recovered, sweeping it under his mustache.

So Hickman knew nothing about Orson Pratt's machinations, and Sam Clemens … maybe Clemens did.

Poe decided to probe a little harder.

"Come, Mr. Hickman," he continued. "Aren't you the *Boatman*?"

"I don't know what in the hell you're talking about," Hickman whined.

Sam Clemens jerked a cigar from out of his inside jacket pocket and bit into it, hard.

"We'll leave that for the moment." Poe shook the open canister of scarab beetles like a maraca as he paced around Hickman and thought. "What if Lee's plan had gone as he'd intended?" he asked. "What would he have done next?"

"It *did* go as he intended," Hickman insisted.

"The Third Virginia Cavalry is here to support Lee in power. There is no United States target worth striking within their range. What is Lee's plan for supporting his fellow-conspirators in the South? Will Mormons invade the Wyoming Territory?"

"I don't know what you're talking about."

"But what I see here doesn't look like a standing army to me, so much as a militia. Or even just an armed citizenry. Effective, maybe, for deterring invasion or oppression but not the sort of force that invades its neighbor."

"There you have it," Hickman agreed.

"So I think the attack will be aerial."

Hickman's evasive look was confirmation enough.

"Perhaps an attack upon Chicago," Poe considered. "Though of course one advantage of an airborne military force would be the ability to attack behind enemy lines. Pittsburgh? New York City? Perhaps the war will commence with an assault upon Boston, to remind the overweening Yankees of the celebrated Tea Party?"

Hickman shrugged. "I don't know," he mumbled. "I ain't never been much for tea."

"The delivery of a team of Danite assassins to President Buchanan's White House?" Poe proposed. "I'd hate to give you any good ideas but of course, you are clever men, and you know your own weapon's capabilities much better than I ever could. All I can hope to do is second-guess you."

"That ain't my part in it," Hickman grumped. "I ain't much of a planner."

"No...? I suppose not. What about ..." Poe let a little suspense build. "What about the phlogiston guns? Why rely on assassins at all, when you could just burn the White House to the ground?"

"What, just the one gun?" Hickman snorted. "It ain't all that impressive, not all by itself."

"Why just one gun?" Poe asked, and then guessed at another connection. "Why one gun, when there are four ships?"

Four ships, Poe thought. He knew that Orson Pratt had built four ships because Captain Jones had told him so. It didn't seem to be uncommon knowledge. But now the number stuck in the back of his mind like a morsel of food he could not swallow. What was there about the number four that bothered him so?

"Hell if I know."

"Rubies," Roxie said.

Sam Clemens looked like he'd bit off and swallowed part of his cigar. It might have been the result of his standing right between the blue and the yellow lanterns, but he looked positively green.

"What about rubies?" Poe asked her.

She shook her head impatiently. "I don't know the details. The phlogiston gun works on rubies but Deseret doesn't have any."

Poe examined Hickman's face. He didn't think the kidnapper had any idea what they were talking about and he had a sudden and terrible insight into why the number four tickled his memory so. He started coughing, tried to stop, and found that he couldn't. He pulled a handkerchief from his pocket.

"Let's step away for a moment and discuss."

"Shall I kill him?" Rockwell seemed eager and Poe wondered whether it was an act.

"Not yet," Poe directed, between hard, violent coughs. "But let's leave the scarabs on his belly as a reminder." He held the handkerchief carefully in front of his face to catch the sputum. There would be blood in it, he knew.

Not yet, he thought. *Let me see this through first and then take me, but just not yet.*

꜠ꓛ꓄ꔋꞍ꜖ꝋꞡ꓆꒦

"You didn't have to poke fun at me," Tam muttered to Sam Clemens as they all moved away from Bill Hickman and huddled around the back of the Danites' steam-truck. "Not with all of them watching."

"Not now, O'Shaughnessy." Clemens didn't look irritated, but he looked distracted and uncomfortable.

The poor idjit had chewed through three of his fancy cigars in as many minutes. *Jesus and Brigit, though, who wouldn't be uncomfortable, with all the talk of phlogiston guns and flying ships?*

Tam was uncomfortable himself. He'd nearly been blown to bits twice in one day by something called a *machine-gun*; first at the hands of an overstuffed circus midget with an unholy affection for someone else's little boy and then by the wee tyke himself. He'd just about had enough of the Kingdom of Deseret.

It made him think of the Molly Malones and the Pinkertons with something approaching nostalgia.

"Yeah, Sam," he agreed, "only I was coming to rescue you, don't you see?"

Clemens ignored him and turned to join the circle with the others.

"So it wasn't right to mock me, is all I'm saying." Tam sighed. He shuffled in close to listen, too, careful that he wasn't leaning over the head of the louse-sized midget. The little bastard had armed himself with every knife he could find.

"It's time for reciprocal revelation," the man everyone called *Poe* was saying. He was saying it to Sam and he was wiping blood off the corner of his mouth with a white handkerchief. The man looked like a walking corpse. "You're the Boatman, and you brought a delivery of rubies to Orson Pratt. How many were there?"

Sam Clemens might not always be nice to his associate, but he knew how to keep his cool. "I'm not saying it's true, Mr. Poe, and I'm not saying it isn't. But I would like to understand your reasoning a little better."

"I took Pratt a delivery, too," Poe explained. "My codename was to be the *Egyptian* but he accidentally called me the *Boatman*. I've seen your amphibious craft and I think the Boatman must have been you. You looked uncomfortable when I mentioned rubies to Hickman. How many did you bring him?" The bony-faced Mormon woman looked fascinated by Poe's every word and Tam wondered what *her* game was.

"How many did *you* bring him?" Sam asked belligerently.

"What I gave Pratt wasn't rubies," Poe said.

"What was it?" This question came from the more manly of the two Englishmen. Tam thought his name was Burton. He looked a little offended, like all this was new information, and he wasn't happy that people had been keeping secrets from him. "In the spirit of reciprocal revelation, I brought Pratt nothing."

"I don't know what it was," Poe said.

"Your profession of ignorance doesn't exactly inspire trust," Sam joked.

"They were some kind of clocksprung devices," Poe explained. "I don't know what the devices were designed to do, but there were four of them and they were built into canopic jars, little Egyptian-looking jars with animal heads."

"We know what canopic jars are," harrumphed Burton.

Poe ignored him. "They might be ether-wave devices of some sort," he said, "but that's almost pure conjecture on my part. How many rubies?"

"Didn't you say that Mr. Pratt has built four of his airships?" the Etonian bastard asked.

Since the fight ended, he'd been followed around by two women, the Mexican gunner and the young Mormon morsel. Tam would happily have instructed either girl in the secret beauties of the Irish avian population but they stuck to the effete little prat with his maimed headgear like blight stuck to a potato. Just the sight of the three of them made Tam want to spit.

The aristo weasel had two women slobbering over him. Poe had the bony Mormon lady making eyes. Sam Clemens and Burton yukked it up like they'd been hatched from the same egg and known each other all their lives. Even the dwarf had the little kid.

Tamerlane O'Shaughnessy was the odd man out.

He felt alone. It surprised him how much the feeling bothered him. *Stop moping, you stupid bastard*, he told himself. *Mother O'Shaughnessy'd die of embarrassment over your womanish ways.*

Of course, on top of being lonesome, good old Missouri Sam Clemens had as much as blamed him for kidnapping the child. Sure, Tam had had the child in his possession at one point, but for that matter, so had Sam.

It had been the dwarf who committed the kidnapping.

It just wasn't fair.

"So what?" he interjected himself into the conversation. "Four ships and four jars, so-bloody-damn-hell-what? Four Horsemen of the Apocalypse. Four cardinal directions, by Brigit. Four arms and legs on a man, four fingers to a hand if you don't count the thumb. How many fookin' rubies, is this a game?" He also felt slightly put out that Sam hadn't mentioned he was carrying around a bunch of precious stones, apparently for some kind of secret trade with the Madman Pratt.

It was like Sam didn't trust him.

But then, maybe he was right not to.

"I don't know how many," Sam Clemens told them. "A small bag full of them. I thought I was best off not knowing the exact scale of the temptation."

"Lee's arming the airships," Burton grunted.

"As far as I know," the older woman said, "Brother Orson's only ever built one working phlogiston gun and it wasn't mounted on one of his ships."

"Consider the facts," Poe said. "Pratt arranged secret meetings in which he took delivery of some number of rubies and four mysterious devices, equal in number to the number of his aerial fleet. *Pratt* took delivery, I say, not *Brigham Young* and not *John Lee*. Our Mr. Hickman there clearly knows nothing about these transactions, so I think we have to infer that there is at least a strong possibility that Orson Pratt is acting on his own in this matter. He as good as said so to my … to colleagues of mine in Army Intelligence. Perhaps he is building additional phlogiston guns to arm all the ships. Perhaps the canopic jars facilitate the arming in some fashion; perhaps they are targeting devices or … who know what they could be?"

"Bombs," Tam guessed.

"Bombs," sneered the dwarf. "Like Hunley and his boys ever made anything so simple as a *bomb*."

"I don't think you can make an ether-wave *bomb* …" Roxie said hesitantly.

"I fear Pratt's action may be imminent," Poe continued. "He was very anxious as to timing when I delivered him the canopic jars. He commented that he was almost out of time. Did he give you any instructions about tomorrow morning, Mr. Clemens?"

Sam Clemens hooked his thumbs into his belt and furrowed his brow. "He wanted me by the Tabernacle at eight in the morning. North side. And the reciprocal revelation?"

"Same place, same time. Something's happening tomorrow morning at eight and he wants us to witness it."

"Or he wants to make sure we're involved," Clemens suggested.

"Or standing on a convenient target," Poe finished.

"We have to get President Young back to the city," the younger, prettier Mormon woman said. "We can't let Lee win. And if we don't stop tomorrow morning's meeting the Twelve and the Seventy will have chosen a new President."

"We also have to move to intercept Pratt," Sam Clemens said. "What if he really does plan to launch an attack first thing in the morning?"

"Any attack might be imminent," Poe agreed. "We may already be too late."

"We split up," Burton announced. "I'm going after the airships. Who's with me?"

CHAPTER THIRTEEN

So I expect you're one cog that's happy to be returning to its ordinary slot in the good Lord's cosmic wonder-machine," Sam suggested. He chewed on a cheap cigar he'd commandeered from one of the vanquished Danites; he'd chewed his way through the entire supply he kept on his person.

That was one more compelling reason to get back to the *Jim Smiley* as soon as he could.

"My people need me in my place," Brigham Young agreed, glaring at Sam like a bear facing down a mastiff. "If you mean something more than that, I suggest you say it plainer. You'll ruin Missouri's reputation for producing straight-talking men."

They rode horses taken from the Hot Springs Hotel & Brewery stable. Ahead of them, *pffft-ankkkhing* across fields of sugar beets and corn, went one of the Mexican Striders; the second brought up the rear of the procession. It was full night and they moved by the light of the half-moon slowly falling towards the western hills, not wanting to attract any more attention than they were already at risk of doing, just by the size of their party and the presence of the two big, clanking fighting machines. Someone's crop was getting trampled, Sam thought. At least it was in a good cause. Or maybe it was okay because it all belonged to Brigham Young. Wasn't this a kingdom, after all?

"You've got us wrong, Mr. President," Sam said. "Missouri doesn't produce straight-talking men, it produces skeptics. And what I mean to say is, I can see how our rescue might tempt you into thinking the hand of Providence was upon you but I would suggest that there are other explanations."

"You mean luck," Young guessed.

Young and Sam rode at the head of the horse-mounted middle of the procession, together with Ambassador Armstrong. Immediately behind them came Orrin Porter Rockwell, slouched over his horse like he was a naturally inborn part of the animal, and then Captain Dan Jones, with the boy John Moses in front of him on his saddle. The midget Coltrane banged along on a horse far too big for him, and behind him came Absalom Fearnley-Standish, his sister Abigail, and Brigham Young's fetching vixen-agent, Annie Web, mixing in more or less among the crewmen of the *Liahona*.

"Luck," Sam agreed. "The diligence of my associate and the persistence of your own loyal people, despite, I would like to point out, your apparent orders to them to stand down. Your own cogs saved you by jumping out of place. I also wouldn't discount the incompetence of our kidnappers, or fail to mention our own manful efforts at overcoming our captors and escaping. Porter Rockwell deserves some kind of medal."

"You don't believe that God acts in the affairs of man," Young asserted. When he wasn't snapping his teeth in anger, he had a kind of dignity that Sam found attractive, and also a little unsettling. Young rode easily and upright even with his chest wrapped in a bandage, like he expected people to look at him and respect him.

He made Sam want to knock him off his pole, just a little. Not hurt him, but maybe get him a little dirty.

"I find that the victors in any contest are generally persuaded that God is on their side," Sam answered. "The trodden down and beaten upon are not often so optimistic."

Young was silent for a moment. Sam listened to the creaking of saddle leather and the soft jingling of stirrups and felt the cool night air on his face. Having spent much of the day in darkness and suffocated by the smell of apples, he experienced this as freedom, pure and undefiled.

"The best friend I ever had in this world," Young finally said, speaking slowly, "was Joseph Smith, Jr."

"The King of Nauvoo."

"Brother Joseph was the President, Mr. Clemens. Jesus Christ was the King."

"No offense intended. I only meant to identify Smith by his common nickname, so you know that I'm paying attention and know the man to whom you refer."

"If you have heard of him, then you know that he was executed by an illegal firing squad in Carthage, Illinois."

"I have heard various views on the legality of the action," Sam acknowledged that he knew of Smith's murder. "No offense. Your kidnapping is not the first piece of mischief to be perpetrated by men calling themselves *Danites*."

"Nauvoo was a kingdom dredged from the mud of the Mississippi River, Mr. Clemens. No one wanted it when we went there, except for the mosquitoes, and without the aid of Heaven, the blood-suckers would surely have driven us out."

"I've seen Nauvoo," Sam said. "It's a pretty town."

"We made it so. And once they had murdered our Brother Joseph, our enemies came for our land. They killed us, they stole all our worldly goods, and they drove us across the Mississippi River into the howling Lamanite wilderness."

"I don't know what a Lamanite is," Sam noted. "But it sounds bad. I'll readily concede that you were mistreated, Mr. Young. That doesn't make you unique, it makes you just like everyone else.

"For thousands of years on this continent," Sam continued, "each Indian people oppressed the next, with tomahawk and obsidian club, human sacrifice and torture and cannibalism. Then the white man showed up with weapons even more vicious—the long rifle and the smallpox germ—and he joined the game. The Spaniards oppressed the Indians, the French oppressed the Spaniards, the Englishmen finally oppressed everyone else and won, and to celebrate the victory they changed their name to *Americans*.

"Someday," he wound up to his dramatic finish, conscious of Brigham Young's cool eyes on him in the darkness and half expecting to have to jump back to avoid a burst of rage, "the next hand of cards will be dealt and somebody else will oppress the Americans. Hell, maybe it will even be the Mormons, but that won't mean that God is on your side, any more than He was on the side of the Iroquois when they sent the Lenape packing out of the Delaware Valley."

"You misunderstand me, Mr. Clemens," Young said quietly. "I am telling you that God was on our side when our enemies drove us out of Nauvoo. I am telling you that when all the world saw as us trodden upon and beaten down, we rode west into the wilderness cupped in the hand of the Almighty God."

Sam nearly swallowed his cigar. "I must be misunderstanding you *now*, Mr. President," he spluttered. "Are you suggesting that you were persecuted and robbed and murdered and chased into the wilderness, as you say—and that it was a *good* thing? That God elected you to defeat?"

"I am suggesting," Brigham Young said, impressively calm, "that God moves in mysterious ways. Uprooting the Kingdom and moving it to the Rocky Mountains was hard, harder possibly than you can ever imagine, Mr. Clemens. Death and starvation and disease dogged our every step. But that move has made us strong and it has given us the space we needed to flourish and grow and become independent. And if your President or Mr. Jefferson Davis or even the Queen of England thinks to coerce us into any particular action with respect to this coming war, or any other thing for that matter … well, they will find that God has taught us to be prepared."

"And has God prepared you for the actions of Mr. John D. Lee?" Sam asked. He felt impudent for his retort, but he was staggered by the things Brigham Young was saying and couldn't leave them without rejoinder.

"God moves in mysterious ways," Young repeated. "We are all cogs in slots in His cosmic wonder-machine, just as you said. Rockwell and Eliza and Annie disobeyed me and they were right to do so, but that doesn't mean they weren't acting as parts of the machine. God is the mechanick, Mr. Clemens, not Brigham Young. I am nothing but a cog that is happy to be returning to his usual slot."

ꓕꓚꓶꟽꟼ0⑥ꟽꟾꓛꓲꓲ

"If it all goes cock-eyed," Sam Clemens had said, "remember whose side you're on."

"I'm on your side, Sam," Tam had shot back. He'd felt like the girl in the corner of the dance hall, looking shyly away from her beau. *Get a hold of yourself.*

"You're in the employ of the United States Army Intelligence," Sam had reminded him, a little preachier than Tam liked. "That makes you on *President Buchanan's* side. And remember this," he'd leaned in close and looked around to be sure that no one was watching, "there's still a war coming. If at any point it looks like Edgar Allan Poe is going to steal Pratt's airships for Jefferson Davis and his cronies, you know what you have to do."

And wasn't Pratt the perfect name for a crazy old bugger living in the mountains, building airships and phlogiston guns and planning on burning down the whole bloody-damn-hell world?

"Kill Poe," Tam had agreed. "Kill Pratt. Kill them all, if I have to."

Sam Clemens had scowled and looked uncomfortable. Good old Sam Clemens, rugged Missouri hard-arse that he was, he was still a bit of an innocent, a bit of an old maiden auntie. "If you have to," he had agreed reluctantly. "But I'd prefer that you steal the ships yourself first, or destroy them."

Then he'd ridden off with His Mormon Majesty Brigham Young and the nasty dwarf and the Mexicans, without so much as a *Please, O'Shaughnessy* or a *Thank you, friend Tamerlane, for coming to rescue me from the godawful Danites who wanted to shoot me dead.* Tam understood that the man had to go show the people of the Great Salt Lake City that he was alive and an innocent man but still, manners were manners.

"Why the make-up?" Tam asked. "Are we going dancing and no one's told me? And here I left me best frock behind on the *Jim Smiley*."

The wheelhouse of the steam-truck they'd stolen from the Danites had two long benches that could have fit four men each in a pinch. Richard Burton sat on the front bench, behind the steering wheel, and drove, his sword across his lap and Roxie Snow beside him. The truck rattled and bounced along a rutted rocky road up and down low hills, a beam of light shot out by its electricks splitting the night in front of it. Burton held tight to the wheel and the others held tight to the benches' arms.

Edgar Allen Poe sat with Tam on the second bench and worked, mostly one-handed, at affixing a false nose to his face with spirit gum. Tam watched the others and tried to be sneaky about the sips of whisky he was taking from the bottle in his coat pocket. He'd borrowed the liquor from the galley of that great dead shrieking behemoth the *Liahona* and if anyone minded, to hell with them.

He deserved a little drink for his efforts (*What man doesn't? but especially clever, dogged Tamerlane O'Shaughnessy.*) and besides, the alcohol helped dull the throbbing pain in his arm, leg, and ear. He'd been having a rough time of it, these last few days.

"I'm impressed that you can do it without a mirror." Roxie smiled.

"I've spent long hours carefully observing women to learn their secrets," Poe said. "Though I have not yet mastered the legendary art of painting my lips using my cleavage instead of my hands."

Tam laughed sharply. He sort of liked Poe. He'd miss the man if he had to kill him. He patted the Hushers to be sure he still had them both, and checked the stiletto against his forearm. Whatever came, he was ready. He'd just have to be sure to take Poe by surprise—the man had taken back his scarabs of death and was carrying them in his coat, now. Tam didn't want to get crosswise with those nasty little Creation-disassembling buggers.

"Maybe you ought to poke into that fearsome huge box the *Liahona*'s boys humped into the cargo bay of this truck for you, Mr. Poe," he suggested. "Maybe there's a spare cleavage in there that you could spirit gum onto your knobby little torso and use to put on your lipstick."

There, that'd teach the ugly southerner that he had to keep an eye on Tam O'Shaughnessy, that the Irishman was not a man to be slighted or ignored. Poe would have to know now that he was being watched with an eagle eye.

But Poe just looked at Tam with a dry stare as he squeezed the nose into place. "*Knobby* is a such a pedestrian word for a body this ravaged by time and illness, Mr. O'Shaughnessy." He coughed several times, hard, to make his point. At least this time he didn't hack up big gobs of blood. "I had expected better from an Irishman. Really, where is that Gift of Gab so famously proprietary of the sons of Eire?"

"I never kissed the Blarney Stone," Tam complained. "I'm a Dublin lad. Never even been to County Cork." And wasn't it more the pity? If he'd had the Gift, he might not be careening through the desert at night in the back of a stolen steam-truck, trading banter with a consumptive secessionist spy. He might be sitting in Parliament, or running a railroad. But Tamerlane O'Shaughnessy's gifts had always lain in a different direction.

"What about *knurled*?" Poe suggested, going to work on a caterpillar-like set of false eyebrows. "*Rugose*? *Scabrous*?" He coughed hard but managed not to lose hold of the eyebrows or the spirit gum.

"Hush," Roxie said. Her voice was surprisingly gentle. Tam wondered what reason she had to show affection to the decrepit codger.

"*Cragged.*" Tam grinned. "*Bumpy.*"

"*Corrugated,*" Poe added, "if it isn't cheating to suggest two different words derived from the same root."

Tam laughed out loud. "We're all driving under the same roof now, Brother Edgar!" If it came down to killing Poe, he decided, he wanted to think in advance of some good fancy words to describe the act. *Decapitation*, he thought, that was a good one. He could say it to Poe just as he swung the blade in for the killing blow, though it'd be better if Poe were tied up. Then Tam could use the fancy word and they could both enjoy it for a minute before it had to be over. *Incineration* for fire and *defenestration* if he could find any windows to throw the spy out of. Tam eyed the silver chain around Poe's neck, dangling something down under his shirt. What was a nice, fancy word for *strangling*?

"Where are we going?" Burton asked from the front bench.

"It's called the Dream Mine," Roxie told them.

"That sounds cheerful," Poe judged.

"A man named Koyle had it dug," Roxie said. "He told everyone he'd dreamed that if you dug a shaft where he said, you'd hit an old Nephite mine, all dug out and just full of precious metal sitting around waiting to be taken away."

"What kind of mineral is *nephite*?" Burton asked. "Is it precious? Like bauxite? Selenite?"

"The Nephites were an ancient people," Roxie informed him. "They lived around here a long time ago."

"Hiya, heya, hiya, heya," Tam chanted, then made his best Indian war-whoop, slapping his hand against his round *O* of a mouth. "I'll admit I may be disadvantaged because I got my schooling in Ireland, but the sisters never told me about Indians digging for bauxite."

"The ancient world is as unexplored and mysterious as is the modern," Burton growled, and took his eyes off the jittering road to shoot Tam a gruff, schoolteacherly look. "Nobody can afford to pat himself on the back for his wisdom just yet. Least of all the Irish."

"Go to hell." Tam took a slug off his bottle.

"Old Bishop Koyle didn't dream of bauxite, anyway," Roxie continued. "It was gold."

"Ah, well, then," Tam said, and he felt himself brighten up. "That's worth a little bit of a drive to see."

"Did they find the Nephite mines and the gold?" Poe asked. The eyebrows were affixed, and now he was attaching a long fake scar running up one cheek.

"Not yet," Roxie admitted. "But they're still looking." She frowned. "You're putting on a lot of make-up."

"Pratt has seen me before, remember."

"Not yet!" Tam felt himself almost squeak with indignation. "Then what's the fookin' point of all this shenaniganning around? I thought we were supposed to be going after the Madman Pratt! I wouldn't have minded a detour for stacks and stacks of gold, especially with one of ours in disguise and ready for a good bit of thieving, or maybe even bauxite, but I can't say as I see the point of a detour for an empty hole in the ground."

"It isn't a detour," Roxie said. "It's a shortcut."

"Mind you," Tam added without a break, "I don't rightly know what bauxite is worth, but in big enough piles anything is worth money. Even shite, don't you know?"

"Buildings ahead," Burton rumbled, "and there's a light in one window. Better explain yourself."

"Slow down," Roxie told him, and she hit a switch to kill the electricks. The bluish beams of light shooting out the front of the steam-truck died instantly and Burton yanked on the brake lever to slow the big truck to a crawl. Tree branches scraped up ominously against the sides of the wheelhouse but the Englishman kept the truck on the road and moving forward, crunching the trees at the road's edges to splinters as it ground over them.

"Jesus and Brigit," Tam cursed, "give the poor bastard a warning next time." He took a drink that he intended to limit to a sip, but that turned into several good swallows. Ah, well. Tam might not have the Gift of Gab but he was enough of a true son of Eire to be able to hold his whisky.

"The poor bastard doesn't need a warning," Burton growled. "The poor bastard is a *man*."

"What are you saying, English?" Tam demanded. "I don't make the mistake of thinking you're the same as that milksop Etonian shite you ride around with, don't you make the mistake of believing I'm afraid of you, you—"

"The mine is operated!" Roxie shouted, cutting them both off. Burton turned his attention back to the road, now a ghostly-silver trail barely discernible in the darkness, and Tam satisfied himself with staring holes in the back of Burton's head. *Throttle*, that was another word for *strangle*, though it wasn't fancy enough to be emotionally satisfying to Tam. *Suffocation*, that was it, but somehow that sounded too sterile.

"The mine is operated," Roxie resumed, "but it's a front. One of the tunnels is a back door, it goes right through Timpanogos Mountain and up to Emerald Lake, where Pratt has his facility. It lets him drive supplies up to the top of the mountain even in winter, and it also lets him drive things up unseen."

"Like what? Like gold?" Tam asked.

"Like rubies and canopic jars," Poe said quietly, "or anything else."

"Who guards the mine?" Burton asked. "Who are you worried about? More of these Danites?"

Roxie shook her head, a motion Tam could only see in the darkness as the glittering of moon and starlight in her earrings. "Brother Pratt has always expressed concerns to Brigham about the Danites, and about the need to protect his facility, in case some Danite faction tried to seize power. He's contracted security to a private firm."

"Melqart's fire, it seems the Madman Pratt had more foresight than all the rest of the Salt Lake hierarchy," Burton commented. "So what private firm's bullets will I have the honor of dodging, then?"

"Brother Pratt insisted he had to have the best," Roxie continued.

Tam felt a sinking feeling in the pit of his stomach. He tried to drive it out with more whisky but it persisted.

"His facility is also the Kingdom's central office of the Pinkerton Detective Agency."

"Aw, fook," Tam cursed.

Burton chuckled. "Something wrong, O'Shaughnessy?" he asked. "Would you like to borrow one of Poe's false noses?"

"Brigit and Anthony fook me right to hell, I've had enough trouble with the Pinkertons to last me a lifetime." Tam felt tired and irritated.

Poe turned to look at him. He looked like a complete stranger, all scarred and hairy, but then he broke the magic of the transformation with a wet, guttural cough. "Of course you have," Poe said. "That gives me an idea."

Absalom Fearnley-Standish quite enjoyed the night ride.

He had little success sticking with Abigail; he wanted to convince her to leave her brute husband and this desert wasteland and come away with him back East and home to England, but she had no interest in the message. Every time he opened his mouth, she spurred her horse away from him, sticking closer to the shaggy Rockwell and showing her brother only her horse's rump.

Absalom was impressed. Before this evening, he would have sworn he was by far the better rider. Life in the Kingdom of Deseret, life as Rockwell's wife, had certainly changed her. He almost didn't recognize his sister anymore, in this rugged, fierce, pistol-slinging woman of the frontier. He was shocked to see how much a person could change in such a short period of time.

He wasn't upset, though. He couldn't be, with Annie constantly at his side.

"That can't be true!" She almost collapsed from giggling at his description of the Horse Guards' Trooping the Colour, and the uniforms of the Yeomen Warders in the Tower of London. "England, the way you describe it, is so romantic! Why, I don't think there's that much uniform and pageantry in all of North America, but there certainly isn't in the Kingdom!"

"No, quite," Absalom agreed, feeling that he'd scored a point with her somehow. "Your Danites just wear black coats for the most part. With different beards, they could be Amish wagoneers from Pennsylvania or fur traders from the Pale of Settlement."

Annie laughed hysterically. "Different … beards!"

Pfffffft-ankkkh! Pfffffft-ankkkh!

Absalom realized that he and Annie had drifted back through the knot of the *Liahona*'s truck-men. The Strider bringing up the rear seemed to be clanking closer. "Egad," he said, gesturing vaguely at the Strider, "I hope there isn't trouble."

"No, my dear," Annie said, "she's just jealous."

"What?"

"Hush!" "Hush!" "Hush!" The word to be silent reached them, passed down the line. Absalom duly fell quiet, puzzled.

They stood in a cluster of tall trees, swaying in the night breezes. Ahead of them in the dark was a knot of long, low buildings and dim lights that might comprise a farm.

Pfffffft-ankkkh!

The Strider stopped. Absalom craned his neck back around and looked up at Sergeant Jackson, who was riding gunner on the vehicle. The big machine's guns seemed to be aimed at a spot unnervingly close to Absalom but he shook his head, reassuring himself that it must be a trick of the light.

"Mr. Fearnley-Standish," he heard a voice at his elbow. Turning, he confronted a small crowd of men, including the Yankee Sam Clemens, the surly dwarf, his mountain man brother-in-law, and President Brigham Young himself. It was Young who had spoken to him.

"Yes, sir." Absalom smiled pleasantly.

D.J. Butler

"Mr. Fearnley-Standish, your unique services are required," Sam Clemens said. His words sounded deferential, but the man's tone always seemed slightly mocking, and it put Absalom off.

"I'm here, gentlemen," he said. "For Queen and country."

"You have an advantage over the rest of us," Clemens offered, which Absalom found intriguing, but unclear.

"We can't be sure how much John Lee knows by now or how much he might have guessed," Brigham Young added, as if this explained something. "And we need a safe place to leave the Ambassador, at least. This is not his adventure."

"Not to mention the little boy," Clemens added.

"Of course." Absalom pretended that he understood. A good face could get you through a lot, he knew.

"The thing is," the dwarf said, "it's you and me, pal. Everybody else around here is famous but you and me are unknowns. So you and me gotta go up to the house to scout it out, make sure there ain't none of them Danites hanging around the place."

"Oh, of course." Absalom smiled stoically. "Shall we take guns?"

"You're going to knock on the door in the middle of the night and ask if you can sleep in the barn," Clemens said in his condescending Yankee way. "Folks around here seem to expect that you'll be armed but it might be best not to show up on the doorstep with an actual full hand."

"I got knives," the midget grunted. "Besides, the whole point of us two going is won't nobody know who we are, anyway."

It all seemed safe enough. Safe as anything could be, in this land of crazed fanatical assassins and constant gun fighting. "Understood." Absalom decided not to mention the little four-shot gun he had tucked into his waistband. He took some comfort from its presence, even if there was no chance of him using it, and didn't want the others to take it away from him. "Of course, I did meet John Lee, in Chief Pocatello's stockade."

Sam Clemens tapped at his own temple with the butt of his cigar. "The encounter has not escaped me, Mr. Fearnley-Standish," he said gruffly. "The logic is that Lee is unlikely himself to be at this particular farm. His minions are likely to able to recognize President Young, the Ambassador, Rockwell, and the rest of us—"

"But not me. Quite." Absalom straightened his coat and adjusted his hat to a jauntier angle.

"This is a good friend of mine," Brigham Young said. "A very good friend. He's a good man, and he'll take in strangers in need. Just make sure that there aren't any Danites lurking around the place, and then one of you can come get the rest of us."

"And if there are Danites," Clemens added, "run like the devil. Discreetly as you can, of course."

244

Absalom nodded. "Shall we go, Mr. Coltrane?"

"Thank you," Young said. Then Absalom and the dwarf turned their horses up the side of an irrigation ditch dividing two fields and headed for the lights.

"So you are Mr. Poe's associate," Absalom said.

"I'm the barker," Coltrane grunted. "Poe is the show."

"Barker?" Absalom asked. "Is a…? Do you mean that you're a *madman?*"

"I'm the guy that works the midway," Coltrane explained without explaining. "I'm also the roustabout."

"Understood," Absalom lied, and then they trotted into the farmyard.

The yard was hard-packed dirt surrounded by a tidy house, a stable, a chicken coop, and a shed and corral that Absalom guessed, from its smell, must be home to a herd of goats. The buildings looked sturdy but simple and the light from the window was the yellow light of oil or kerosene or wood-fire, not the blue of electricks. The farm might have been a hundred years old, except that Absalom knew that a hundred years earlier the valley had been occupied by Indians who lived in holes in the ground and ate pine nuts and lizards.

"Maybe it's best if *you* knock," Coltrane suggested.

"Yes, agreed." Absalom handed his reins to the dwarf, dropped to the ground and approached the door. In the shadows of the yard he checked his small pistol and was reassured to feel it in place.

He rapped hard on the door and listened as feet crossed floorboards. The man who opened the door and filled its frame was solid in the shoulders and belly, like a boxer. His head was completely bald and he had a curly beard under his jaw and chin. He looked like any yeoman farmer from Dorset or Kent.

"Good evening," Absalom said.

The man stepped across the threshold and grabbed Absalom by the hand. His grip wasn't an ordinary handshake but something odd, with his thumb squeezing insistently down over Absalom's first knuckle. "Brother Boaz," the man said urgently, and he stared into Absalom's eyes.

"Er, no," Absalom smiled. "My name is Fearnley-Standish. My friend and I are traveling through the valley and looking for a place to stay. We hoped we might share your fire tonight."

"Invite your friend inside, Heber," Absalom heard a voice from inside the farmhouse.

The man called *Heber* trembled, his head quivering slightly, almost imperceptibly. He kept staring Absalom in the face and Absalom wondered if he was walking into a house of sick people, or insane, but decided the fellow was probably just old.

"It would be a great kindness," Absalom said cheerfully. He smiled.

Heber sighed and stepped back inside, making room for Absalom to pass. Absalom walked inside the low house, enjoying the smoky warmth and the smell of a meaty stew that came from a large pot hanging over the fire.

"Thank you," he said.

"I'm sorry," Heber answered. He stared at the heavy boots on his feet.

Then Absalom saw John D. Lee. He stood behind the door, smiling a smile that might have been handsome on another face. Between his jug ears and over the two cocked pistols he held pointed at Absalom his smile looked vicious.

Three more men in black coats stood in the corners of the room, all pointing guns at Absalom. He swallowed uncomfortably.

"Come now, Brother Heber." Lee kept his voice low and he grinned. "You should never apologize for hospitality. Besides," Lee's grin vanished into a stony glare, "I saw you try to warn the little limey off."

"I say," Absalom gulped.

"Isn't it time you invited your friend into the house, too?" Lee suggested in a catlike purr. "It will be a lot easier that way."

Absalom turned and looked out the open doorway. The dwarf Coltrane still sat on his horse in the yard. Absalom couldn't see his face in the shadow, but if the midget was holding back, he must suspect something was wrong. Absalom didn't want to invite Coltrane in. They weren't friends but they were allies, and Absalom didn't want to be the kind of man who betrayed an ally into a trap, even when he was in a hard position himself.

"Go on," Lee said.

Absalom wanted to be Richard Burton. Damn the man, he was infuriating and Absalom hated him, but Captain Richard Burton was no coward. Besides, would Lee really shoot him? He must guess that Young and the others were outside and gunshots would warn them off.

Lee raised his pistols and pointed them at Absalom's head.

"Run!" Absalom shouted, and tackled John D. Lee.

He knocked the Danite chieftain back against the wall with a shoulder and then jabbed him several times in the jaw with his fists. Lee didn't shoot, as Absalom had expected, and the man called Heber joined the fray, grabbing Lee and throwing him against the wall.

Then something heavy crashed into the back of Absalom's skull. He saw stars and planets and then the wooden planks of the floor, filthy and stinking of sweet pine, rushed up to whack his head.

The room spun around him for a minute and he heard more sounds of scuffle.

"Goddamn midgets!"

A drop of blood hit the floor right in front of Absalom's eye, then another, then a dwarf. Coltrane struggled but ropes were thrown around him as the farmhouse door slammed shut. "Dirty yellow cowards!" he snapped, and then his captors banged his head against the planks. "Rotten sons of bitches were waiting in the corral and the coop, too," he muttered to Absalom.

Absalom tried to say something reassuring and full of bravado to the dwarf but the effort almost made him throw up and no words would come out.

"Don't do anything foolish, Heber," he heard John D. Lee say. "Think of your family." Lee's boots paced slowly across the planks to Absalom's face, their heavy *thuds* reverberating like the relentless beats of a drum. They stopped with the toes pointing right into his eyes.

"Mmmrrrrroolpff," Absalom protested. He felt vaguely cheated—the Foreign Office had never prepared him for this—but also proud, for not surrendering.

"I told you," he heard Lee say, "that if you invited your friend in, it would be easier."

One of Lee's boots swung away, slowly—

then kicked Absalom in the face, smashing him into darkness.

ꝥꞮꝘꞮꞶꝘꝊꝎꞶꝈꞨꝶꞮꝶ

Burton scrambled stiffly out of the scrub oak and onto the gravel, pressing himself against the plascrete wall of the Dream Mine. The knife wounds in his leg and his arm agonized him and he kept careful control over the fencing saber he carried in a scabbard on his belt, so it didn't scrape the plascrete.

The building rose above him like a staircase in several tiers, with windows overlooking the valley. At Burton's level were a wide veranda, a front door and windows as for an office building, but only if the office in question belonged to a bank or a police station—the windows were all covered with long iron bars. Oiled paper blinds behind the glass kept Burton from seeing any detail but he heard the voices and footfalls of several men inside.

Below Burton was the lowest tier, which had a large bay door. According to Roxie, it opened and closed to permit vehicles entry. Now Roxie and Poe emerged from the trees on the other side of the veranda. Poe coughed, as gently as a man dying of consumption could, and spat into the bushes, carefully not emptying his lungs into the white cloth he held. There was something mysterious about that cloth—Poe had warned Burton not to look directly at it during the fray. Roxie came behind Poe, carrying the canister of scarabs. Burton hadn't seen them in action but Poe seemed to think they were deadly.

Burton had encouraged Roxie to join him on his side of the fracas; after all, he was armed, and an experienced fighter, and Edgar Allan Poe seemed to be more of a spy than a warrior. Burton drew his Colt 1851 Navy revolver and checked the cylinder to be sure each chamber was loaded and capped. *Oh, well.* The woman was in love with another man. It was her choice, even if the man in question was doomed.

And besides, he told himself, Burton was in love with another woman. Or at least, he was committed to her. He was committed to going home and marrying Isabel and settling down. He was committed, and he was starting to think that he even almost wanted to. His bandaged arm and leg both twinged at the thought of more action.

All he had to do now was survive the Kingdom of Deseret.

He cocked the pistol as Tamerlane O'Shaughnessy came lurching up the steps onto the veranda. The man held a crumpled sheet of paper in one hand and a whisky bottle in the other. Burton would have sworn he'd seen that bottle full when he'd taken the wheel of the steam-truck and left the Hot Springs Hotel & Brewery, but it was empty now.

The Irishman was tipsy and he was singing. Burton thought he recognized the tune as an old war-ballad. "If the song should come, we'll follow the drum, and cross that river once more …"

Burton could still hear the men inside talking, and he thought he could make out one of the voices say, "Did you hear something?" He grinned, preparing himself for the moment of decision.

As he stumbled onto the top of the stairs, O'Shaughnessy dropped the bottle.

Crash! It shattered instantly on the plascrete.

The talking inside stopped and O'Shaughnessy dragged himself to the front door. "That tomorrow's Irishmen may wear the sash my father wore!" he finished with flourish, rapped hard on the door, then took two steps back.

He flattened the paper, smoothing it out against his own chest, and grinned.

The door opened and two men stepped out. Two was the perfect number, with two men the plan would go without a hitch, even if they were tall, strong-looking gents, with serious, square jaws like Burton's. One held a rifle in his hands, a Henry, and the other a double-barreled scattergun.

"What do you think, lads?" the Irishman asked in a sliding, imprecise voice, stabbing one finger into the calotype on his chest. "Doesn't look like me at all, I reckon. Besides, what kind of idjit detectives are you, if you haven't figured out yet that my name isn't bloody-damn-hell McNamara?"

Henry and Scattergun both raised their weapons and stepped forward.

Burton slid out from hiding, a little behind Henry, and pointed the Colt at his man. He watched Poe do the same, ridiculously holding up his wadded-up handkerchief. What was the man going to do, suffocate the Pinkerton?

Roxie followed in his wake, holding the canister with both hands.

"It's that Mick Samuelson was looking for," Henry said.

"Philadelphia warrant, isn't it?" asked Scattergun. "I think there's a reward."

Poe and Burton nodded at each other.

"Good evening," they said together.

The plan was that one man would turn to Burton and one to Poe, and both would be neatly captured.

Instead, both Pinkertons wheeled and pointed their guns at Burton. It was the curse of his deep voice; they hadn't even *heard* Poe.

Burton squeezed the trigger.

Bang!

Henry fell back bleeding, losing his grip on his rifle as it went off—

—*Bang!*—

—harmlessly, the bullet winging away into the night.

Burton saw Roxie leap into action, tossing the brass scarabs all through the office door and slamming it shut. Poe grabbed for Scattergun's shoulder and Burton swiveled to aim at the man with his 1851 Navy, but they were both late—

—*Boom!* the scattergun went off.

Poe jerked the man back, dragging him to the ground in some sort of combat maneuver that might be kung fu or karate.

Burton sank to the ground, a searing pain in his side.

Boom! Bang!

Burton and Scattergun both fired pointlessly into the night sky.

Then the screaming started inside the offices of the Dream Mine.

�⅂ω40⊛ω8

Absalom opened his eyes to the upside-down sight of the Danites taking away several big knives from the dwarf. There was a long straight one, like a short sword, that he thought was an Arkansas Toothpick. There was a Bowie knife, with the notch out of its tip so that the point hung below the hilt, and another knife in Coltrane's boot. Then the black-coated men walked to the other corner of the room and conferred. Absalom thought he saw half a dozen of them now, though his vision still swam and he knew he might be miscounting.

The midget saw Absalom's eyes open. To Absalom's surprise, Coltrane popped free another knife, out of the back of his belt apparently, and held it out to Absalom. It was a small, sharp, one-edged affair, with a wooden hilt and no cross-piece. It might have been a kitchen knife for paring potatoes.

Absalom shook his head, which was hard, since he was basically resting on his head, upside down on the wooden floor. He had a gun and he didn't really know how to fight with a knife.

Coltrane mouthed some words silently that Absalom couldn't make out and Absalom gave in. He took the knife and slipped it into his pocket.

Just as he finished, Lee and his men came back.

"Good to see you awake, milord," Lee cracked.

"I'm not a lord," Absalom objected. "My family has a little land and less money, and technically my uncle is a Baronet."

"Isn't that what the French call you all, though?" Lee smirked. "Milords?"

"I thought they called us *rosbifs*," Absalom said. "They protest but obviously they envy us our robust diet. We sometimes call them *frogs*, also a reference to diet. Mostly we call them *prisoners*."

Lee guffawed and slapped his knee. "You're funny, milord. I'm going to call you *milord*, anyway. I like it."

"As you please."

"What's the contingency plan if you two don't come out of this place?"

Absalom wondered if there were some tactic he could adopt, some ruse he could pursue to confound the Danite thug. He screwed up his brows but none came to him, and Lee began to look impatient.

"I said—"

"There is none," Absalom said. "Sorry, bump to the head, I'm a little groggy. How long have I been out? There is no contingency plan. If the farmhouse was clear, we were to come out and tell our comrades."

"Brigham Young and Sam Clemens."

"Yes. And if your men were here, we were to feign innocence and ignorance and sneak out at the first opportunity."

"Shit," observed one of Lee's men.

"How long was I unconscious?" Absalom asked.

"Not long," whined one of the black-coated men.

"Shut up!" Lee snapped to his subordinate. He turned back to Absalom, his face in a growl. "Here's what you're going to do … milord. The dwarf stays here. Any misbehavior, the dwarf is the first one to get it, understood? The dwarf and the good people who own this farm." Lee gestured into a corner and Absalom saw the man named Heber, who had tried to warn him, gagged and tied hand and foot.

"Understood," Absalom agreed. He tried to seem calm, like Burton would. Well, maybe not exactly like Burton. Burton would be roaring and charging up and down the floorboards like a bull with a saber, killing men. But Burton wouldn't be afraid, at least, and in that, Absalom tried to emulate him.

"Wells here'll go with you," Lee continued. Wells stepped forward. He was a tall man, dressed in black from head to foot, with thin dark hair sweeping back from a high forehead. He carried a long rifle. "You'll go back to your friends and you'll tell them all's clear and they're to come in, got it?"

"I've got it."

"Meanwhile, the rest of us will arrange a little welcoming party." Lee twisted his face into an ugly leer. "Any tricks, Wells shoots you and then the dwarf and the farmer get closely acquainted with the handiwork of Mr. Jim Bowie." He brandished the fighting knife he'd taken from Jed Coltrane.

"Understood." The wheels of Absalom's brain spun wildly, trying to generate a plan that didn't involve leading his sister and Annie into the farmhouse, or getting himself shot.

The Danites cut Absalom loose and marched him out the door, Wells on his heels. He avoided making eye contact with either the midget or the farmer, for fear he'd give away either his hopeful reflection on rescue schemes or his gut-wrenching fear.

Exiting the farmhouse, the temperature dropped. After weeks on the road, it still impressed him how cold the desert got at night. The sudden cooling of sweat on his forehead made Absalom realize how hot and stuffy the inside of the house had been.

"This way," he said politely, and marched out along the irrigation ditch.

Wells walked behind him, which put Coltrane's knife and the pocket it was tucked into conveniently out of the Danite's line of sight.

Absalom slipped the knife into his hand.

He kept spinning the wheels. They kept failing to catch on anything clever or insightful.

Absalom stopped walking. "Those are my companions over there," he told Wells. He could see the Striders, silhouettes jutting out around a stand of trees where three fields met. "Will you wait here for me?" He doffed his hat politely with his left hand.

Be brave, he told himself. *Be a fighter, like Burton.*

Wells spat on the ground. "I reckon not. I reckon I'll follow you on up closer, so I can hear what you and your companions say to each other. And make sure you talk good and loud, hear?"

Be fearless. Be a bull with a saber.

"Of course."

D.J. Butler

Be the warrior Annie wants.

Absalom stabbed with Coltrane's knife, aiming for the Danite's jugular.

CHAPTER
FOURTEEN

L ie back, Captain," Roxie instructed him, "and think of England."

Burton struggled to sit up in the office chair. "Who's bringing up the steam-truck? Tell me it isn't O'Shaughnessy."

Roxie plucked another pellet from Burton's side and tossed it to the plascrete floor, where it hit with a gentle *plink*. "You object to giving the wheel of a steam-truck to a man who's been drinking?"

Burton snarled against the pain and spat on the floor to clear his head. "I object to giving it to *him*."

"Not to worry, then," she told him, wrapping a bandage around his chest. "Poe's driving."

"Ekwensu's slippery shell!" Burton cursed. "Let's hope the wretch lives long enough to get back here."

"Captain Burton." Roxie looked at him reproachfully. "Don't be a sore loser." She wrapped some sort of cloth around him as a bandage. It had the sting of alcohol.

Burton growled and grumbled wordlessly, but nodded. "It's my nature, Mrs. Snow … Mrs. Young … I was never cut out for the soft conversation of the civilized."

"You can still call me Roxie," she said, and tied the bandage off.

He shrugged back into his coat and limped with her across the veranda. At the top of the stairs, they gathered up O'Shaughnessy, who was droning on and on about the pipes that were calling him. Burton didn't dislike the Irish, not any more than he disliked any other race of men, and he decided that, on balance, he almost *liked* O'Shaughnessy's singing voice. He helped the other man up and they staggered together down the stairs, to stand in front of the bay doors that now gaped open.

Blue lights jostling up the road showed that Poe had survived the hike down to the steam-truck and was on his way back.

"I've been meaning to ask you," he said to Roxie, pointing to the row of squiggles over the top of the bay door. "What language is that? It's everywhere in this Kingdom but I haven't heard a language spoken other than English and Spanish."

She chuckled slyly. "Why, Dick," she said, "I'm surprised to see you so easily stumped. That's perfectly good English. It says *Koyle Mining Corporation.*"

Burton squinted at the letters. "It's a cipher, then," he guessed. "You've taken as a nation to writing in code. It's like the tangled streets of a medieval city, a deliberate device to keep outsiders out."

"On the contrary," she told him, "it's a system to make writing the English language simpler."

"Simpler!" he snorted. "Some of us find the Latin characters simple enough."

"Yes?" she asked innocently. "How do you write the sound *fffff?*"

"*Eff,*" he retorted, then caught himself. "Or *pee-aitch.*"

"Or?"

He thought, feeling that he was being baited. "Double-*eff.*"

"And what sound does *gee-aitch* make?" she pressed him.

"Dammit, woman," he rumbled, "what's your point?"

"The point," she explained, gesturing at the row of characters that allegedly identified the owners of the mine, "is that those characters are the Deseret Alphabet. They are used to write English, in a manner that is simple, logical, and consistent."

"Once you know the damned code," Burton growled.

"Yes," she agreed, "once you know the alphabet."

"I did not know you Mormons went in for Websterism," Burton complained.

The steam-truck rumbled up out of the trees and clattered to a puffing halt in front of the big door.

"Oh, we are reformers, alright," she told him. "But that is the least of our surprises."

"You people," O'Shaughnessy belched, "are so fookin' *boring!*" He staggered to the side of the steam-truck and started trying to climb up one of its big India rubber tyres.

Burton examined the letters. "Your *kay* resembles the Egyptian hieroglyph of a woman's breasts," he said. "What is that lightning-bolt-and-cross pictogram that follows it?"

"Sound it out, Dick," she suggested. "That's the *oi* in *Koyle.*"

Burton shook his head. "Was this scheme dreamed up by your Madman Pratt, too?" he asked. He dragged the Irishman over to the ladder and shouldered him up it by main strength. His injured arm, leg, and side all hurt, though none of it, he reminded himself, hurt half so much as having a spear thrust through his head.

Roxie climbed the ladder nimbly. "Actually, it was his brother Parley. With some others."

Burton followed. "And Parley Pratt is at present doing what? Rendering the contents of the Library of Congress into this efficient alphabet of his?"

Roxie sat on the front bench inside the wheelhouse. Burton kicked O'Shaughnessy into a crumpled pile on the second bench and dropped beside him.

"Parley's dead," she said quietly. "He was killed two years ago."

Poe started coughing. He didn't look well and Burton did him the courtesy of pretending not to notice.

"Thoth knows it'd be easy enough to get killed in this wild place," he said. "If the rattlesnakes, bears, or coyotes don't get you, the Shoshone or the Pinkertons or the Danites will."

"Parley was killed in Arkansas," she said. "Orson has never been the same since."

Poe was still coughing. Roxie patted him gently on the back.

"I hope the guilty man was brought to justice." Burton expressed his sympathy a little roughly but he meant it.

"I'm not sure about justice," Roxie said, "but there was certainly revenge."

"Sometimes the distinction between the two is fine."

Roxie nodded. She looked sad. "And sometimes there is a huge gulf between them. Some of the rough men, Danites and others, of our Dixie—that's the southern part of the Kingdom, where Brother Brigham is trying to grow cotton and wine grapes—ambushed a wagon train passing through from Arkansas. Parley's killer, a bitter old man named McLean, was with the wagons."

"Your men killed McLean, I take it?"

Poe hacked violently into his handkerchief. Burton could smell the blood and mucus.

"They killed every last person in the wagon train aged eight and older. Over one hundred people, men, women, and children."

"Great God of Heaven," Burton murmured.

"The Danites who ambushed that poor wagon train," Roxie said, her voice barely above a whisper, "were led by John D. Lee."

Burton's heart ached. He wanted to say something but tears stung his eyes and he didn't trust himself to formulate words. He was astonished at his own reaction and more than a little embarrassed.

D.J. Butler

Poe straightened up, his breath rasping in his lungs. He hurled his handkerchief out the wheelhouse window, took the wheel, and without saying a word put the steam-truck into gear.

The truck rattled forward, under the big letters in the Deseret Alphabet and into the dark-gaping maw of the Dream Mine.

ᘜᏕᎣ᙭ᘺᏇᘘᎰ᙭ᘓᎱᎱ

Absalom plunged the knife into the Danite Wells's throat. The resistance the blade met sickened him; it felt crunchy and elastic, as if he were cutting through the joints of a chicken.

He shuddered and let go of the knife handle.

Wells staggered back. His face was pale under the moon and washed with dark, deep shadows but Absalom clearly saw the look of surprise, anger, and fear in the man's eyes. Blood poured down his chest. Absalom felt a burning mixture of shame and pride, knowing that the man was doomed, and it was Absalom who had killed him.

Richard Burton couldn't have done it any better.

Wells stumbled, but kept his footing—

—his breath came in wet gasps—

—he slowly raised his rifle—

Absalom ducked reflexively and started to scuttle sideways, but then realized that he couldn't let the rifle go off; Lee would kill Heber Kimball, not to mention the dwarf Coltrane.

Absalom lunged and jerked the rifle out of Wells's hands.

Wells windmilled his arms and stared. He clawed at his thigh, and Absalom saw that he wore a pistol holstered there. Absalom couldn't let that be fired, either.

Wells slipped the string off his pistol.

Absalom closed in, grabbing the Danite by the lapel of his coat and reaching for the hilt of the knife that still protruded from the other man's neck.

Wells jerked the gun from its holster—

—and Absalom gripped the hilt of the knife and drew it across the Danite's throat in a single swift motion.

Snick!

Blood gushed from Wells's throat and poured over Absalom's shoes. It smelled of salt, and meat, and iron, and death.

The Danite dropped his pistol from nerveless fingers, then collapsed to the earth.

Absalom let the knife slip from his hand. Then he fell to his knees and began to vomit.

256

⅂⅃◯⅂Ⱳ◲◎Ⓦ⅃◖⅃⅂

"We need a plan," Roxie pointed out.

"Recover the canopic jars," Poe suggested.

"Sequester the rubies," Burton added.

"Burn the fookin' place to the ground," Tam threw in, focusing to keep his words from slurring. *Best not to sound too drunk, me boy.* "Excuse me, I meant conflagrate it to the … terrestrium." He looked out the window of the steam-truck at the tunnel walls. They were rough and rocky and propped up with heavy timbers but the tunnel was surprisingly large, for a mine. Well, it wasn't really a mine, was it? But it looked like it had been bored by an enormous drill, rather than cut by picks. And of course, it was huge, so big the steam-truck rattled up it at top speed. "Terrarium?"

"Any of the three would do," Poe noted, and coughed once. He and the woman Roxie sat on the front bench together. He drove and she kept a hand on his shoulder, stroking him like a bloody-damn-hell lapdog. "Or anything else that would prevent the launch of his ships come sunrise."

"We should split into two parties," Burton suggested. "At least."

"Agreed," Poe said. "I propose to drive the steam-truck into the facility and try to bluff my way through to achieving any of our objectives. Perhaps Roxie can join me, and corroborate my Pinkerton disguise."

"You don't look like a fookin' Pinkerton," Tam complained. "You look too clever to be a Pinkerton."

"I could follow on foot," Burton suggested. The Englishman sounded like someone had pissed in his tea, but then, he'd been stabbed twice, so Tam had compassion for the man. "Or is there another way in? The coal fumes from the trucks must get out of the tunnel somehow, mustn't they?"

"Ventilation shafts," Roxie explained. "But they go straight up."

"There's doors," Tam pointed out, jabbing his finger at one in the wall as they passed it. Mother O'Shaughnessy hadn't birthed any blind pups and Tam's drinking hadn't yet gone that far.

"Those are doors to let emergency maintenance workers in," Roxie said. "They're there in case the main tunnel is blocked and something needs to be dragged out or extinguished. They open automatically in case of fire in the tunnel but otherwise they're locked."

"And now we're back to my plan of burning the place down," Tam pointed out.

"Can anyone pick the lock?" Burton asked. He looked pointedly at Roxie and at Poe.

She shook her head. "Annie's good with mechanical things. I'm more of a people person and a woman of words."

"Seduction, forgery, and narcotics, in other words," Burton said with a brutish leer, "but nothing useful."

"Stop the Brigit-blessed truck," Tam grumbled. He felt sick from all the motion anyway. "*I'll* open the lock."

Poe braked the steam-truck and Tam stumbled out. He took a moment once his feet touched the gravel floor of the tunnel to fill his lungs with air and let the walls stop spinning around him. Outside the truck, he could now see that the steam and coal smoke jetting out the back did indeed flow directly up into shafts overhead. The air filling the main tunnel itself was cool and very breathable.

Burton hit the ground behind him, saber clinking against the gravel (and didn't he strut like that bit of steel made him all important and fancy?). "Wait until we're sure he can do this," the Englishman called over his shoulder to Poe.

Tam saw that Poe had conveniently stopped beside a door and he walked over to it. The door was a very ordinary-looking affair, solid, with a brass doorknob and a small, very modern-looking keyhole to its lock.

Burton followed him. "Aren't you too drunk to do this?" he asked gruffly.

"I'm not drunk," Tam objected, drawing one of the Maxim Hushers. "I'm Irish." He pointed the gun at the lock and emptied the cylinder at it.

Zing! Zing! Zing! Zing! Zing! Zing!

Bullets whined through the tunnel and into the darkness but Tam paid them no attention and the explorer was unfazed.

Clang!

The doorknob hit the gravel. Burton stepped forward, hooked a finger into the ragged hole that the mutilated lock had left behind, and jerked the door open.

"We're in!" he called to Poe and Roxie. He drew his long Colt pistol with one hand and his rapier with the other and disappeared into the open doorway.

"Sure, and who gets the credit?" Tam muttered. He thumbed open the compartment surrounding the Husher's cylinder and stumbled after Burton, doing his best to reload while on the move. And a little bit tipsy.

�167WHOⱭW8

Absalom Fearnley-Standish staggered into the grove of trees. His arms and chest looked strangely blotched in the moonlight and it was only when he got close enough for Sam to smell the iron-loamy stink of blood that he realized why.

"I've killed a man," Fearnley-Standish murmured. He seemed distracted.

"I hope it wasn't the dwarf," Sam said. "I was beginning to feel fond of him."

The Stridermen kept their watch in their big, clanking beasts, but everyone else rushed around the Englishman. The Mormon girl, Annie, pushed harder than the rest, elbowing aside even Brigham Young to get to his side, where she pushed her shoulder under his arm as if to keep him on his feet. He didn't resist.

In his place, Sam wouldn't have resisted, either.

"Coltrane was alive, last I saw him," Fearnley-Standish protested mildly. "He gave me this knife." He held up an empty hand, fingers smeared with blood.

"I see," Sam said. "What happened?"

They stood in the grove of cottonwoods, trees tall enough to more or less mask the presence of the Striders, but also tall enough to block out most of the moonlight. Sam would have liked to use Pratt's Fireless Darklantern but he was afraid it would be visible from the farmhouse.

The Englishman shook himself and snapped to a sort of attention. Sam couldn't be sure in the darkness but he thought the fellow was squeezing Annie Webb's shoulders rather more tightly than was strictly necessary to avoid falling down. "There are Danites in the farmhouse," he informed them. "And the outbuildings. They have Heber Kimball and his family tied up, and Jedediah Coltrane as well. They sent me out to bring you in. I was not to let you think anything suspicious was happening."

"Is that your blood, Mr. Fearnley-Standish?" Brigham Young asked. Sam found his voice surprisingly tender.

The Foreign Office man shook his head. "They sent one of their men to watch me and make certain I did as they asked. I, ah ..." he gestured with his empty fingers, making a vague motion that might have been meant as a stab or a slash. "I killed him."

"What was the man's name, do you know?" Young inquired.

Fearnley-Standish cleared his throat. "Ah, Wells, I think."

"Son of a bitch!" Orrin Porter Rockwell snapped.

"Poor Wells," Young said thoughtfully. "So they got to you, too."

"They got to a lot of folks," Annie Webb said. She was snuggled as close into Absalom Fearnley-Standish's side as a person could be without actually being in the same set of clothes. Sam snorted at the silliness of his own envy.

"It's like I was trying to tell you, Brigham," Rockwell grumbled. He sounded like a hungry bear.

"Hush now, Port," his wife urged him, and the frontiersman fell quiet.

"We need a plan," Young announced, sounding ebullient and determined in the darkness. "Port, have you ever been to Heber's farm?"

"Begging your pardon, Mr. President," Sam intervened. "But it seems to me that your enemies have made our lives easier. We were looking for a quiet place to stash some of the more egregiously civilian members of our party. John D. Lee has tipped his hand and shown us where he's lying in wait, which makes the whole rest of the valley safe and fair game for us. Our plan now is the same as our plan was before, only now we go to a different friend's house of yours. Or a wife's, whatever is comfortable for you."

"Aye," puffed Dan Jones. "Or better still, pick a farm that doesn't belong to someone in your family or anyone else close to you. The minute he sees you're alive, any loyal man would be happy to hide John Moses and the Ambassador for you in his shed."

"To open the blind eyes," Young recited gently, "to bring out the prisoners from the prison. I'm not leaving Heber Kimball and his family in there. Or Mr. Coltrane. Who sees human beings as mere cogs now, Mr. Clemens?"

Sam was astounded. "That dwarf came out to your Kingdom planning to spy on you, steal from you, and, if necessary, commit acts of sabotage!"

Brigham Young looked at Sam. His eyes were in shadow, and Sam felt like he was looking into infinitely deep wells, rich with the knowledge of human folly. "Is he the only one who came to Deseret with such plans, Mr. Clemens?" Young asked.

Sam hung his head. "No, sir," he admitted. "But I believe I had good motive for my actions."

"Most men believe they do," Young agreed.

Sam chuckled wryly. "I think you've stolen my line, Mr. President." He *really* wished he had a Partagás to chomp on.

"In any case, Coltrane is my ally now and I won't abandon him. Also, he came to the rescue of young John Moses Browning, more than once, and for that he deserves to be rescued himself."

"Amen," Dan Jones added.

"If joo are worried about your friend Heber, I suppose that rules out simply blowing the farm to esmithereens with my Estriders," Ambassador Armstrong observed. "But I wish joo to understand that my bodyguards are estill at your disposition. As am I, of course."

Fearnley-Standish cleared his throat again. "I believe we're all at your disposition now, Mr. President," he said, "whatever our prior political positions may have been. I think one of the tactical difficulties with any plan we adopt at this juncture is that if I don't return up that irrigation ditch shortly, with at least you by my side, and maybe even without Ambassador Armstrong, Mr. Clemens, and Mr. Rockwell, the Danites hiding in the goat shed will tell Lee and he'll kill all his prisoners."

Brigham Young smiled. "Oh, that's no problem," he said. "That's no problem at all."

�158W@04WTCII

Burton strode purposefully, shoulders back to keep him at his full height and pistol raised and ready. *Fitzzing* blue electricks globes lit the passage, embedded into the ceiling at intervals of twenty feet. It was enough light to see by but he worried that shooting would be difficult, especially against moving targets that shot back. He kept his gaze nailed to the end of the passageway ahead; at least in this plascrete tunnel he didn't need his peripheral vision for anything.

His whole body hurt. He kept going.

"You're a brave man," the Irish thug whined behind him. When he wasn't actually singing, Burton decided, he didn't like the Irishman's voice. "And you're a fast walker, aren't you?"

"Jamshid's crook! I've been stabbed twice and shot with a scattergun today," Burton reminded the other man. "What's slowing *you* down?"

"I've been shot twice and had my bloody-damn-hell ear bit off, is what I've done!"

"Unless the missing ear is somehow slowing your pace," Burton growled, "I think that still means I've had the worst of it."

"Do you hate me because I'm Irish?" Tam wheedled.

"A man serves his own country and cause without hating the countries and causes of other men," Burton snorted. "Even the Irish."

"Mother O'Shaughnessy taught me better than that," Tam said, and his words slurred grossly. "She taught me that every man serves himself, and himself only."

The passage ended at a staircase, steps leading up to the left and down to the right. Burton stopped to let O'Shaughnessy catch up.

"Milton puts that doctrine in Satan's mouth."

"Brigit love you," the Irishman grunted.

"Is your pistol loaded?" Burton asked him.

"It is." O'Shaughnessy brandished his strange, silent gun. "Just finished, and the second is still full, all six chambers."

"I'm glad you can count," Burton snarled softly, "because when I get to three, you and I are both going to step out onto the stairs, pistols first. You will turn and look down the stairs, and I will look up."

"Why's that, then?"

"We killed the Pinkertons at the bottom of the mountain," Burton reminded him. "I expect that if we are to see more of them, it's likely that they will be coming down at us from above."

"What's that mean, you reckon you're the better shot?"

"I know I'm the better shot," Burton hissed. "I would have taken out the lock with one bullet, not an entire cylinder."

"Ah, that's just a question of style," the Irishman grunted.

"One," Burton riposted. "Two."

On *three* they stepped onto the stairs. Nothing. Burton began briskly marching up, O'Shaughnessy trailing behind.

"Are we going to walk to the top of the bloody mountain, then?"

"We'll take the first lift we find," Burton promised. He felt like he was talking to a child. *Was this what being a father was like?* he wondered. Maybe he didn't want to get married after all.

"There might have been a lift if we'd gone down, too," the Irishman wheezed.

"There might have," Burton agreed. "But if there's no lift at all, we need to be going up. Besides," he took a deep breath himself, "you clearly need the exercise."

"I'm not a weakling," O'Shaughnessy protested, "I'm just a bit drunk."

"Keep your pistols aimed down the stairs, then," Burton urged him. "But you told me before you weren't drunk. Just Irish, you said."

"I'll let you in on a secret, Dick," the Irishman said. "It's the same fookin' thing."

They climbed past several more passages, all leading off to the left. Burton could see that each ended in a dark doorway and he guessed they were further maintenance access tunnels and didn't waste his time exploring them. He was feeling winded and lightheaded himself when he stepped onto a longer stretch of flat corridor, wider and taller and better lit by two miniature, man-height Franklin Poles against the right wall.

Between them was a glass door beyond which lay a dark shaft. The glass was bound and surrounded by brass, and a brass control panel to one side framed a lever in a vertical slot with three positions: *UP, NO CALL,* and *DOWN.* Burton thumbed the lever from *NO CALL* into the *UP* position with a loud *click!* and checked the percussion caps on his 1851 Navy while he waited for the tipsy Irish thug to catch up to him.

Hishhhhhhhh …

The lift descended into view from above. It was small, fit to hold maybe four men, with three walls paneled in wood and brass, and a brass accordion gate replacing the fourth wall and meeting the lift door. It all gleamed of shine and polish and only Burton's close watch and sharp eyes caught the furled edge of a coat on one side of the lift, betraying at least one passenger.

"Back!" he hissed to the Irishman.

O'Shaughnessy's eyes were stupid with drink but something propelled him against the wall, back first, and he filled both his hands with silenced pistols.

Burton raised his pistol.

The lift stopped—

—*Bang! Bang! Bang!*—

—and Burton started firing.

The Colt 1851 Navy punched three holes through the glass and shining wood in a tight pattern that should have placed all three bullets into the neck of the man hiding there. He collapsed forward into the middle of the lift but Burton paid him no attention. He was already shifting his aim to the second man, who spun into view holding a Sharps carbine and raising it to his shoulder.

Bang!

The Sharps fired first and Burton felt the bullet bite into his hip. He staggered back, losing his grip on the Colt as he pulled the trigger.

Bang!

Burton's shot missed and the bullet tore away up the tunnel uselessly. The pistol clattered to the floor. Burton fought to regain his footing and bring the saber up into a guard position, pointless as that would be against a rifle, but his wounds were too much and he flailed backwards until he collided with the wall.

The man with the Sharps stalked forward out of the lift. He was clean-shaven, with a cleft chin and the determined look of a professional in his eye. He kept the muzzle of the Sharps pointed squarely at the center of Burton's chest.

"Drop the sword," Sharps growled.

Zing! Zing! Zing! Zing! Zing! Zing!

Tamerlane O'Shaughnessy's first shot hit the Pinkerton in the side of the head, but he kept firing. Every bullet hit and the gunman crumpled to the floor under a tsunami of instant, nearly silent death.

"I reckon *you'd* have got him with one shot," O'Shaughnessy said with a lopsided grin. "I promise I'll try harder next time."

Burton stooped to recover the Colt, hopping on one leg like a crane and wincing with pain. "I've reconsidered my view," he said, trying to speak gently, but knowing that it came out surly. "Shoot as many bullets as you want."

"I'd give you a shot of my whisky," the Irishman offered, "only I drank it all."

Pain seared Burton's hip and thigh but he forced himself to walk with as much dignity as he could muster into the lift. "Think nothing of it," he brushed away the offer, knowing he wouldn't be quite so cavalier if there were actually a bottle to hand. "I've had worse."

"I can see that you have," O'Shaughnessy agreed, nodding pointedly at the scars on Burton's face. "Only I doubt you had to walk out of that jungle on your face afterwards, did you?"

D.J. Butler

Burton checked his hip in the lift. It bled, but not profusely, and the bullet had entered, missed the bone, and exited again. He'd live. They dragged the bodies out into the hall and then wiped blood off their shoes on the dead men's clothing.

"Try not to step in the blood," he urged O'Shaughnessy.

"Do you reckon me that big an idjit, then? I'll not be painting a bright red trail behind us wherever we go. Mother O'Shaughnessy might have raised a numbskull or two but she didn't name them Tamerlane."

Both men climbed gingerly into the lift together. Burton shut the brass accordion door and heard a click outside as the external lever popped back to its NO CALL setting. Inside, a brass panel set into the wooden wall contained another lever running past five markers: GATE, TUNNEL, BAY, LAKE, and TOWER. The lever was currently set at TUNNEL.

"It can't have been just bad luck that these two men stumbled upon us," Burton ruminated, examining the panel.

"No, I reckon they're expecting trouble," the Irishman agreed. "Maybe they've seen what happened at the mine entrance, or they called down and got no answer. Then you called the lift with that switch outside, and they jumped on to see what they'd find."

Burton nodded. "I suggest we go to the Bay, one level up from where we are now."

"Bit of a gamble, isn't that?" the Irishman asked.

"Anything we do is a gamble," Burton agreed. "I'm gambling that there aren't other Pinkertons waiting for us at the Bay level, either because there aren't others waiting anywhere, full stop, or because they're waiting at a higher position."

"I'll wager on the same horse," O'Shaughnessy deferred to him. "If we actually had a horse, mind you, I'd gladly force the beast up the tunnel with me on its back, because I don't mind admitting I'm a wee bit nervous. But I can't do any more of these stairs."

"No more stairs," Burton agreed, and began reloading the 1851 Navy.

When they had both reloaded, he shoved the lever to BAY.

Hishhhhhhhhhh!

The lift slid smoothly upward and the lever in the panel climbed to show their progress.

ꚜᛤᘔꕷᘯᚺᛤᘔ⸘ꕷ⸘

Jed Coltrane's hands were free. He'd cut his own bonds before he'd handed the one knife the Danites had missed in searching him to the Englishman, and he'd kept his eyes shut and his head down since then.

264

Now he opened his eyelids a crack and examined the room.

Danites in long coats stood at every window, peeping out past the animal skin curtains that covered them, and one more waited behind the door. Jed counted six of them, including the leader with the jug handle ears, Lee, who paced up and down the center of the floor rubbing his hands together like he was warming up to pray. A single kerosene lantern burned, shedding its oily stink and its wavering yellow light from the hook by which it hung from the center beam of the ceiling.

Jed lay piled in the corner by the chimney with the farmer and the rest of his family. They all had their hands tied and a few of them had bruised faces or bloody lips but they wore patient, serious expressions on their faces. Maybe they were sure help was coming. Or maybe they were just ready to die.

Jed wasn't ready to die, not by a long shot. He wasn't sure what it was he thought he had to live for, exactly, but whatever it was life brought him, he hadn't had enough of it yet. He looked for a way out, and it wasn't hard to find. The Danite at the nearest window watched the yard outside and not the prisoners, obviously relying on the fact that they were tied up and had been beaten. Either end of the cabin's long plank table or the rough wooden bench running along the wall would give Jed plenty of platform from which to launch himself into the air and through the window. The Danite would never see it coming, and then Jed would be out in the night and running for freedom.

He was an acrobat, after all.

Hell, maybe he ought to escape, to warn Brigham Young and Sam Clemens and the others. Jed had no reason to be confident that the young Englishman had somehow pulled it off. For all he knew, John Moses might be merrily on his way into the trap at that very moment.

But if he jumped out the window, he'd be leaving prisoners behind. They had no one else to help them … that wasn't right.

Dammit, Coltrane, what's happened to you?

He clenched his jaw to keep from gnashing his teeth and giving away the fact that he was awake. *Don't go soft now, Jed Coltrane,* he browbeat himself. *Those are real guns those men are carrying and they'll happily blow you full of holes to make a point, much less to snatch the keys to this Kingdom they want so badly. They're willing to burn down the whole damn show. They won't bat an eye at having to snuff out a rousty like you.*

You can come back for the farmer and his family, or tell Brigham Young and he can send his people back. It's his problem, anyway, not yours. Just because you went all soft on a little kid once doesn't mean you have to go soft on everybody.

Count to three, then go.

One. The Danites kept their watch strictly. The man at the nearest window was fixed on the back pasture and wouldn't even see Jed until he was flying past.

Two. "Ain't they a bit late getting back?" a big-shouldered, red-haired Danite asked his chieftain.

"Patience, Brother Robison," John Lee answered. "We'll give them a few more minutes."

Three.

Jed stayed put.

Dammit! he cursed himself.

"Hoo-whee!" the man standing beside the doorway called out and opened the door wide, letting in a rush of cold night air. Every Danite in the room turned into the breeze, pulling his pistol or readying his rifle to shoot.

Jed had another clear shot at the window and still he did nothing.

He looked at the farmer Heber Kimball. As if the old man were echoing Jed's own thoughts, he shook his head sadly.

Brigham Young came into the room first, hands raised in surrender. The Mexican Ambassador followed, and Orrin Porter Rockwell, and then Sam Clemens, and finally the Englishman Fearnley-Standish, all holding their hands up and bowing their heads in meek submission.

"Shit." The curse escaped Jed in a whisper but it escaped him. No one seemed to notice except the farmer Kimball, who turned and shot Jed a curious look. Jed winked back at him and dropped his eyelids back to slits.

"You've got us, John," Young said gruffly. "You've surprised me here like you surprised me in the Beehive House. Now let me surprise you."

"With what?" Lee asked. "A burst of pointless temper, followed by an even more pointless offer of forgiveness? Save your breath, whatever it's worth to you. Jesus may be able to forgive me, Brigham. All you can do is promise not to bring me to trial. And even if I believed you, your promise is meaningless now, because as of tomorrow morning, you won't be President of the Kingdom anymore."

Absalom Fearnley-Standish edged over to the knot of prisoners beside the fireplace and sat down. The Danites paid him no mind.

"What if you fail?" Young asked.

Lee laughed, harsh. "If I do, you won't be there to see it. You'll never see another sunrise, Brigham. I'm going to take you outside now, purely out of courtesy to Sister Kimball, and kill you in the goat pen. Of course, I don't know how long Sister Kimball will appreciate my courtesy, that's entirely up to Heber. Once you're dead, he'll have to choose to be with me or against me, like the Savior said. Naturally, there will be consequences, whichever choice he makes."

"We have to move," Fearnley-Standish hissed in a soft whisper. Jed barely heard the words, they were so soft, and Heber Kimball shook his head to clear it from the distraction of the Englishman's voice.

"You're not the Savior." Brigham Young's voice was gentle.

"Neither are you." John D. Lee's voice was hard and flat. It was the sort of voice you'd use to accuse another rousty of gaffing a card game.

"We can't … be by … the chimney." The Englishman was still whispering out of the corner of his mouth, shooting out his words in staccato bursts like the bullets out of John Browning's *machine-gun*. The Danites, transfixed by the confrontation in the center of the room, didn't hear him, and Jed and the Kimballs ignored him. His eyes began to twitch frantically.

Brigham Young turned and paced deliberately across the room in Jed's direction, the cabin floor creaking under his steps. He looked like Daniel in the lions' den, Jed thought, except the only man in the room who carried himself like a lion was Brigham Young. He was a lion in a jackals' den, maybe.

Young stopped himself in front of the fireplace, then stopped and turned to face Lee.

"Shoot me here," he told his adopted son.

"Aren't you troubled you'd make a mess of Sister Kimball's floors?" Lee asked, but he drew a pistol from the holster at his hip. "But why do I ask? Consideration of others has never been your strong suit."

"The blood of Brother Brigham would make this a holier temple than you'll ever set foot in, John Lee!" the farmer's wife snapped. "Don't you worry about my floors!"

"My Brother Joseph died in a jail cell," Young said quietly, "surrounded by his friends. Dying in a cabin surrounded by my friends would be no less honorable."

"Move!" The shouted instruction came from the Danite by the nearest window, the man Jed had been planning to slip past. Now he pointed a pistol at the prisoners and urged them to their feet.

Jed pretended to wake up, then carefully held his unbound hands together as he scrambled to his feet and followed the Kimballs as they shuffled across the creaking floor to the far wall.

"You happy?" he grunt-whispered to Fearnley-Standish. "Now we ain't by the chimney."

The Englishman had a look of pure consternation and worry on his face. "He'll die," he whispered.

"Who, Young?" Jed shot a look over his shoulder. The President of the Kingdom of Deseret stood with his back to the chimney and his hands over his head. John D. Lee stood in front of him with his pistol drawn but not yet raised. All eyes in the room were on them. "Yeah, he might. But he's only getting what he chose."

"He'll die." The Englishman patted the waistband of his pants like he had an upset stomach.

"Hey," the red-headed Danite Robison said, "what about Wells?"

"Do I get last words, John?" Young asked. He stood directly before the stone column of the chimney, his arms spread wide like wings, and he edged forward slightly, taking small steps that brought him closer to the man holding the gun on him. His eyes were calm, Jed noticed. He was one steel-spined son of a bitch, Brigham Young. "A last meal? Brother Heber is tone deaf, but will you let him sing 'A Poor Wayfaring Man of Grief' for me, anyway?"

"You're no martyr," Lee said. "You're no Joseph Smith. You're just in the way."

"The chimney," Fearnley-Standish murmured, and suddenly Jed guessed what he was worried about.

John D. Lee raised his pistol—

and Jed tackled him. He hit the man knuckles-first, missed his grab at the jug ears, and tumbled to the floor.

Bang!

Lee's shot went wide, the bullet biting into the wooden ceiling.

Jed rolled, racing for a window. The room around him bustled into action, guns swerving and men barking, but unfortunately all the guns were in the hands of the men who wanted Jed dead. He came out of his somersault reaching to plant his foot on a chair and leap for a window and freedom—

—and a booted foot caught him in the midriff.

Jed crashed hard into the log wall of the cabin. The room tipped to one side before his eyes and then spun around in a greasy yellow kerosene swirl, and when he could see again, he was looking up the barrel of a heavy rifle at the snarling face of the Danite Robison. Behind his attacker, Young and Clemens and Rockwell and the Ambassador all stood still, guns to their heads.

So much for the little rebellion he had started.

So much for worrying about other people. You should have run when you had the chance, Coltrane.

"Go to hell," he drawled to the Danite in his best cracker accent.

"Kill the dwarf," Lee said.

The powerfully-built Danite raised the rifle and grinned. "This is for Wells," he snarled.

Pip! Pip! Pip!

Robison's head exploded, spurting a fountain of blood out one temple. He dropped the rifle, took two jerky steps forward and then toppled to the floor. Jed turned to stare at the source of the shots, with everyone else.

They had come from Absalom Fearnley-Standish. He stood upright, if trembling a bit, and in his outstretched hand he held a tiny derringer, a little four-shot lady's gun. In any other moment, Jed might have found him silly looking, with his scalloped hat brim and badly scuffed city boy shoes and the look on his face, part scared, part determined, and part totally insane. Trembling as he was from the close scrape with death, though, Jed was happy to have a champion of any appearance whatsoever.

The short yaps from the derringer faded and Fearnley-Standish lowered his gun. His face shone with sweat and his eyes trembled and Jed wondered if the other man might be just a little bit drunk.

"Mr. Lee," the Englishman said slowly, tugging at his waistcoat and jacket in effort to smooth them that was doomed to failure. "The first step in any successful negotiation is the making of an offer. We are all reasonable men here, President Brigham Young more than any of us. Please tell us what you want and why you want it, and I'm sure that together we shall all be able to find common ground."

"Kill them both!" John D. Lee barked.

Danites cocked pistols all over the room.

KABOOM!

The chimney exploded.

CHAPTER FIFTEEN

KABOOM!

Two Danites standing nearest the chimney collapsed under the barrage of flying stones. Then the ceiling around the fireplace caved in and Young, Armstrong, Rockwell, and Clemens all disappeared from Absalom's view.

"Not that easy!" John D. Lee raged and waded into the mess of fallen timbers, one hand clawing at the rubble and the other holding a pistol high.

"Get outta here!" the dwarf Coltrane shouted. He wheezed a bit and sounded generally thrashed but he had a knife in his hand and he started cutting ropes off the hands of the Kimball family.

A Danite with a scattergun stepped close to the knot of prisoners and raised his weapon. "Stop right there!" he growled, aiming at the midget.

To Absalom's own surprise, he didn't hesitate. He raised his derringer and took aim at Scattergun's neck.

Pip!

Scattergun toppled sideways and then Coltrane was on him like a dagger-wielding ape, stabbing him twice in the face before Absalom pulled his gaze away—

—and found himself staring down the barrels of three long pistols in the hands of two furious-looking men.

For a split second Absalom considered the very real possibility of his own death and found that he wasn't terribly troubled. He'd carried out his duty to his family and he'd served his country well. If he died on the errand of his Queen, he joined thousands of greater men than himself in a shared patriotic glory. A faint smile crept across his lips.

Crunch!

A long, laced-up boot spun sideways, crashed into the temple of One Pistol, flipping him over like a rag doll thrown by a petulant child. A swirl of skirt like a pinwheel followed the boot, and a flash of petticoats and sleek legs, and as Annie Webb landed her other boot came down hard on the Danite's throat.

Snap!

Two Gun's eyes slipped sideways for a moment in surprise as his comrade vanished under an onslaught of petticoats. When the moment ended, his face twisted into a snarl, his eyeballs rolled forward again to target Absalom—

—*Boom!*—

—and his head exploded.

Blood and worse spattered over Absalom's face and chest. He resolved not to think about it; he had business to take care of.

He heard the shouting of men and gunshots outside the farmhouse.

He tucked the derringer into his waistband and strode across the floor toward John D. Lee. The square-headed man shoved a timber out of his way and unearthed Brigham Young, who stared up at him with a fierce, unyielding brow.

"I'm not leaving!" he heard Heber Kimball shout behind him.

Men with knives closed in on either side of Absalom. One spun suddenly backwards in a nearly perfect circle as Annie Webb's toes crunched into the underside of his chin; the other disappeared in a cloud of red mist that spattered Absalom even further.

Rat-a-tat-tat-tat-tat-tat!

Through the missing wall, Absalom glimpsed one of the Striders only a dozen paces away and he realized that Master Sergeant Jackson was watching over him.

John D. Lee straightened up. He cocked and aimed his pistol at Brigham Young's forehead.

Absalom had vaguely imagined that he'd pick up a fallen pistol or other weapon from the floor as he crossed it, but there hadn't been any. So when he reached John D. Lee, he simply punched the man as hard as he could in the jaw.

Bang!

Lee staggered sideways. His gun went off and the bullet sank into the wreckage of the roof and disappeared. He turned, off-balance, raised his pistol—

—and Absalom punched it aside, sending the gun flying.

The Danite stared.

Absalom took off his hat and tossed it aside. He raised his fists into guard position in front of his face.

"Son of a—"

Boom!

Indistinctly out of the corner of his eye, Absalom saw Heber Kimball blast with a scattergun, knocking down a Danite who came charging into the farmhouse door.

Shooting and shouting continued outside, but inside the farmhouse was as still as the eye of any hurricane. Soft groans came from the rubble. Absalom knew that Young was still alive and felt optimistic that Armstrong and Clemens might be equally lucky. It wasn't that heavy a roof, after all.

John D. Lee eyed his pistol where it lay, across the ravaged room.

"Are you man enough to fight without it, Mr. Lee?" Absalom dared him. "Fisticuffs, like gentlemen, though I hesitate to sully the word by associating it with you!"

Lee flared his nostrils. He shrugged out of his coat and tossed it aside onto the floor.

"My ancestor Richard Lee emigrated from England and made a fortune on this continent in tobacco," he snarled slowly. "Thomas Lee founded the Ohio Company that opened up the great inner reaches of this land for the civilizing touch of the white man. Francis Lightfoot Lee and Richard Henry Lee signed the Declaration of Independence that severed the noxious umbilical that tied us to the tyrants of Old England." He pushed his shirtsleeves up over his forearms, revealing a surprising amount of wiry, corded muscle. "And when your whining grandfathers objected, Light-Horse Harry Lee rode roughshod over their lobsterback underlings at Paulus Hook, Camden, and Yorktown, and sent them weeping back to their kidney pies."

Lee spat on the floor and raised his fists.

"Then you can consider this a repayment," Absalom said.

He punched first, straight for Lee's nose. It was a light punch, to which he didn't fully commit, because he wanted to test Lee's guard.

Lee turned it aside easily and punched back hard, turning with his shoulders and throwing a fist at Absalom's stomach—

but Absalom easily stepped aside.

He punched for Lee's temple with a right cross that glanced off the other man's shoulder and then they both pulled back into defensive stances.

Lee started circling to his right. He had a wary look in his eyes now. Absalom saw the dwarf Coltrane scramble over the rubble of the fallen roof, so he circled to the right too, and drew Lee away into the center of the room and away from Brigham Young and the other trapped men.

Lee charged, hurling punch after punch at Absalom's sternum. Absalom caught the flying fists against his forearms, again and again—

—ducked under the punches—

—slammed his own knuckles into John D. Lee's belly—

—and caught a sharp punch to his own jaw.

Absalom staggered away. His vision spun and he fought to keep his guard up. By luck more than by skill, his flailing hands managed to slap away two more punches before his vision calmed enough for him to focus on Lee.

"You're in over your head," Lee barked.

Outside, the battle continued, many reports of handguns, and the booming of the larger firearms mounted on the Striders.

The thrill of the fight rushed through Absalom's body, almost making up for the blow he'd taken. He saw Annie watching from the side of the room; she looked like a coiled spring, ready to hurl herself into action. He saw the Strider outside, too. It traded shots with a knot of men in the farm's outbuildings, but it held its position and Absalom felt it was keeping an eye on him.

Absalom didn't want to be rescued, especially by beautiful women. He wanted to rescue *them*, by George.

"Ha!" he spat out his contempt, and jumped forward punching again.

Lee stood his ground and met Absalom's jabs with his left hand guarding and a right uppercut for Absalom's jaw.

Absalom swerved, took the punch on his shoulder.

He buffeted Lee on the cheek, backhand. It was a little irregular and bad form, but it connected.

Lee headbutted Absalom in the forehead.

The attack was so fast, Absalom didn't see it coming. One moment, he was swiping the other man across the face, and the next, the space inside his head felt infinite and echoed with pain and his vision narrowed to a tiny tunnel, the only image in which was the sight of John D. Lee's hammer-hard head pulling away after the blow.

"Ugh," Absalom said, and fell back.

He kept his feet under him, though not by much, and he staggered and slipped like a dancing marionette.

"Ouch!" someone yelled as Absalom stepped on him.

He lurched forward again, trying to raise his hands to intercept the—

POW!

The punch hit him squarely in the nose, and it was bigger and louder and more painful than the exploding chimney.

He punched back, without form or discipline. His head hurt so much, he couldn't even feel his hand and he had no idea if his fist connected.

Thud!

Lee punched him in the stomach.

"Unnph!" Absalom gasped, and he doubled forward. He was still on his feet, but only barely, and he knew the killer, bout-ending punch was inevitable now, was surely about to land on his face. He felt humiliated. Annie would rescue him, or if he fell maybe Master Sergeant Jackson would simply squeeze the trigger and blow John D. Lee to smithereens, but he, Absalom Fearnley-Standish, had personally failed.

Abysmally.

The expected punch didn't arrive. Instead, Lee grabbed him in a clinch hold, pulling Absalom tight to his own chest.

Absalom dimly heard a snick and then felt a cold, metallic line against the side of his neck. *Is that a knife?* he wondered.

"I'm leaving now." John D. Lee's voice was gigantic and booming in Absalom's ear and inside his empty, quivering skull. "Anybody tries to stop me, I kill the Englishman."

ꚱꟽ Ⱳ0ꞪⱲ⅃Ɔ��H

Hishhhhhhh!

The rock surface skimming past the accordion gate and punctured glass of the lift door disappeared first at the top, and then the gap in the stone slid down until it filled the entire door. Tamerlane O'Shaughnessy stood beside Richard Burton in the center of the lift.

At Burton's suggestion, they didn't try to hide, and just stood with their heads down. Hopefully, Burton had lectured Tam during the lift ride, their concealed faces would create enough uncertainty to give them a small margin of initiative if anyone were waiting for them.

Hopefully, Tam thought but didn't say, the bloody-damn-hell Pinkertons wouldn't just shoot first and then examine their faces later. After all, Burton openly held a saber in his hand.

The sword and the man's mustache made Tam feel like he was in some mad piratical pantomime. He half expected to be made to walk the plank at any moment and he was half tempted to shoot Burton the first moment the man turned his back, only he didn't think Sam Clemens would like it, and after all, he and Burton were on the same side now, more or less.

Tam had punched through the linings of both pockets of his coat, so he could keep his hands in his pockets, each filled with a loaded Maxim Husher ready for action. He was beginning to feel sober again. He itched all over, ached, and was grumpy. He didn't like the feeling and he disliked it even more than he usually disliked the sensation of sobering up. He felt light-headed and a little sick. He wondered if something was wrong with him.

Besides the two gunshots and the missing chunk of his ear, of course.

No one waited for them at the Bay level. Burton quietly slid the doors open in two quick movements and they both looked out.

The Bay was a single vast chamber, thirty feet tall at least and large enough to hold several good-sized village greens. It was lit by the blue light radiating from Franklin Poles that jutted from the ceiling, upside down like iron stalactites, illuminating everything and leaving the floor unobstructed. Obstruction was provided by the stacks of lumber and iron and brass and piles of crates that stood all around the chamber like toys in an untidy child's room. Several steam-trucks, of various sizes and no consistent make or appearance, stood haphazardly in the Bay as well, motors stilled. To one side a plascrete ramp, wide enough for two steam-trucks to drive abreast, led up through the ceiling into a darkness that looked like the darkness of night outdoors. *There's your exit, me boy,* Tam thought.

Directly across the Bay was another opening in the cavern wall. As Burton and Tam watched, a steam-truck rumbled into the Bay and ground to halt, idling its engine. Half a dozen tall men in long coats stood around it with guns and one old man with hair so white and wild that Tam could see it from the lift.

"That's our steam-truck," Burton said in his lecturing way, as if it wasn't obvious.

"No wonder there weren't any Pinkertons to welcome us," Tam answered, showing he was just as smart as the Englishman. "They all went over to welcome the truck."

Burton shut the gate and jammed the control lever up to the *LAKE* slot.

This ride was short, but it felt extremely fast and violent to Tam. Burton looked unfazed and he glared down at Tam as the Irishman bent at the waist, leaned with one hand against the wooden panels of the walls and breathed deeply.

"Are you well?"

Tam answered by throwing up, a thin stream of sour bile that he spat into the corner of the lift. The space well and truly reeked now, blood and sweat and bile, not to mention the urine released by the Pinkerton who had died in the lift.

"Well enough." Tam straightened and wiped polluted spittle from his chin with the back of his hand. "Right fookin' cheerful, in fact. Now I've made some room for them, I'm ready to eat me a Pinkerton or two."

He grinned at the Englishman and opened the lift door.

They hobbled out into cold night, weapons first, and Tam sucked in the freezing air to catch his breath. It helped, though he still thought he might throw up again.

They stood outside, next to a large, long brick-shaped building made of plascrete and fitted with few windows. Of those few, even fewer showed any light. Before them was a sward of wild meadow grass and flowers, silvery-gray in the light, that fell gently down to a long, narrow lake, a shimmering silver pan. Halfway down the meadow, a gaping hole that must be the ramp into the Bay below lay at the end of a gravel road that led past the lake and disappeared at its end, apparently dropping off a cliff. The lake was fed by a glacier, a ribbon of shining white that climbed up a boulder-strewn field to a jagged rocky ridge above.

Tam followed the ridge around with his eyes. The complex stood in a big horseshoe-shaped bowl and was lidded over with the most amazing field of stars Tam had ever seen. The sky looked more star than void between and though the moon was down, he felt he could see perfectly. *Keep your wits about you, me boy,* he told himself, but he was still stunned by the sight.

Even more amazing than the stars, though, was the sight directly above Tam. The brickish building was punctuated by a single tower, something like the steeple of a village church. It rose into the darkness, gray and forbidden, and at its height it bulked out into some sort of platform. All along its length ran metal rods. The rods emerged from the plascrete just above the ground and ran vertically up towards the top of the tower. They were the thickness of Tam's wrist, but they disappeared from sight before he could see any end of them. Smaller horizontal rods linked them to each other at intervals (and what could those possibly be for, then? They looked like the world's biggest seamstress was building a hoop skirt around the tower, and hadn't yet got to the crinoline).

Clustered around the platform, hanging in mid-air … *flying* … were four enormous objects. *Airships,* Tam thought. Each bore four external pods like an animal's four feet, paws down, and a golden light glowed in a dim ring, cupped into each paw.

"Hell and begorra."

"Utnapishtim's beard," Burton added.

"They look like Viking ships. They look like big bloody-damn-hell Viking ships with feet out the sides that can *fly.*"

Burton harrumphed. "I would have said Sumerian magur-boats, but in the essentials, we're agreed."

Tam chuckled. "You smug English fook, with your Queen and country. We've done it, don't you see?" He pointed with a gun. "That up there is the world's one and only flying airship fleet!"

Burton grinned, looking even more like a pirate. "Let's go up to the tower and take a closer look, shall we?" He slapped Tam on the shoulder. Tam would have been embarrassed to admit how good the friendly smack felt.

They held their breaths and hobbled back into the lift. Burton pressed the lever to *TOWER.*

Hishhhhhh!

Tam vomited again.

"Ach!" he spat on the lift floor. "Anthony's knuckles, I don't know what's wrong with me!"

"Injuries," Burton promptly suggested. "Sleep deprivation, physical exertion. Have you drunk enough water? You might be dehydrated. Altitude sickness, of course. We must be at eight or nine thousand feet of elevation here, judging by the way my ears feel."

"Fookin' hell, you make me sound like a little girl. Altitude sickness, really?"

"Really," Burton affirmed, furrowing his brow. "And, of course, you drank an entire bottle of whisky in short order. All things considered, it's amazing you've made it as far as you have."

"A single bottle is nothing," Tam bluffed. "I drank whisky from Mother O'Shaughnessy's breast." He leaned against the wall and breathed deeply, spitting sour strings out of his mouth. His own tongue tasted like he'd been cleaning a stable floor with it.

Hishhhh … the lift stopped moving. The door still faced a solid sheet of plascrete.

"Damn!" Burton cursed.

"Lift broken?"

"Or we're discovered. Let's hope it's the lift." Burton jiggled the control lever out of the *TOWER* notch and back into it. Nothing happened.

"We can't stay here, we'll be shot like rats." Tam shot his eyes around the lift and spotted an indented square in the ceiling that looked like a trapdoor. "Emergency exit, right there," he said.

"I'll go first," Burton suggested. "Maybe there's a ladder in the lift shaft. Or we can climb up the ropes."

"Like hell," Tam snapped. "We're both of us shot full of holes and I'm sick to boot but you've had it worse than I have. Said so yourself. Give me a bloody-damn-hell hand, I'm going up." He grinned. "For Queen and country."

Burton made stirrups with his hands and hoisted Tam towards the ceiling. The mustached man grunted and ground his teeth but didn't complain or even wince as Tam pushed open the trap door. He snaked his arms up through the open space and wedged his elbows into it, dragging his body up.

He brushed aside a loose cable and struggled to come to the top of the lift carriage. Taut cables locked into the carriage top near him shot straight up, but not into darkness as he had expected.

Tam stopped. "Aw, shite," he said. "Harris."

"Higley," the Pinkerton corrected him. "Hello, McNamara. Top of the evening to you."

"O'Shaughnessy," Tam sighed. "Listen, have you seen my friends? I seem to have lost them all in this great bloody complex of yours."

The rooftop of the lift carriage was level with the exit from the shaft. Four men stood in it, each holding a Henry rifle. Three of the men pointed their guns down at the lift. Higley held the muzzle of his weapon pressed directly against the lift cable.

"Ah," Higley chuckled, "you Irish are great liars. Come out slowly with your hands up and tell your friend in the carriage he's next. You try any funny business, any delay, any sign of a weapon, and I'll squeeze the trigger and drop you both to the bottom of Timpanogos Mountain."

ꝏℲⲦⲰⲎ0ⲢⳐⲤ𐤉𐤉

Sam Clemens regained consciousness to the sound of gunfire. Some of it came from handguns but there was bigger artillery in the mix, he could hear it.

It took him a moment to remember where he was, and then another to realize why everything around him was dark.

He tried to move and discovered that his arms were free. He pushed, shifted planks away from his head, and found himself in a pile of rubble on the farmhouse floor. Yellow light from a kerosene lantern overhead illuminated a scene Sam had not expected to see.

Jug-eared, square-headed John D. Lee held the Englishman Fearnley-Standish hostage. He edged sideways towards Sam, facing off against an irate-looking bald man holding a scattergun aimed straight at the center of Fearnley-Standish's head, as if he thought he could punch through both men in a single shot, and beside him hunched a woman who looked the part of his wife and hefted a heavy iron skillet in one fist. Young Annie Webb was with them, Annie who had been such a sweet conversationalist at Bridger's Saloon, but who now held her skirts and petticoats hiked up with both fists clenched and gritted teeth, as if, of all things, she planned to *kick* Lee. Poe's dwarf stood at bay in the corner of the room with a knife held up defensively in front of him, apparently protecting a huddle of children.

"Anybody tries to stop me, I kill the Englishman."

Lee's grip on Fearnley-Standish was not the conventional hostage-taking maneuver. He held the other man like one tired boxer clinches another, pinning Fearnley-Standish's head to his own clavicle, and holding a Bowie knife to the side of the Englishman's neck.

Sam clambered out, coughing at the dust his movements threw up. Lee stepped closer to him, and he saw what the other man was after.

A pistol lay on the floor between them.

Lee switched his knife to his other hand, pointing the tip now against Fearnley-Standish's collarbone, and reached for the gun—

—Sam grabbed it—

—Lee snatched the other end, and pulled.

Sam held tight and was hauled to his feet.

"Don't let go!" Annie shouted. Sam didn't.

Sam sneezed, blowing sawdust out of his hair and mustache. To his relief, he found he was holding the grip-end of the pistol and Lee was holding the barrel.

"Let go or I'll stab him!" Lee barked. He yanked again, but Sam held tight.

"I believe the threats customarily belong to the man with the trigger end of the weapon," Sam quipped. He pulled at the gun too, but couldn't wrest it from the Danite chieftain's grip. They tugged back and forth like children struggling with a knotted rope over a mud puddle. The loaded gun between reminded Sam not to laugh at the thought.

Beside Sam on the floor, Brigham Young struggled to free himself. Heavier timbers lay across him than had pinned Sam, and he was still stuck. "Heber!" he roared. "If you could stop trying to commit murder for just a minute, you might free me!"

The farmer looked abashed. He rushed to Young's side and started heaving at the largest of the beams. His wife, though, stayed right where she was.

"I think one of us should stick to the plan of committing murder," she grumbled, taking an experimental swipe at the air with her skillet. "Or at least battery."

Brigham grunted, a sound that might have been agreement.

Sam and Lee struggled.

Bang! Bang! The shooting outside continued.

"I'll give you five hundred dollars," Sam offered. "Just let the Englishman go and leave the Kingdom tonight." That would be an expenditure he'd be happy to account for to the green eyeshade boys in Washington.

Lee eyed the efforts to free Young like a wild horse fighting the bridle. "I'll give you all of Iron County!" he snapped back. "Just let go of the gun!" The Danite didn't relinquish his hold on the English diplomat.

Sam really wished he could bring himself to pull the trigger. Any other man in the room would have killed John D. Lee by now. But Sam couldn't do it. His brother Henry had died in government service, in a riverboat accident, of course, but it was much too close to dying as a soldier in uniform for Sam ever to feel cavalier about taking another man's life.

"Somehow, I doubt Iron County is worth five hundred dollars," he huffed. He was panting from the effort of wrestling now and sweat from the back of his hands trickled onto the pistol grip, making it slick and harder to hold on to. He wrapped his second hand around his first, to tighten his hold.

"Give yourself up, Brigham!" Lee shouted. "Give yourself up and I won't have to kill this English fellow!"

The farmer Heber grunted and shoved aside the pillar that had Young trapped, exposing at the same time Ambassador Armstrong, who lay very still. Brigham Young rose to his feet. He was dirty and battered, but he stood upright in a strong motion, like a bear rising to sniff the wind, or a lion announcing its presence on the savannah. He sucked air in through his nostrils and his chest swelled.

"You don't *have* to kill him now, John," he rumbled, his voice low and threatening like a storm cloud. "Don't pretend you're a puppet. Be a man. Choose. Lay down your arms, and you might still be forgiven."

"Choose?" Sam couldn't help himself. "What kind of cog *chooses*?"

"Shut up, Clemens!" Young barked at him.

"You're right, Brigham," Lee laughed. "I *am* choosing. Hell, I chose years ago and now we're just playing out the consequences. Surrender, or I'll *choose* again, choose to stick this boy like a pig."

Sweat poured down Sam's forehead and neck and chest now, too. *Any moment,* he thought, *I'll lose hold of this gun, and Lee will start shooting.* He half wished the farmer's wife would go ahead and brain the Danite with her pan.

"He's dead." The farmer knelt by Ambassador Armstrong, checking the big black man's pulse and breathing. "He didn't make it."

Ire flashed in Young's eyes. "I can't save you from hell, John," he snarled. "I can't even save you from the Mexicans. But if you start running right now, I can promise you that I won't be the one chasing you."

John D. Lee spat on the floor. "*That* for your promises, Brigham!" he shouted.

Sam felt his hands start to slip off the pistol—

—Lee grinned triumphantly and jerked at the gun—

—Sam stumbled back—

—and Absalom Fearnley-Standish punched John D. Lee in the kidney.

"Aaaagh!" Lee hollered, throwing his head back and tearing the revolver out of Sam's grip. Now Sam saw that Fearnley-Standish was biting the Danite as well, his teeth sinking into Lee's neck until blood flowed.

Lee stabbed the Englishman. He missed his neck, stabbing down instead shallowly across Fearnley-Standish's collarbone and into his chest.

Fearnley-Standish lost his grip and staggered back.

Lee raised the knife to stab again—

—and Mrs. Kimball smashed him with her skillet.

Crack!

Sam heard Lee's elbow break under the hammer of the heavy iron at the same moment he tumbled back onto the rubble from which he'd emerged.

"I ain't gonna leave nothing for the Mexicans to take!" she shouted. She raised the skillet again—

—Lee staggered sideways in the direction of the door, fumbling with the pistol to bring it up into position and cock it—

—Annie Webb launched herself past the enraged farmeress, spinning like a thrown saucer, boots-first in attack.

Bang!

Smoke poured from Lee's pistol and Annie fell back, hitting the floor hard in a tangle of arms and legs with the Englishman.

Lee stepped forward, raising his pistol to fire at Brigham Young, and the dwarf snatched it out of his hand, sailing through the air in a leap worthy of any circus acrobat.

Heber Kimball grabbed his scattergun and swung it around to shoot at Lee but Lee didn't wait for the shot. He ducked out the farmhouse door and was gone.

Boom!

Heber's scattergun kicked a hole in his own door, knocking it back open again, and then Mrs. Kimball threw her frying pan out the door on the Danite's heels.

"And good riddance!" she shouted.

Outside, the shooting sounds grew fainter and more sporadic, as if maybe the firefight was ending and drifting away from the Kimball farm.

"The day is ours," Brigham Young pronounced. He sounded very grave when he said it and also very tired, and then he turned to the farmer. "Heber, I'm going to have to leave Ambassador Armstrong with you, along with one or two other people."

"Of course," Heber said at once. "And the meeting tomorrow morning? The Twelve are supposed to be there, and the Seventy, to replace you."

Young's face darkened. "I'll get into the Lion House tonight," he glowered, "and send out messages. I'll hold that meeting tomorrow morning, all right, but it will be the trial of John Lee and Bill Hickman."

"But what about Port?" Mrs. Kimball pointed out.

"Rockwell!" Sam snapped. He ached and his lungs wheezed, but he sent himself to shifting timbers. Other men joined in and it was he and the dwarf Coltrane together who slid aside a wide plank to reveal the mountain man. He lay dirty and still under criss-crossing beams, with a trickle of blood at one corner of his mouth.

"You alright, Rockwell?" Sam asked. He was a little reluctant to touch what was in all likelihood a dead body but the dwarf wasn't so finicky. He slapped Orrin Porter Rockwell twice, once across each cheek. Young's bodyguard didn't stir, until suddenly his lips cracked open and he spoke.

"No ... bullet or blade ... shall harm thee," Rockwell intoned slowly, without opening his eyes. "And not no fallin' ceilings, neither."

⑆⑅⑇⑉⑈⑃⑄⑊⑉⑇

"And what happens," Poe asked, "if we succeed?" He coughed, feeling his lungs tear and bleed from the force of it.

The steam-truck rattled up the long tunnel towards the top of Timpanogos Mountain. Timber supports flashed by in the truck's forward lights like the ribs of a gigantic whale through whose innards Poe now traveled. He wondered whether he was being swallowed or regurgitated by the thing.

"We restore Brigham," Roxie said. "He will have to administer justice, of course. Some men will have to hang or be exiled, but for all his gruffness, Brigham Young is a soft touch. Most of Lee's rebels will just go back to their wives and children. I don't know what he'll do about someone like Brother Orson."

She looked away, out the window.

"I mean *us*," Poe said. "You can be evasive if you like, but I know that you know that I mean *us*. I want to talk about our future, together."

"You're dying, Edgar." She turned back to face him. In the blue glow of light emanating from the dials and meters of the steam-trucks control panel, Poe saw tears gently sliding down her cheeks.

Poe slammed his fist in frustration against the steam-truck's wheel. "Does that mean I am incapable of love?" he demanded.

He bit back further words that welled up in his throat, about her unfairness, and about the injustice of the universe. What kind of tyrannical God would make him suffer this torturous love for this woman for so many years and then take it away, just at the moment he was about to touch it?

"Of course not," she said softly. "But it means that you have no future at all."

"Is that the glorious secret doctrine of the Mormons, then?" he pressed. "You dragged your wagons across the plains from Nauvoo, scattering your dead along the way like seeds to the wind, for the mighty and seductive call *death is the end, o man, gnash your futile teeth and despair?*"

"No," she admitted. "But whatever afterlife there is, I am bound to Brother Brigham in it."

"Oh?" Poe couldn't let that one lie. "And when we first met, weren't you bound to the King of Nauvoo?"

"Things change," she acknowledged. "It isn't wise to resist the inexorable."

Poe pounded his fist against the control panel. "And is there no choice in it? You were Joseph's, you are Brigham's … may you not choose to be mine?"

"There is always choice," Roxie said, "for all of us. I choose fidelity to the promises I've made." She hesitated. "Fidelity after a fashion. Such fidelity as I can manage. I choose service to the whole and to the greater good. I choose to play my part in the plan."

"Edgar Allan Poe be damned." He started coughing again, his chest shuddering and shaking with the effort. He spat out the window, tasting the blood and phlegm on his tongue even after it was gone.

"I hope not," she replied softly. "Edgar Allan Poe be saved, and even healed."

"You believe in miracles, then?"

"I do," she agreed. "I also believe in the surprising genius of Orson Pratt."

The light ahead shifted, the tunnel suddenly turning, leveling out, and debouching into a large space stacked with crates, like a warehouse. Men stood arrayed loosely around the opening, including an old man whom Poe recognized instantly as the Apostle Pratt.

"This seems surprisingly direct," Poe murmured. "It can't bode well."

"Follow my lead," Roxie urged him.

Poe shifted the truck out of gear and attached the brake. Pratt shuffled around to Roxie's side of the steam-truck and squinted up into the cabin.

"Sister Young!" he squeaked.

Poe did his best not to cringe or gnash his teeth.

"Brother Pratt!" she hallooed back. "My apologies for the late hour!"

"My condolences for the death of your husband," Orson Pratt responded. "I'd have thought you might be in widow's weeds by now, comforting your sister-wives in the Beehive House or the Lion House."

"I would," she agreed, "only Brother Lee asked me to bring you something."

Pratt frowned and shook his head. "I'd have thought that snake would have plenty of strong backs to do his work without troubling the bereaved women of the Great Salt Lake City," he harrumphed. He held up his hand, inviting her down. "Come visit with me. That fellow there can unload the materials, whatever they are."

Roxie took his hand and hopped lightly down. "Oh, that's my cousin Jared. He's new to the valley and offered to help me. Jared, come join us, would you, please?"

Poe fought off a coughing fit by force of will as he climbed down.

"I didn't know your cousins were members of the Kingdom," Pratt said. He arched his bushy eyebrows, which made them jump almost to the top of his bald head.

"Jared isn't," Roxie clarified her lie. "He's come to tell me about a death in the family. An aunt. I'm to have a small inheritance, it seems."

Pratt's men climbed into the back of the steam-truck and dragged out the crate they found there, beginning to lower it to the ground.

"Honest Jared," Pratt mumbled in vague approval.

"He's something of an amateur technologist," Roxie continued. "I hoped you might like to show him the *Teancum.*"

"Your airships are famous, sir," Poe played along, affecting enthusiasm and doing his best to imitate Roxie's Massachusetts twang in his voice. "They were all the talk at Fort Bridger, flying airships and phlogiston guns!"

Pratt chuckled. "I'm pleased to entertain, sir. Perhaps I can entertain you tonight even further."

"How's that?" Poe asked.

"Oh, Jared would be thrilled to take even a short ride aboard one of the airships," Roxie gushed.

Pratt's men pried apart the crate with crowbars and stripped away the cotton batting inside, revealing what Poe had known was in there all along.

The Seth-Beast.

It stood stiff and erect, like a shining steel sculpture of a dog, life-sized if the dog in question were a very large hunting hound or a small pony. It wasn't quite a dog, though; very long, donkey-like ears sprang up at either side of its head, square at their extremities, and the tail that shot straight up into the air from its hindquarters forked at the end. Its muzzle, too, had a little of the anteater about it, or maybe the sloth, curving downward slightly at the nose, over powerful jaws bristling with long steel teeth. Hinges and ball joints all over its body hinted at the movement the machine was capable of.

"My goodness!" Pratt ejaculated. "Brother Lee didn't make this. No one in the Valley, not even John Browning, made something like this!"

"I don't know where it came from," Roxie said. "I do know that John has been dealing with southerners a lot today."

Pratt paced a circle around the Seth-Beast, examining it closely. The whistle on Poe's breast felt very heavy.

"And how does it *work*?" Pratt asked. "Where are the *controls*?" Poe would have sworn that the long hair standing up at the back of his head stood up even straighter as he examined Hunley's craftsmanship, like curious antennae.

Roxie shrugged and shook her head. "He didn't say."

Pratt stopped pacing and clapped his hands together once. "Well," he said, "there'll be plenty of time to play with this new toy later. As I was saying, your arrival here is very timely. Tonight ... or rather, tomorrow morning, you will be witness to a unique spectacle, a great first time event in the history of mankind." He turned, and gestured to his men at the Seth-Beast. "Leave this here, gentlemen; we can deal with it later."

D.J. Butler

"What's that?" Poe asked uneasily in his false twang.

Pratt turned back to face them, and he held a gun in his hand. Not a weapon of any sort that Poe recognized—it was bulky and square, to be held in two hands, and its muzzle was far too big for anything resembling an ordinary bullet.

"Why, Mr. Poe, the complete destruction of the Great Salt Lake City, of course," Pratt said calmly. "By aeronautical assault and phlogiston rays."

"No!" Roxie gasped.

Poe considered, and couldn't see any reason that the obliteration of the Mormon capital would serve Lee's interests. "I thought Lee wanted to be President," he said mildly, dropping the false accent. No point denying his identity, since Pratt had obviously recognized him. "Either his plan is so Byzantine I cannot penetrate it or it is misconceived."

"*Lee's* plan!" Pratt snapped, and then chortled. He'd have looked jolly, without the exotic and sinister gun in his hands. "Wrong *twice*!"

What did that *mean?* Poe wondered, but couldn't guess. "*Your* plan, then," he said. "Why do you want to destroy your home?"

Pratt nodded to his men and they swooped down on Poe and Roxie, drawing guns and grabbing with hard-knuckled hands. Roxie shot Poe an imploring look and he held his face impassive. This was not the time to resist. The men began dragging Poe and Roxie away. There were so many of them, they lifted the two prisoners off the floor entirely.

"I'll keep the explanation simple," Pratt shouted over the heads of his hired thugs, trailing in their wake. "John D. Lee killed my brother. Brigham Young, in his infinite wisdom, forgave John Lee."

"For that you will murder the entire city?" Roxie shouted back. Her face was twisted in anger and surprise and pain.

Pratt ignored her travail. "Lee has done me the favor of punishing Brother Brigham for his virtue," he further explained. "Tomorrow morning, I, in turn, shall punish John Lee for his vice!"

286

PART THE FOURTH

ⵝⴹⴷⵀⵟⴳ

TEANCUM

CHAPTER SIXTEEN

B e good for the Captain and Mrs. Rockwell," Jed told John Moses. He sniffed a little but he told himself he wasn't crying. It was just cold at night in the desert, that was all, and it made his nose drip a little.

"Can't you come with us?" the little boy asked. He sobbed openly.

Jed shook his head. *Suck it up, Coltrane.* "I got things I gotta do," he said. He wasn't exactly sure whose side he was on now, really, but he knew Poe wanted him to help Brigham Young and that seemed like the generally right thing to do. At least, all the pit vipers and crazy people seemed to be on the other side, and that was a pretty good weather vane. "You got things you gotta do, too. You gotta get home, so your poppa and your two mammas and Captain Jones can all stop worrying about you."

John Moses nodded slowly. "And being brave is doing what you gotta do, even when you're scared."

"Especially when you're scared."

"Don't you let my silly brother talk you into any notion that I'm leaving," Abigail Rockwell told her battered, bear-like husband as she wrapped her arms around his chest and squeezed him once. She shot a look of pure venom at the Englishman that made Jed flinch, even though it wasn't aimed at him. "And don't you even try."

Annie Webb flared her nostrils in indignation but Fearnley-Standish answered before she could.

"Do dot worry, dear sister," he said. The poor bastard's nose was smashed nearly flat and the injury had taken away his power to pronounce the letter *N*. "I have do such idtedtions. Besides, my brother-id-law has gived do iddicatiods of beigg susceptible to my limited powers of persuasiod."

Jed hugged the little boy and then let Abigail Rockwell pry him away. She climbed into a buckboard with Mrs. Kimball at the reins, Mr. Kimball and his scattergun at her side, and the body of Ambassador Armstrong arranged on the floor.

Captain Jones grabbed the dwarf's hand and shook it vigorously.

"Any time you need a berth, boyo," the Welshman said gruffly, "come find me."

Jed nodded. He was numb. "Get him back to John Browning safe," he mumbled.

"Aye, of course I will." The *Liahona*'s skipper joined the others on the buckboard.

Jed turned and followed Sam Clemens and Brigham Young across the stubble-splashed field towards the nearer of the two Striders. The knives at his belt and in his boot were a comforting weight. He had been particularly happy to find one of the dead Danites armed with a Colt Vibro-blade, and he now wore the weapon openly, like a sword.

He caught up to the other two men as they reached the Strider. It crouched low to board its passengers while the other stood guard.

"I don't understand how we were trapped, Mr. President," Clemens was saying. "What good is having a prophet along if he can't warn us of ambushes?"

"A prophet isn't a fortune-teller," Young snorted. "No man walks around knowing his future all the time."

"Oh?" Clemens gave Young a boost and helped him clamber up onto the bent leg of the Strider. "Then what's a prophet for? I mean, other than to warn people against wearing fornication pants?"

Young scrambled over the side and into the carriage of the Strider. "A prophet carries the word of the Lord, Mr. Clemens," he barked, "but it's the Lord who decides what that word will be, not the prophet."

"Seems like the other fellers are the ones as have the prophet," Jed muttered. He hadn't meant it to be audible, but he was cranky and his words came out kind of loud. When Clemens and Young both owled their heads around to look at him, he explained. "They found us awful easy, is all I'm saying."

Brigham Young coughed. "Yes, well, that's my fault."

"Explain, o swami," Clemens urged him.

"Heber Kimball is my closest friend and has been for years," Young offered. "Anyone in the Kingdom would know that, and certainly Lee. Aside from one of my own houses, with one of my own wives, there was no more obvious place for me to go for help. In hindsight."

Sam Clemens started to laugh. "Prophetic hindsight!" he guffawed, and climbed into the carriage himself. "I might have to get myself a signboard and go into the prophet business with you. Or against you. Set up shop across the street."

Jed hopped easily up the outside of the Strider. "Shut up, Clemens," he growled.

Sam Clemens jutted out his jaw. "I didn't realize I had a midget in my chain of command."

"That's me, Jed Coltrane, circus freak," the dwarf conceded. "Jest 'cause you're taller don't mean you're right."

Clemens shut his trap and chewed on Jed's words.

"Just because you're short doesn't mean you can be a boor," Brigham Young bristled.

"Jest 'cause I'm helping you don't make you my prophet," Jed shot back.

All three of them fell silent then, until Sam Clemens again began to laugh.

"So that's settled," he chuckled. "Everyone is his own man."

"I ain't!" Orrin Porter Rockwell snapped, hurling himself into the carriage just as the legs extended and the carriage rose into the air. "I'm Brigham's man, come hell or high water, or even undeserved kicks in the teeth."

"What about the kicks you actually earn?" Clemens asked.

Pfffffft-ankkkh!

"I don't know whether the Strider will hold four passengers," Young said warily, looking over the side of the carriage at the harvested field falling away beneath them.

"What's the word of the Lord on the subject?" Clemens needled him again, but his voice was gentler this time.

"You ain't got four," Jed grunted. "You got three and a half."

"Don't joo worry," the Striderman at the controls called back over his shoulder. Ramirez, Jed thought the fellow's name was. And the gunner's name was Polk, which was a queer name for a black man from Mexico, but that's life. "She'll hold."

The other Strider bent low to pick up its passengers. That was the pilot Ortiz and the gunner Jackson, and they'd carry Absalom Fearnley-Standish and the Mormon girl Annie, who wouldn't stop making eyes at him.

"Where to, Mr. President?" Clemens asked, jolly again.

"As close in to the Great Salt Lake City as we can get," Young rumbled. "I don't think we'll be able to take the Striders all the way, they're too conspicuous."

"Don't you want publicity?" Clemens asked.

"Not the kind that comes from getting shot," Jed guessed sourly.

"The *Jim Smiley* is parked in a lot on the east side of the city," Clemens suggested. "That's my steam-truck. She's distinctive, but a lot less distinctive than the Striders. Lee and his boys might not know her."

"They know her," Young said grimly. "But it can't hurt us to have the option. Let's go get your steam-truck, Mr. Clemens."

The other Strider rose to its height. Absalom Fearnley-Standish sat in it like a Turkish pasha, between two women. He waved, and the Striderman pilots exchanged arm gestures, and then Ramirez turned his machine and began *pffft-ankkkkhing* across the fields.

"It also can't hurt us to have a supply of decent cigars," Clemens added.

ꓛƧ√ꓩⱯꓷ

The Pinkertons had taken the jar of scarabs. They'd missed the hypocephalus, folded up as it was like a handkerchief, and also the whistle, which looked innocuous. And they couldn't take away his baritsu training.

Passing the top of a stairwell leading down, Poe made his move.

He simply stepped sharply to his right, planting one foot in front of the fleshy-jowled Pinkerton holding him on that side, and leaned with his body into the man's elbow. Jowls missed his footing, then missed the floor, crashing hard onto the second step and bouncing down the stairs, wobbling face first.

Before he hit, Poe was already turning to the burly guard holding his left arm. Burly grabbed for Poe's coat—

—Poe raised his tied hands, as if the knotted rope binding them were a weapon with which he could parry—

—and Burly grabbed the rope.

Poe fell back, pulling Burly, who was much larger than Poe himself, forward with the power of his own lunge. He curved his back to hit the floor rolling and tipped Burly up and over his head with a direction-prompting kick into the man's crotch.

"Ooomph!" Burly gasped and let go of the ropes.

Poe badly wanted to grab the whistle around his neck and blow it but he resisted. That was his ace in the hole, and he was afraid he'd get the notes wrong—it was so blasted hard when you couldn't actually *hear* them yourself—or it would take him too much time to get them just right. And once the Pinkertons realized what he was trying to do, surely they'd take the whistle away.

No, the whistle had to wait.

He blocked a charging hatchet-faced man with a heel in the man's midriff, kicking off immediately and using the impetus to roll to his feet.

Beyond the crowd of stampeding Pinkertons, Poe saw Orson Pratt again draw his strange weapon.

Two fingers to two beady eyes knocked another Pinkerton to the ground and a quick chop to the throat took down a fourth.

Zottt!

The blue light of the electricks in the hall was pierced and empurpled with a sudden red wave erupting out of Orson Pratt's weapon. A beam as thick as Poe's calf burst from the gun and lanced into the plascrete wall beyond Poe. The plascrete bubbled instantly under the touch of the ray, exploding into blisters, melting and running down to the floor. A thick stench, like the foulest stink of a tar pit, assailed Poe's sinuses.

The beam snapped off.

Poe seized another Pinkerton by shoving one finger up each of the man's dilated nostrils, pulling his body forward over Poe's knee and slamming him head-first into the melted segment of wall as Poe deflected another man's punch with the elbow of his other arm.

The reek of scorched flesh cut sharply into the tarry smell and Nostrils shrieked in pain.

Poe turned to run.

"Stop or I kill her!"

Poe burst into a paroxysm of coughing and stumbled.

Hands grabbed him and he batted them away, but his will evaporated and he didn't have the strength. Big-knuckled men with bruised faces and wounded pride in their eyes dragged him back and held him before the Madman Pratt.

Pratt held his gun to the back of Roxie's head. The thing didn't have a trigger that Poe could see, but it bore some sort of bolt or lever on the side and Pratt kept one thumb carefully on top of it.

"Aaaaaagh!" Nostrils continued to howl. Out of the corner of his eye, Poe saw that the man's head appeared to be stuck to the melted plascrete of the wall.

"The phlogiston gun." Poe felt crushed.

"Bit of a misnomer, of course," Pratt huffed. "It doesn't shoot out phlogiston, not like you'd think with that name. Phlogiston is already in everything that exists. It's in you, in me, in the plascrete, in the air. It's the stuff that burns out when something is incinerated, and what is left behind is the calx."

"I've heard this," Poe muttered. He could get away himself, but the price would be Roxie's life. Hers was a death he had fantasized for ten long and lonely years, and now he found it too high a price to pay. "Ether rays."

"*Ether* rays? Ha! Ether comes in *waves*, son! All my weapons do is fire a ray, a simple beam of refracted *light*, that causes the phlogiston in any targeted object to ignite and rapidly consume itself," Pratt continued. He sounded like he was lecturing, and liking it. "*Phlogiston gun* is as ridiculous a name as *Calx gun* would be. *Light beam gun* or *ray gun* would be less preposterous."

"Aaaaaaagh!" Nostrils kicked against the floor and shuddered. The other Pinkertons looked away from him uneasily.

"I don't think anyone finds your weapon ridiculous," Poe murmured. He shook himself mentally, trying to shrug off the feeling of defeat and find a way forward, any information or advantage he could manage to squeeze out of the moment. Pratt hadn't reacted to the *ether rays* gambit but it had been a shot in the dark.

"The gun's real name is the *Pratt Ruby-Refracted Matter Enkindler*, of course." Pratt's voice sounded like he was just getting wound up and might continue forever. "Named in honor of my brother Parley Pratt and not named after myself, which is why its nickname is the *Parley*. A sophisticated man such as yourself, a writer, even, will be able to appreciate the ironic pun in the nickname. Not that you should care."

"I do appreciate it. I appreciate it enough that I shall not ask you for a parley, now or ever. And at least if you shoot me with that thing," Poe said, "I can take comfort in the fact that I didn't bring you the means of my own destruction." He coughed again, so hard he nearly shook himself free from his captors.

Pratt laughed, and patted the Enkindler. "No," he agreed, "Mr. United States did. What you brought me was for the *ships*."

The ships? That was surprising. The Kingdom of Deseret had been famous for its airships for several years, since they'd first been spotted (and fired upon) by miners in the silver fields of Colorado. One had flown over the *Liahona* as it entered the Kingdom just ... well, just yesterday now, though it seemed like ages ago to Edgar Allan Poe. Pratt didn't need any devices from Hunley in order to make his ships fly, obviously.

Therefore he needed the devices to make the ships do something else. But what? Something that required ether-wave devices? Something Pratt didn't know how to make the ships do on his own?

"Are you really willing to destroy your own ships?" he asked, and scrutinized the Madman's face for a response.

Pratt cocked a wary eyebrow. "You're playing games," the inventor snapped.

Poe said nothing and watched Pratt's face twitch.

"Hunley would never have sabotaged the canopic jars!" Pratt barked. "He knows I'd never give him the schematics if he did!"

"You *didn't* give me the schematics," Poe pointed out. "And you never intended to, did you? You wanted me on the ground, a known and fixed target, so you could destroy me. You wanted that for me and Clemens both."

Pratt grinned, a crooked, shifting thing that belonged on the face of a beggar or a drunk. "I can't very well have you running back to your governments and telling them that I double-crossed you, can I?" he pointed out.

"Why not?" Poe asked. "Before I could get back to Richmond and tell anyone what you'd done, you'd have your revenge. Even if Hunley or Jefferson Davis or Robert E. Lee wanted to stop you, they couldn't."

"Aaaaagh!" Nostrils screamed again, shuddering. Orson Pratt snorted, raised his Parley and pointed it at the suffering man. He clicked the firing bolt once.

Zottt!

Nostrils burst into flame, writhing as his body burnt to cinder. Poe didn't let himself stare.

"Yes, but what about *after* my revenge?" Pratt pointed out. "I plan to survive the downfall of the Kingdom and, wherever I decide to go, I'm not interested in living my life under the threat of a bounty offered by the United States of America."

Poe didn't care about Pratt's plans following the mass murder he had planned. He wanted to know what the canopic jars did. Could they be an energy source? Could ether-waves power a device, including an airship? "With the canopic jars in place, how far will your ships take you? Could you get to Mexico City?"

Pratt laughed. "You drop your hook into the fishing hole hoping there's a big trout down there in the darkness somewhere," he said.

"I have a hook," Poe said. "I have to try." The fact that Pratt had realized he was being probed and cut off the line of conversation didn't mean that the guess about the canopic jars being a power source was wrong, of course, but it didn't confirm the guess, either. He sighed. It was so much easier to *write* a clever detective than actually to *be* one.

"What you don't yet realize," Pratt continued, "is that the fishing hole is home to a terrible monster." He gestured to the Pinkertons. "Hit him a little bit, but don't kill him. If he tries anything—anything at all—kill *her*. After you've all had your fun, throw them in with the others."

Pratt handed his Pratt Enkindler to the nearest Pinkerton, turned and walked away. The Pinkerton, a heavy man in a bowler hat, sneered and shoved the muzzle of the weapon into Roxie's side.

The first fist rammed Poe in the belly and knocked him against the plascrete wall, only a foot from where the Pinkerton's skull, now embedded in the ruined material, smoldered away. The blow kicked all the air out of him and triggered his coughing reflex at the same time, so Poe gagged and sucked in and choked on air, his stomach retching up bile and his lungs forcing out blood in the effort. Punches to the face prevented him from even spitting out the polluted fluids, so the sour vermilion mess bubbled from his lips and spattered all over his chin and face and shirt as Poe went down, unresisting and defenseless, with his eye fixed on Roxie.

Her face was dark with despair and she looked beautiful.

The plascrete floor filled his vision and then pressed against his face. The blows didn't stop and blood, phlegm, and bile oozed betweens his lips and puddled warm and sticky around his head.

After a while, Poe breathed again.

He was picked up and dragged, knees scraping on the floor. Blue light globes whizzed by him impossibly fast, and he thought they might be stars. Was he in the ether, then? Was he stung to death by the Scorpion and racing around the outline of its celestial body, waiting for the abyss to take him?

Then there was a door.

Had he come a million miles?

A hundred feet?

He was hauled through the door and dropped to the plascrete again. *Slam!* A buzzing noise, and for a time he drifted. It was the first day of creation, he decided, and if the world was without form and void, then the buzzing sounds must be the Spirit of God hovering upon the waters. He knew that if he waited long enough, he would eventually hear the Lord's first words and then the firmament would divide the waters.

"I think he's awake," turned out to be the creative incantation. That didn't seem quite right to Poe, but with the words came light, shaky, elusive, and painful, but enough to see by. Light and a plain of stone.

"Mrarmgaaaarble," he tried to say, but failed. Creation responded, though, in the firmament that seared his body, throwing a violent mass of blood and sputum from the waters below into the waters above and out upon the dry land. Poe didn't feel able, in clean conscience, to pronounce creation good.

"Ick, he's in bad fookin' shape, though," was the second mantra of creation.

"Poe?" He recognized Roxie's voice.

"Mmmmmmalive," Poe managed to mumble. His lips felt like they had been flattened under hammers. Man, created in the images of the gods after having been run over by divine steam-trucks. "I'm alive."

"Worse luck you," complained another voice that Poe now recognized as belonging to the Irishman O'Shaughnessy. "I was hoping you were dead, for your sake."

ꓶƐꓴꚁꙄꓶꓚ

Pffffffft-ankkkh! Pffffffft-ankkkh!

The two Striders trundled along at a surprisingly good clip, bobbing up and down as they went like they were picking worms out of the soil. They weren't as fast as the *Jim Smiley* on a straight flat road, of course, but the chicken-like legs and claws meant that the things could run like wild animals across the landscape, leaping irrigation ditches, high-stepping over tangled brush, and vaulting wooden fences. Occasionally, one of the pilots cut it too close and a big metal claw reduced a shed or a root cellar or a gate to splinters and rubble in a single blow.

The Mexican machines were impressive but Sam was pretty sure they couldn't swim. The *Jim Smiley* had them there.

The big metal chickens headed closer to the mountains, looming up like shadowy giants to block out the stars. Sam had seen plenty of mountains back East but nothing like these enormous sprawling Himalayans. It wasn't just the fact that they were tall that made them imposing, it was the fact that they were *suddenly* tall—they sprang out of the valley floor and shot another mile or more nearly straight up into the sky, like a row of teeth around an immense cultivated tongue.

Pfffffft-ankkkh!

In the absence of a binnacle, Sam watched the stars to keep his bearing, more by habit than by necessity, since the mountains were such unavoidable landmarks. They circled around the southern edge of the Great Salt Lake City (Sam could see the blue glow of the city center's many Franklin Poles from miles away), staying off the roads and away from farmhouses where light showed. Crossing the farmland at a run showed Sam the vastness of the Mormons' network of irrigation canals and small roads and he was duly impressed. He was a man who prided himself on valuing industry almost as much as he valued innovation.

The Mormons had both, in spades. It was too bad, he thought, that they were so hopelessly strange. They might have made good Americans.

The night sky was clear but as the Striders veered left across the wide, flat benches of the mountains' foothills, turning to come at the city on its east side, Sam chanced to look to the south and saw what he took for flashes of lightning, striking over and over again in the same spot, high up in the air.

"That's a queer-looking storm," he observed. The sight of the city coming closer made the *Jim Smiley* feel imminent, and he could almost taste a Partagás on his tongue. "It's awfully local to the top of that mountain. Maybe there's a vein of metal up there attracting all the electricity. You ought to send prospectors, Mr. President."

"That's no storm," Rockwell growled. "That's Timpanogos."

Sam gulped. "Pratt's place?" He watched the lightning flash some more and realized that the "storm" was even more local than he had at first imagined—the lightning appeared to be striking over and over again in exactly the same place. "Is it possible those flashes are our comrades, putting an end to the threat of an airborne assault upon Chicago?"

"Your Irishman's a lightning wizard, then, is he?" the dwarf asked belligerently. "O'Franklin, was that his name? Now he's jest shooting lightning bolts at Pratt and his airships? That's quite a show, then, and I'm sad I'm missing it."

"It's possible," Young said. His voice was cold and hard. "There's a darker possibility."

"That's how he charges up the airships," Rockwell offered.

"With lightning bolts?" Sam was dumbfounded. Most electricks were powered by some sort of generator that turned motion into small amounts of electricity—the motion of a turning, steam-powered engine, for instance, or the motion of falling water. To reach out and harness the fire of heaven directly was a Franklinesque act, if not a downright Promethean one. He felt no small amount of awe and his teeth ground upon each other over and over where by rights a good Partagás should have been.

"Jebus," Coltrane muttered. "Heaven help Chicago."

"Or us," Rockwell offered. "There's no guarantee he's planning to attack a *Gentile* city."

A pall of silence settled over the carriage.

The Striders turned north. They tramped through the foothills above the farms now, so there weren't any more ditches or fences to jump or sheds to avoid. Mule deer scattered at the Striders' approach, and dog-like creatures that might have been coyotes.

"What was your offer, then, Mr. Clemens?" Brigham Young asked. His voice sounded deliberately cheerful.

"Excuse me?"

"I can guess what the English had to offer," Young said. "And the secessionists, for that matter—either of them might have offered me land, to the north or south of my Kingdom, that would have been very valuable. But I don't want the Wyoming Territory."

"Who does?" Sam agreed. "But what about Colorado, with its silver fields?"

"Is that the Union's offer, then?" Young asked. "Join with us to prevent secession, and you can have the silver of the Rocky Mountains? Couldn't I get the same thing from the Southern states, in the event of their victory?"

"You certainly could," Sam conceded, "and the victorious United States could offer you land all the way from St. George to Mexico, so land promises are cheap. Which is why the Union didn't send me to promise you land."

"No?" Rockwell sounded curious.

"No," Sam continued, "my offer is one trainload of fornication pants, sizes to be specified by a duly appointed agent of the Kingdom."

Young snorted, then began to laugh.

"I don't mind fornication pants myself," Rockwell said, shrugging, as Young continued to guffaw. "The buttons up the front make it easier to empty your bladder quick and sometimes that can be a real advantage."

"Urination trousers." Sam grinned, knowing that he was reeling them in. He was, after all, still on a diplomatic mission, and when the evening's crisis was over, whoever was still standing in the Lion House would have to make a decision about the war. "Micturition leggings, if you prefer."

"Pissing pants!" Rockwell barked, and he started laughing, too.

The dwarf just shook his head like he thought everyone around him was crazy.

"All pants to be delivered by train to the Great Salt Lake City," Sam finished. He jabbed an imaginary cigar at Young's chest for emphasis. "On the new Transcontinental Railroad, one hundred percent owned and operated by the Kingdom of Deseret."

Young stopped laughing.

"All land to be provided and all track laid at the expense of the United States government," Sam added. "Along with rolling stock up to five million dollars in value, complete training in railroad operations for up to two hundred persons of your choice, and a ten year maintenance guarantee for the entire length of the track."

"President Buchanan really wants me in the war on his side," Young observed.

"President Buchanan really doesn't want a war at all," Sam disagreed. "And he thinks that the best way to avoid one is to have the Kingdom of Deseret on his side from the beginning."

"Patrolling the skies over Richmond and Atlanta," Young guessed.

Sam shrugged. "If need be. Maybe simple telegraph messages from you to Richmond and Atlanta would suffice."

"The telegraph doesn't connect to Salt Lake yet," Young pointed out.

"Oh, did I forget that part?" Sam asked coyly. "Of course we'd connect the Great Salt Lake City to the American telegraph network first. I'm told it could be done in a matter of mere weeks."

Young was silent for a minute. Sam leaned into the cool dry air of the night, feeling his hair ruffle and imagining himself as the victorious figurehead on the prow of a mighty ship of state.

"Your gift is something of a Trojan horse," Young finally said.

"I missed the part about the horses," Rockwell grunted. "How many horses?"

"The United States has no interest in infringing on the sovereignty of the Kingdom of Deseret," Sam said quickly. "The railroad would carry no troops, unless you wanted them."

"I'm not worried about guns."

"What, then? Fornication pants?"

"Yes," Young snapped, "fornication pants! And Southern cotton and French wine and Virginia tobacco and manufactured goods from the mills of the North! And anything else that would make my people soft and weak and dependent on a Gentile for anything!"

Sam rocked back on his heels. "That's commerce, Mr. President," he said. "We're all dependent on each other." He gestured down at the valley below. "You could trade your sugar beets, your wheat, and whatever else you grow, make, or dig out of these mountains, and get the things your people want."

"What they *want*, maybe. But I can't get in trade the things my people *need*," Young growled. "Independence. Pride. Freedom from persecution. Open borders and commerce work very well, Mr. Clemens, when you are a powerful people with wealth. They're not nearly as useful to a small, persecuted folk like us."

"You're afraid of persecution?" Sam asked, slightly mystified. "It'd be *your* railroad, you could decide who rides it and who has to walk! How would you be any worse off than you are today?"

"I do worry about persecution," Young admitted, and he pounded the side of the Strider's carriage with his balled fist. "And I am right to do so! More than Gentile bullets, though, or Gentile tar and feathers, I worry about Gentile trade goods. I worry about my children and grandchildren, and the seductive power of material things. The first step on the road is fornication pants, Mr. Clemens. The second is fornication. And at the end of that path, my people will cease to exist, not because they have been murdered but because they have become your people, and snuffed out their own unique lamps to do so."

Sam opened his mouth, found he had nothing to say, and closed it again.

As the Striders dropped out of the foothills, past the first tall Franklin Poles and into the outskirts of the Great Salt Lake City where Sam's steam-truck waited, Sam began to hear gunshots. Sam tried not to think about who was shooting whom, and prepared to switch vehicles.

The lot where the *Jim Smiley* was berthed was unattended and the gate locked, but from the height of the Strider's carriage, Sam found he could easily step onto the broad top of the plascrete wall surrounding the lot and from there it was a short jump onto the steam-truck's deck.

"The gate's locked," Young bristled as Sam stepped across the gap and onto the plascrete.

"I'll pay for all the damages," Sam acknowledged. He paced to his left, looking for the shortest possible jump.

"Wait for me," Young barked, and scrambled after him. On the wall, he straightened his jacket and nodded to the Strider's pilot. "No offense, Private Ramirez. Your skills are impeccable, I'm sure, but the ride is a little bumpy."

The Striderman saluted, and Rockwell and Jed Coltrane followed Brigham Young up onto the wall.

"Shall we lead the way dowd to the Liod House?" Absalom Fearnley-Standish called from the other Strider.

Sam looked at the exhaust pipe and saw, of course, no smoke. "It'll take us a few minutes to get her going!" he called. "Keep an eye on the street!"

He jumped down to the metal deck of his craft, landing softly on his rubber soles and rolling forward on bent knees. He had spirits in the galley that would get the fire started quickly, but of course the fire would take time to heat the boiler and build up enough steam to move the *Jim Smiley*'s tyres.

Which was why Sam had had the *Smiley* built with a special emergency starter, an electricks device the engineers had built to his specifications that basically hurled lightning bolts through the boiler to superheat its contents in just a few seconds. He flicked the switch on in the wheelhouse, hearing two heavy thuds on the deck behind him as he did so, and headed below decks as the dwarf Coltrane dropped onto the *Jim Smiley* with a tumbling flip, landing on his feet without a sound.

Sam heard the electricks of the emergency starter hum as he hit the engine room. He checked the water levels, saw the rising pressure gauge with satisfaction, and was happy that the Danites weren't as sabotage-minded as Captain Richard Burton. He was even happier that he'd talked the United States Army into equipping the *Jim Smiley* with the biggest electric battery on wheels in North America, if not the world. It would take a week of normal driving to recharge, but this was exactly the sort of emergency he'd in mind. Well, maybe not *exactly*.

He ducked into the galley for a bottle of something flammable and a fistful of cigars.

Coltrane trotted down the stairs as Sam threw a bottle of high-proof whisky into the furnace. The little man rolled up his sleeves and nodded.

"I shoveled a lotta elephant shit," he said. "I figure I can shovel coal."

"It might make a nice change," Sam agreed, biting on his Partagás with a sense of cosmic relief. He handed the dwarf a cigar too, struck a match, lit Coltrane's smoke, and then tossed the match into the furnace.

Poof!

Sam checked the pressure gauge again. "Here we go," he told Coltrane, and headed up to the wheelhouse. "Join us when the furnace is full."

Sam gestured at the co-pilot's chair inside the wheelhouse but Rockwell and Young both declined to sit. He happily released the brake and put the *Jim Smiley* into gear, backing away from the parking lot gate in order to have as much of a run at it as possible.

He wasn't sure, but he thought the gunshots sounded closer.

ꓹƐ⅃ꓩꙶ☉ꓪꓛ

KRANG-NG-NG-NG!

The piles of coal in the boiler room's boxes jumped like popping corn in the pan and Jed tumbled to the hard metal floor.

"Ouch. You're getting old, Coltrane," he muttered to himself, rubbing a bruised elbow as he stood back up. He shoveled coal into the boiler until it wouldn't take any more, then he shut the grate, jammed the shovel into a convenient coal box, and headed back up the stairs to the deck.

He heard trouble brewing in the gunshots and he patted the vibro-blade at his belt to reassure himself.

The *Jim Smiley* rolled down the empty streets of the Great Salt Lake City. Jed emerged from below decks facing backward and saw one of the two Mexican Striders bringing up the rear of the little procession. They seemed to be slowing down, and so did Sam Clemens's steam-truck.

Jed turned around. Ahead he saw the curving lower side of the big egg-shaped Tabernacle and the other Strider leading the way. Absalom Fearnley-Standish and his girlfriend rode in it and as Jed looked at him the Englishman took off his mutilated hat and waved it back in salute.

Beyond Fearnley-Standish, around the base of the egg, Jed saw war. He moved forward into the wheelhouse to see it better.

A large brick building of some kind, like a storefront, faced the Tabernacle. Twin rows of three-foot-high brass letters decorated its façade, one in the strange Mormon gobbledygook they called *Deseret* and the other in English, reading *ZIONS COOPERATIVE MERCANTILE INSTITUTE.*

Most of the windows had been shot out of the front of the building, leaving the street littered with glass and fragments of wood, and bodies, in both blue and gray uniforms. A flag Jed didn't recognize flew over the battered Institute, blue and gold and showing an Indian holding a bow and a single white star. Men in blue uniforms crouched inside, showing themselves only to fire carbines at their besiegers.

The soldiers outside the Institute wore gray. They advanced in ranks upon the men in blue, crouching behind Franklin Poles and carriages and creeping up in tandem with their metallic clocksprung horses, the horses shuffling low to the ground in postures impossible to flesh and blood animals, providing their riders cover with their heavy gleaming bodies.

"There, Mr. Clemens," Brigham Young said. "There is your commerce."

"They're not shooting at your people," Sam Clemens said. "They're shooting at each other." He shifted the steam-truck into neutral gear and eased down on the brake handle until the *Jim Smiley* rolled to a halt. "But where to?"

The front Strider clanked alongside the steam-truck, and Fearnley-Standish waved his hat again. Annie Web, beside him on the rumble seat, looked dressed for a picnic or a dance but held a long rifle across her lap. "Chadge of plads, gedts?" he called.

"It's all death, just the same." Young stared at the gun battle. "And they're blocking our access."

Jed looked again, and realized it was true. The men in gray were fighting from the Lion House, and a number of them crouched in its bushes and behind its walls, and even inside the building, shooting out of its windows.

"They're probably wearing fornication pants, too," Sam Clemens quipped, and he winked at Jed.

"We need to get the message out that I'm still alive," Young said.

"And that I'm innocent," Clemens added.

Fearnley-Standish nodded. He looked very serious, almost like he was posing for a daguerreotype.

"That's the place to do it from." Young jabbed his finger, pointing at the Lion House. "George Cannon always has one of his clerks sleep in the message room on a cot, in case we need to send out instructions or an announcement in the middle of the night. We need to get in there, wake that clerk up, and announce to the Kingdom what's been going on."

"Do problem!" Fearnley-Standish leaned forward and said something to his pilot, and the Strider lurched into motion again, heading straight for the fracas.

"Fool!" Clemens snapped. He put the *Jim Smiley* into reverse, wheeling it around in the street and narrowly avoiding colliding with the second Strider. Ramirez made the vehicle chicken-walk backward in the nick of time, and then Clemens had the steam-truck rolling the other direction, crashing over the curb onto a sidewalk and shearing a couple of saplings into toothpicks.

Jed rushed across the deck to the back end of the truck and stood beside the big paddlewheel's casing to watch the action.

Boom! Boom! Boom!

The Striderman at the gun controls—Jackson, the woman—fired on the soldiers in gray. Her aim was deadly; two of the clocksprung horses exploded, rocketing into the air and collapsing into metal shavings as they were hit, one taking its rider with it. The third shot plowed a furrow in the glittering plascrete sidewalk at the feet of two soldiers.

Every gray-capped head turned and looked at the intruders.

Ramirez moved his Strider into a support position, Polk firing past the lead Strider and blasting craters in the street.

Boom! Boom!

Jed wondered where all the Mormons were. He'd seen them in the daytime, every one of them, it seemed, armed to the teeth. Why were none of them on the scene now, assisting one side or the other, or trying to quiet the fight? The one or two people on the street not in uniform that Jed spotted were in the corners, scurrying for cover.

Maybe the conflict was just too big. Or maybe they'd been ordered to stand down.

Then every gray soldier who could manage turned where he stood, crouched, or lay and began firing at the Striders.

Bang! Bang! Bang!

Ramirez and Ortiz whipped their vehicles around in the storm of bullets and the grays began to leap into the saddle.

Rockwell jumped to the back rail with Jed, raised a pair of long Colt pistols, and fired at the secessionist Virginians.

"Left!" Jed heard Brigham Young yell. "We can get around to North Tabernacle and get in through the Beehive House!"

The Striders split left and right. Ramirez and Polk vanished between tall brick warehouses, and Ortiz and his company ducked as his Strider jumped in long goose-like steps down a ramp that led underground. Clocksprung-mounted riders turned and followed each Strider, drawing the bulk of the force away.

Other cavalrymen, a dozen of them, kept after the *Jim Smiley*.

Rat-a-tat-tat-a-tat-tat went their hooves on the street, sounding altogether too much like John Browning's *machine-gun* for Jed's comfort.

"We have company!" Rockwell yelled. He anchored his hips against the railing of the steam-truck and leaned into each shot he took, stealing every inch of range he could, heedless of the shots that came back his direction.

Jed wished he had a gun and tightened his grip on the hilt of the vibro-blade.

The *Jim Smiley* raced forward the length of another city block, the six riders behind closing.

"Into the wheelhouse!" Sam Clemens barked over his shoulder. Jed obeyed.

"No bullet or blade!" Rockwell shouted his defiance, reloading at the rail in a swarm of hot lead.

"Now, dammit!" Clemens shouted, and the mountain man reluctantly came forward and joined the others at the wheel.

Clemens snapped his fingers to catch Jed's attention, and pointed at a switch on the control panel. It had a small symbol like a lightning bolt engraved in the metal next to it, and a keyhole. Clemens took a key from around his neck, inserted it, and turned the key. Nothing obvious happened.

"When I light my cigar, flip this switch," Clemens said to him. "When I light the cigar, and not before. Got it?"

"Sure," Coltrane said. "Is that a weapon?"

Clemens grinned and pulled a fresh cigar from his pocket. "It's the brake on the Ikey Heyman," he said. "The rest of you, stay in the wheelhouse, no matter what, and *don't touch the walls.*"

Coltrane didn't know what Clemens meant, and didn't know what to expect. Just to be prepared, he drew the vibro-blade and put his thumb on the switch.

Rat-a-tat-tat-a-tat-tat, the men in gray drew nearer.

Sam yanked on the brake handle and the *Jim Smiley* shuddered to a halt in the middle of the street. "When I light my cigar," he repeated. "Don't touch the walls. And don't shoot! Guns always mess everything up."

Sam Clemens walked out onto the deck of his steam-truck and waited, cigar in one hand and match in the other.

"My guns?" Rockwell looked at Brigham Young like a kicked dog. "Do it."

"He's crazy," Rockwell muttered, but he holstered his pistols.

"Don't shoot me or nothing," Jed contradicted the mountain man, "but I think he might jest be the least crazy man on this truck."

The cavalrymen dismounted. Sam Clemens held his hands by his chest in plain sight, and the men in uniform swarmed up the sides of the vessel. They looked angry and they rushed up the *Jim Smiley*'s two ladders holding nothing back, with murder in their eyes.

Clemens stood calm and smiling, like he was out at the fair, having a nice day of it. He looked as happy, Jed thought, as any shill ever had. Jed himself felt very uncertain, and shifted from foot to foot on the black rubber that matted the floor of the wheelhouse.

"You, there!" demanded one of the grays, a young man who appeared to be in charge. "Who are you?"

Soldiers rushed towards the wheelhouse. The last of the cavalrymen jumped onto the bottom rungs of the ladder. Sam Clemens struck the match slowly and deliberately on the rivets of his fornication pants and held the little flame to the tip of his cigar.

Jed flipped the switch.

Crack-ckz-ckz-ckz-ckz-ckz-ckz!

CHAPTER SEVENTEEN

Burton propped Edgar Allan Poe up in his lap and dabbed blood away from the other man's face. The American had been beaten badly. Under the bruises and cuts, he was pale as chalk, his face sweated, and he trembled with each breath.

Poe was dying.

"I'd put the hypocephalus under your head," Burton joked, "but it's flat, and would give you no comfort. The Egyptians made lousy pillows." He knew Poe had it worse than he did, but he hurt, too, arm, leg, and chest. He hadn't been in this much sheer physical pain since the night he had a spear thrust through his face.

He grinned with pride at the memory.

Poe twisted his face into something that resembled a smile. "Putting a cloth … under a man's head … doesn't make it a pillow," he gasped, "any more than putting a man in a stable … makes him a horse." He coughed hard and flopped his head to one side to spit more of his life onto the floor.

Burton chuckled. "I'm willing to admit we don't know what the hypocephalus was for and call it a draw if you are," he offered. "I'd love to borrow your specimen and take it back to London with me. You could come lecture on it for the Royal Geographical Society. We could debate the issue again."

"It's a fabrication," Poe croaked.

Burton laughed. "You Americans. Not enough antiquities of your own, so you fake them!"

"Not every country has an Empire full of ruins to ransack," Poe said, and then collapsed into bloody wet coughing again.

"You gents are awfully fookin' jolly for men about to die," the Irishman O'Shaughnessy complained. He sat slumped against the plascrete wall, beak-like nose protruding between his bony knees.

The room they were in was long and cold. It was windowless and devoid of furniture other than two long tables in the center, with benches affixed to either side. Burton guessed it was something in the nature of a mess hall, and he sat cradling Poe on the table while the woman Roxie examined the room's only door. The door was a single slab of plascrete, featureless as far as Burton could see.

"Is any other response appropriate in a man?" Burton wanted to know, puffing out his chest.

"I reckon not." O'Shaughnessy slumped.

"I don't know how the door is locked," Roxie said, "but it's done from the outside. Maybe it's barred, I didn't notice on the way in. But it won't budge, and there isn't so much as a keyhole, doorknob, or hinge showing on this side of the door."

Poe groped feebly at his jacket with both hands. "Help me sit up," he mumbled.

Burton pulled the other man to a sitting position and stayed next to him, an arm around his shoulders. Poe fumbled into a coat pocket and produced a folded yellowing cloth. He opened it, and Burton saw the circles, figures with raised arms and animal heads that marked this as Poe's hypocephalus. He put his hand over it to restrain Poe.

"Keep it," he said. "The Society isn't going to be interested in a fake."

Poe shook his head, weak but impatient. "Weapon," he said. "It's a weapon."

"Is it an explosive?" O'Shaughnessy asked. "If it blows up like dynamite, that and the kiss of fortune from sainted Brigit might just get us through this door."

Poe looked slowly around the room. "Hypnotic," he said slowly, and shook his head. "No good, no good."

Burton wondered if the other man were delirious. He had seemed lucid before, though battered and weak, but men often lost their reason in their final moments. Roxie turned away from the door with a look of devastation on her, Burton now saw, rather plain, angular face, and he wished he had some way to shield her from Poe's imminent death. Not that she was a wilting flower and needed protection, but because that was what a civilized man did for women. As if to belie his thoughts, Roxie crossed the room and gathered Poe in her arms, taking him from Burton almost by force.

"And what if it did do some good?" O'Shaughnessy demanded morosely. "What if we could get out of this hole? Would it matter? What are we doing, anyway?"

"Are you serious?" Burton snorted, rising to his feet. "Varuna's saddled seal, man, we're trying to save all our countries from disaster!"

"Oh, yeah?" the Irishman grimaced. "You're trying to save the English mill owners, aren't you? That's *your* cause, Burton, remember? Queen and country! Remind me again what you're doing for the poor suffering Irish."

"Yes, you bloody-minded idiot, I'm trying to help the Irish!" Burton meant to keep his temper, but found himself roaring. "If the United States splits into two, how many Irishmen do you think will fight and die on each side?"

O'Shaughnessy shrugged and looked away.

"And how many Irishmen will fight in Britain's armies and navies when she invades in support of her ally?" Burton wanted to pummel the other man in the face to make his point, but he controlled himself at least that much. "The only thing your country exports is its people—how many Irishmen do you think will die torn to shred by guns? How many will sink in burning ships? How many will die of infection in freezing, mud-floored camp hospitals?"

"More than one," O'Shaughnessy admitted sourly.

"More than one!" Burton bellowed. "Then for the sake of those *more than one* Irishmen, you whimpering sot, not to mention for the sake of your own wretched life, do you think you can be troubled to bestir yourself to help us escape?"

The Irishman leaned forward and vomited on both their shoes.

"Surya's golden arms!" Burton shouted. In rage, he kicked the plascrete wall, right beside O'Shaughnessy's head.

"I'll help, I'll bloody-damn-hell help!" the Irishman gasped. He staggered to his feet, propping himself against the wall with his shoulder blades. "I don't really have a choice, do I, unless I want to just lie down and die. Only I don't see what the point of my help would be. I haven't got dynamite or a drill, or the tiny brass beetles, or anything else. But if you want me to run and smash my own fookin' head against the door over and over again until it breaks or I do, I will."

The exaggerated, desperate glare in the man's eyes, the tangled thatch of red hair, and the drips of vomit on his chin made Burton laugh.

"You're right!" he surrendered, throwing up his useless hands. "There's nothing we can do! We're trapped!" He pointed at the door that penned them in and wagged his finger at it, as if scolding the architecture. "That door has us buried in here as effectively as any avalanche. But sooner or later Pratt's men will open the door and we owe it to ourselves and our various countrymen to be ready to take action when they do."

"Unless they just want to starve us to death," O'Shaughnessy muttered.

"What kind of action, Dick?" Roxie asked.

Burton ran both hands through his hair and tweaked his own mustachios. "What weapons do we have, other than fists?" he asked.

Roxie shook her head. "Nothing."

"I've got a knife," the Irishman admitted, looking down at his bile-spattered shoes.

"A knife?" Burton was impressed. "How did the Pinkertons fail to find a knife on your person?"

Tamerlane O'Shaughnessy grinned. "The Pinkertons failed," he said—

—and snapped his hand forward in a quick gesture, like he aggressively wanted to shake hands—

—*Snick!*—

—and a knife blade popped from his sleeve and filled his hand. "Because they're born idjits and then the Agency trains them to be even stupider."

"I accept your analysis," Burton harrumphed. "That knife blade won't get us through the door, so we'll need to make a plan. Poe's manifest unwellness should allow him to distract at least one man." Burton gestured around the room, like it was a chalkboard and he was sketching out a plan of battle. "Obviously, you'll want to attack your man here inside the room, with the possibility of luring more men in. If I position myself beside the door, I should be able to take advantage of the commotion and get behind our enemy."

"No need," Poe groaned. He waved Roxie away and climbed gingerly down off the table, setting each foot on the floor like he was sticking it into a pot of boiling tar.

"Will your hypocephalus do something besides hypnotize a man, then?" Burton asked gruffly. He found that he felt protective of Edgar Allan Poe, and wanted the man to lie back down and rest.

"Better," Poe said. With a hand that shook like a falling autumn leaf, he reached inside his shirt and pulled out a long, thin, silver whistle.

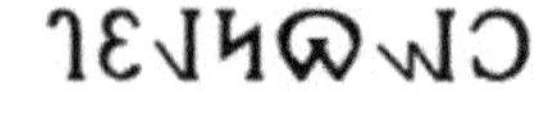

K-k-k-k-k-RANG-ng-ngchhhhhhhhhh!

The Strider's gigantic chicken-like feet slammed onto the plascrete ramp down and planted. The Strider wobbled, but under Ortiz's expert hands it kept its balance and slid forward, like a child on ice skates, unsteady but upright. Sparks flew up in sheets from where the metal scratched the plascrete.

"Get dowd!" Absalom yelled, and followed his own advice.

Ortiz heard him too, or already saw the ceiling coming on his own, and the Strider dropped into a crouch as it passed underground and into the warren of parking bays that surrounded the Tabernacle. Absalom cringed but the plascrete slid by safely several feet over his head.

Master Sergeant Jackson never ducked. As the Strider turned to scuttle underground, she swiveled widdershins, keeping her assortment of guns aimed at the clocksprung cavalry on their heels. As they descended, she adjusted her aim up to compensate and fired.

Boom! Boom! Rat-tat-tat-tat-tat!

One metal horse exploded into flame in the barrage. Its companions swerved aside or balked, buying seconds that might become precious. Absalom took aim with his Danite-pilfered pistol and fired off a single shot.

The Strider turned a corner and the horses were out of sight before Absalom could see if his shot hit anything. He cocked, steadied his aim and waited, watching parked steam-trucks and plascrete pylons rush past out of the corner of his eye. The blue light from the electricks globes in the ceilings and in the walls flickered but provided plenty of illumination for gunplay.

Three clocksprung cavalrymen *clattered* down into the hangar bay. Absalom exhaled gently and squeezed the trigger again and again, imagining a clay pigeon flying directly away from him and into the chest of the lead rider.

Five shots rang out in quick succession and the soldier tumbled off his horse.

Absalom sat back, took his powder flask from the pocket of his coat and set about reloading.

"Stay down!" sweet Annie Webb urged him, pulling gently at his shoulder and trying to drag him low into the carriage. Absalom only grinned recklessly at her and began thumbing lead balls into the pistol's cylinder.

Boom! Boom!

Consuelo Jackson fired her big gun. Shattered lights exploded and chunks of plascrete tore from their place and scattered across the floor.

Annie pressed herself against the edge of the carriage and raised a rifle she'd taken from one of the Danites at Heber Kimball's farm.

The cavalrymen in gray fired back. Bullets *whizzanged* off the outside of the Strider's carriage, and Absalom hoped they had succeeded in drawing enough soldiers away from Brigham Young's office so that the man could get in and send the message he needed.

"Ortiz!" Jackson yelled, waving her fist as the mustached Mexican pilot looked over his shoulder. *"Allá!"*

Absalom looked where she had gestured and saw familiar doors. This was the entrance by which he'd come into the Tabernacle, a million years ago, yesterday. Ortiz dropped the carriage lower, the Strider running with knees bent low to the ground and its great claws gouging at the plascrete floor. Bullets whizzed by the Strider's carriage, sparking on the walls and ceiling.

Annie rose up to shoot again with her rifle.

"Dot dow!" Absalom shouted, and dragged her down.

Bang! Her shot whipped away in the artificial cavern and then the Strider lurched under the low entrance—

Jackson leaped out of the gun platform and threw herself to the bottom of the carriage—

—*CRUNCH!*—

—and the Strider didn't quite get low enough. The carriage crashed into the top of the doors and smashed Absalom's shoulder.

"Aaaagh!" he cried out.

CHANG!

Master Sergeant Jackson's gunning platform disappeared, ripped away by the plascrete.

The Strider lumbered up the large concourse toward the main chamber of the Tabernacle. Absalom threw himself against the back wall of the carriage between Annie, raising her rifle high, and Master Sergeant Jackson, now drawing and cocking her sidearm.

"Ortiz, hijo de puta que eres, me destruyiste todo!"

Ortiz only grunted in reply, intent on the twin levers with spring-actions grips that controlled the Strider's legs. Steam and foul black smoke jetted in tight tendrils from cracks where Jackson's guns had been torn away. Absalom smelled petroleum, and something burning. The carriage walls felt hot to the touch and he heard a faint, strained whining from the machinery.

Clocksprung horses burst into the concourse behind and below the Strider, and Absalom and the two ladies traded shots with them. With the joggety-thump motion of the big Mexican machine, Absalom wasn't at all surprised that his shots missed.

"Hold on!" Ortiz shouted in English, and Absalom took the cue. Not having a railing in front of him, or anything else to grab onto, he wrapped one arm around each of the women and they in turn anchored themselves to the Strider.

Ka-chunk!

The Strider took a particularly long step—

—the ground fell away beneath it—

—the cavalrymen reigned in their machine-beasts, stopping at a crumpled banister overlooking a ten-foot drop—

—the Strider sailed through the air and involuntarily Absalom began to scream, the ladies screaming with him, "Aaaaaaagh!"

CRASH!!!

The Strider hit the ground in an explosion of brass, steel, wood, and stuffing. The machine staggered as Ortiz lost his grip on one of the levers and the corresponding leg went limp. Then Ortiz regained control and the Strider righted itself, racing down into the center of the well of the

Tabernacle, claws chewing their way through the Tabernacle's seating like a thresher through ripe grain.

The Strider pulled away from the men of the Third Virginia Cavalry, but now it was at a lower elevation, and everyone sitting in the carriage was exposed. The men on the metal horses raised pistols and rifles and began to fire.

Absalom ducked between the two women. Improbably, his mind began to wander, considering which of the two he found more attractive, and just as he was imagining them both on a picnic blanket upon a sheep-cropped green sward beside a sluggish river in the May warmth, cutting together into a savory mince pie—

—*Bang!*

Ortiz slumped forward at the controls. Both levers pushed forward under the weight of the man's body and the Strider stumbled and fell, crashing to its knees. The three passengers rattled around like balls in a roulette wheel but none of them rolled out.

"Take the controls!" Jackson shouted.

Annie ignored her and both women poured lead out of their weapons up at the cavalrymen, who now streamed around the Tabernacle's seating and into separate stairway aisles, rushing for the downed Strider.

Absalom grabbed Ortiz to drag him out of the way, certain that at any second a bullet would take him in the back. Each moment seemed surreal to him. Nothing at Harrow, at Cambridge, or in his Foreign Office training had ever prepared him to kill men, handle dead bodies, or operate heavy machinery. The only thing distinguishing the last twenty-four hours from a nightmare was the fact that Absalom really *was* doing all these things, as well as being shot at, stabbed, punched, chased, and slammed into plascrete walls.

With two very attractive women at his side.

Absalom rolled Ortiz's corpse out of the way, shoved his long pistol into his waistband and squeezed into the pilot's seat.

He grabbed the two levers. Experimentally, he moved the right one forward and the carriage shuddered as the battered Strider shifted its right leg forward. Absalom squeezed the spring-triggered handgrip and the Strider's chicken-claw clenched, gouging up plascrete and squeezing three seats into sawdust and metal shavings.

Bang! Bang!

"Hurry!" Annie shouted in Absalom's ear.

Absalom played with the levers some more, feeling intensely the sweat under his arms and on the back of his neck. He could move the legs forward and back, side to side, but the Strider stayed kneeling, lurching from one side to another with loud metallic grating sounds, like a man having an epileptic seizure. He needed to be able to flex the knees. He needed another control …

He looked down, and found it. Two pedals, cupped to grip the pilot's toes nicely, between the two levers. He stuck his feet into them—

—lead sliced the air to ribbons around his head.

"Ahorita!" shouted Master Sergeant Jackson—

—*rat-a-tat-tat-a-tat-tat* galloped the clocksprung horses.

Absalom pulled the pedals back, strained at the levers, and made the Strider stand up. The carriage automatically leveled out with the motion, staying upright rather than tipping and dislodging its riders. *It must be weighted,* he thought, *to automatically adjust to changes in gradient.* Absalom could hear the metal horses and didn't risk a look back. Toes and elbows and hands operating in as close a harmony as he could manage, he started jogging forward.

"Yee ha!" whooped Annie, and crouched down in the carriage to reload.

"Más rápido!"

Absalom knew enough Spanish to realize that meant *faster.* He went as *más rápido* as he dared, much faster than he would have thought prudent. He launched the Strider's legs out in front of him like missiles, clutching clawsfuls of plascrete and floor and dragging the vehicle forward as if by the strength of his own arms.

He hit the floor at the bottom of the Tabernacle, lurched in two steps across it, and then bent the Strider's knee sharply to get up on top of the Tabernacle's stage. The enormous wooden podium exploded into sawdust as the Strider's claw punched through it.

"They're still coming!" Annie shouted, and fired over the side.

Bang! Bang!

Absalom risked a quick glance back and saw that she was right. The cavalrymen weren't gaining on him anymore, but he wasn't leaving them behind, either. Their horses coursed around the wreckage he was making of the Tabernacle like a pack of wolves running down a moose. He turned back around and worked his arms faster.

Ka-RANG!

He slammed the shoulder of the Strider into one of the enormous Franklin Poles lighting the dais. It flew backward, uprooted like a tree in a hurricane, and hurtled into the bottom rows of the Tabernacle's seating. As the Franklin Pole detached from the stage, there was a bright blue flash of light—

—FITZZ!—

—all the light in the bottom half of the Tabernacle died—

—and where the tossed Franklin Pole slammed into a row of seats, smoke wisped into the air.

Egad, Absalom thought. *Now you've lit their Tabernacle on fire.*

Distracted by this realization, Absalom almost missed the end of the stage in the sudden darkness, but he just managed to plant his claw right on the lip of the platform and jump. He took the space between the stage and the slope on the other side in a single bound, smashing through seats and railings and very nearly losing his grip on the edge of the plascrete well. The horses, because they had to turn and find stairways in the gloom, fell behind twenty feet.

Absalom fixed his eye on a doorway halfway up the Tabernacle, a well of darkness in the artificial gloaming. "I'm headigg for that exit!" he shouted, barely hearing his own voice over the whine of the machine and the splintering sounds of the chairs he trampled. "Do you have explosives od the Strider?"

"Jes, I have *un poco de* dynamite!"

"Get it ready dow!" he shouted.

He concentrated, sprinting with his arms. The levers must operate the legs by intermediaries of gears, he knew, but it was still an effort, and his arms weren't used to it. They ached.

Shots from behind the Strider exploded in front of it, spoiling the nice, ordered rows of seats even before the Strider plowed into them and crushed them beyond recognition. At least the horsemen were shooting up now, which made it virtually impossible for them to hit anyone in the Strider's gravity-perpendicular carriage.

"Light the dydamite!" Absalom shouted to the two women.

Fitzzzzz.

"What are you doing, Absalom?" Annie Webb called, a note of surprise in her voice.

"Brace yourselves for a bit of a tumble," Absalom called back. "Id three … two … wud …"

He jerked both levers and both pedals back and deliberately tripped the Strider.

As he hoped it would, the carriage automatically rolled back as the Strider rolled forward, staying parallel to the plane of the earth, so when it hit the plascrete it hit it flat, like a sled—

—plowed into the doors Absalom had aimed for—

—*POW!*—

—knocking them open, sliding through in a wake of sparks—

—and grinding to a halt on the other side, with the big legs of the Strider still choking the doorway and partly blocking it shut. Partly but not entirely.

"Throw the dydamite!" Absalom shouted, and leaped from the carriage. His legs felt like jelly and his arms felt like sacks of flour. He pressed forward by sheer will, drawing the pistol from his pants and turning to watch for any clocksprung-mounted soldiers that might make it through the obstruction he'd just thrown in their way.

Richard Burton couldn't have done it better, he thought smugly.

D.J. Butler

Master Sergeant Jackson threw the dynamite into the doors, then grabbed several things out of the Strider that looked like rifles. She and Annie came scrambling over the top of the carriage, following Absalom.

Rat-a-tat-tat-a-tat-tat, horses clattered to the doors.

"In there, men!" one of the soldiers shouted.

KABOOM!!!

ꓶꓛꓦꟼꟼꟼꓭꟼ

Poe blew his whistle and it made no sound at all.

Tam cringed back away from the man as he huffed and puffed into the little sliver of metal, ready to pop his knife out if the whistle produced anything dangerous, like, say, carnivorous beetles or jets of fire or flying poisonous serpents to make even St. Patrick cry himself to sleep.

But Poe screwed up his face in concentration and wheezed in and out and nothing happened. Not even a sound, much less anything that would actually knock down the door or kill Pinkertons or get them out of the locked room.

"If I tell you I'm disappointed," he grumbled, "will it hurt your feelings?"

"Obviously the whistle is ultrasonic," Burton snapped. The others all nodded their heads and Poe kept contorting his face around the whistle.

"Does *ultrasonic* mean *broken*?" Tam persisted. "Here, I'll show you how to fookin' whistle!" He stuck two fingers in his mouth and blew, *hyoooooo, whup!*

CRASH!

The racket came from the other side of the door and Tam yanked his fingers from his mouth. *Careful, me boy, don't bite your own hand.*

"What in Brigit's knickers was that?"

"Apparently, your whistle just killed our guards," Burton said dryly. "Go on, whistle some more. This time, why don't you cut out all the intervening steps and just sink Pratt's airships?"

"Ha, ha," Tam said, and got ready to spring out his knife.

Poe coughed long and hard. The gob of blood and mucus he spit on the floor was the size of a baby's head, and Tam retched at the sight and smell of it. Clearing out his lungs seemed to have a salutary effect on Poe, though—the man straightened up, and looked better than he had since they'd been thrown into the cell together.

"Remove yourselves from the vicinity of the door," Poe suggested. He leaned on both Roxie and Burton to limp across the room himself, and Tam retreated into the far corner. Whatever was happening was beyond him and sounded dangerous. Mother O'Shaughnessy had taught

316

him not to be a coward but she'd also taught him not to be an idjit, and only an idjit ran *toward* the danger he didn't need to.

Then Poe blew his silent whistle again.

CRASH!

The plascrete door snapped in half and something big and shiny and metallic and monstrostastic, the size of a small horse but with a strange head not quite like a dog's, punched through and slammed into the room. It landed on its four claws and stopped, staring at Poe. Tam thought he could see and hear the thing breathing and he shook himself. *It's your imagination, you idjit,* he told himself. *The thing is obviously clocksprung, like any plantation worker or twenty-four-hour-mule.*

Still, it made an impression. "Bloody-damn-hell," he observed.

"Ha!" Burton said, and slapped Tam on the shoulder. "Well done, O'Shaughnessy."

Tam peered around the corner and out into the hall. Two men lay on the ground, mangled beyond any ability of even their mothers to recognize them. "How did you do that, then?" he asked Poe. "You couldn't even see them."

"I didn't have to see them." Poe shook off Roxie's efforts to help him and shuffled towards the door on his own wobbling ankles. "The machine is very sophisticated."

Tam grunted appreciatively, remembering the little beetles. "This machine, on the other hand, is simple enough." He bent and picked up one of the Pinkerton's pistols. "Point and shoot."

"An important desideratum in anything, and especially in a weapon," Poe agreed, then burst into coughing.

"You look like hell, Poe." Tam squinted closer at the gun as Burton picked up the other man's firearm. "There's something wrong with this pistol. Where do the percussion caps go?"

Burton laughed. "It's a good thing you Irish are so amusing," he snorted. "It goes a long way to make up for your ignorance."

"Fine!" Tam snapped. "Then where does the percussion cap go, Mr. English Genius?"

Burton snapped open the cylinder of his pistol and shook out six brass cylinders. "This is the Smith & Wesson Model 1," he said, and he sounded as smug and holier-than-thou as any priest. "Its bullets come in brass cartridges, with powder and percussion cap built right in. They load thus." He demonstrated, reloading the cylinder and snapping it into place.

Tam examined his own pistol. "Bloody hell," he marveled at it. "You can say this for the Pinkertons, they have interesting guns."

The dog-machine *clicked* past him and out into the plascrete hall, Poe limping in its trail with Roxie fussing at his side. Tam and Richard Burton both ransacked the Pinkertons' bloody pockets, coming away with handfuls of shells and a scattergun, which Burton passed to Roxie.

"Only two shots," the Englishman said.

"That'll do nicely." She nodded, taking the scattergun on one hand and wrapping the other arm around Poe's trembling chest.

Ahead of them, a man in a long coat turned the corner into the hall. He had just enough time to look up and reach for his gun before the dog-thing was on him, knocking him to the ground under its weight and biting for his throat.

"*Aaaragh!*"

Blood spattered the walls and the Pinkerton fell silent.

"How did it do that?" Tam asked, astonished. "You didn't even touch the whistle."

Poe spat blood on the floor and nodded shakily. "It's a very sophisticated machine," he agreed. "Horace Hunley is a true genius."

"I think I've seen enough of true genius on this trip to conclude that it's overrated," Burton growled. "If every true genius were shot on diagnosis, we wouldn't be in this pickle."

"There'd still be a war in the offing," Roxie reminded him.

"What do you call the thing, then?" Tam wanted to know. "I can't keep thinking of it as a doggie."

"Are you blind, O'Shaughnessy?" Burton barked. "It's obviously a Seth-Beast."

"Obviously," Tam muttered.

"Also called the Typhonian Animal," Poe added.

"Or the sha!" Burton finished, with a trap-like snap of his heavy jaw. He grinned a row of teeth at Poe, and the American grinned back.

Tam felt left out and a little bit disrespected, but he was still impressed. "It's tremendous," he said. "Have you got another?"

�

Crack-ckz-ckz-ckz-ckz-ckz-ckz!

The men of the Third Virginia danced spastically like puppets before they fell, blue sparks running along the metal of their belt buckles and guns and in their teeth. Triggered by sparks in their cylinders, their guns started going off.

Bang! Bang! Bang!

Bullets ricocheted off the metal deck of the *Jim Smiley* and shattered glass windows in the streets storefronts. The show was spectacular but getting shot in the bargain was not part of Sam's plan.

"Shut it off!" he shouted to the dwarf Coltrane, who complied.

Instantly, the sparks stopped and the cavalrymen lay still. Sam smelled ozone and gunpowder and burnt flesh. "I hope they aren't dead," he said, looking around himself at all the fallen men, "but either way, we need to get them off the deck."

Upon inspection, though some were burned severely, none of the cavalrymen turned out to be dead. They thudded as they were trundled off the steam-truck and hit the ground below. Sam would have preferred a gentler treatment of the unconscious men but, after all, they had been trying to kill him, and he had saved their lives, or at least some of their lives, by keeping Rockwell in check. Really, they owed Sam a debt of thanks, and one that they would never acknowledge, so on balance he didn't feel too bad.

"Should we take their horses?" Rockwell asked, staring at the burnished metal beasts. "If they were … uh …"

"Meat?" Sam suggested.

"Flesh," Brigham Young growled.

"Alive," Rockwell agreed, "I'd take 'em."

"Do you know how to operate one of those machines?" Sam asked the mountain man.

"No."

"Then now's not the time," Young decreed, and resettled himself in the wheelhouse.

Sam took the wheel again.

"You've got good timing," he said to Coltrane. "You'd be a good mate on a steam-truck."

"Yeah?" The dwarf kept running his eyes around the streets, expressing a nervousness Sam felt.

Sam released the brake and the *Jim Smiley* rolled forward. "I might be looking for a mate after this is all over."

"You're the second steam-truck man to offer me a job tonight." Coltrane scratched the stubble on his jaw. "I ain't used to this much favorable attention."

"Would it feel more comfortable if I rode you out of town on a rail first?" Sam quipped, turning the truck back in the direction of the Beehive House. "I could demand a bribe, shut you down anyway, rough you up, and then warn you never to come back. Would that make you feel at home?"

Coltrane chuckled. "Yeah, it would. You ever worked as a carny, Clemens?"

"Call me Sam. No, my heart was always on the river. But I've never turned down a good show and it's hard to get a better show than a carnival." He sucked at a cigar and offered another to the short man. "Just have to avoid the gaffed games. Of course, even the rigged games are part of the show."

"Damn straight," Coltrane agreed, and took the cigar. "And call me Jed. But I don't figure you for a fellow who gets hoodwinked much."

"I'm certainly a fellow who does his best to avoid it," Sam agreed. "That doesn't stop the hoodwinkers from trying."

The edge of the Beehive House rolled into view and Sam braked the *Jim Smiley*. Shooting continued on the far side of Young's two conjoined houses, but it was more sporadic now. "Is it worth me driving the truck somewhere else to draw off attention?" he asked. "Or hiding it?"

Brigham Young smiled fiercely. He looked an awful lot like a heavier, Yankee version of Richard Burton, Sam thought. Minus the scars on the sides of the head and plus approximately fifty wives. "Not worth it, Mr. Clemens," Young said. "In fifteen minutes we'll have sent our message and it will be too late to stop us. Everyone will know that I'm alive, you're innocent, and John D. Lee is a scoundrel."

"I could drive the *Jim Smiley* across the yard," Sam offered. "Crash it right into the window of the message room."

"There are still men fighting over there," Young said, sounding grumpy even at the suggestion. "This is my house, Clemens, with my family inside. We'll just walk through. If anyone tries to resist, my family will help us. Besides," he hefted a pair of pistols he'd taken from electrocuted cavalrymen, "we're armed."

"Yes, Mr. President," Sam agreed.

They crossed the north lawn of the Beehive House with guns in hand, other than the dwarf, who carried a big vibro-blade, thumb on the switch. A man with a long coat and rifle stood on the porch, and Brigham Young walked straight up to him and leveled both pistols at his chest.

"Welker, isn't it?" he asked.

"President Young!" the man gasped. He was barrel-chested and tall despite short legs and Sam thought he looked like he ate surprisingly well for a man who lived on the frontier. "You're not dead!"

"Are you with me or Lee?" Young asked, cocking his guns. Sam looked around the porch, half-expecting to be spied on. Coltrane must be sharing his suspicions, he thought; the dwarf looked itchy.

Welker promptly turned his rifle around and handed it to Young, stock-first. "I'm your man, President Young," he said. He turned and knocked three times at the door. "Thank God you're back." He opened the door, revealing a parlor lit only dimly by electricks turned down low.

"Not everyone!" Young snapped. He uncocked one pistol, stuck it into the waistband of his pants, and handed Welker's rifle back to him. Just in case, Sam cocked his own guns and kept an eye on the guard.

Welker nodded and stepped aside, and Young stomped into his home. Rockwell snatched back Welker's gun and pushed himself into the man's face.

"You're coming with us," he growled. Welker backed away, nodded, and followed Brigham Young.

The chairs and sofas in the parlor were very nice, and the room was empty of life.

"Why did you knock, Welker?" Sam asked. "Everyone's asleep."

Welker hesitated, then shrugged. "Manners," he said. "It isn't my house."

"People knock on doors before entering in the Kingdom of Deseret, Mr. Clemens," Young growled. "For my bodyguards, it's protocol."

"Yes, but he didn't enter, did he?" Sam pointed out. "And this is your house, isn't it, Mr. President?"

"In ten minutes it won't matter," Young said, barreling through the parlor and down a long hall. "In ten minutes they'll be able to shoot me dead and it still won't matter. Lee will be held accountable and the Kingdom will avoid entering this ridiculous war."

The long hall was lined with doors, all of them shut. Sam wondered what time it was and guessed the hour must be nearing six in the morning. If this were a farm, everyone would be up by now.

One door opened in the hall, directly in front of them, and a young woman appeared in it. She wore a long white nightgown that covered everything but her head and hands, but Sam still blushed and looked away, out of habit.

"Father!" the young woman gasped, and threw herself on the gruff President's arm.

"Get inside your room, Elizabeth," he harrumphed at her.

"But …"

"I'll explain at breakfast."

She looked at Sam Clemens and Welker and Rockwell and the midget Coltrane and their bristling guns, and hesitated. She was a slightly-better-than-plain-looking girl, Sam thought, strong enough to be some frontiersman's wife, and fair enough to have her pick of such rough men. Here she'd probably end up as one of a trio of girls on the elbow of some toothless, doddering old fart. She met his gaze and he blushed again and looked away, feeling vaguely embarrassed.

"Do you need help, father?" Elizabeth asked.

"The day I need help from one of my daughters," Young snapped, "is a dark day indeed for the Kingdom of Deseret!"

He moved on, Sam followed, and they left Elizabeth behind them.

They passed a window and then another, looking out onto the orchard between Young's houses and the Tabernacle, and then Coltrane tagged at Sam's sleeve. "Something's wrong," he muttered.

Sam looked out at the orchard. Other than the flare of gunshots off to the left, by the Mercantile, it was still and quiet, but for a faint wheezing and pumping sound. "Those glass bells," he agreed. "The pumps, or whatever they are. They're still working. Should they be stopped for the night?"

"I ain't sure that matters, but I figure it might."

"I think they might be pneumatics," Sam pondered.

"I ain't sure," Coltrane scratched his head slowly, "but I reckon you must mean either rheumatic, or pneumon ... pneumonic? Pneumoneristic? You mean they're sick? There's something wrong with them?"

"I mean they're pumps to create pressure. I think it's good they're still going, because the message system will work."

"I don't trust Welker."

"I don't either." Sam considered. "Don't take this the wrong way, Jed, but I calculate that you might be a touch more inconspicuous than I would be, if you were to go missing from the party here."

"Is there a *right* way to take that?" Coltrane grinned. "But I agree."

The dwarf jogged back down the hall the way they had come and disappeared. Sam hurried and caught up to the others. They were in the Lion House end of the two buildings, now, by the crenellated entrance through which Sam had originally come. Shattered windows and bullets in the plaster of the walls bore witness to the Third Virginia's using the room in their gun battle. Outside, gunfire still flashed and shoes echoed.

Young hammered at the door of George Cannon's communication room with the butt of one pistol.

"Go away!" called a voice, faint through the door.

"Is that Lindemuth?" Young roared. "Open up, you maggot!"

"Is that...? Who's there?" Lindemuth called, the door still shut.

"Open up!" Young bellowed. "Or I'll seal you for time and all eternity to every fat, man-hating shrew in the Kingdom!"

"President Young?"

"I'll seal you to a man, Lindemuth! I'll kill two birds with one stone and seal you to John Lee himself!"

Sam elbowed his way past Welker and Rockwell and raised one of his pistols. "With all due respect, Mr. President, I worry we may not be able to wait."

Bang!

The action of the pistol felt alien in Sam's hand, but the resulting progress was satisfying. Sam's bullet blew both the lock and doorknob off the door and kicked the door open, revealing a thin man in suspenders and a knotted tie cowering at the message table. Behind him gleamed the brass trap doors over the bank of circular glass cubbyholes that Sam remembered from only the day before.

Young glared at Sam fiercely. "Thank you," he said, without softening his expression. He turned and barreled through the door. "Lindemuth!" he barked. "Pens and ink and a stack of blank message slips!"

The clerk scurried to comply and Young shoved aside papers on the room's central table, clearing the entire space.

"I trust you gentlemen all know how to write?" Young asked, shrugging out of his jacket and rolling up his sleeves.

"So long as the writing's short," Rockwell said.

"I'd have said the same," Sam agreed. "But it would have been funnier."

"'*I am alive and John Lee is a traitor*'," Young dictated. "I trust that's short enough." He grabbed a pen and bottle of ink and stationed himself at the end of the table. "I will sign my name to each. Lindemuth will shove them into the message transmitter as fast as we can create them."

CHAPTER EIGHTEEN

Jed Coltrane slipped out a window. It was easier than trying to find a door; he just tipped up a big pane and crouched in it like a gargoyle for a minute, checking his exit route. Outside the Lion House, or the Beehive House, whichever it was he was now leaving, a man in a long coat paced in the bushes, rifle in both hands. He looked too alert to be a casual sentry—the man had obviously been warned to expect something.

Jed's uneasy sense that he was playing a gaffed game ratcheted up a notch. He was in deep shadow, invisible to the guard (who was watching for people breaking in, anyway, and not for people trying to break out), so he waited.

When the man passed, Jed jumped onto his back with the piano wire looped between his fists.

The man fired his rifle twice, but he couldn't get it swiveled around tightly enough to get a good shot at Jed. The sound of his shots was lost in the general firefight noise, and then he was collapsing on the green grass, unconscious.

You really ought to cut the bastard's throat, Coltrane, Jed told himself, but hell, the guy might have family, so he didn't. He put the wire back into his pocket and crept out into the park to reconnoiter. The bellows inside the glass bells still pumped up and down, but unlike in the daytime, nothing whizzed through the glass tubes overhead. He wondered what the bellows did—maybe they circulated the air inside the Tabernacle or powered the electricks? Poe would have a good guess.

Of course, if he kept coughing up blood like he had been last time Jed had seen him, Poe might not live long enough to ever see the bellows.

The area outside Brigham Young's twin houses was well lit by a series of Franklin Poles running up South Tabernacle and North Tabernacle, as well as Poles dotting the open park space. Ahead of Jed was the Tabernacle, the gigantic plascrete egg that seemed to be the center of the Kingdom of Deseret. Faint lights shone through its glass doors, lights that flickered a bit, if Jed was not mistaken, and were yellow. It was almost like the enormous building might be on fire.

Off to his left, Jed saw the *ZIONS COOPERATIVE MERCANTILE INSTITUTE* building and the gunfight that enveloped it. Men in gray on clocksprung horses were leaping in through the front doors and windows now, shattering glass and splintering wood as they went. He didn't see any of the Massachusetts soldiers in blue, and guessed they must be running away, out the back doors of the building.

If they weren't being outright massacred on the inside.

Jed felt very nervous, and armed himself with the vibro-blade. He didn't know how much of a charge the weapon's electricks carried, but as long as the juice lasted he'd be able to cut through just about anything.

To his right, where North Tabernacle Street crossed along the edge of the glass bellows park, the *Jim Smiley* idled on the grass, in the shadow of a couple of big cottonwoods. Her lights were all off but Jed knew just where to look and could make out a wispy plume of steam and smoke trickling out through the trees' interlaced leaves. It was like some kind of Indian trick Clemens had pulled, making sure the truck's vapors were sifted by leaves before they went up into the open sky, and Jed admired him for it. It might not be a bad life, being mate aboard the *Jim Smiley*.

Clocksprung horses moved into view. Six … seven … eight of them, Jed counted, and there were real live horses, too, and men mounted on them. They passed the *Jim Smiley*, without seeming to notice the big steam-truck, and trotted to the first of the glass bells.

One of the men on horseback raised his arm, and the clocksprung riders urged their mounts forward—

—*Crash! Crash! Crash!*—

—shattering the bells.

"Jebus," Jed muttered. He crept through the trees along the side of the Beehive House for a better look. Why were the soldiers and Danites (if that's who the other men were, but hell, every man he met seemed to be one) smashing up the bellows? They did it roughly, too, not like rousties sloughing the show to move on to the next town, but like cops letting you know that you hadn't paid them enough and you'd reach a little bit deeper into your kitty if you wanted to play in their town.

Jed growled involuntarily and tightened his grip on the Colt vibro-blade.

Without meaning to, he realized he had come all the way to the side of the *Jim Smiley*. He hadn't meant to—he'd intended to creep back the other way, to watch what happened to Sam Clemens and the others, make sure they weren't walking into an ambush—but the action had been irresistible.

He turned to head back the other way and across the park, the Tabernacle's doors burst open.

Three figures stumbled out, drawing with them huge puffing clouds of smoke and the orange tongues of hungry fire. From the top hat of the central silhouette, the poofy skirt of the one on the right, and the queer Striderman getup of the third, Jed immediately recognized Absalom Fearnley-Standish and his angels. The Strider gunner (he could tell her body from Ortiz's a mile away) carried a bundle of bulky things in her arms, like short poles.

"What happened to the Strider, then?" he muttered to himself.

The horsemen in the garden stopped, saw Jed's three allies, and immediately opened fire. Clutching his hat, Fearnley-Standish turned and dashed back into the burning building, coattails flapping. He and the two women hid inside the door, drew pistols, and began firing out. The horsemen took cover, behind park benches, trees, and the clocksprung horses themselves.

Jed looked left, to where he knew Sam Clemens and the others had gone. Who knew what was happening to them now? Jed had basically abandoned his post, and they might be prisoners or dead.

On the other hand, maybe Welker was totally trustworthy and they were just fine. The fact that he and Sam Clemens had had the same hunch didn't mean the hunch was correct. Young had been confident in Welker and confident that he was about to get his message out and turn the tables on the Danite insurrection. And if someone didn't step in to help Absalom Fearnley-Standish and the two women pronto, they would be roasted alive or pumped full of lead.

Jed climbed the ladder of the *Jim Smiley*, up over the huge India rubber skirt, across the metal deck, and onto the rubber matting on the floor of the wheelhouse. He had watched Clemens operate the machine, and it had been no big deal—gear, wheel, and brake, Jed could manage. And he knew the furnace was full of coal.

Jed sighted down over the front of the steam-truck at the fifteen or so men whose backs were turned to him, shooting at his allies. He needed a way to get them all, or as many as he possibly could, and hand-to-hand fighting was not going to do the trick, not even with his Colt blade.

But the *Jim Smiley* might—Jed started to laugh when he saw that Sam had left in its place the lightning bolt key, the one that had activated the steam-truck's defensive electricks. Jed flicked on the lightning bolt switch, electrifying the vehicle. Sparks *crackzed* off the deck and hull of the craft where stray hanging Cottonwood branches touched it, and one of the trees caught fire. Jed released the brake, shifted the steam-truck into gear, and rolled forward.

The horses, the flesh and blood ones, saw him coming first. Two of them yanked up their pickets and bolted before any of the Danites or the Third Virginia heard the clank-and-hiss of Sam Clemens's truck and turned around.

And then it was too late.

Bang! Bang!

Crash!

Crack-ckz-ckz-ckz-ckz-ckz-ckz!

Bullets smashed out windows of the *Jim Smiley*'s wheelhouse, banged off her metal hull and sank into her heavy rubber. Jed stayed low—easy enough—looking over the control panel of the steam-truck just enough to be able to steer at the thickest knots of Danites and cavalrymen he could find.

Men threw themselves on the *Jim Smiley*'s ladders and shrieked in pain as they were flung off again, electrocuted. The craft's ponderous tyres rolled over man and machine alike, crushing clocksprung horses into their component parts and simultaneously turning them into lethal transmitters of the steam-truck's deadly lightning currents. The heavy rubber reduced hollering, struggling men into smears of goo on the grass. The air reeked of ozone and blood and smoke, gunpowder and otherwise, and the night rang with the screams of men and horses.

Just as Jed wondered how long the electricks would hold out, he heard an enormous *SNAP!* and the crackling sound that told him the deck was electrified ended. He spun the wheel, aiming for a cluster of four men who fired at him with rifles and pistols, and then he turned and ran.

Across the deck he pelted, looking for targets—

—bullets cut the air around him.

Jed saw two men, one mounted on a clocksprung horse and the other trying to mount up. He thumbed the vibro-blade's switch to *on* and hurled himself through the air.

Hummmmmmmm, sang Sam Colt's deadly blade.

Jed landed in the empty saddle of one of the horses. While the man whose mount he'd boarded cursed and reached for a pistol, Jed swung the vibro-blade in a neat arc—

—slicing through the head of the other horse—

—and cutting off one leg of its rider.

Jed wasn't used to fighting with knives that met no resistance and his own momentum pulled him forward and off the horse. He scrabbled with his free hand at the sculpted metal saddle horn and missed, tumbling to the ground and narrowly avoiding impaling himself on the humming weapon.

The mutilated rider screamed and fell backwards onto the ground in a spout of red blood. His horse kicked aimlessly with its back feet, then kicked again, and again, trampling its own severed head with its razor-sharp metallic front hooves. Jed rolled, narrowly avoided being crushed by the clocksprung horse, and then the other cavalryman got a bead on him with his pistol and started firing.

Bang! Bang!

Jed threw the vibro-blade. It wasn't meant to be a throwing weapon, it wasn't especially balanced and it wasn't weighted in the tip. But Jed was a carny who had done his time at every conceivable kind of joint, including throwing knives at beautiful girls, and Jed knew the secret of throwing any sort of knife at all, even one that would chop your finger off if you so much as touched its tip.

He threw the vibro-blade by the handle, overhand, so the blade launched out from his shoulder in a straight line, and not tumbling like a weighted knife. He let his extended index finger drag along the knife's hilt as he threw, truing up his aim at the center of the cavalryman's chest by simply pointing at him.

Bang!

Pain lanced through Jed Coltrane as a bullet hit him in the stomach.

Fhoomp!

The vibro-blade slammed straight into the center of the man's gray-breasted uniform, punched a hole right through his entire chest, and hurtled straight away like a perfectly pitched baseball, into the air.

"Aaaagh!" One-Leg kept screaming, thrashing around in a growing puddle of his own arterial spray.

The standing soldier dropped his pistol, stared down at the bloody hole in the middle of his chest, looked at Jed with an expression that was half-accusation and half-puzzlement and then toppled forward, crashing face-first into the grass.

"Aaaagh!"

Jed grabbed the dropped pistol and turned on One-Leg.

"Shut up!" he yelled, and put the man out of his misery.

He almost vomited from the pain, and looked at his own belly. Black blood soaked into his shirt from a neat little bullet hole. Jed probed around his side and back and couldn't find an exit wound. *The bullet's still inside you, Coltrane, you idiot,* he thought. *Not that it matters, because as soon as they can recover a teaspoon's worth of organization, these boys'll jump on you and cut you down.*

Jed cocked his borrowed pistol again and turned to face whatever he had coming.

But the wave of attacking soldiers he expected didn't materialize. Instead, through blurring vision, he saw men in gray running away and men in long coats chasing down skittish, fleeing horses. And Absalom Fearnley-Standish, scalloped hat on his head and pistol held high, charging in silhouette out of the inferno of the Tabernacle with an angel to each side of him, blasting at the few holdouts among the Virginians and the Danites and driving them away. Behind them, grinding in the opposite direction and plunging into the wall of flames, went the *Jim Smiley*.

"Thanks, old girl," he mumbled a farewell. The beheaded clocksprung horse finally wound down and toppled over, and Jed sat down on its flank, holding one hand over his wound. The sweat on his forehead felt cold and clammy even though the fire in the Tabernacle rose higher, flames exploding out the balconies and windows of the upper stories.

Absalom and the two women found him there a minute later. They looked concerned. He felt like he was seeing them through water, slow and distorted and slightly out of their true positions.

"Thack you, Mr. Coltrade," the Englishman said, doffing his hat and making a slight bow. "I believe you saved our lives."

"Eh," Jed grunted. "I'm gonna need a doctor."

� ꓴꓷ

Poe's machine led the way (and wasn't there something perfect and poetic about that, an ultra-advanced machine that was shaped like some kind of ancient Egyptian monster, and all the human beings enslaved to it?), bounding up plascrete corridors and tearing to shreds the Pinkertons that got in its way.

That turned out to be an awful lot of Pinkertons. Their deaths, by claw and fang and sheer pounding mass of bloody-damn-hell steel, cheered Tam's heart considerably. He still felt sick.

Poe stalked along in the Typhonian Animal's wake, grim as death, alternating inaudible toots on his whistle and wet, sucking coughs by which he smeared the foul and nauseating contents of his chest on the floors and walls of Orson Pratt's facility.

Roxie stalked at his right side, a pistol in each hand (But hadn't the scattergun been a work of art, for the two shots it provided? And after she'd killed one man and winged another, Tam had been more than happy to finish off the wounded fellow with a knife to the belly.), and Burton marched at his left.

Tam followed in the back. It gave him a good view of the carnage ahead of him and when he stopped to retch, belly empty and aching and lungs burning like fire, which he did every few minutes, he could do it without being stared at. Also, following at a distance let him use his sharp ears to good effect, to hear the *creak* when a fat-eyed Pinkerton opened a door to try to get the drop on him—

—Bang!—

Tam sent the man to the hell he deserved.

Or the soft squish and slap of shoe leather as men crowded in waiting down a side passage—

—Bang! Bang! Snick!

—and Tam added three more widows to the rosters of the beneficiaries of the Pinkertons' pension and insurance fund.

Abruptly, he caught up to the others. They had stopped in an open area not quite expansive enough to be a room, arguing. They stood beside another lift door, with its brass and glass panels and its accordion gate and beside that a plascrete door labeled *STAIRS*.

"If we get onto the lift again, we trap ourselves." Burton's voice was as hard as a punch to the jaw. "We did that before, and played right into their hands."

"You said no more fookin' stairs!"

"And going up the stairs doesn't trap us?" Roxie demanded. "Do you imagine there are exits halfway up the tower, if we need them?"

Tam heard the *click* and *shuffle* of boot heels on the plascrete behind him, and turned in time to plug another bloody-damn-hell Pinkerton twice with the Model 1.

"I imagine," Burton snarled, "that even if we find ourselves surrounded, in the stairwell we'll have a fighting chance. No one will be able to simply cut the rope and drop us to our deaths!"

Tam shuffled wearily to the Pinkerton and took his pistol, shoving it into his coat pocket with the others he'd taken from dead men in the last few minutes and then sliding more brass-jacketed cartridges into the Smith & Wesson. He liked the Model 1, maybe even more than he had liked the Hushers. It reloaded much easier and sometimes, like this evening, killing was a game of volume.

"Can he even *make it* up the stairs?" Roxie shouted, waving at Edgar Allan Poe. She had a point there, Tam thought, and besides, he was puking up his own guts—from the altitude or the injuries or the alcohol, whichever it was he didn't care—and the thought of climbing the mooring tower up to the airships on foot didn't appeal to him.

For that matter, he wasn't entirely sure he wanted to go to the mooring tower at all. Why not go down, get a truck, and get the hell out of Deseret? Go to bloody-damn-hell California, rob Californian banks of their queer rectangular dollars and look for the easy life? But he looked at Poe, dying on his feet, and Burton, shot all to hell and still fighting for his precious chubby Queen, and Roxie, who'd seduced two different men to come to the aid of her husband (and did a woman ever look finer than when she had a pistol in each hand and blood in her eye?), and found that he couldn't walk away.

"Shite."

D.J. Butler

He pressed the lift's lever from NO CALL to UP.

No sound, no motion.

"Damn!" Roxie shouted.

"It doesn't fookin' matter, does it?" Tam pointed out. "The lift's dead. We're walking."

He dragged open the plascrete door.

Poe nodded, wiped blood off his lips and blew into the silent whistle. With a click and a clatter of metal nails on the hard floor, the Seth-Beast pushed past Tam and crashed up the stairs.

"Come on, then," Tam said, and he offered his shoulder to Poe.

"Thanks." Poe's voice was a gravelly whisper. Together, they limped up the stairs.

Bang! Bang!

Burton and Roxie fired at enemies Tam couldn't see before slamming the door shut.

"You know," Tam grunted, Poe heavy on his arm, "that pony-dog thing's so big, if you called it back here, I could sling you over its shoulders and you could just *ride* up to the top of the tower."

Poe shook his head, spat a squirt of blood onto the floor like bright red tobacco juice, and kept climbing. "We need it to go first," he said slowly.

Like an exclamation mark to the dying man's words, a door slammed at the top of the stairs and then screaming began.

"Right you are," Tam agreed, and did his best to pick up the pace. He hurt and hefting the American slowed him down, but Mother O'Shaughnessy hadn't raised any quitters.

"Here," Burton said gruffly, "let me help." The Englishman shoved himself under Poe's other shoulder and together they hauled the American right off his feet. Tam still hurt like hell and the going was still slow.

"Brigit's secret belly," Tam chortled, "aren't we a pretty choir of angels, all of us dying and just trying to get across the finish line before we do?"

"Speak for yourself," Richard Burton grunted.

"But really," Tam said, "you did promise me no more stairs."

"Or better still," Roxie suggested, "shut up."

The stairs climbed back and forth in a regular Z-shaped pattern. The interior of the stairwell was dimly lit by a small electricks globe at each landing but it was enough glow to walk by. It was enough light to shoot by, too, at least for Roxie, who brought up the rear with her two pistols. Once they reached the second landing, Tam heard the door below open and the whisper of men plotting against them.

"Pinkertons," he said softly, and before he had closed his mouth on the end of the foul word, Roxie stood at the stair's banister and was firing down into the well.

She kept a steady pressure on the men behind them and when her pistols ran dry Tam mutely dug two more out of his pockets and handed them to her.

"This really isn't my strong suit," she observed, taking them.

"No?" Burton sweated under their shared burden, and left a spattered trail of his own blood on the plascrete behind him. "Perhaps you can go down and offer the gentlemen a doctored drink."

"I thought I might seduce them," she countered. "Men are so easy that way." *Bang! Bang!* "I think it's because of their boundless vanity."

The air inside the stairwell, thick and artificial to begin with, stank acridly of fired bullets, blood, bile, phlegm, and sweat. It was half the reek of a hospital and half the airborne ordure of battle.

"Is it vanity, woman?" Burton snarled. "Or pride in accomplishment? Men brewed beer, tamed the horse, captured fire from heaven, built the pyramids, learned to sail the oceans, invented writing, music, theater, dance, government, and philosophy, and discovered mathematics. Maybe men have something to say for themselves, after all."

Roxie laughed, a light, almost frivolous sound that was given a murderous edge to it by the gunshot punctuation she rained down on the following Pinkertons. *Bang!* "Why, Captain Burton," she fluttered, "you make it sound like all those accomplishments belonged to a single fellow!"

"A single man may accomplish many great things!" Burton nearly shouted with the effort. Tam willed him to shut his mouth and keep carrying his half of the American but he wasn't about to open his mouth and say anything out loud, for fear of getting shot by the irate explorer. "Think of Newton! Or your own Benjamin Franklin! Or Alexander the Great, by Ravana's ten heads!"

"And what each of those men has in common," Roxie pointed out, *bang! Bang!*, "is that a woman gave birth to him."

"Not without the help of another man, she didn't!"

"True," she agreed, "but a paltry, sad kind of help, five minutes of sweat for which the man no doubt patted himself on the back forever after."

Burton growled and pushed harder up the stairs.

At the top of the stairs bright blue light flooded in through an open door mixed with the sounds of gunfire and angry yelling. "Hold him," Tam muttered to Burton, and shoved Poe entirely onto the Englishman before getting a reply. As much as anything else, Tam wanted a breath of cold air that didn't smell of plascrete and bodily fluids. He shoved his head around the corner into the cool light recklessly, though he made sure to poke out the Smith & Wesson Model 1 at the same time.

He saw the top of the mooring tower. It was a great flat space, a square, and above each of the four corners of the platform floated one

D.J. Butler

of the strange, Viking-like airships, tethered by a metal pole jutting up from the tower's corner and inserted below the prow of the ship. They were stuck to the tower by pins through their tails, as if they were gigantic bugs in some naturalist's collection. Blue bolts of lightning ran up and down the bits and crackling ozone mixed into the compound stink that already blocked Tam's nostrils. More electricity jolted and snapped about the edges of the platform and Tam remembered the lightning rods he and Burton had seen climbing up the outside of the tower. Rope ladders dangled from the hind end of each ship. One of the four ladders was anchored to a big iron mooring ring at the nearest corner of the platform but the others dangled free. The names of the ships were painted on the side in that Mormon gibberish-writing, just like the name of the *Liahona* was.

Lightning flashed from the tops of all four anchor poles towards the center of the space above the tower, like interlocked fingers or a great bloody-damn-hell spider's web of electricity. Noticing it, Tam flinched and tightened his grip on the Model 1. *You stupid bloody idjit,* he told himself. *As if you're going to shoot the lightning.* He felt the hair on the back of his neck and head both stand straight up and he screwed his porkpie hat on a little tighter, in a vain attempt to tamp it back down.

In the center of the mooring platform was a plascrete shed; Franklin Poles at its corners cast bluish light over the platform, though the area was lit much more by the wild electricity snapping free through the air than by the domesticated shining of the Poles.

Seven or eight men huddled inside the little building and fought through its doors and windows the steel-gleaming, four-legged mock-Egyptian apparition of death that stalked them. With sticks and knives and guns they fired at it, but it was winning—the bodies of as many men lay torn and broken on the floor, and as Tam looked, the Seth-Beast shoved its head and forequarters through a window, shattering iron shutters into scrap and removing the head of a screaming Pinkerton in a single bite. Bullets fired by the Pinkertons streaked and sparked harmlessly off its armored flanks.

"Fookin' hell," he called back to Edgar Allan Poe. "It's eerie how that thing of yours doesn't make a noise, even while it's chewing men to pieces."

"You'd prefer it to say *woof,* I suppose?"

"I'd prefer it to do *something,* is all I'm saying. Besides generate minced Pinkerton, I mean. Not that I object to the mincing at all."

"Yes, well," Poe mumbled dryly, "I promise to take your criticism to Mr. Hunley next time I see him, though I can't make any representations about the likelihood or imminence of that possibility." He spat a quid of thick blood against the wall.

Bang! Bang!

"If you're quite finished chatting," Roxie snapped, "we're about to have company by the tradesmen's entrance."

"Hell and begorra!" Tam shouted, and pointed with his Model 1. The others crowded into the stairwell exit with him and looked. The airships, all of them, were sliding up the metal antennae that rooted them to the tower.

No, not all of them. Three of them, and they gave the impression of being pushed free of the tower and into space by the electricity itself. The fourth, the ship nearest the lift and stairwell exits, almost behind them, did a queer little St. Vitus' dance of a rattling motion, shaking against its anchor pole but not pulling free of it.

Then one of the three departing ships reversed course and sank back down toward the platform. "That's Pratt!" Roxie shouted, and Tam saw the frayed old man standing against the airship's railing with one of the big Pinkertons. The old fellow shouted at the Pinkertons on the platform, they shouted back, and Tam couldn't hear any of their words over the crackle of the electricity.

But he saw that Pratt's companion was carrying a queer-looking gun. *Bang! Bang!*

A bullet snapped past the Irishman and into the open night air like a rocket-powered mosquito. Behind Tam, Roxie fired into the stairwell and the muzzle flash stuttered white in the corner of his vision.

"Go!" she shouted. "Out!"

Poe blew silently on his whistle and lurched out onto the platform, leaning on Tam (though Tam hadn't really invited that again, had he?) and Burton both. He reeked of illness and death. Pratt's ship touched down and the big man next to him dropped onto the platform, gun held high. It was that damned man from the Deseret Hotel, Herman or Hardison or whatever his name was.

"Duck!" Tam yelled, but the Pinkerton wasn't aiming at them.

Poe blew—

—the Seth-Beast wheeled away from its assault on the Pinkertons in the center shed and charged the big man—

—*Zottt!*—

—a bright red ray lanced through the center of the mechanical animal-thing, slicing it into two pieces in a single shot. As if a magnetic force holding together a box of springs had suddenly been shut off, the creature sprang to pieces, bits rolling and rattling away across the plascrete.

Poe dropped the whistle from his mouth and yelled something high, strangled and wordless, a cry like a paid mourner's that ended in a strangled cough. The man with the ray-gun heard him, stopped and looked in their direction. Pratt heard too, looked up at them, and then disappeared from the airship's railing.

Herbertson, or whetever, looked up for Pratt, didn't apparently see him, then turned and advanced on Tam and the others.

"Get into the other ship!" Burton barked, and began shooting at the Pinkerton.

"It isn't flying for a reason," Roxie protested. "There's no point."

"It should have phlogiston guns," Poe coughed. "At least we can fire at the others."

"England!" Burton yelled, and charged left across the platform, shooting at Harrison.

"Shite!" Tam cursed, and then ran right, firing his Smith & Wesson at the Pinkerton. He'd never charged to a war cry before in his life.

It was satisfying.

Behind him he heard shooting and he looked over his shoulder as he ran, to see Roxie emptying a pistol into the stairwell and then dragging the pale, sweating, trembling, bent Edgar Allan Poe, hacking his lungs up at every step, toward the fourth airship.

ꓕƐ𐐷ꓧⓆᴎꓛƐ

At the sound of footsteps in the doorway Sam grabbed his pistol.

It was George Q. Cannon, the stubble on his fleshy jaw taking some of the punch out of his square beard. He was in his shirtsleeves, suspenders askew and the tail of his shirt hanging down over the seat of his britches. The short hair he had was pulled this way and that, like a haystack after a dry storm.

"George!" Young snapped, finishing another scrawled signature and setting aside the finished message into the stack with the others, a dozen already completed by the impromptu communiqué production line, the ink still drying on the first ones.

"What's going on?" Cannon asked. "Where have you been? We ... I thought you were dead!"

"I would have been, too, if Bill Hickman had an ounce of integrity!" Brigham Young snorted.

"I don't understand." Cannon's eyes narrowed. "Was Hickman part of the plot against you? Did Bill Hickman kidnap you? Is he in league with the Massachusetts men?"

"Massachusetts men?" Young laughed, a sound like rolling thunder. "Heavens no, George, the Massachusetts men have nothing to do with the plotting against the Kingdom! It was John Lee who ordered my killing, and Hickman was to have done it!"

All the talk of killing and plots made Sam nervous, especially since the gunfire outside continued unabated. "Only Hickman gaffed the game in his own favor," he offered, and then realized that his whispered conversations with the dwarf Coltrane had lured him into carny slang. "I mean, he was playing his own game against Lee," he explained. "He held us hostage as chips to play when he made his own demands."

Where was Coltrane, anyway?

"And by the grace of God you escaped Hickman," George Cannon said. His accent sounded wrong when he looked this rumpled, Sam decided. The Liverpudlian tones went better with a starched collar and necktie.

"Exactly!" Young snapped out another signature.

"Well," Sam reckoned, "exactly how much God has to do with our escape has been a subject of some discussion."

"Mr. Clemens is a skeptic," Young snorted, "and a cynic. He's a thoroughly modern man, George, you'd like him."

"I'm only as skeptical as the facts force me to be," Sam said in his defense. "It tells a sad truth about our universe that I find the facts generally compel me to be a misanthrope."

"Get over here and operate this machine of yours, George, you and Lindemuth both," Young barked, signing another slip. "You know I was never any good with Orson's devices."

Cannon walked around the table, looking at the message slips being written. *John D. Lee is a traitor,* Sam printed carefully, making sure to use his best legible copperplate hand—who knew who was going to have to read these messages and just how literate they would be? He blew on the slip and set it beside the others awaiting signature.

"No, your gifts have always been the classic ones," George Cannon agreed. "You've inspired the hearts and minds of men, and sometimes known them, but this age of steam-powered machinery and electricks is a bit beyond you. You'd have been a good Nephite, Brother Brigham, or a good Hebrew patriarch, or a good Spartan, even."

"Are you saying I'm not a good Mormon?" Young growled, inadvertently crumpling a message slip in his hand. "That I'm old-fashioned, a relic?" He held the pen in his hand like a dagger.

George Cannon stood by the wall of cylindrical message tubes and rubbed his fingers over a series of brass hatches. "Not really a man of the nineteenth century, perhaps," he admitted. "That's not entirely a bad thing."

"Only a fool focuses on his own century!" Young gnashed his teeth. "God's work is eternal, the prize is eternal, a life and all things that make one eternal round, George! Why should I care about steam-trucks and message tubes and … and …" his eye roved the room looking for other examples, "fornication pants, when God has commanded me to focus on the eternal salvation and progression of his family!"

"Are they so incompatible, Brigham?"

"Load the machine!" Young shouted, red in the face, and he thrust a handful of slips at Cannon. "Stake Presidents first!"

Cannon dutifully put each slip into a canister and loaded a series of message tubes, chosen apparently at random from the gleaming bank.

"Help me understand, Brigham," George Cannon continued. "Why are you so convinced that a man can't drive a steam-truck and wear Levi-Strauss's trousers and still be in God's good graces?"

"Let's not get too personal," Sam objected. He wrote again that Brigham Young was alive and John D. Lee was a traitor.

"Distractions!" Young huffed. "Temptations! The frivolities of this world, the putting of pleasure and convenience before the daily necessities of prayer, introspection and obedience to the commandments of God!"

"A man can be tempted to fornication no matter what pants he's wearing, Brigham." Cannon smiled the smile of a salon wit. "He's probably worst tempted when he's wearing no pants at all."

"You've seen England!" Young raged. "You've seen the United States, damn it all! Do you really believe that those societies live the way God wants His children to live? In squalor and desperation and sin and pollution of every kind, cutting each other's throats and stealing each other's virtue?"

"England isn't perfect," Cannon admitted, closing the brass doors almost, but not quite all the way. "Neither are the United States, nor the Southern states that feel bullied by the North and want to secede. Nor is the Kingdom of Deseret."

"Not yet!" Young snarled. "But we will perfect the Saints, in time! That's God's work, to bring about our immortality and eternal life, and I thought you were my fellow-worker, George!"

"Have you considered the possibility," George Cannon said mildly, "that John D. Lee's uprising was not an attack against the Kingdom, but only against yourself?"

"What are you talking about?" Young asked.

Sam's heart sank. *Where was Coltrane?* He tried to keep his eyes from jumping to the room's windows. The gunfire outside seemed to be dying down now, and even that felt ominous to him.

"Have you considered the possibility that Lee might not be alone?" Cannon continued. "That there might be others, a sizable group of men, even, who worry that your leadership, inspired as it may have been in the past, may be leading the Kingdom of Deseret in the wrong direction?"

"Any man fool enough to reach out his hand to steady the Ark will suffer Uzzah's fate!" Young thundered.

"Instant death?"

"Smitten by the hand of God!"

"Have you considered the possibility that such a movement might have a leader and it might not even be John D. Lee?"

"Send the messages!" Young shouted. The President of the Kingdom of Deseret grabbed a pistol off the table he was working at and pointed it at his clerk, pulling back the hammer with his thumb.

George Cannon shut one of the trapdoors. Sam expected to hear a *hiss* and see the canister inside the tube disappear, but nothing happened.

"Another!" Sam grunted, involuntarily. The President of the Kingdom glared at him, then spun back to Cannon.

"Another!" Brigham Young himself shouted.

George Cannon closed another tube, then another, then another. No *hiss*, no canisters disappeared.

"Are the tubes broken?" Sam asked. He remembered standing with Tamerlane O'Shaughnessy outside the Lion House and watching the network of glass tubes radiating outwards from this office. "The device must work by pressure, right? If any of those tubes is broken, it might stop the cylinder from going through. Try a different tube."

"Try a different tube!" Young waved his pistol around vaguely.

"None of them will work," Cannon said. He was calm, despite the pistol in his face, and Sam had to admire the man. "Don't waste your time."

"*You're* the traitor!" Young bellowed.

Cannon shook his head slowly. "I love the Kingdom," he said, "and I would never betray it. That's why *I* recruited John D. Lee and made him part of my plans to save Deseret."

"Lee!" Young gasped.

Sam felt like a fool.

"That's why I had Lee's men smash up the pneumatic bells in the yard," Cannon added. "When he told me you were alive, I knew you'd have to come here and you'd want to get word out that you were still alive. But until those bells are repaired, no message will get in or out of the Great Salt Lake City, unless it goes by hand."

"Then I'll get them out by hand!" Young shot back. "Like a hundred Paul Reveres in the desert, I'll send out a single Elders Quorum and warn the entire Kingdom in an hour!" Sam wondered if he was bluffing.

"And that's why," Cannon's voice rose higher in pitch and became more nasal. He sounded emotional, like he was coming to the climax of a real stem-winder of a sermon. His body, though, looked relaxed and unthreatening, standing in his shirttails with his arms at his sides. "That's why, I'm afraid, you simply cannot be allowed to leave this room alive, Brother Brigham."

"Ha!" Young roared. He still looked like a lion, towering over the smaller man. Cannon looked neater and more composed than the President, somehow, despite his dishabille. "You're forgetting that I'm the one with the pistol and the armed men at my back!"

"No," Cannon said. "I'm not."

CLICK.

It wasn't one *click* that he heard, really, but a whole series of simultaneous *clicks* that all together were so loud they sounded like an ax sinking into a tree trunk. Sam turned slowly.

John D. Lee, bruised and beaten about the face but holding himself upright with cold fury in his eyes, stood inside the room. He held a cocked pistol in one hand and his other arm hung limp at his side. Five men stood with him, in the room, in the doorway and in the hallway beyond, all with guns aimed at Brigham Young and his companions.

"Lee!" Young roared.

"Drop it, Brigham," Lee drawled slowly, and for the first time Sam could hear a little Virginia in his voice. "Or Welker and Lindemuth get to see the great eternal round before you do."

Lee kept his gun on Young but his men pointed their firearms at the message clerk and the bodyguard.

"Don't do it," Sam said, but he wasn't sure who he was saying it to, or what he meant.

Young gritted his teeth. "Wraaagh!" He tossed his pistol heavily to the ground.

Sam raised his hands, as did Brigham.

"Port," Young said, and his voice was almost gentle.

The shaggy frontiersman stood gripping the table with white knuckles, right beside his two large pistols. An ink-blotched, crumpled message slip in front of him bore the poignant message, scrawled in large, child-like capital letters, *I EM A LYVE. JON LEE IS A SUMBICH SNAYK.*

"It ain't right, Brigham," Rockwell grunted, and shook his long-haired head.

"Porter, do as I say," Brigham Young said.

"No bullet or blade," Rockwell reminded him.

Lee swiveled one of his pistols and pointed it at Welker's head.

"Port!" Welker cried.

"Please," said Brigham Young.

Rockwell gritted his teeth and slowly raised his hands.

"Get their guns," Lee said.

Welker and Lindemuth scooped up all the pistols lying on the table and George Cannon bent to pick up the pistol Young had dropped onto the floor. Then the clerk and the bodyguard stepped away from the table—and turned, pointing their guns at Young, Rockwell, and Sam.

"Dammit!" Rockwell roared.

"You see what I mean about the facts compelling me to misanthropy." Sam joked but he felt sick to his stomach.

"I do indeed," Cannon agreed.

"Can I smoke?" Sam asked. He didn't know what to do but he wanted to buy time, for himself and, if the poor bastard wasn't already dead somewhere or in Danite hands, for Jedediah Coltrane.

"Be my guest."

Sam struck a lucifer on the snaps of his jeans and lit a Partagás from his pocket. He imagined the action as a clever signal to the dwarf that he was in trouble and needed help, needed something like the electrified *Jim Smiley* to come to his rescue. Of course, if the dwarf was watching through the windows and couldn't figure out that all the guns pointed at his head meant that Sam needed help, then he was an idiot and was going to be useless in any case.

He sucked a puff of smoke but it didn't really calm him. "Now what?"

"Now, Mr. Clemens," George Cannon said, "I make you and your government an offer."

Sam was caught off guard. "Me?" was all he managed to spit out.

Cannon nodded. "There's a war coming. Don't you want the Kingdom of Deseret on your side?"

Sam chewed his cigar and tried to think. "Why the change of heart, Mr. Cannon? Only yesterday, I was being framed for a murder so that you could go to war against my government. What happened between then and now?"

"*You won* is what happened, Mr. Clemens. You're here with Brigham Young, and the Southerners and the Englishmen are not. Your craft, the *Jim Smiley*, is an impressive and ultra-modern piece of engineering and it has conquered my heart. And Captain Everett's Virginians, though they remain in the field, have done a surprisingly poor job against the men from Massachusetts, and the Mexicans."

"You don't care whose side you're on," Sam realized.

"Correction," Cannon said. "I don't care whose side I'm on, as long as Deseret is with me and it's the *winning* side."

"You're going to hell!" Rockwell spat on the floor.

"Why, George?" Young asked.

"For Deseret, of course," Cannon explained. His eyes and mouth were earnest, even pious in their expression. "Deseret needs the war and it needs to be on the winning side."

"You're insane," Sam judged. "Nobody needs war, except undertakers."

"You're wrong," Cannon insisted. "*We* need the war. We need a winning ally who will need us, share with us, take us in, and love us, and then after the war, trade and mingle with us. We need to be part of the world, in and of it and not sequestered away in some godforsaken corner like dervishes. The United States drove us out once, but if it is the cost of winning this inevitable war, they will take us in their red, white, and blue arms again. It will be a gain for the United States and it will be a gain for the Kingdom."

"Fool," Young cursed him.

"The modern world is inevitable, Brigham," Cannon told him. "It's already here and knocking at our door. We can't run and we can't hide, and if we fight it we'll be destroyed. We must embrace the world, and it must embrace us."

Sam hesitated. Wasn't Cannon offering him exactly what he'd come here for? With Pratt's airships and the phlogiston guns, whatever war there was would be short. Lives would be saved, the Union would be saved. "President Buchanan's offer to the Kingdom of Deseret is the gift of a transcontinental railroad," he said, "and sundry supporting materials."

"Perfect," Cannon said. "I accept."

The stocky Liverpudlian raised his pistol and pointed it at Brigham Young's head.

"No bullet or blade!" shouted Orrin Porter Rockwell, and leaped.

CHAPTER NINETEEN

he Englishman looked like he'd charged without a second's thought but somehow he'd chosen the right direction. As he sprinted, firing, he moved behind the plascrete shed in the center of the mooring platform. Several of the men inside the shed saw him and began throwing themselves against windows to take aim at Burton, but Harrison's view of him was cut off by the little building—

—which meant that he turned the ray gun against Tam.

Higley, that was the man's name. *What a stupid bloody-damn-hell clodhopper of a name.*

Zottt!

Tam threw himself flat. The plascrete hurt like a giant's fist punching him in the stomach, chest, and chin simultaneously but the phlogiston gun's killer beam missed, turning the air over Tam's head to fire and incinerating the hairs on the back of his neck.

Tam fired back with the Smith & Wesson. His shots were a little wild but he didn't care. He had to give Higley something to think about, force him to dodge just a little or take cover, or Pratt's weapon would make this a very short fight.

He fired and then he rolled sideways, tumbling shoulders-over-elbows and trying to keep the Pinkerton in his sight and his pistol pointed more or less in the other man's direction.

Zottt!

The heat of the killer beam made Tam's face sweat and then sparks exploded above and behind him. Higley stopped shooting and staggered back.

Tam was puzzled but relieved and kept moving. He looked for Burton and saw the man dragging one of the Pinkertons bodily out the window of the shed, punching him in the jaw with the butt of his pistol.

Sparks rained down around Tam and he wondered why. He saw Higley do a little uncertain jig, moving to one side and then the other, and then the Pinkerton turned and broke into a run to his left.

He's hit the lightning rod, Tam thought.

Then: *He's hit the bloody-damn-hell lightning rod!*

Tam scrambled up and into action, galloping right on two legs and a hand, and bringing the Model 1 into play, squeezing off shots at Higley as he ran straight at the man. The imminence of death slowed his perception of time, like honey had been poured over the entire scene, and in Tam's imagination the electric prickle on the nape of neck became the sharp poking of a thousand needles.

Higley raised the ray gun.

Tam squeezed the trigger again and his heart sank as he heard the loud *click*—

—CRASH!!!

The lightning rod smashed into the plascrete floor of the mooring platform like a fallen tree wreathed in St. Elmo's fire. Tam felt something that was part fire, part knives, and part gigantic vibrating tickle in the soles of his feet, and then he was thrown sideways, the rush of electricity tossing him onwards in the direction in which he was already moving, towards the edge of the platform.

Higley flew headlong in the same direction, losing his grip on his weapon.

Tam hit the edge of the platform, grabbed at it, missed—

—and then caught himself with one hand on a metal bar that ran around the outside of the tower, horizontally just beneath the lip of the mooring platform.

The Smith & Wesson left his other hand on impact and disappeared into the darkness below, along with Tam's porkpie hat. Fire raged through the wound in his arm and bile bubbled up through his lips.

"Fookin' Brigit and fookin' Anthony and every other fookin' saint help me now!" Tam squealed, hating himself for the little girl sound that came out of his throat. He spat against the plascrete tower wall and coughed for breath, expecting a ray gun beam to slice him to pieces at any second.

No beam.

He grabbed with his other hand for the bar and steadied himself a little.

Tam's head spun. He hurt, he felt sick, he was exhausted, and he wanted a drink.

You were bloody-damn-hell right, Burton, he thought. *All of the above.*

He snaked up a hand and grabbed the plascrete. It was his uninjured arm so he managed to drag his chin up to the level of the mooring platform for a better look. At least the bar wasn't electrocuting him, he realized with relief. Why was that? Maybe the electricity all came out of the metal when the pole fell, he guessed. Hell if he knew.

All four airships were gone now. The Franklin Poles had gone dead and Tam realized that he could still see because the sky was beginning to gray over with the coming of morning. The shed in the center of the platform was quiet and he saw that the lightning rod, when it had hit the plascrete, had smashed into the wall of the shed, too. He wondered if Burton and the Pinkertons inside were dead.

Higley wasn't dead, though. He stirred, brushing at his face like he dreamed of being caught in a swarm of flies. The Pinkerton groaned.

Pratt's ray gun lay on the plascrete, halfway between Tam and Higley. Its gaping muzzle, grossly oversized by comparison with any normal firearm, stared at Tam like a viper. It looked ready to bite (but wasn't any gun a biting beastie, and the trick was to be on the tail side, and not get the fangs?).

"Hell and begorra." Tam spat bile out of his mouth and tried to dig his good elbow into the plascrete. It took several tries because, with the vertigo that twisted his vision all around every time he tried to focus on anything, he kept slipping and missing his mark. The fact that his toes dangled over an abyss that, as he could see out of the corner of his eye, might as well be bottomless, didn't help. As he finally got the elbow firmly planted and hoisted himself with a sharp cry of pain up onto it, he heard a louder groan from Higley.

The Pinkerton propped himself up on one forearm and shook his head.

Anthony's teeth! Tam clawed at the plascrete with his nails like a dog, trying to drag himself forward faster. The hiss of his breath through his teeth was too loud, like a hurricane in his own ears, and he imagined Higley could hear it, too.

He flopped chest-down on the platform and sucked in cold air, pain lancing through his bad arm. The air smelled ozone-fried and full of death, like meat charred to cinders by an electricks cooker.

"Dammit!" Higley cursed, and Tam heard a scraping sound.

He didn't waste time looking up, just threw himself in the direction of the ray gun. He lunged, fingers out, paddling across cold plascrete like he was swimming, and raised his head. He and Higley locked eyes—

—and grabbed the gun at the same time.

Better than no loaf at all, Tam thought. Only Higley had the bloody-damn-hell tail end of the snake.

Tam threw himself back, praying to Brigit that he wasn't hurling himself off the platform to his death. He wrapped both hands around the barrel of the ray gun and pushed it up with all his wasted, pain-wracked strength, trying to get the viper mouth away from his throat, above his head.

Zottt!

Tam felt his hair burst into flame but his head wasn't incinerated. He smelled plascrete melting, a horrible tarry bubbling stink, and then his shoulders hit the mooring platform floor and it was solid.

And Higley came crashing down on top of him.

Zottt!

The ray gun fired again, over Tam's head, and he smelled the burning stink more intensely, and then Higley let go of the gun—

—it rattled away across the plascrete and stopped, spinning, right at the new, melted, edge of the platform—

—and Higley's big heavy Pinkerton body slammed into Tam, the first point of contact being the bigger man's knee crunching into Tam's crotch.

"Aaagh!" Tam screamed.

Higley head-butted Tam, maybe on purpose or maybe not, but it hurt like hell. Then the Pinkerton reached over Tam's shoulder, trying to crawl past him for the gun.

Tam grabbed Higley's head. He wrapped his fingers in the other man's hair and yanked back as hard as he could.

"Damn Irish!" Higley bellowed, and punched Tam in the jaw.

Tam lost his vision. He knew he wasn't unconscious, because he could still feel Higley's hair clutched in his fist, and the Pinkerton's knee as he pummeled Tam again in the balls, but he saw a bright flash of light and then blackness.

Tam snapped his hand forward.

"Let go!" Higley snarled, and punched Tam again, this time in the throat.

Tam lost his wind and vomited at the same moment, and had the horrible feeling of his lungs filling up with his own bile—

—and as the stiletto leaped into his hand, he shoved it forward, hard, at the spot where his best guess told him Higley's neck would be. Whatever he hit, it had the satisfying resistance of human flesh.

"Glagh!"

Hot blood spilled over Tam's face and chest and arms and Higley lurched sideways, screaming and coughing. Tam coughed, too, spitting out bile and blood and gasping to get whatever slivers of tainted air he could into his lungs. He couldn't see, he vomited again, he took an elbow in the face, and he didn't let go.

He slashed again, and stabbed. Sometimes he hit flesh and sometimes he hit plascrete, but he kept stabbing and coughing and spitting and sucking air until the hunk of flesh he grappled had stopped moving, and finally his stiletto blade hit the plascrete one last time and its blade snapped off, sticking into the palm of his hand like a giant splinter.

Tam coughed, spewing out blood and bile and what felt like half his lung. "Fookin' hell!" he shouted, and then he wiped blood from his face with his sleeve, which was almost as bloody.

Vision began to return, under a dark gray sheet and streaked with blue sparks almost as heavy as the overhead field of electricks had been. For good measure, Tam smashed Higley's mangled face against the plascrete, shattering the dead man's nose, and then he rolled away from the body and vomited some more.

He was surprised he had anything left to throw up, but then he was surprised even to be alive, at this point.

"Seamus fookin' McNamara!" he gasped. "Idjits!"

Tam lurched to his feet, found his sense of vertigo hadn't recovered, and fell to the hard plascrete again.

He yanked the broken blade from his hand, wincing as more blood gushed out, wiped blood off his forehead, and out of his eyes, and looked around again. The sky grew ever lighter. Off in the distance in mid-air he saw flashes and he dimly thought that some sort of battle was being waged in the clouds.

"I hope Poe is sticking it to that bastard Pratt," he spat, and looked around for the ray gun. He found it, teetering on the edge of the abyss.

He crawled this time, staying low and moving slowly, and made it all the way to the gun without collapsing. Below, the creeping light of morning showed a blue lake and the gray, bowl-shaped arms of the mountain around, with a silver skunk's tail of snow connecting the two. It was a long way down, and as Tam grabbed the ray gun he pulled away from the drop, sinking back to the floor and breathing heavy.

Bang!

He heard a gunshot elsewhere on the mooring platform, and Tam rolled over to look. He saw Richard Burton, standing but looking more like a mutilated corpse than a man, with blood and bandages all over his body, and a half-reloaded Smith & Wesson Model 1 in his hands.

A big-shouldered Pinkerton leaned against the shed with his back to Tam. He held a long Henry rifle in his hands, and he pointed it at Burton.

Tam thought about standing, but didn't dare risk it. Biting back a groan with his bloody-coppery-tasting teeth, he tightened his grip on Orson Pratt's ray gun, as much as he could with his battered and sliced hands, and started dragging himself on one elbow and two knees in the direction of the little shed.

Crash!

The message machine room filled with shards of flying glass and splinters of wood, and Sam staggered back, raising an arm to protect his face. Something long and spear-like punched George Cannon in the chest and hurled him across the room toward the door, scattering his minions out of the way likes Swiss skiers before an avalanche barreling down the slopes of Mont Blanc.

Rockwell hit the ground where Cannon had been, looking like a dog whose bone had been yanked from his jaws and thrown across the yard. He stumbled, knees wobbling, and tried to recover his balance.

Bang!

Cannon's bullet disappeared in the confusion. The turncoat Welker raised his pistols and a knife appeared in his throat. He staggered sideways and rotated, cocking and firing his pistols alternately as he turned and sank to the floor, a deadly Fourth of July cracker with blood spilling down his shirt.

Bang!

Lee shot Welker in the forehead, blowing him to the floor before the other man shot the Danite chieftain, and then turned his attention grimly to the rest of the room.

Orrin Porter Rockwell got his feet under him again. The wild man hurled a table onto its side with a titanic grunt and then tackled Brigham Young and Sam Clemens both simultaneously, knocking them towards the upended table and shelter. Sam resisted out of reflex but the back of his knees struck a horizontal table leg and he sat down, hard, slamming prone onto his back. He spat his Partagás straight up into the air as he hit, like the explosion of a tobacco landmine.

Crash!

Another window exploded inward, showering Sam with glass again. His face felt like it had been shaved by a drunk with farm implements and he coughed out the last wisps of cigar smoke from his lungs and cheeks with a sense of disappointment. A figure wrapped head to toe in leather crashed into the room in the cloud of shards, a pistol in each hand.

Rockwell pulled a knife—

—the figure fired, both guns blazing and throwing lead at John Lee, George Cannon and their cohorts.

"Surround them!" Lee yelled to someone in the hall behind him, and he backed into the message room doorway, leaving Lindemuth behind, who collapsed under the withering fire of the leather-clad figure. Staring up at the specter of death, Sam found himself uniquely situated to appreciate the voluptuousness of this angel of punishment, and then he recognized it—*her*—as the Mexican Striderman, Master Sergeant Jackson.

Sam struggled to sit up, wishing he still had the brace of pistols in his hands.

Another spear hurtled in through the window over the shoulder of the dwarf Coltrane, who rolled in with a humming Colt vibro-blade in his hand. The spear struck John Lee in the shoulder and knocked him spinning out into the hall, but Sam noticed that there was no blood. A spear that size should have taken off the man's arm entirely, but there wasn't a drop.

Then he saw the spear that had knocked George Cannon down. It was long, light and forged of steel, and it ended in a rubber cup. Sam laughed. "Where did you find a weapon like that?" he asked no one in particular, shaking his head. "A squadron of militant plumbers?"

Coltrane slammed the door shut and jumped aside to avoid bullets that snapped through the wood immediately, punching holes and sending in shafts of yellow gas light.

"Anyway, it did the job," he answered his own question, reminding himself of his electrified steam-truck deck.

Absalom Fearnley-Standish backed into the room through one of the broken windows, frock coat skirt first and pistols last, firing out after himself. Cute little Annie Webb, who had so entranced Sam in Bridger's Saloon, came in the same moment by the other window.

"They're behind us!" Absalom cried. He had acquired a distinctly more manly ring to his voice despite the broken nose.

"They're on every side!" Annie added. She kicked at a man following close on her heels, sending him flying away into the darkness.

Only it wasn't darkness. Behind Annie Webb, Sam realized that he now saw the grayish light of early morning. In that half-light he saw the Third Virginia and Danites, taking up positions in the street and at the Mercantile, facing the Lion House. A glance out the other side's windows showed him more men taking up positions in the Tabernacle's gardens.

"So much for the poor performance of the Virginians!" he shouted. "Quick, before they settle in! Where's your Strider, Sergeant?"

"The one, she is destroyed," Jackson said simply, and grabbed another table, knocking it over in front of the windows facing South Tabernacle and the Mercantile. "The other, joo tell me, but *tengo miedo que* she is lost."

Rockwell tossed a third table on its side, creating a sheltered area walled in on three sides by heavy wood. Sam hoped it was heavy enough.

"The *Jim Smiley*, then," Sam suggested. "We can run—"

"Burned up," Jed Coltrane grunted. The dwarf shoved his vibro-blade straight through the plaster wall into the hallway, cutting a long horizontal slash at knee-level. A man's voice outside screamed and cursed, and Jed somersaulted away, throwing himself behind a chair and then scooting around a table end into the sheltered space. "If it's any comfort to you, she did a lot of damage before she went."

"Burned up?" Sam demanded, disgruntled. "How in mercy do you burn up that many tons of steel and India rubber? Was she hit by a *meteorite?*"

"Near enough," Coltrane agreed. Absalom Fearnley-Standish crouched beside him, sharing the cover of the tables, and handed the dwarf a long pistol. Both men began pouring powder and reloading. Up close, Sam could now see that the little man bled from a belly wound and breathed through flared nostrils.

"You hit, Jed?" he asked, stupidly.

"We can't go, anyway," Rockwell said, and his voice was profoundly sad.

"What are you talking about?" Sam asked, and Rockwell pointed at Brigham Young. Only then did Sam realize that the President of Deseret hadn't moved since the shootout began and he looked at the man, half-expecting to find him dead.

Young wasn't dead, but he looked bad. He lay on his back, a thick shard of glass lodged in his neck and blood streaming down his chest from what looked like a bullet wound in his shoulder.

"No bullet or blade," Rockwell said, even sadder. "Brother Joseph made his promise to the wrong man."

CHAPTER 31

Poe scrambled up the rope ladder in as seamanlike a fashion as he could manage, though the effort nearly killed him and twice he spit blood into the void below. Despite her flounced skirts, Roxie was more nimble. He thought he might die of shame, only, of course, the consumption was going to kill him first.

The consumption was going to kill him no matter what he did. That knowledge gave Poe a certain freedom. Somehow, it also helped him shrug off the lingering pain of the beating the Pinkertons had given him an hour or so earlier.

He dragged himself over the railing and managed not to fall to the deck. A few deep breaths—as deep as he could manage, anyway—and his swirling vision recovered, and then Roxie was beside him, pistols in her hands. Behind and below them, gunfire and yelling continued on the mooring platform.

There was no one on the deck of the ship. The craft curled up and inward fore and aft, like a Viking vessel but with no dragon's head. It had a brass mast, from which hung a sail of no fabric that Poe recognized. It shimmered slightly in the thinning darkness, as if electrified, and it looked thinner than any ordinary cloth. On the near—aft—side of the mast was a small stand that looked like the control panel of a steam-truck, with a wheel and binnacle. In the prow of the boat, mounted just inside the great inward curve, was some sort of cannon. At their feet was an open hatch.

"What does the sail catch?" he wondered, dragging the rope ladder up behind them to prevent unwanted pursuit. "It can't be *wind*, can it?"

"Look at the controls!" Roxie shouted, ignoring him, and jumped feet-first down through the hatch and into the hold below.

"Ether waves?" he speculated, and chuckled at himself.

Poe shuffled across the deck to the gun. He was no mechanick, but he'd spent enough time with Hunley and his devices that he knew what details to look for. The cannon was large and built of shiny brass, with a seat directly behind the barrel and a sighting guide over the top of the cannon. Halfway along the length of the barrel, Poe saw a glass panel and within it, gleaming dully by the crackling light of the sail, the vermillion glint of rubies. Below the gunner's seat, large, crisp-toothed gears appeared to give the gun the ability to turn three hundred sixty degrees horizontally and at least some amount out of the plane of the ship's deck. Levers by the side of the seat clearly connected to the gears to control movement and another lever on the side of the weapon's barrel, like the bolt of a rifle, must control fire. A clear glass tube rose up from the deck of the ship within the gear works, and blue light snapped and crackled inside it. India rubber cables ran across the deck to the control panel like snakes, dormant but ready to strike if stepped on.

So the phlogiston cannon was probably fire-ready.

He turned and scanned the horizon, easily spotting Pratt's other three airships. They moved away from the mooring tower, out of the high valley in which Pratt's facility was nestled, and out into the broader Wasatch Mountains. He squinted, making the best use he could of the first pale cracks of dawn, but saw no one on board the ships other than Pratt himself.

How were the other two flying, then?

Poe coughed, spat on the deck, and limped back to the control panel. He arrived just as Roxie emerged from the hatch, shaking her head.

"There's no one aboard," she confirmed.

"I can detect no one aboard the other two, either," Poe said. "How on earth is Pratt controlling them?"

They looked together at the control panel, and Poe immediately knew the answer to his own question.

"Hunley," he gasped.

The controls looked simple enough. There was a wheel like on any terrestrial ship, and beside it a binnacle, glowing blue around its rim and containing a simple compass whose needle was a stylized brass bumblebee. There was a broad, wool-padded belt-and-shoulder-straps harness that bolted into the center of the wheel for the pilot. Beside the wheel was a small knob-headed lever marked *PITCH AND YAW* that appeared capable of moving in all directions; next to it was another level like a steam-truck's throttle, currently at the lowest position in its range; buttons marked *WEIGH* and *DROP*; and from a solid block of brass beside the ship's wheel protruded a monkey's head that Poe knew all too well.

"What do you think this does?" Roxie asked, touching the *PITCH AND YAW* lever without moving it.

"Controls pitch and yaw, is my guess," Poe suggested dryly. "That would let you alter your elevation, as well. And there you have acceleration. But the monkey is the interesting thing."

"How so?"

"Because Horace Hunley made it and three others like it, and this is the one that I smashed against my cabin door in the *Liahona.*"

Zottt!

Poe looked up from the controls to the phlogiston gun, but it was dormant, and he knew from the reddish light playing against its side that a phlogiston weapon must have been fired on the mooring tower.

"So what?"

"So," Poe said, "I think this is how Pratt is flying the ships. This is what Horace Hunley did—he built four devices that communicate, somehow, with each other. Ether waves, possibly, or anyhow, that's what Robert hinted to me once."

"You love Robert," Roxie said.

Poe sighed. "As much as a man can love another man," he said, and felt broken and heavy as the words came out. "For years, he has been my only human connection, the only person to know my secret." He looked at her, frail and diamond-hard and plain and beautiful. "I wish it had been you."

"Go on," she said, and rested a hand on his arm.

Poe looked at the monkey's head to recover his train of thought. "So one of the canopic jar devices must be the master and the other three are slaves—forgive the expression—so that the person in the right ship can control the other three."

"So Pratt can pilot the entire fleet by himself. So he doesn't need anyone else to help him get his revenge."

"Yes." Poe looked at the controls again. "But I must have damaged the monkey-headed jar, so hopefully we'll have local control of this craft, whatever it's called."

"It's called the *Ammon*, actually."

"As in the Egyptian god?" Poe was amused. "Identified with the sun and with Ra? You Mormons love your Egyptian things, I must say. Robert was wise to suggest that I disguise myself as an Egyptianeer."

"Mostly we identify Ammon with chopping off arms," Roxie said. Poe didn't know what she meant. Still, he was happy to be with her and he felt like she forgave him, and he forgave her, too. Besides, she smiled at him, so even though he was dying and he didn't understand the joke he threw back his head and laughed.

Zottt!

A bright flash of blue light snapped behind them—

—and the *Ammon* hurtled directly upward, into the morning sky.

They both staggered. Poe grabbed the wheel for support and Roxie threw her arms around Poe's waist. Together they contrived not to fall as cool air whistled through their hair, and then suddenly they were several hundred feet higher than they had been, and the *Ammon* slowed its ascent and started to drift.

Roxie started to the edge of the ship, but Poe caught her arm.

"What's happening?" she shouted.

"It doesn't matter!" He pointed at Pratt's other three ships, disappearing down around a gray cliff below and to the north of them. "Burton can fend for himself—we have to stop the Madman!"

"His name is Orson!" she cried. "He's no madman!"

Poe dragged Roxie to the wheel, though the effort made him cough up half a lung. "Since you feel that way about it, I propose that you man the wheel and I man the gun!" He grabbed the monkey, ripped the canopic jar from the socket in which it was nestled and tossed it overboard. "Just in case," he said.

Then he lurched across the deck, back to the gun.

"If I am to *man* the wheel," she shouted after him, "then I insist you *woman* the gun!"

Poe laughed until he bled, then dragged himself into the seat. "We must endeavor to take Brother Orson by surprise!" he called over his shoulder. "I shall not fire until we are close, or until we are fired upon!"

Roxie waved an acknowledgement and grabbed the controls.

The *Ammon* slid forward and Poe looked to the craft's sail. It billowed forward as if puffed by a following wind, but whatever made it move wasn't the night air over Mount Timpanogos, because it billowed *into* the wind. As it billowed, it lit up and sparks crackled up and down its gossamer surface. As Roxie turned the airship's wheel, the mast and sail turned, turning the ship with them.

"Extraordinary," Poe murmured. *If only men of genius such as Pratt and Hunley could collaborate away from the terrors and pressure of war,* he thought. *What marvels might they accomplish?*

Of course, it could be suggested that the terrors and pressures of war were the very things that pushed such innovators to their most spectacular results. Poe sighed, and then he coughed. He grabbed the phlogiston cannon's gunner's seat for stability and let the world around him swoon. *Hold on to yourself, man,* he thought. *At least long enough to stop this atrocity.*

The *Ammon* suddenly pitched to its right, which was at Poe's shoulders. Poe lost his grip on the back of the gunner's seat and tumbled hard to the deck. He slid across the wood, terrifying images of himself catapulting into the void filling his mind's eye—

—but then the ship righted itself.

Poe rolled onto his hands and knees and saw a gray cliff wall, passing within arm's reach of the left side of the ship. Ahead of the *Ammon,* the last of Orson Pratt's automaton fleet turned left and disappeared from view around the peak they were all skirting.

They hadn't come far in the night, Poe thought. The Great Salt Lake City must be just around that bend.

"Sorry!" Roxie shouted. "This *manning* business is surprisingly difficult!"

"I heard those same words from my step-father once!" Poe yelled back, and climbed into the seat again. "He was caning me at the time!"

Poe saw now that the gunner's seat had a leather belt, and he strapped himself in, his fingers aching and trembling, and the effort making him sweat. Roxie moved the *Ammon* forward, accelerating as her confidence increased. The cliff brow to his left dropped and Poe began to see blue sky and brown valley floor beyond the end of the rock. He examined the gun more closely; it was exceedingly simple. There was a lever labeled *LEFT* and *RIGHT*, a lever labeled *UP* and *DOWN*, and a bolt labeled *FIRE*.

Orson Pratt's inventions were spectacular but his genius had a pedantic, talking-down-to-children quality to it. After all of Horace Hunley's mysterious devices, manipulated by unlabeled buttons or long sequences of whistled notes that were inaudible to human hearing, Poe found it more than a little refreshing.

He rehearsed looking down the barrel, raising and lowering and rotating his seat with the whirring and clicking of gears to take aim at spots along the cliff wall. He wished he could take practice shots, but he needed as much surprise as he could possibly arrange. Preferably, they'd slide up behind Pratt utterly unnoticed, either because he'd be focused on his target on the ground or because he'd assume the *Ammon* was malfunctioning but attempting to respond to its remote ether-wave instructions, simply lagging behind the rest of the fleet.

"Try to stay low!" he hollered to Roxie. She acknowledged with a wave, then hunched down slightly behind the ship's wheel.

The *Ammon* rounded the cliff and drifted through a notch between two peaks.

The view took Poe's breath away. Gigantic rock shoulders to either side could have shattered the little airship with a shrug, or by shaking free the boulders that clung precariously to their heights and dropping them right through the plank floor and copper bottom sheathing of the *Ammon*. Mountains to the east aligned perfectly at the same moment, letting through a rush of bright yellow sunshine, and the airship rode the light forward like it was sailing a river of pure honey, the morning warmth tickling Poe's cheek and ear and then the back of his neck as the *Ammon* turned. Below passed a saddle, thousands of feet above sea level in elevation but below the timberline, and furred with evergreen trees that looked black in the first light of the day. Poe saw a cluster of big-horned mountain sheep winding their way up out of the pines and onto the shattered-rock slope at the base of the cliff to his right.

Then the saddle fell away, Roxie turned them to the right again, and below and before the *Ammon* stretched out the Salt Lake Valley. The lake itself looked like a sheet of hammered steel, great inland salt sea that it was. It covered the distant half of the valley. The nearer side was a grayish brown shade of desert summer, fields mostly heavy with crops, trees sparse and dusty even at their greenest. The natural grasses of the Wasatch Mountains were tall and yellow in color but they disappeared with the fields and ditches into a general colorless smudge, cut by roads and irrigation ditches into a great, man-made grid. Ahead, against the eastern wall of the valley, shone the Great Salt Lake City, sparkling like steel and china as the sunshine hit it. It wasn't all that big, Poe thought, not from the air and from this many miles away.

ZOTTT!

A hot beam flashed past the *Ammon* and carved into the side of the nearest cliff. Rock exploded out from the cliff face, improbably bursting into flame and smoking as it fell.

"Roxie!" Poe shouted, but she was already reacting. The *Ammon* leaped forward like a racehorse given its head, and yawed down, plummeting at a sharp angle to the ground.

"Are we hit?" Poe bellowed, and yanked at the lever to swivel his aim at Pratt's ships, which seemed to come level and then rise above the *Ammon*, as they stayed in their plane and the *Ammon* rocketed downward.

ZOTTT!

The next phlogiston-consuming bolt passed harmlessly overhead, narrowly missing the top of the mast.

"Aim high!" she yelled back, and raced straight at Pratt's trio of craft.

And then Poe saw the genius of her maneuver. The other ships fired again, several times, but the *Ammon* was too low for them to hit it without changing their pitch or yaw. Pratt adjusted as the *Ammon* raced forward and one of his ships turned and began to tilt in Poe's direction, but he was managing three vessels, not one, and the guns as well as the steering, so there was only so much he could do at once.

Poe took aim at the ship that was turning and tilting and fired.

ZOTTT!

A miss, and a wave of heat emanated from the barrel of the phlogiston gun. The firing lever stayed depressed, and though Poe banged at it with the heel of his hand, it inched its way back into ready position at its own leisurely pace.

It might be an automatic delay designed to give the barrel time to cool before firing again, Poe thought. He started counting.

"Evasive action!" he shouted to Roxie. She must have had the same thought, for as he shouted the *Ammon* was already banking to one side and slowing, then banking again and speeding up, the angles irregular and the speed constantly shifting.

ZOTTT!

Another miss from one of Pratt's craft and a field below Poe burst into fire, dirt and rock exploding upward and leaving a crater where once a plank bridge had crossed a broad irrigation ditch.

The firing lever of Poe's gun *snicked* back into ready position. A slow count of twenty. "Give me a good shot!" he yelled.

In response, Roxie pulled up the prow of the *Ammon* and launched the ship straight forward like an arrow, at the copper-shining underside of the nearest of the three.

It was less than ideal, Poe thought. He had no idea whether Pratt was aboard his target ship or not. But it was a clear shot and he couldn't let it pass. He sighted carefully and depressed the firing lever.

ZOTTT!

BOOM!

The back half of the targeted ship burst into flame and the vessel pitched wildly to one side. Poe stared, hoping to see some sign of a single wild-haired old man falling overboard, but Roxie was already moving evasively again and Poe saw nothing that gave him any hope.

"That's the *Stripling Warrior!*" Roxie shouted.

"So?"

ZOTTT!

The beam lanced by close enough to the *Ammon* that Poe felt its heat crackling in his false beard. Nervously, he yanked off the beard and then the eyebrows too, picking at the spirit gum with his fingers and keeping one eye on the slowly-resetting firing lever of his phlogiston gun.

"So," she shouted again, "it's one of the older ones. Pratt will be on the *Teancum!*"

"Now you tell me!" Poe threw a wad of spirit gum and hair overboard as the *Ammon* pitched to one side. Roxie must have strapped herself in too, he thought. Good girl. But what in hell were these queer names? "Which one is the *Teancum?*"

Roxie laughed and pointed ahead. "One of those two!" she shouted.

Poe squinted; they had come out west above the valley and were now turning back eastward and angling up again, so the morning sun shone bright into his face. He could make out two ships but the glare of the sun kept him from making out any detail.

He could tell, though, that one of the two ships hung back and hovered in place and one circled to get around the *Ammon*, tilting to maneuver its gun into position.

"That one!" he shouted, and pointed at the further, hovering airship. Roxie nodded and accelerated towards it, slipping side to side to present a difficult target to the nearer ship as it tried to fire at them.

ZOTTT!

It missed, but narrowly.

ZOTTT!

The airship hovering still fired as well and very nearly hit the *Ammon*. Poe blessed Roxie again, a thousand blessings in his heart for each of the thousand times he had cursed her name over the years.

Pratt must have practiced his gunnery a lot, to be such a deadly shot when firing from a remote platform. Or did the canopic jars contain a targeting system of some sort, as well? Poe shook off the introspection; with both targets' gun just fired, now was the moment.

"Charge!" he yelled, and Roxie opened the throttle.

Poe held his fire, sighting along the barrel. He knew he had a slow count of twenty from when the first of the two enemy guns fired, and he jumped into his count at *five … six … seven … eight …*

The *Ammon* passed under the flat, copper-plated belly of the circling craft. Poe shot a glance up at its hull to confirm that it wasn't the *Teancum*, but all he saw was the pseudo-alphabet the Mormons called *Deseret*, and he spared no more thought for it.

Twelve … thirteen … fourteen …

He'd only get one shot before he had to pull away, so he needed to make it good. Poe sighted at his target craft, smack in the center of the hull, so the sun in his eyes wouldn't make him fail. It started to move, but slowly, and Poe easily kept his sight fixed on the middle of the huge target. He wouldn't be able to miss.

Sixteen … seventeen …

Then the *Ammon* dipped into the shadow of one of the Wasatch Mountains, and Poe saw his target for the first time free of the sun's glare. There was no one at the helm.

"Wrong ship!" he shouted.

Zottt!

It was a smaller sound, but the unmistakable noise of a phlogiston gun being fired. Not one of the huge cannons, maybe, but the little one, the one Pratt had nicknamed *Parley*.

From above and behind him, Poe saw the phlogiston-igniting beam of ruby-red light bite into the gun barrel in front of him, slicing through the brass, igniting it, dissolving the barrel and leaving behind a charred ruin.

"Evade!" he shouted. "Evade!" He scratched at his safety harness with trembling, weak fingers, and managed to free himself barely in time to avoid a second swipe of the ray gun that incinerated the gunner's seat.

He scampered down along the deck in Roxie's direction, patting down his pockets in search of any kind of weapon. Roxie stared over her own shoulder at the ship that fired on them, and now, with the sun at their backs, Poe saw the Madman Pratt at the rail of his airship, dark goggles on his face to shield his eyes from the sun, firing his Enkindler at them.

"No!" Roxie howled.

Great god of heaven, Poe thought, *she's not watching where she's going—*

—CRASH!!

The *Ammon* collided with the—whatever the name of the remaining ship was, Poe had lost track—ramming it amidships with its copper-sheathed prow. *Like battling triremes,* Poe thought abstractly, *we're fighting like the Ancient Greeks, though thousands of feet above the ground.*

The blow threw him back along the deck, and he smashed into the control panel and wheel of the *Ammon.* Roxie was securely belted in, struggling with the wheel with one hand and trying to draw a bead on Orson Pratt with a pistol in the other. Poe had to catch himself, grabbing the wheel with one hand and jamming his fist in the slot where the monkey-headed canopic jar had been.

Surely, he thought, *we'll fall.*

But the *Ammon* ground her sister-ship under her flat keel, snapping its mast into splinters and then gliding almost majestically between the two shattered halves, which fell apart like a cracked egg and then dropped before Poe's eyes to the valley floor.

"I'd say you *womaned* that airship pretty thoroughly," Poe gasped. His breath came in sucking gusts that rattled his chest, and he spat tendrils of ropy blood and phlegm. The wind snatched them away before they reached the deck.

"Oh?" she asked, and pointedly cocked her pistol. "And how would it have looked had I *manned* it, Edgar?"

Poe got his feet under him and looked down, across the slanting deck of the airship. Buildings of the Great Salt Lake City carpeted the valley floor below them now and the broken airship fell into two ragged pieces down onto unsuspecting sleepers, or shopkeepers opening their stores at the crack of dawn. There was some sort of commotion in the center of the city, around the Tabernacle—*Bang! Bang!*

Roxie's pistol exploded in Poe's ear as she took pot-shots at Pratt, continuing to crank the *Ammon's* wheel and bringing the airship around to charge it at the *Teancum.*

Poe focused on the action around him. He patted his pockets again and found what he was looking for.

"We've got to get closer!" he cried, and started to cough.

Pratt raised his Enkindler to fire again.

CHAPTER
TWENTY

P oe staggered to the railing, the balled-up cloth in one hand and the other fist thumping his own chest. He shook, he trembled, cold sweat poured down his body. He felt like he was breathing through water.

The *Ammon* closed on the *Teancum* and Orson Pratt raised his Parley again. Poe saw the swept-up hair, the matted beard, the black glass disks for eyes and the mad, piratical grin, but what he watched closely was the inventor's hands.

Pratt squeezed the firing lever on the Enkindler—

Poe let his body fall—

—*Zottt!*

The beam of hot light scorched the air above Poe but Poe ignored it. He hit the deck rolling, and as he came to his feet he snapped open the hypnotic hypocephalus, fixing it directly in Pratt's gaze across the closing gap like a shield and running his fingers across it in the simple but peculiar pattern that Hunley's mesmerist had drilled into him.

Pratt fell like a sack of potatoes.

The gap shrank at an alarming rate.

"Turn!" Poe shouted.

"I can't!" Roxie yelled back.

Poe looked over his shoulder just long enough to see that Orson Pratt's last shot had entirely dismasted the *Ammon*. Then he flung his body to the rail and wrapped his arms around it to brace for the impact.

CRUNCH!!!

Poe rolled over the side. His toes scrabbled against copper sheathing and for a mad second he thought he was going to fall—

—below him he saw the Third Virginia Cavalry, firing on one of the buildings beside the Tabernacle, one of Brigham Young's own houses, he thought he remembered from Robert's briefings—he was going to fall to his death through Brigham Young's own roof and nearly laughed at the thought—but then Roxie was there and dragging him up the side. He hacked and coughed and fell onto his own blood and phlegm on the deck.

"You weigh nothing, Ed," Roxie told him.

"Corpses generally don't," he said, affecting a gallant grin that was ruined by the wet, bloody coughing fit it provoked.

"Orson!" she shouted, and leaped to the rail.

Poe shook his head clear and followed her. The *Ammon*, dismasted, hovered still in the air a thousand feet above Salt Lake City. Below, the Virginians advanced on Young's residence, guns blazing. Not only his residence, Poe remembered, that was the Lion House, where Young lived and worked. That was where Young and Clemens and the others had gone to send a message out to Young's people to end the coup.

The Virginians must have Young holed up inside.

Below the *Ammon* and above the Great Salt Lake City floated the *Teancum*. Orson Pratt's flagship had had the worst of the collision with its sister; Poe could see that two of the cup- or foot-like protrusions of the *Teancum* hung shattered at its flank, and the airship drifted slowly down, pitching over onto one side as it did so. It was ten feet beneath the *Ammon*, sinking and drifting laterally.

Poe grabbed the rope ladder and hurled it over the side.

"Save Orson!" Roxie cried, following him over the railing. "He may be able to cure you!"

"To hell with Orson Pratt!" Poe coughed, hitting the tilted deck of the *Teancum* hard and staggering forward. "And to hell with me!"

"What are you doing, then?" Roxie clattered after him to the phlogiston cannon mounted at the front of the ship.

"I'm saving your President!" Poe shouted. The *Teancum* sagged to one side even further as he spoke. "Take the controls! Try to correct the pitch!"

He and Roxie both turned to look at the control panel as he said the words, and Poe saw Orson Pratt, conscious. The old man clung to the bottom of the *Ammon*'s rope ladder, now seven or eight feet off the *Teancum*'s deck and rising as the *Teancum* sank. He held his Enkindler in one hand and fumbled, trying to get his other hand to the firing lever while hanging on the rope ladder by his elbow.

The old man saw that he was noticed. "Too late!" he cried shrilly, and aimed the Parley—

Bang!

Roxie shot Pratt in the chest. The Madman shrieked and dropped his ray gun, which fell past the *Teancum* and disappeared. He slumped and his blood flowed down the ropes, but he held on to the ladder as Poe and Roxie descended.

"Fools!" he shouted, and then Poe ignored him.

"You're a hell of a woman, Roxie!" Poe shouted across the angled deck of the *Teancum*. "There isn't room in this world for the both of us!" He climbed into the gunner's seat and saw Roxie similarly strap herself to the helm.

"You're wrong again, Edgar!" she called back. "There isn't room enough in this world for *either* of us!"

Poe chuckled and cranked the gun around to aim at the siege below. "Give me as steady a platform as you can!" Smoke billowed out of the Tabernacle, threatening his visibility.

"Give them hell!" she yelled back.

ꓘƆꓤ�15Ɔꟼ

"Hell!" Jed shouted and ducked.

Bullets whizzed over his head and he stayed down, his hands full of knives and his loaded pistol at his side. The big tables they crouched behind caught the bullets that struck and held them fast but the air above the tables was a deadly cloud of lead hornets. Outside the Lion House was light but inside was darkness.

And pain.

Jed's belly hurt like hell but he hadn't had the worst of it. Brigham Young was dying. Jed felt sad enough about that, because he seemed like an ornery cuss and Jed kind of liked ornery cusses, but worse than that was Jed's impression that Young's death meant their defeat, and then John Lee and George Cannon would have their war. After, of course, they killed Sam Clemens and Jed Coltrane and everyone else who knew about their plot.

Sam worked over Brigham Young's body, wrapping strips of his own shirt and jacket around the man's bloodied neck and chest, keeping the big glass shard in place and trying to stanch the bleeding.

Steel flashed low in one of the windows and Jed threw a knife. The blade *clanged* off the steel harmlessly and disappeared into the bushes. Jed grabbed the pistol and cocked it.

A hat appeared behind the steel and then Jed realized what he was seeing. It was one of the Virginians' clocksprung horses and it crouched sideways in the window like a barrier. A soldier—no, two soldiers—sheltered on the machine's other flank and their pistols snaked over the top of the horse and began firing into the room. Their angle and position pointed their barrels into the sheltered area among the tables, and Jed scrambled with the others not to be in the line of fire.

Orrin Porter Rockwell, hair and beard wild around his face like a halo around Blackbeard the pirate's head, jumped to his feet to get a better angle and fire down at the two soldiers. A bullet struck him, and then another, and he collapsed to the floor beside his master.

"Egad," Absalom Fearnley-Standish said. He pressed his back against one of the tables. Jed saw over his shoulder that more brushed-metal horses advanced in the street. They shone implacable and solid in the morning sunshine blazing down South Tabernacle.

"Throw your hat!" Jed told him, and switched to the Colt vibro-blade.

"Beg pardod?"

"Your hat!" Annie Webb jerked the damaged top hat off his head and pressed it into his hand.

"At the horse!" Jed whispered, and nodded to indicate the direction he meant.

Fearnley-Standish nodded, stood, and threw the hat.

Idiot, to stand up like that. Brave, but an idiot.

Bang!

The soldiers fired at Fearnley-Standish, his hat splintering into black shreds in mid-air and the man himself ducking and tumbling backward. Jed didn't know if he was hit or trying to dodge and didn't wait to find out. As the Englishman stood, Jed rolled forward and jumped, taking advantage of the distraction to hurl himself high onto the wall of glass tubes and brass doors—

—glass shattered around him as men firing from the hall saw him—

—he swung like an ape, thumbing the vibro-blade on, almost dropping it with the stabbing pain in his gut—

—and landing on top of the two soldiers in the window. He piled onto them with both his feet on one man's neck and with the humming blade he lopped off the other fellow's hands with a single swipe.

The mutilated soldier screamed, the other man barked, and guns swiveled to point at Jed.

"Aw, hell," he grunted, and stuck the vibro-blade into the second soldier.

ᒐᘓᒍᑫᗅᗄᒍᗄ

Tam hurt and he could only see out one eye. He thought it was because the other was covered in blood and not because the eye had been destroyed, but he hurt so bloody-damn-much all over his body that he couldn't be certain, and he couldn't spare a hand to wipe away the blood and find out for sure. Besides, Mother O'Shaughnessy had taught him to always stay focused on the task at hand.

He needed his left hand for crawling; in his right he held Orson Pratt's ray gun.

Now that he saw it up close, the thing didn't have a trigger at all, not like an ordinary gun. It had a grip and a sort of bolt on the side, which must be how the thing was fired. Too bad he hadn't been able to watch Higley as he worked it, but Tam had had other things on his mind at the time.

Higley. Tam chuckled to himself. *Fookin' bastard.*

He was close enough to the Pinkerton and to Richard Burton now that he couldn't miss the one, and didn't think he'd hit the other.

"Who's your boss?" the Pinkerton was demanding, pointing a big rifle at Burton's chest. Burton did a good job of not looking at Tam and giving him away. The Englishman had been caught reloading the Smith & Wesson. He had some shells in the cylinder, but obviously didn't have time to snap it into place, raise it and fire before he'd take several shots in the chest.

"Her Britannic Majesty, Queen Victoria," Burton sneered, "is my *sovereign.* I don't have a *boss.*"

Tam levered himself up onto his knees. He swayed a bit, but managed to wipe blood from his eye with his elbow. He was pleased to discover that he'd been right—both his eyes still worked (not that he needed more than one, not for this task, not at this range, did he?). He dropped the muzzle of the ray gun to point it at the Pinkerton's back and examined the bolt on the side of the weapon.

"Funny you think there's a difference," the Pinkerton shot back. He was a thin man with no hair and big ears. "She ain't gonna save you now, you know."

Tam fired.

Zottt!

The big-eared Pinkerton burst into flame. His rifle went off anyway—

—*Bang!*—

—but the shot missed, because Burton was already jumping to the side, snapping the Model 1's cylinder into place and aiming—

—not at Big Ears, but behind him—

"Ha!" Tam shouted—

—was Burton aiming at Tam?

Bang!

The shot didn't come from Burton's gun.

Bang!

That was Burton's gun and Tam heard a heavy thud and another man's body hit the platform in front of him.

Tam dropped the ray gun, finding that his arms suddenly didn't work. Puzzlement. He was cold, and his limbs felt far away. Then he noticed something in his jaw, a numbness and a pressure. He opened his mouth and blood spilled out.

Tam fell over.

He saw only blackness, but he heard scuffling boots. Arms grabbed his chest and then he heard Burton's voice. "Easy, O'Shaughnessy," Burton said gruffly. "Good man."

"Don't let them have me," Tam tried to say, but blood was spilling from his mouth and down his throat and he wasn't sure he was getting the words out. "Don't let the fookin' Pinkertons have my body."

ꓵꓵꓬꓩꓕꓭꓩꓕ

"Get them now!" John D. Lee cried in the hall outside. "We're running out of time!"

The shouted commands to the Danites assailing him captured Absalom's own thoughts perfectly. Brigham Young was bleeding to death. Orrin Porter Rockwell—his own brother-in-law, he thought, begrudging the title less than he expected to—lay face-down and still. Really, that should have been a cost-free victory for Absalom, allowing him to grieve with his sister and still bring her home to England, but instead he found that it made him feel sad.

The dwarf Coltrane, flinging himself out the window with a crackling vibro-blade in his hand, was the last sight Absalom had seen before he fell over backward, stumbling and knocking himself down on the outside of the tables. Then he'd heard the cacophony of gunshots outside explode into a riot, and Lee's shouts from the hall.

This might be it, he thought.

He cocked both his pistols and stumbled to his feet, lurching toward the message room door. The wish in the top of his mind as he did so was that he could be acting out this scene without the broken nose—he felt that he was doing and saying heroic things, but with the silly voice of a man with a chronic head-cold. The wish made him feel slightly embarrassed and he ran faster.

He expected to die instantly, cut down by gunfire from all sides, but he didn't. He could see out of the corner of his eye that Coltrane had come back over the clocksprung horse, and that the dwarf was bleeding and maybe unconscious. Still, he was drawing the fire of the soldiers outside, sparing Absalom.

And for some reason, Lee's Danites hadn't charged through the door yet. Throwing caution to the wind, Absalom charged them instead.

He rushed out into the south lobby of the Lion House and found himself looking at the backs of George Cannon and John Lee. Their men were pressed against the walls and behind upturned chairs, firing their pistols—

—not into the message room, but up the hall, into the Lion House.

Down that hall came a charge the sight of which made Absalom Fearnley-Standish let out an unprecedented noise. It was partly a roar of triumph, because he knew when he saw the charging party that they were allies. He didn't know if they could turn the tide against the soldiers and Danites combined, but the arrival of any assistance at all at this crucial moment heartened him. He and his friends had held the fort, and now the day might still be theirs! The sound was also partly a laugh, because the allies were the most improbable, even impossible soldiers he had ever seen. And, finally, the sound was also partly a quizzical harrumph of animal delight, thrilling purely at the physical appearance of the saviors rushing to his aid, pistols high and firing.

They were a crowd of beautiful girls, scandalously dressed in nightclothes and without even a smudge of makeup. They sheltered in the doorways of a long hall and fired at the Danites with pistols and rifles. Absalom stepped to one side, to be sure none of their stray shots could whistle through the hall and strike him down.

Absalom felt an urge to simply clap his gun to John Lee's head and blow out the man's brains, but he mastered his wrath, split his aim between the two pistols, one each on Lee and Cannon, and forced his voice into a calm, Wellington-worthy baritone.

"Good evedigg, gedtlemed," he said, and smiled. He regretted that he had no hat to doff and, for that matter, no third arm to doff it with, and he regretted even more that he'd been punched in the nose.

John Lee spun around like lightning, and Absalom saw too late that the other man had a pistol in his hand, too. He felt the pistol nearly as soon as he saw it, thrashing across his own cheek and jaw and knocking him back.

Bang! Bang!

Absalom fired but missed. He saw Cannon rushing out the door and he tried to aim at the little man, but Lee pistol-whipped him again and he dropped both his guns. Lee raised his pistol a third time, cocking the hammer and drawing a bead on Absalom's face.

"Damb," Absalom cursed.

ZOTTT!

The street outside the lobby's windows, South Tabernacle, exploded into flame. Lee staggered and Absalom seized his chance, kicking at the Danite's knees. As John Lee fell back and tried to recover his balance, Absalom grabbed his own fallen pistols and started firing.

Bang! Bang!

They were wild shots but he was firing point-blank and Lee ran from them. Absalom looked over his shoulder just long enough to see the women in nightgowns overwhelming the remaining Danites, and then he crashed out the doors on John Lee's heels and into the street.

At the last moment, it occurred to him to worry about the Third Virginia, but he needn't have. The explosion, whatever its source was, seemed to have targeted them. A ditch of flame and wreckage ran in a straight line down the middle of the street, and scorched men and machines lay in it and to either side. Absalom turned to look at the message room windows and saw that Annie Webb and Consuelo Jackson fought hand to hand with cavalrymen among the shattered glass. He spared a single pistol shot, hitting Annie's man in the back of his thigh, and then he turned to follow Lee again.

John Lee was no coward. He sprinted straight for the fire and, as Absalom watched, jumped through it. His movements were lopsided because one arm still hung useless at his side, but his legs were strong enough to get him across and he landed heavily on the other side.

Absalom knew he'd never make the leap; he was no long jumper. He shot his pistols instead, emptying every last bullet he had remaining and missing with every shot. Lee ducked, he weaved, and he stumbled, but he disappeared from view on the other side of the street, running in smoke and flame.

ZOTTT!

Remembering the talk of airships and phlogiston guns, Absalom looked up in time to see a great flying thing, like a Viking ship, snap off its flame-ray from a second shot. This time the shooter had targeted the soldiers on the other side of the message room, in the garden between it and the Tabernacle, and he had reduced their horses to slag and the men to charred heaps.

Burton, Absalom thought. *It must be Burton.*

He raised an empty pistol and waved it in salute at the ship, and then he saw that something was wrong. The airship had four appendages like stubby legs that were turned-down cups glowing within in the shape of luminescent golden rings, only two of them were smashed to pieces and evidently not working, because the ship was slowly sinking and drifting to one side, apparently out of control.

It drifted down toward the Tabernacle.

"Burton!" he gasped, and lurched towards the impending collision. He raised a hand, too little, too late, and much too far away.

The airship hit the wall of the Tabernacle. The impact looked incongruously gentle from where Absalom stood, but the Tabernacle was already burning and as the ship struck, flames erupted from the point of contact, and then the airship exploded in a ball of flame.

KABOOM!!

Whatever didn't burst into flame and evaporate crashed through the wall of the structure, and then the ship was gone.

Absalom dropped both his pistols, stunned. Armed women in nightgowns rushed past him, chasing Danites and cavalrymen who scattered from their path, but he could only stand in the bright warm sunshine of the early morning and stare at the flames and the ruin all about him. Numbness settled over him. He'd come with Burton as a diplomat to the Mormons, fighting with the man every step of the way, and now the Mormon capital burned and Burton burned with it, like a dead Viking chieftain aboard his warship. It was fitting, somehow, but it was horrible, and it was not what Absalom had expected or wanted.

When he was finally able to move, Absalom reached into his coat pocket and took out his Patent Metallic Note-Paper-Book. Without even opening it to remind himself of all the offenses of which he had once kept meticulous track, he took two weary steps over to the flaming rut that ran down the center of South Tabernacle and threw the Note-Paper-Book into the fire.

As it burned, pages browning and curling up into ash shavings, he heard the *cloppity-clop-clop* of horses' hooves about him. Absalom looked up to see Chief Pocatello at the head of forty or fifty of his men, in rattling bone-and-metal breastplates, with long Brunel rifles rising high like knights' lances from special stirrups beside each rider's boot.

The Third Virginia, or what was left of it, might have rallied and resisted, but it didn't. The Virginians' commander, Captain Morgan, fled first, vanishing away down one of the city's right-angled streets, flamboyant facial hair bouncing with the gallop of his clocksprung horse. His men followed, catch-as-catch-can and mostly on foot.

"Oh, good," Absalom said, mostly to himself. He raised one hand to wave it at Chief Pocatello, who waved back and grinned. "The Iddiads are here."

ᎾᏌᎯᏫ᷐ᎳᏳ

Richard Burton loaded his Smith & Wesson Model 1. It was fancy enough, but he missed his 1851 Navy, which was much more handsome and just as deadly. With the loaded pistol tucked into his pocket, he dragged every Pinkerton body he could find into the hut at the center of Orson Pratt's mooring platform and stacked them like cordwood. He ached all over, which made it slow work, and he slowed it even further by frequently stopping to check the saw-toothed, rugged horizon for any sign of returning airships.

But no airships returned, and no other people appeared to disturb his work.

Last of all he dragged in Tamerlane O'Shaughnessy. The Irishman had been crazy and a criminal, but he had fought and died bravely at Burton's side. Burton propped O'Shaughnessy into sitting position on top of the stack of dead men like a king on his throne.

Then, emboldened by the cool hush of the morning, he went down into Pratt's facility. He found his own Colt (loaded) and sword in a pile that included the Irishman's two silenced pistols. They were stolen from the Pinkertons in Bridger's Saloon, Burton thought, but that seemed to make them all the more appropriate as trophies.

He found a galley, too, and appropriated a bottle of whisky.

Back up on the mooring platform, Burton took several slugs of the whisky, then tucked the bottle into O'Shaughnessy's dead hand and laid both Maxim Hushers on the Irishman's lap.

Then he ransacked his memory for every scrap of lyric he could think of and gave the corpses the best rendition he could of "Danny Boy." He thought the rictus on O'Shaughnessy's face looked almost warm, and certainly pleased.

Then Burton stepped back from the plascrete shed, picked up Orson Pratt's hand-held phlogiston gun, and burned the shed, Tamerlane O'Shaughnessy, and all the trophies of victory to calx. In less than two minutes, the entire pile was a heap of smoking ash.

He found the Danite steam-truck in the Bay, its furnace reasonably full of coal though its tender was empty. A few minutes' driving down the tunnel, more recklessly than was really called for, and he burst into daylight again under the Deseret squiggles that Roxie Snow had taught him to read as *Koyle Mining Corporation*.

Hell of a woman. He wondered where she was, though only idly and for a moment, because he found that thoughts of her quickly and surprisingly turned to thoughts of Isabel. He'd had enough adventure to last him for a good long while, he realized, and enough of these Hades-damned Mormons, with their Danites and their plotting and their phlogiston guns and their airships.

"Kaveh's apron," he grumbled to himself, "I'd like a cup of hot coffee, a bit of Welsh rarebit, *The Sunday Times*, and my feet before a hot fire."

And Isabel in a nice house frock.

The Dream Mine's long gravel drive ended at the highway, and Burton turned right, toward a shoulder of the mountain that shrugged down before him and blocked the Salt Lake Valley from view. The highway rose to the shoulder and then hugged it all around, and at the furthest point out, right above a sodden, muddy, burnt and blasted ruin that Burton recognized as the remains of Porter Rockwell's Hot Springs

Hotel and Brewery, he saw a Mexican Strider, southbound and coming his way.

He stopped the truck parallel to the Strider, which also stopped, and crouched to bring its crew and passengers level with the steam-truck's wheelhouse.

Pfffffft-ankkkh!

Absalom Fearnley-Standish sat in the carriage of the Strider, with Annie Webb by his side and three Stridermen in uniform about them.

"Good mordigg, Captaid Burtod!" Fearnley-Standish called through a broken nose. He sounded happy and manly, despite the ridiculousness of his voice, and not the sniveling, whining, petulant child Burton was used to dealing with at all. He also sounded surprised.

"Good morning, Ambassador!" Burton called back. "Someone's hit you, I see!"

"Dod't soudd too edvious whed you say that!" Fearnley-Standish laughed. When the laughter ended, a grin remained, with a touch of regret in it. "I thought you were dead."

"So did I." Burton grinned his best piratical grin. "More than once."

"I forged my commissiod letter, you dow!"

"I know," Burton said, and he looked over his shoulder down the road south. "Relocating to Mexico, are you?"

"Lookigg for Johd Lee," Fearnley-Standish said cheerfully. He pointed at his nose. "I have him to thack for the dose."

"Lee killed *nuestro* Ambassador Armstrong," one of the Strider's crew added. Burton recognized her by her voice as Master Sergeant Consuelo Jackson. "Our President will expect *la justicia*."

"Lee's a Dixie man," Annie Webb added, and Burton saw that each woman had a hand on one of Absalom's elbows. "So we're heading to St. George to try to cut him off."

"I came lookigg for my sister," the Foreign Office man continued, "add foudd her. Odly she's happy here, so I deed a dew task."

"A new *quest*!" Burton suggested. "I am sorry to hear about the Ambassador."

Jackson and the other Stridermen nodded solemnly and crossed themselves.

Burton couldn't help looking at the two women holding Absalom Fearnley-Standish's arms and smiling.

"It isd't a perfect arradgemedt," Fearnley-Standish said ruefully.

"No arrangement is," Burton agreed. "Godspeed, Absalom."

"Godspeed, Dick."

They waved and Burton put the steam-truck into gear and rolled north, into the Salt Lake Valley.

ᒋᔕᘺᕁᏯᔑ

Dick Burton stomped gamely across the lobby of the Deseret Hotel. He wore his gun and sword openly, in the Deseret fashion, and the shiny Order of the Nauvoo Legion medal that Brigham Young had pinned to his chest three days earlier appeared never to have come off since. "Clemens," the Englishman growled.

"Burton!" Sam snapped right back at him, flashing his best grin around the unlit Partagás he was chewing. "You look so spry, I almost suspect it doesn't hurt you to walk anymore!" The bandages were all under Burton's clothing, but Sam knew they were there. The man was a walking infirmary.

"In the best tradition of the American West," Burton told him, "I'm self-medicating." He pulled a flask from his coat pocket. "Care for a shot?"

"Thanks, I believe I will," Sam said, though it was early morning yet and he intended to drive the steam-truck himself.

"Surely you're planning on wearing your medal," Burton said. "Or does the democratic egalitarianism of your President Buchanan prohibit it?"

"Oh, sure I am." Sam wiped his mustache dry, handed back the flask and fished around in the pockets of his fornication pants … his Levi-Strauss denim pants. "When the right opportunity presents itself."

"It is something of a formal occasion, after all."

"We're just *leaving*," Sam objected. "In this country, the principal formality of departure is remembering to lock the door behind you."

"Ha!" Burton didn't seem able to have even friendly, casual conversations without growling, snapping, and barking. "We're envoys, setting out with important messages to our governments. The Kingdom of Deseret is to side with peace. She will intervene against any party commencing hostilities and if Jefferson Davis and his Southern leaders are to secede, they will do so through peaceful negotiation. There will be few greater occasions in this century."

"Good thing I'm such an accomplished liar," Sam said. He pinned the medal on his jacket, noticed that it was askew, and tried to reposition it to achieve something approaching the military crispness of Burton's medal.

"Virtra's dusty belly, man!" Burton roared. He pulled the medal from Sam's hand and fussed at it, pressing it neatly into place parallel with Sam's shoulders.

"Thanks, Dick," Sam said. "You'll make some woman a fine wife one day, if you can ever bring yourself to shave that mustache."

"What are you talking about, *liar*?" Burton demanded. "Young has promised that he will intervene on the side of peace and that's the message we're to bear!" He took another sip from his flask and then put it away.

"Without the airships," Sam laughed, "who cares if he intervenes? Without Pratt's fleet and his phlogiston guns, Deseret is a gaggle of badly-armed mountain men who only fight part time at best."

"There's John Browning," Burton pointed out. They exited the hotel doors onto South Tabernacle, nodding at the desk clerk, who was still arranging for their luggage to be carried behind them. "His *machine-gun* is impressive."

"No more impressive than the work of Sam Colt or Horace Hunley or Isambard Brunel." Sam shook his head. "No, with Pratt's four ships destroyed and him dead and no one else in the know on how to squeeze rubies and get out his phlogiston-burning rays, Deseret is a paper tiger at best."

"Only three ships were destroyed," Burton pointed out.

"Yes," Sam admitted. "And the fourth disappeared, with Pratt on it and *persona non grata* in the Kingdom."

"Then lie," Burton said. "Lie like hell. Lie like hell, for heaven's sake. The cause is worthy."

"True," Sam agreed. He took a lucifer from the box in his jacket, sparked it off the rivets on his Levi-Strauss pants and lit the Partagás. "I'd take another sip of that bourbon, if there's any left."

They walked down South Tabernacle. In the five days since Brigham Young's return to his office, the street had been repaired and most of the windows but the avenue's many trees remained blasted and withered stumps, or bare baked earth, and much of the old plascrete still had black scorch marks on it, obscuring the sparkle.

"If only you Americans had put in your transcontinental railroad or your telegraph earlier," Burton commented as they neared the Lion House, "we'd have been spared the journey."

"There won't be a railroad," Sam said, "not for a while. And Young still isn't convinced about the telegraph. Young doesn't really want either of them in the first place and, at least for a little while, he'll need to keep outsiders out of the Kingdom, to avoid giving away his bluff. Besides, don't you want to get home to your fiancée Isabel? And to writing your books?"

"I do," Burton admitted. He looked slightly embarrassed as he said the words. "I have in mind a memoir of this journey, though I don't know whether anyone would believe it."

"Sell it as fiction," Sam suggested. "I think you'll find you can tell a lot of interesting truth, if you're willing to stoop to writing novels."

Burton guffawed and slapped Sam on the back and then they had arrived.

The *Jim Smiley* sat idling on the grass beside the Lion House, surrounded by the accordion-filled glass bells, repaired, restored to operation and pumping away softly. The glass tubes overhead hung silent, many of them shot to pieces on the night of what had begun to be called the Battle of the Tabernacle. The Tabernacle itself sat silent and still in the background, a burnt out hulk and the final grave of Edgar Allan Poe, Eliza Snow, Sergeant Ortiz, and others whose names Sam didn't know. It, and the splintered, bullet-riddled shambles of the Lion House, were the last two things untouched by the hand of any repairmen.

The *Jim Smiley* had been pulled from the Tabernacle's wreckage toasted but mostly intact. Captain Dan Jones and John Browning and others had been hard at work on it since the morning after the battle, and now it stood shiny and gleaming in the morning sun, looking as good as new with coal smoke and steam puffing gently from its exhaust pipes.

A crowd stood around the steam-truck, dressed in long coats, high hats, and gloves on the one hand and crisp bonnets and dresses on the other. Beyond and around the crowd stood horse-mounted Shoshone braves, looking just as formal, in their proud and savage fashion. A calotypist stood to one side with his boxy tripod-mounted device, and Brigham Young and Heber Kimball (both nearly as bandaged as Burton was, Young's neck wrapped in white all the way up to his jaw like a cravat) and Chief Pocatello stood in front of it, in a small cleared space.

"We have a lot to talk about still, Sam Clemens," Brigham Young snarled to Sam as they shook hands. Then the President of the Kingdom of Deseret broke into a broad grin. He clasped Sam's arm, and then Burton's.

"You won't persuade me." Sam grinned as he spoke, covering up his fear of death and nothing and his unresolved questions about his brother Henry. "But I'm inclined to let you keep trying."

"You'll always be more than just a cog to me."

"Don't believe him," Pocatello said with a straight face. "He says that to all the girls."

"And it works!" Heber Kimball roared. "They all marry him!"

Sam and the English explorer and the Mormon prophet and Heber Kimball and the Shoshone chief together froze and showed their teeth while the calotypist counted down from three and then the flash powder flared and told them they could relax again.

"Any sign of Cannon?" Burton wanted to know.

Heber Kimball growled like a bear, but Young shook his head. "It doesn't matter," he said. "There have always been dissidents and there always will be. The machine rolls forward, whatever the individual cogs decide to do."

Sam couldn't decide whether to shake his head or nod or what to say, so he smiled and grasped Young's hand a final time and turned to his steam-truck.

"The last time I was aboard your vessel," Burton said, blushing, "I was up to no good."

"Ha!" Sam snorted. "Me, too!"

Dan Jones stood on deck, feet squarely under his shoulders and hands clasped behind his back, with young John Moses beside him and the dwarf Jed Coltrane. As Sam and Burton climbed the ladder onto the *Jim Smiley* Jones gestured to the porters of the Deseret Hotel, who had finally caught up. Sam's and Burton's travel cases were shoved up the side of the *Jim Smiley* and stowed below decks in short order.

"You gents planning to ride all the way to the United States?" Sam asked.

"Or England?" Burton added. Sam arched an eyebrow at the explorer, and he pointed at the steam-truck's paddle-wheel. "I know she floats, Sam. I've seen it myself, remember?"

Sam laughed.

"Just to Fort Bridger, boyo, if you don't mind," Captain Jones said. "We wanted to say good-bye, the boy and I."

John Moses said nothing but stuck close to Jed Coltrane.

"You said you could use a hand," the dwarf reminded Sam.

"I can," Sam agreed. "And the pay is terrific. At least until they shut down my expense account."

A one-horse buggy rattled to a halt among the Shoshone, and as Sam turned to look, Orrin Porter Rockwell nearly fell out of it, and then hobbled, half-leaning on his wife, over to the side of the *Jim Smiley* and up its ladder. He reached the deck grunting and sweating, with her on his heels, smiling. She looked as fine as any Sunday stroller in crinoline and hoops, though more deeply tanned than a conventional belle, and he looked like he always did, in buckskins and furs, with knives and guns hanging all over his body.

"Orrin Porter Rockwell," Sam said, shaking the mountain man's hand. "I've never seen a human being take so much damage and keep moving."

"No bullet or blade," Rockwell averred proudly.

"Have you had any news of Absalom?" Burton asked Abigail, bowing slightly.

"Last I heard he'd been spotted in St. George," she said. "They were heading east into the red rock country, and thought they were hot on the trail."

"I wouldn't worry about him," Burton said, radiating confidence.

"I don't," she agreed. "Not anymore."

"We want to come along," Rockwell grunted, and then Sam noticed that two young men from the crowd were dragging a large trunk between them from the buggy to the steam-truck. "Hell, you smashed my hotel all to pieces, I think you owe it to me."

"You aren't worried about the security of the Kingdom?" Sam gestured in Brigham Young's direction.

Rockwell shook his head. "Lee and Hickman and Cannon are gone," the mountain man said. "Brother Brigham's got good men around him now and besides," he grinned, "I'll be back."

"We thought we should go back to England and spend a little time with my family," Abigail explained. "Especially since there's no telling how long Absalom will be gone on his errand."

"His *quest*," Burton jumped in. "I hope you will allow me to accompany you. I'll be collecting my thoughts and memories into notes. I plan to write a memoir of this journey, and your assistance would be invaluable."

"I ain't ever wrote a book before," Rockwell guffawed. "Hell, I ain't hardly read one. But I'm game to try!"

Sam took the wheel of *Jim Smiley*, marveling how perfect it looked, and unaffected by the truck's charge into the blazing inferno of the Tabernacle. Either the wheel had survived unscathed and been cleaned to perfection, or someone had lovingly produced a perfect replica. The same went for all the rest of the controls, and the entire interior of the cabin, with one tiny exception—

—in the center of the wheel, which had previously been a blank disk, was affixed a discreet brass beehive.

Sam laughed.

"What's the mate do, then?" he heard Coltrane say, and he realized the dwarf was standing at his elbow. "It might be best if I, uh, don't have to mingle too much with the Shoshone, boss. I ain't sure jest how much they know, but they kinda have reasons to be unhappy with me."

Sam handed the little man a Partagás, took one for himself, and lit them both. "Shovel coal when we need it," he said. "Stay away from the Indians. Eventually, take the wheel so the captain can nap. For now, see to our passengers. Especially any minors we have aboard. I believe there may be some hard candy somewhere in the galley."

"I believe there may be." Coltrane affected a very sloppy salute, grinned a lopsided grin and hobbled off, holding his chest stiff to avoid irritating the bandages on his healing belly wound.

Sam released the brake, shifted the *Jim Smiley* into gear and turned left up South Tabernacle, towards the mountains, Fort Bridger and the Wyoming Territory. Chief Pocatello mounted his horse and the Shoshone fell in around the steam-truck like pest-eating birds on the back of a rhinoceros.

With the morning sun in his eyes, Sam leaned out the window of the wheelhouse to wave at Brigham Young, Heber Kimball, and the entire crowd. His passengers leaned over the steam-truck's railing and waved too.

"Good-bye!" everyone shouted.

"I'll be back!" yelled Sam.

"We'll be ready for you!" roared Brigham Young.

The End

For Now

FEW AND BRIEF OBSERVATIONS ABOUT HISTORY IN THE REAL WORLD

I stole my title from one of my protagonists.

In real life in 1860, Captain Richard Burton, East India Company man, linguist, Nile explorer, swordsman, falconer, and erstwhile ersatz hajji (ahem), traveled to Salt Lake City. He wrote a book about his journey, called *The City of the Saints*. Burton was a clear-eyed and unshockable observer, and this book is well worth reading even today. Here's my favorite bit, from his description of meeting Brigham Young:

> *Altogether the Prophet's appearance was that of a gentleman farmer of New England—in fact such as he is: his father was an agriculturist and revolutionary soldier, who settled "down East." He is a well-preserved man; a fact which some attribute to his habit of sleeping, as Citizen Proudhon so strongly advises, in solitude.*

Burton's real-world journey is the seed from which this gonzo action steampunk fantasy sprouted.

Edgar Allan Poe is the father of both detective stories and weird fiction. He also dabbled in cryptography. In the real world, he died in 1849 in Baltimore. He died strangely: delirious, not wearing his own clothes, and muttering about someone named "Reynolds." His end has never been satisfactorily explained, and theories include sickness, madness, intoxication, and even a rough kind of electoral fraud called "cooping," in which unwilling voters were forced multiple times through the booths, and beaten, or even killed, if they failed to cooperate.

Eliza R. Snow was almost certainly not to blame.

Sam Clemens's brother Henry did in fact die when the steamboat he was working on, the *Pennsylvania*, exploded. Sam had dreamed of Henry's death a month earlier, and these experiences left him with an abiding curiosity about psychic phenomena and the other side; he was a member of the Society for Psychical Research. He was also curious about technological advancements, becoming a friend of the inventor Nikola Tesla and patenting three inventions himself.

In real life, like Richard Burton, Sam Clemens traveled to Salt Lake City and met Brigham Young, writing about the experience in his book *Roughing It*. His most famous comment on the Mormons he met, though, is probably this one, about polygamy:

> *With the gushing self-sufficiency of youth I was feverish to plunge in headlong and achieve a great reform here—until I saw the Mormon women. Then I was touched. My heart was wiser than my head. It warmed toward these poor, ungainly and pathetically "homely" creatures, and as I turned to hide the generous moisture in my eyes, I said, "No—the man that marries one of them has done an act of Christian charity which entitles him to the kindly applause of mankind, not their harsh censure—and the man that marries sixty of them has done a deed of open-handed generosity so sublime that the nations should stand uncovered in his presence and worship in silence."*

The inventors in *City of the Saints* deserve a short note.

Isambard Kingdom Brunel built railways, bridges, tunnels, and the first propeller-driven transatlantic steamship. In 2002, he came second to Sir Winston Churchill in an extended survey to identify the greatest Briton ever.

Eli Whitney invented the cotton gin, one of the key advances in the industrial revolution, which also had the effect of strengthening the economic basis of slavery. I don't think Whitney, a Massachusetts man, intended that outcome, so in *City of the Saints* I instead made him the inventor of the clocksprung technology that ended slavery and resulted in Harriet Tubman's exodus to Mexico.

Hiram Stevens Maxim did invent the first silencer; he also invented the first portable, fully automatic machine gun, which inspired Hilaire Belloc's famous couplet: "Whatever happens, we have got / The Maxim gun, and they have not."

Sam Colt manufactured the first commercially viable mass-produced revolver.

Horace Hunley was a New Orleans lawyer who built hand-powered submarines for the Confederates during the American Civil War. His invention career and legal practice both terminated when he personally

took command of one of his ships during a routine exercise and it sank.
Orson Pratt was a mathematician and astronomer. He was also one
of the inventors of a primitive odometer that the Mormons attached to
the hub of a wagon wheel to measure miles traveled as they crossed the
plains westward.

Parley Pratt was one of the principal movers on the committee that
developed the Deseret Alphabet.

John Moses Browning, finally, was an Ogden kid and son of a
gunsmith who became arguably the most influential gun designer ever.
His M1911 pistol was the standard-issue sidearm for American armed
forces from 1911 to 1985 and is still widely popular today.

While we're on the subject of guns, let me admit to an anachronism:
the Henry rifle was not in fact available in 1859, but began to be
manufactured in the early 1860s. In a story stuffed with ray guns, flying
Viking ships, and flesh-eating scarab beetles, it seemed a small sin to
nudge the Henry forward a few years.

Brigham Young may or may not have really denounced Levi-Strauss
jeans as "fornication pants." His proposed State of Deseret was rejected
by the United States Congress in favor of a significantly smaller Utah
Territory in 1850, which was still twice the size of present-day Utah, of
which he was the first governor.

George Q. Cannon was an Apostle, a Territorial Delegate to the
United States Congress, a newspaper publisher, mission president, and
writer. His long presence in the upper ranks of Mormon and Utah
leadership without ever becoming head of either the church or the
territory may be why he was called by some the "Mormon Richelieu."

Orrin Porter Rockwell was a frontiersman, accused assassin,
sometimes lawman, and saloon owner. Joseph Smith did promise him
that if he was loyal and didn't cut his hair, "no bullet or blade" would
harm Rockwell. He remains a beloved and quirky figure in Mormon
popular consciousness today.

John D. Lee has not fared so well. Though in his lifetime he was a
beloved leader and believed to possess rare spiritual gifts, he was involved
in the deservedly infamous Mountain Meadows Massacre, an atrocity for
which he was—eventually—shot by a firing squad. Lee maintained to the
end that he was a scapegoat.

Bill Hickman, a Mormon frontiersman like Lee and Rockwell, wrote
an autobiography confessing to a number of murders and implicating
Brigham Young. It's not clear how much of his book was pure fiction;
neither he nor Young were ever charged for any of the crimes to which
Hickman confessed. On a personal note, Bill Hickman murdered one of
my wife's ancestors, Isaac Hatch, and if I have made Hickman out to be
an illiterate, gap-toothed, coward, well … he deserved worse.

Ann Eliza Webb was, after an earlier marriage and divorce, one of

Brigham Young's polygamous wives. She left Mormonism and became an early feminist critic of it, though the accuracy of her book has also been contested. She had a rough life, and in making her a kung fu chick in this novel, I mean no disrespect; I would like to imagine Annie Webb as a freewheeling, high-kicking, happy young woman, and not the serial divorcée estranged from her own family that she became.

Eliza R. Snow was a teacher, poet, historian, and polygamous wife. She was the first secretary of the Nauvoo Female Relief Society and later, in Utah, president of its successor organization. Her radical theological poem "Invocation, or the Eternal Father and Mother," is included in today's LDS hymnal under the title "O My Father." In that poem, Snow writes: "In the heavens are parents single? No, the thought makes reason stare! Truth is reason, truth eternal, tells me I've a mother there." She was an adventurer of the mind, heart, and spirit, and in my view has always been the true and profoundly romantic heroine of *City of the Saints*.

If You Liked ...

If you liked *City of the Saints*, you might also enjoy:

Lincoln's Wizard
Tracy Hickmann and Dan Willis

Best of Penny Dread Tales
Edited by Quincy Allen and Kevin J. Anderson

Flux Engine
Dan Willis

Blood Ties
Quincy J. Allen

About D.J. Butler

D.J. Butler (Dave) is a novelist living in Utah. His training is in law, and he worked as a securities lawyer at a major international firm and in-house at two multinational semiconductor manufacturers before taking up writing fiction. He is a lover of language and languages, a guitarist and self-recorder, and a serious reader. He is married to a powerful and clever woman and together they have three devious children.

Dave has been writing fiction since 2010. He writes speculative fiction (fantasy, science fiction, space opera, steampunk, cyberpunk, superhero, alternate history, dystopian fiction, horror, and related genres) for all audiences. In addition to *City of the Saints*, he is the author of a gonzo action-horror serial about a bar band comprised entirely of damned men, *Rock Band Fights Evil*, and a dark science fiction tale about guilt and ritual murder, *Crecheling*. His novel *The Kidnap Plot*, a steampunk fantasy adventure for middle readers, will be published by Knopf in 2016.

Read about D.J. Butler's writing projects at:

http://davidjohnbutler.com.

Other WordFire Press Titles by D.J. Butler

Crecheling

Rock Band Fights Evil:

Hellhound on My Trail

Snake Handlin' Man

Crow Jane

Devil Sent the Rain

Our list of other WordFire Press authors and titles is always growing. To find out more and to see our selection of titles, visit us at:

wordfirepress.com

CPSIA information can be obtained
at www.ICGtesting.com
Printed in the USA
BVHW081132280120
570505BV00004BA/76

9 781614 753476